Lasting Promise

CAN TWO BROKEN SOULS FORGE A LOVE
STRONG AS THE FRONTIER?

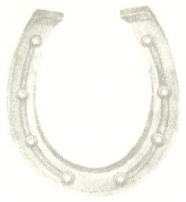

also by

SUSANNA LANE

Imperfect Promise

Enduring Promise

Lasting Promise

CAN LOVE SURVIVE SECRETS
BURIED DEEP IN THE PLAINS?

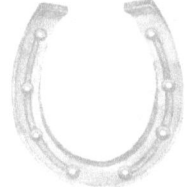

SUSANNA LANE

WESTERN WRITERS OF AMERICA SPUR AWARD WINNER

HAT CREEK

HAT CREEK

An Imprint of Roan & Weatherford Publishing Associates, LLC
Bentonville, Arkansas
www.roanweatherford.com

Library of Congress Cataloging-in-Publication Data
Names: Lane, Susanna, author
Title: Lasting Promise/Susanna Lane | Promises #3
Description: First Edition. | Bentonville: Hat Creek, 2025.
Identifiers: LCCN: 2025947305 | ISBN: 978-1-63373-084-4 (trade paperback) |
ISBN: 978-1-63373-085-1 (eBook)
Subjects: | BISAC: FICTION/Romance/Western | FICTION/Western | FICTION/Women
LC record available at: https://lccn.loc.gov/2025947305

Hat Creek trade paperback edition October, 2025

Cover Design by Casey W. Cowan
Interior Design by John Bredesen
Editing by Staci Troilo & Rachel Santino

Hearty thanks to Roan & Weatherford Publishing for promoting my Promise Series. And many, many thanks to Casey Cowan for his continued support of the historical western genre.

Always mindful of my husband's loyal support, I sense his presence beside me, even as the end came too soon. You will always missed and always loved.

I'm very grateful for the encouragement of my sons and their wives.

My many friends on Hawks Trail in Georgia have dried my tears and brought sunlight to my life. They are simply the best.

Last, but not least, I deeply appreciates K.S. Jones and Deborah Swenson for their consummate support, wise opinions, and big hearts.

PREFACE

WITH REGARD TO *Lasting Promise,* please note, as in all my works, the characters are fictitious, having been placed in the context of the story scenes. Any of the characters' names are strictly part of my imagination, and any similarities to real life are coincidental. I stay true to research for setting and backdrop, using accurate details unless it is necessary to embellish them in terms of storyline or events. A few geographical locations are nonexistent or altered in description to accommodate the storyline.

As to the writing of a story, there are some key features I adhere to. First, I always write from research and outline. I never begin a story without first having an eye on historical background, if for no other reasons than plotting and realism.

One of my chief tasks is to flesh out characters so that they are believable. Along with that, every character is flawed or has had a problematic background, thus promoting emotion and drama while keeping the pages turning.

Writing dialogue that is real, especially within the setting and time period, is certainly one of the most important things for an author to achieve. And I'm a stickler for crisp POV and use third person so that there is freedom to invite DPOV into character development.

Where do my ideas come from? That is a question often asked and most authors cannot tell you. Why? Because much of an author's personal experience is already built before the story reaches the writing stage. Also, an author is able to step outside of the box and solve problems. In real life, we have little or no control over the endings.

In terms of historical western writing, survival, bravery, and determination are universal themes. In the case of my "Promise" series, each backstory revolves around a core theme with several common themes.

In *Imperfect Promise*, courage, sacrifice, and honor are at the forefront. In *Enduring Promise*, courage, fidelity, and determination illuminate the main characters. *Lasting Promise* portrays the characters as brave but sacrifice and jealousy loom large. And in *Distance Between Stars*, courage, sacrifice, and final surrender are overriding themes.

ONE

CAPTURING INDIANS

Fort Benton, Montana
June 1879

BY THE STARES that followed him, Gus Quaid figured he'd drawn attention he didn't want. Wearing his dust-covered buckskins, his rifle resting across his lap, he rode past townsfolk who stopped to gaze in his direction. Usually, he wouldn't care. But this time was different. The fewer who knew his business, the better.

The sight of a woman with long black braids sent flashes of the renegades he'd helped the Army round up. Remorse tugged at him because he'd been part of it. Yet he also knew that times had changed since he'd become a scout. The same heat of anger cooled with time.

There'd be no lodging at old Fort Benton. After a storied history, it had closed. A new town sprang along this side of the Missouri. Nudging his horse into a faster gait, he guided the animal, along with his pack horse, around two plain-dressed women who picked their way across the mud-baked road. Gus offered the women a courteous nod, then moved on. He grinned beneath his shaggy beard, taking perverse pleasure in their discomfiture as they averted their faces.

When I.G. Baker's mercantile came into view, he turned his attention to the considerable greenbacks and gold he expected to find in Baker's vault. He was honor-bound to see it returned to the rightful owner. After he continued along Front Street, he passed the freight barn, then the row of wagons that lined the boardwalk. At the sudden blast of a riverboat, his horse skittered sideways. After a few words, he urged his jittery Appaloosa onward. The day after tomorrow, he'd board one of the steamers with the burden of Enders's money. Once he reached the plains, he'd be alone, and if he wasn't careful, he'd be prey to road agents. But towns worried him more. Every kind of no-account collected in places like this.

For now, he set that aside and imagined the taste of warm beer on his tongue and the touch of a woman for the night. Paying for a woman's affection had its merit. Still, the notion sickened him on some level where civility still perched. His preference would be to hear a woman's soft conversation over a table and vittles. But that kind of woman wasn't likely to be found.

A gray-haired man limped toward him after he dismounted at the livery. "You ain't no soldier. Not a freighter neither. Peg you for an Army scout." He swiped his gritty hands over his work pants.

"That important for you to know?" Gus replied.

"Nope. Just wonderin',' what with you wearin' buckskins and moccasins. That Springfield, them revolvers, generally mean business."

Gus poked his tongue into the pocket of his cheek. *Nosy son of a bitch.* "Keep my business to myself. Take care of my two horses and tack. I'll take along the rest."

"Surely will. Don't think you'd like the Centennial. Might try the Choteau House."

"Thanks. Think I'll do just that. How much do I owe you?"

"Ten dollars for the week."

The man rocked back on his heels and waited. Gus raised one eyebrow. "Seems high since I'll only be here a few days."

"Make it three dollars, then. Both horses."

With haggling over, Gus shrugged. "Guess I got no other choice."

Gus reached for the money tucked inside his boot, peeled out three dollars, then slapped them onto the man's bony, outstretched hand. Without a word, the liveryman nodded, then led his mounts away. The man's cackle followed Gus as he headed toward the hotel, his gun belt in plain view, rifle in hand, with his saddlebag slung over his shoulder.

Three women stepped back from him as they held their calico skirts aside to avoid his touch. He wended his way around them, then saluted with two fingers to his brow. One offered a prune-faced smile to match her sour expression. As he scrubbed a hand across his face, he was reminded it'd been a long while since he'd used a razor.

A sidelong glance brought his attention to a pretty, dark-haired woman who'd stepped around a pile of horse dung while she made her way to the other side of the street. She wore a prim black dress, buttoned to her neck, and looked like she might be in mourning. From his vantage, she had the poise of an angel, yet something about her struck him as haughty. He shrugged. She wasn't the kind of woman who'd look at him once or twice. Besides, he was already thinking about a sweet, soiled dove for tonight.

THE SMELL OF tobacco, whiskey, and men's sweat filled Gus's nostrils while he stood at the bar of the Red Lace Saloon. The stink didn't bother him as much as the loud-mouthed rowdies. After the second beer went down, he was struck mellow. Peering over his shoulder, he took in the gamblers through the haze of smoke. Some tossed coins down while others studied their hands. A soldier sat alone, his whiskey for company.

The piano player lifted his head after the barkeep nudged him awake. The sleepy man's fingers struck up the tune "Oh, Susanna," but the notes failed to drown the hoorahs, cuss words, and grumbles from the diverse men at the tables and bar. Cussing was something most men kept to themselves around women. Any women. *That included the one in the shiny green dress looking in his direction.* What he could see appealed to his baser side. Their gazes met. Her eyes were red-rimmed from either opiates or lack of sleep... or both. Her hair was the color of a ripe red apple while her face creased with the lines of time. He looked away, but not fast enough. Damn... she headed directly for him as he gulped the last of his beer.

"Got some time if you need somethin', sugar."

Slurred words were proof enough she didn't care to know what kind of man he was. He'd be just another man in a long line of clients. With a mouth smeared with rouge, she frowned and waited for his reply. After some consideration, he was bone-tired, and she wasn't appealing. "Maybe later."

"Suit yourself." She tossed her mane of hair, then sashayed away in search of another client.

Just as he figured he'd call it a night, he sensed someone watched him. He lifted his eyes away from his empty glass, only to see the same woman with dark hair... the one who'd crossed his path. His breath hitched at her beauty. A coiled braid rested over one shoulder, and she still wore that prim black dress, pearl buttons to her throat. The woman in black began a regal descent from the landing above, leaving him to swallow hard. He didn't need to turn around to know all eyes followed her.

Her attention stayed on him until she reached the bottom, then she stepped into the bowels of all manner of men. Men who didn't deserve her. With his stare riveted on her, he caught a glimmer of amusement in her eyes. His stomach clenched. A proper-looking woman with a pure face. He'd pay well to have her beside him for one night.

Her deep blue eyes turned from him, then she surveyed the room. His heart stopped when her focus returned to him with an almost imperceptible wrinkle of her nose that crushed any hope she'd spare him any of her time. It was a clear dismissal he should've expected, given he was in need of grooming. She appeared to be a lady who shouldn't be here. But she was here—leaving him to suppose she was for hire.

Just as he decided her a pompous whore, she walked near enough for him to breathe in the scent of lilies. Before he thought to speak, the words died on his tongue after she discounted him, then walked around the tables. His stare followed her to where she entered a room at the far side, then closed the door behind her. He squinted to see the word, *Private*.

Thinking was hard when a man like him had been both snubbed

and attracted to the same haughty woman. He looked over his shoulder to give thought to how long before she'd return. Then he made a decision... one he might later regret. *Hell.* He'd take whatever she'd offer. The question that niggled was how to approach this beautiful, arrogant phantom.

After the bartender refilled his glass, he picked it up, swallowed, then mulled over whether to make a fool of himself. Glass in hand, he made his way around the tables, then stopped in front of the closed door.

"Hey. You can't go in there. Off limits, mister," the piano player snapped.

Jaw taut, he ground his teeth then slapped the glass on the piano top. Clearing his throat, he rapped on the door to the sound of hoots and guffaws. From the corner of his eye, he saw the piano player shove back his chair.

"Maybe I'll let the lady decide," he muttered. When there was no response, he turned the handle, then entered the dimly lit room before he kicked the door closed behind him. His attention settled on the woman seated in a tufted green chair behind a mahogany desk. She raised her head then her eyes narrowed. She said nothing but simply watched him. A nervous twitch of her lip suggested she was nervous as he gazed at her proper dress and porcelain skin.

If she could read his thoughts, she'd know how much he itched to relieve her of the confines of that black dress. She was both alluring and dignified. And as untouchable as a butterfly. She was something of an enigma, yet maybe worth his effort... if he managed to breach her icy wall.

A corner of her mouth lifted while she studied him like he were a fly. If she expected him to turn tail, she was wrong. Instead, he crossed his arms, then she raised an eyebrow. The door opened behind him, admitting a cacophony of guffaws while they held each other pinned.

"Back out, mister. I got a shotgun pointed at your spine. The lady don't want to be bothered by the likes of you."

"That so?" Gus kept his eyes on the woman's dainty hands, now gripping a little derringer. "Ma'am. Guess it was my mistake. Just thought you'd share a bourbon with me. If you've a mind."

She sighed, then leaned around his frame to address the bartender. "William. I'm just fine. I'll take care of this. I'd be interested in hearing what the man has to say for himself."

The door slammed shut while Gus kept his eyes on her derringer.

"Might as well pull up a chair from that wall, mister," she said. "And then we'll figure out if I want your company or not."

After he dragged the chair close to the desk, he took a seat, then watched while she set the derringer into a fancy box. From the set of her chin to her beautiful hair, he felt like he'd been granted an audience with a queen. Still, he'd like more than a bourbon from her. "Name's Gus Quaid."

Her head tilted. "Don't know you. What exactly do you want, Mister Quaid? And may I remind you it isn't polite to enter a room without invitation."

"I apologize. Though, as I recall, I knocked. Miss?"

"I'm Victoria Barrett, and I'm certain I'm not what you think."

Gus was glad his beard hid the heat in his face. She'd nailed him. But she'd also changed his mind about wanting her in his bed. Her husky voice, like fine whiskey, was almost enough to soothe his soul. "Just what are you certain of?"

"You've been watching me. I see your kind come and go, Mister Quaid. I know what you think. What you want."

"Maybe I can change your mind. Would you consider having dinner with me, Victoria Barrett? Or that bourbon I suggested? I've heard the Centennial has good food. I'd be very interested to hear what you're doing in a saloon... over supper."

"A saloon?" She inclined her head, then offered him a brilliant smile. "Your invitation is one of the strangest I've ever been offered. I'm not the preacher's daughter. If that's what you're getting at. But what I am... is particular."

"You're not a whore from where I'm sitting. Too refined to be here."

"You have a lot of assumptions. So, let me tell you what I think. You've been away from civilization for a while. You need a bath. Just maybe once you clean up, we can talk over dinner. As it happens, I'm staying at the Centennial. You are correct about the food there. Six o'clock, Mister Quaid. And if I'm not there, you have my answer."

Gus stood to leave, then considered whether to break into a laugh or a salute. Neither seemed would give him an advantage. As he headed to the door, he was stopped by her next words.

"Gus. Most call me Tori."

"That name suits you."

After he left the saloon, he walked toward the Choteau House, giving thought to that bath she suggested. As he drew closer, he took a turn, then headed for the barber. It was about time he had a shave and trim before he forgot what he looked like beneath the hair. A bath took on new urgency. *Tori.* As much as he looked forward to being with her, something niggled about Tori. Those beautiful blue-gray eyes hid something. *Fear. Caution. Secrets. Lies.* He shook his head, resolved not to think of her after tonight. After all, he would be on the riverboat.

AFTER GUS QUAID left, she mulled over his size. And a lot more. Certainly, he was handsome beneath all that hair. Besides that, she just may have found a protector. It didn't sit right in her gut to use him for her own purposes—but she'd become an opportunist, and he presented an opportunity. Yet that didn't mean she didn't have a conscience. She'd never shied from using a man. This time felt different.

"*Tori suits you.*" Gus Quaid had said. She'd read men for much of her adult life. This man was tough behind his simple manner. If he found out the truth about her, it might prove bothersome. Tori poured herself two fingers of bourbon at the table beside the window, then called herself every name she could think of for agreeing to meet this stranger for dinner. But then again, what harm could come of conversation and sharing a supper? *None.* Besides, he might turn out to be of use to her. Whenever trouble came, she'd outlasted it. That was her best attribute.

He was broad-shouldered, like someone used to hard work. She noticed how he'd ducked when he'd stepped through the door. Sure of himself, to boot... but plain-spoken and direct as any drifter she'd ever met. She might be able to count on him. Maybe not. Time would tell.

She'd bet her last dollar he was far more civilized than he let on. Refinement slipped from his words before he could call them back. Now why would a man hide his distinguished side beneath those buckskin clothes? After she gave thought to the possibility he had a wife somewhere, she was surprised at how that bothered her.

No. He wouldn't be the kind to leave a wife. Still, her momentary flare of jealousy had nothing to do with reason, nor did he figure into any permanent plan. With that thick beard and straggly hair, he was handsome in a rugged sort of way. The kind of man she needed. A man she could wrap around her finger.

Tori stood before the Cheval mirror in her hotel room, then turned this way then that, to admire the plain black and gray dress with pearl buttons she'd decided to wear tonight. The rounded neckline offered a demure peek at her decolletage. She draped a blue wool wrap around her shoulders, clutched her reticule, then stepped into the hall.

Just as she inserted the key, someone cleared his throat. She whirled and came up short, hardly able to suck in a breath at the sight of the tall, handsome man dressed in a gray chambray shirt and clean-pressed denim pants. He stood at the top of the stairway, his gaze steady. With hair as straight as a poker, it managed to complement his rugged, lean face. Gus Quaid cut a fine figure of a man no matter what he wore.

As she strolled toward him, she could hardly hold back her grin. She looked him over from his polished boots to his deep-set black eyes. His hair gleamed like a raven's wing in the sconce light. While he didn't move, he did follow her every step as she approached. Nearing him, she didn't miss the whiff of bay rum. Their gazes held a moment before she looked toward the wall, avoiding his penetrating stare. She was as nervous as a schoolgirl.

"I like it when you smile," he said.

"You sure are full of surprises."

One of his eyebrows lifted, clearly waiting for her to say more in a way of explanation.

"I wasn't sure what I might see if you shaved."

"And?"

"I'd be dreadfully familiar if I told you how handsome you are."

"I'd be damned brazen to come out and say you are beautiful enough to steal a man's breath."

He offered his arm, then they descended the stairs together. For once, she felt she could trust a man. *This forthright man.* She'd been wrong before.

"THE SUPPER WAS very good. Thank you, Gus."

"You still haven't finished your pie."

"The stew filled me. I usually don't eat all this much. From the looks of it, you certainly enjoyed the food. Have to admit. I'm not used to watching a man eat."

He leaned back in his chair to observe the delicate way she sipped her tea. "Huh. I don't have the best table manners. To have a meal with a woman isn't my usual. I mostly eat at a campfire or just stuff my mouth with dried jerky while in the saddle."

"Do you have a home? Family?"

He flinched at her question. He leaned forward, his fists balled against the table. "My house is in Belle Fourche. No family."

"So you have no wife?" She continued to stare at her pie.

"Tori. Look at me when you ask questions."

Ever so slowly, she lifted her eyes. Her lips pressed into a thin line, while her flushed face suggested she hadn't meant to ask about a family. He usually didn't care to answer that question... until now.

"Don't often discuss her. My wife is dead. I seldom spend much time at my home because I work with the Army off and on. That's all I intend to say about it. But know this—some men, maybe ones you know, would woo you then bed you whether they had a wife or not. I'm *not* that kind of man. I don't want you to think I am. It would be insulting."

"All right. I accept that."

"But you'll be sleeping alone tonight."

Her chin jerked up, then her eyes narrowed. "Yes."

He sucked in a breath, then sipped the tepid brew. He cocked his head as he studied her. "Fair enough. This might surprise you. I'm glad you turned me down. I'd rather recall you like this. A lady having supper."

"You're leaving?"

"Day after tomorrow. Soon as I finish up some business."

"Where are you going? If you don't mind me asking."

"Long riverboat trip then across the plains. After I see you to your door, it will be goodbye."

"Then, farewell, Gus Quaid."

———————

THE NIGHT HELD a sliver of moon. A blackness sprayed with a swath of stars peeked through clumps of clouds and held him mesmerized. His head lay atop his folded arms while he stared at the vastness framed in his window. From this vantage on the bed, he gave thought to her. Counting the cracks in the ceiling had done little to help him sleep.

Her scent still washed through his senses while her grin sent a spasm through his gut. Presumptuous is what she'd called him after he'd pressed his lips to her cheek, then they'd parted. He'd almost turned back to take her mouth in a real man's kiss. Just to prove he could. Damn. Even after her dark blue eyes narrowed at his *presumption*, he found her breathtaking. He wasn't one little bit sorry.

After she'd turned from him, she stepped into her room, then closed the door in his face. He'd stood there for some time in the hopes she'd reconsider. Her change of heart wasn't in the cards. On the way back to his hotel, he whistled a tune, then gave thought to the red-headed woman at the saloon. But there was too much to compare with the softly defiant woman who'd managed to intrigue him. The whore in the saloon may have fallen short on appeal, and the lady in black would stay in his head for a long while.

He turned his thoughts to business. The first thing tomorrow, he'd retrieve Bryce's money and gold from the safe. Before he left, he'd see to his gear and, particularly, his two horses. The plan to disembark at Fort Randall meant he'd have a long ride before he reached the train at Columbus. The fewer towns, the better.

Where would Tori be? A vision of her with another man set his teeth on edge. His last thought before he fell asleep was how much he'd like to cross paths with her again.

TWO

NO

FORT BENTON FELL away from sight while he leaned forward at the rail, his gaze on the changing shoreline. The tents, log houses, hotels, and saloons were no longer visible but were still impressed in his mind. His thoughts turned to his time working with the Army.

After one disappointment after another, he had begun to realize he'd never find her. Rounding up renegades who'd escaped capture was an excuse to look for his captive wife. This time, like all the other times, he'd come up dry. The heat of his fury had long since passed, replaced with respect for their plight. He couldn't blame them for seeking freedom. But he could blame the ones who'd taken her.

He turned, crossed his arms, then perused his fellow passengers. A group of men smoked while some chattering ladies strolled the deck. Most were what he'd expected—haggard men, down on their luck, ragged farmers leaving behind failed farms. One well-dressed man wore a sidearm. Maybe he looked for trouble. Maybe he protected his possessions. *Like him.* His property was in the captain's safe, for now.

His regard followed a bedraggled woman who walked beside a boy he judged to be about twelve or thirteen. Her plain dress and straw hat suggested she was poor. Maybe she left behind a husband buried on the prairie. None of their stories mattered, but speculating kept his mind from wandering back to Tori.

Just before he headed to the lower deck to check his horses, he drew up short at the sight of a well-dressed woman in a deep gray and blue dress, hair glistening in the sun. Gripping a hat in one hand, she faced the steep Missouri Breaks as the ship plowed ever faster. When her face turned toward the woman and child walking by, he had a good look at her profile. No mistaking her. *Tori was here.*

The woman who'd kept him awake had boarded the Nellie Peck— *quite the coincidence.* Damn her. Was she playing some sort of game, or did she have some nefarious intent? Clenching his teeth, he wondered if there was some way she'd found out about the money he carried. Maybe he was a horse's ass and had played into her hand.

While he watched her, his traitorous legs moved in her direction. At least, that's what he told himself. He stopped beside her and waited. Out of the corner of his eye, she appeared to be unaware of his presence, her focus level on the hills. That slight twitch of her lip signaled she knew he was here.

He cleared his throat. *Loudly.* "Miss Barrett."

With a slow turn of her head, she looked up with those dazzling blue eyes. "Mister Quaid."

"At least you remember me."

"Let's say you made an impression."

"Huh. From the sound of it, you'd rather forget." Her grip tightened on her reticule. "Surely, I had no idea you'd be on the same boat, Miss Barrett. Unless I miss my guess, you decided to follow me. I'd like to know why."

"It slipped my mind. Now, if you'll excuse me."

Just as she started to walk away, he latched onto her arm. Her blue irises were hard and cold as ice. "Join me for supper in the dining room tonight. It's not the Centennial, but it'll do."

She tugged her arm free of his grasp. "As you said. We best go our own way."

Just as he was about to challenge her, the man he'd seen with the revolver had joined another man, both armed and both looking toward them. They casually passed, tipped their hats, then moved on. There was something about the slight nod of her head that told Gus she recognized them. Her mouth thinned then her hands trembled. She was downright scared.

"Yes, Mister Quaid. I believe I'd like that supper. I'll be along at six. If that suits?"

"That'll do just fine, ma'am."

This sudden change in her demeanor after those two strangers walked by suggested there was trouble. And he didn't know how they were involved. Those two men had something to do with her sudden change of mind. He poked his hat farther back on his head as he watched her saunter toward the row of cabins shaded beneath the upper deck. *Yes, indeed, Miss Barrett, though I'm not sure I'm willing to stand between you and whatever trouble is following you.*

Unfortunately, he figured he'd already been sucked in.

NOT FOR THE first time, Gus gave thought to the woman as he waited for her in the cramped dining room. Several long, crude wood tables and benches were set up for the twenty or so passengers. A few smaller, more private tables were situated at each corner of the room, where he'd managed to claim one. *Where was she?* Tori Barrett was an enigma with her quicksilver mood that kept him off his center.

Whatever the track of her thinking, he figured he'd just follow along until he rid himself of this misplaced attraction to a woman he didn't trust. As much as he was drawn to her, he wasn't about to be fooled into doing something stupid. While deep in thought regarding what to do about Tori, a gray-haired woman wearing a stained yellow apron offered him a pinched smile.

"What can I get you?" she asked without preamble.

"I'm waiting for my guest."

"Best hurry your guest along. The captain don't like folks havin' to wait for a spot to eat."

"All right. Tell me the choices, so I'll know."

"We got stew and biscuits. Got salt pork and potatoes. Got some apple pie and coffee if you don't wait too long. That goes fast."

In the midst of the pretense of considering the options, Tori walked in. He didn't need to look across his shoulder because all eyes had turned in her direction. With her usual poise, she approached the harried waitress with a bright smile, apologized for being late with a mellifluent sweetness, then asked to have the stew.

As always, she was full of surprises. She wore a charming grin and a pretty yellow dress with pink flowers, a dazzling picture of pure innocence. The contradiction between now and his former impressions kept him off-balance. Then his gander settled on the slight scoop of her neckline, having him wonder which Tori she was tonight. "I'll have what the lady is having. Stew's fine."

The waitress harrumphed, then returned to the kitchen. He stood, slid out her chair, then waited while she seated. After he'd taken a chair across from her, he crossed his arms. "Thought you'd changed your mind."

She glared in his direction. "Once it's made up, I never change it."

Throughout supper, he forked his food while she prattled on about how she planned to head for Omaha then on to San Francisco to start an undetermined business. Tori picked at the thick stew, then nibbled the biscuit. He was more than amused at how she plowed into the pie. She spoke of her Virginia origins but said little else about her past. And he damned well wished he knew more.

Except for her pain-filled expression at the mention of the War, she gave up little of herself. Instead, she commented on the dreadful smell of the river and her cramped but acceptable quarters. He'd already concluded she wasn't a pampered, frail woman. For certain, this woman was both cunning and manipulative. In a sudden flash of memory, Lark came to mind. That set him to wonder if Miss Barrett was on the run. It seemed like it.

"Mister Quaid. You seem far away. I'm blathering. You don't seem to be the kind used to that sort of thing. I must bore you."

Gus tilted the mug of coffee to his lips and thought about how he'd respond. "As a matter of fact... no. But I don't mind. Just not used to talking to ladies. In fact, I'm not around folks much. Out on my own, there's not much chance for pleasant conversation."

"I'm sorry."

He raised his eyebrow. "I didn't want your pity."

Drawing a breath, she folded her hands against the table. "The ticket clerk said it'd take six or seven days to get to Fort Randall, then could be another week or even more to Omaha."

"Huh. If that's a round-about way of asking where I'm headin', all you had to do is ask. I'm getting off at Fort Randall with my saddle and pack horse. Thought I'd already mentioned that."

"So, you'll ride into the wilderness from there."

"Rather not talk about where I'm goin'."

Gus hoped she didn't work for thieves, but just in case she did, he'd already said too much. Those men wearing guns could be part of a band of road agents. He hated to think she worked with them.

"I didn't mean to intrude. Just curious."

"There's a lot of dangers out there. You can't trust a lot of folks. Best to keep your intensions to yourself, Tori. Staying to your own business might save your life."

"I'm beginning to see that. The dangers, I mean. For instance, today, I saw a long line of mounted Indians following a trail beside the river. Do they attack these boats?"

Her sudden change in questioning had him strangling back a bark of laughter. From the look of her tautened mouth, she was dead serious. "The short answer is maybe. Depends. Don't think they would do that on the reservation. We're passing through their lands, so they naturally keep an eye on us. Can't blame them. You don't need to worry."

"You wear a gun."

"Out here, most men do. Even some women. I'm thinking you carry your little derringer in that reticule of yours."

One corner of her mouth tilted upward, and he had his answer. "I've learned to be ready for anything. Out here, as you say."

"Good." Satisfied he'd chipped away at some of her secrets, he was still left with an uneasy feeling about Miss Tori Barrett.

"Well. It's gotten late and the waitress has her hands on her hips. Suppose that means we need to make room."

He nodded, grabbed up his hat, then stood. He jutted his chin in the direction of the doorway. "I'll see you safe to your room. Tori, don't wander out on deck until daylight."

While they strolled at an unhurried pace, he found her grin came more easily. Once they reached her room, he took the key from her hand to unlock the door. "Wait here while I make sure it's safe." A quick look inside assured him it was empty. After he returned to the threshold, he nodded. "Goodnight, Tori. Keep your door locked."

"About the cost. Of the meal?"

"Already paid."

"Thank you."

"I thank you for your company. Don't get much chance to converse over a meal."

There it was again. That nervous little twitch of her lower lip. Even if he *was* thinking about settling his mouth on hers, this woman was different. He never knew what to expect from this lady. After a slight movement of her arm, her gun was leveled at him. His jaw hardened.

"I already told you. I've no intention of hurting you. Best get that through your head. Another thing. If you ever pull that little gun on me again, I'll take it from you... just to show how easy it would be. Better plan to use it when you draw it, lady. If you do, make sure it's for a good reason."

She dropped her chin, then averted her eyes. "I'm sorry I misjudged you for a moment. Trust comes hard for me."

"Keep in mind that I'm not the kind who'd ever hurt a woman." He stepped aside, then waited for her to pass him.

She turned. "Gus?"

Her sweet voice fit the girlish grin, as well as the image he wanted her to be. A river of heat moved to where it shouldn't. He held up a finger. "One question."

"You said you've spent most of the time alone. You said your wife is dead. How did she die?"

A welling pain rose, chilling the warmth of her company. "She's dead. A long while back. Taken by Sioux about eleven years ago."

"That's why you work as a scout."

He couldn't tolerate another question, no matter how innocent. "Best get some sleep. I gave you one question. Right now, I'm resisting that kiss you don't want me to give you."

Her door closed. After he heard the click of the lock, he headed for the lower deck where he'd find a whiskey for a price... any price was fine at the moment.

FOR THE TENTH time, she touched her derringer beside the bed. Sleep evaded her, even as she yawned. Determined to stay awake to think about the two men who'd looked familiar. *One of them was Ben Irons. Silas's man.* There was no secret about what he wanted from her. The money she'd taken from the safe. Money she planned to keep because it was rightfully hers.

Damn Silas and all men. How had she missed seeing him board the ship? The other man must work for Silas, as well. Gus's presence gave her a sense of safety. But he'd said he was going only as far as Fort Randall. Ben hadn't cornered her yet. Once Gus was gone, she'd have no one to protect her. The law was thin, especially where women were concerned.

They might have her arrested once they got to Pierre. It made her sick to take advantage of Gus's charity and kindness. To stay alive, she had no other choice. She bit her lip, then closed her eyes. *Just a little sleep.* Then she'd think about how she could avoid the trouble ahead.

She didn't know how long she'd slept before she struggled to breathe. The smell of sweat and taste of salt nauseated her. There was a large hand pressed hard against her mouth and nose. When she tried to move, she found she couldn't. Pinned beneath the man above her, she shoved, but he wouldn't budge. Her mewling plea was ignored.

Ben leaned close to her ear and growled, "I guessed you recognized me. Best not struggle, or I'll hurt you."

Her eyes widened at the threat because she knew what this man was capable of doing. She nodded beneath his cloistering hand. He eased away while she gasped for air.

"Silas wants his money. Where is it?"

"I don't have it."

His fist rose above her. She rolled to the side of the bunk to reach for her derringer. He stopped her with a vicious tug of the neck of her nightdress before he wrenched her from the bed. Breath whooshed from her chest when he slammed her against the wall. She could neither scream nor draw in air as he squeezed her throat. Spots floated in her vision.

"Let's try this again. Before I take away my hand, these are your options. You give me the money and come along back to Virginia City like a good girl, or I take the money and leave you with nothing but the clothes you got on. Maybe they'll find you in the river. Matters not to me, *Miss High and Mighty.*" He released her with a shove.

From where she landed against the bed, she caught sight of the door that swayed with the rise and fall of the boat. If she could run to the deck, she might find help. If he tore apart the cabin, it would be a futile search. The captain was kind enough to hold her money in his safe.

Her hand pressed against her sore throat. "All right. I hid the money."

He backed a step, considering her admission.

She used that opportunity and all her strength to shove him backward. Quick as she could, she rolled across the bed, out of his reach, then sprinted for the door. He was faster. When he yanked her back by the hair, pain shot through her scalp. She wilted against him.

"Where is it?" he growled.

"I'll get it from the captain tomorrow. Is that satisfactory?"

"I'll count on it. Otherwise, you won't like what happens next." He shoved her backward. "Tomorrow. No tricks. Else you'll be the one to go to jail for stealing."

Ben's red face and wild brown eyes told her he meant what he said.

She rested her head against the wall and waited. At the sound of his fading footsteps, she gulped in long drafts of air. She stumbled to the door. With an unsteady hand, she reached for the bolt, but it hung at a lopsided angle. Her options dwindled. He'd come with another man. Now her salvation was in Gus.

She leaned forward to examine her mottled face in the mirror. Brushing her hand across the red skin of her throat, it was no doubt badly bruised. It was dangerous to stay here. There was no law on the ship. Besides, she'd be seen as a scheming thief if Ben had his way. There was no protection except for her derringer. *I'm sorry, Gus. I need you.*

"You're all I have right now."

GUS LAY ON his bunk with his arms folded beneath his head, his revolver and holster draped over the headboard. His saddlebags were hidden from view. The money and gold bags were safe and guarded in the captain's quarters. Still, the only sure protection were his weapons.

In just a few days, they'd reach Fort Randall then he'd be on his way into Nebraska. He sucked in a breath, imagining the smell of the grass of the open plains. A sound of footsteps alerted him to someone's approach. He rolled to his bare feet, then waited with his revolver in his hand. Someone had stopped outside his door. Revolver cocked, he prepared for a fight. Instead, there was a light tap, then another.

"Who is it?"

"Tori."

Christ. After sliding the bolt free, he opened the door to find her in a plain dress and shawl, clutching her reticule, her face chalk white in the moonlight. Fear was written in her big-as-saucers eyes and pursed mouth.

"May I come in? I know it's late."

"If you didn't look so damned scared, I'd ask you to wait till mornin'. Come in."

She stepped inside. "I wouldn't bother you if I had any other choice."

Gus closed the door, then slid the bolt. After he passed her, he shoved his revolver into his holster, then turned to face her. What he saw was a woman who'd been terrorized. His anger boiled inside when he took in the sight of her.

She shook from her head to her boots, and her hair looked like she'd been in a wind storm. The buttons at the neck of her dress were unfastened as though she'd dressed hurriedly. When her shoulders slumped, he swallowed what little spit he had in his mouth and hoped she hadn't come to exchange her body for his help. That would disappoint him in ways he couldn't name.

Taking her arm, he led her to the only chair. "Sit down. I'll pour a glass of water."

Once he returned to her side, he handed her the glass, and it shook in her hand. She gulped water like she'd just been in the desert. When he turned up the lantern to have a better look at her, what he saw sent raw fury through him. *She'd been attacked.*

She looked up, giving him a glimpse of the red imprint on her neck. The son of a bitch had nearly strangled her. God Almighty, whoever did this would pay for it. The first thing he aimed to find out was why and who. Right now, he suspected it had something to do with the fancy-dressed men he'd seen on deck.

He hunkered in front of her. "I can see what must've happened. Tell me who did that. I'll need to know what's going on. *All of it.* No lies."

She tried to look away from him, but he captured her chin and forced her to look into his eyes. "If you don't tell me, I'll find out my own way, which will make things worse."

THREE

SPILL OF TRUTH

"I'M IN SOME trouble, Gus. I don't want you involved except to keep watch until I can figure out how to get away from *him*. The man who sent two of his employees after me."

"This *man*. Is he your husband?"

"*No*. But he wants something from me that I plan to keep. Once I'm away from this boat, I'll hide. In California. Start a new life."

Gus took in her defiant expression and the pallor of her skin. Her eyes glistened with tears. "I can't be of help if I'm blind. I don't know who this man is. Or what he wants. So, you'll have to tell me."

"He's dangerous."

He ran a finger across her cheek, and she flinched. Her lips quaked at his steady perusal. With one knuckle, he lifted her chin higher for closer inspection of the red impression on her neck. "Yes, he is. As long as I draw breath, he won't do that again. I'll see to it. Tell me his name. In fact, tell me all of their names."

She looked away.

He dropped his hands, sighed, stood, then crossed his arms. "There isn't any point in you being here if you won't talk. I can't help if you're evasive. These secrets aren't useful. This game you're playing could end badly for you. Throw down your cards, Tori, or go back to your room."

She kept her face averted. "All right. The man who attacked me is Ben Irons."

"That's a start. How does he know you?"

"He works for my former partner. In Virginia City."

"What does he want?"

"*My* money."

"I see."

"No. You don't. But if you could just see me safely to Omaha, I'd be willing to do whatever you ask."

His laugh was bitter, even to his own ears. "I'm not going to Omaha. I'm getting off at Fort Randall. I'll keep an eye out until then, but that's where we part company."

"If you could see your way clear to escort me as far as Omaha, I'd be grateful. *Very grateful.*"

"Maybe you'd care to spell out your meaning because I'm not sure I like much about what you might be suggesting."

"I'll give you what you asked for. Back at Fort Benton."

A roiling of his stomach started to transform into a full-on need to heave up last night's vittles along with the whiskey he'd drank. *She was for sale, after all.* And he didn't like it one little bit. He moved around her to reach for his gun belt and holster. Near enough to see her cringe at his nearness.

She stood. He sensed her eyes follow him to where he bent over a trunk, then hefted his saddlebag, draping it over his shoulder. His eyes narrowed on hers. She looked like a woman about to break into an all-out cry. That he couldn't handle.

He waved his hand. "After you."

"Where are we going?"

"You've just invited me to your cabin. Isn't that so?" He didn't leave her enough time to object. Instead, he perversely enjoyed her stunned expression. He gripped her arm, then propelled her through the door, locking it behind him.

"You can't stay in my room," she retorted as she trotted beside his long strides.

"No?"

"It wouldn't look right to the others."

He gripped her arm, and Tori skipped to keep up. "Maybe you should've gave it thought before you invited me. At least now I know what you really want from me. Protection. Hope you're worth it."

The door was part-way open, swaying with the motion of the boat. The bolt hung from the hinge. He released her, then watched her back away from him as he dropped his gear to the floor beside her valise. Now he understood why she'd come to him. She wasn't safe, and he'd been her only recourse. When she fumbled with her reticule, it was certain she tried to reach her derringer.

"If you pull your gun on me, I already told you I'd take it from you. You still don't trust me, Tori. And I sure don't trust you. If you don't believe that I won't hurt you, you damn well shouldn't have come to me for help." He advanced toward her.

She shook her head, then stepped back until she met the wall.

He snatched her purse from between her fingers, then tossed it to the bed. "Tell me everything. Then we'll broker our own deal."

"No. It's not like that. You misunderstand. I—"

"I?" He grazed her face with the back of his hand, and she jerked her face away. "So. You don't like my touch." *Christ, how he hated to torment her. But this was the only way he could dig out the truth.*

"I don't like your touch because you're being perverse. And cruel. You aren't the man I thought."

"If I'm to save your pretty ass from robbery and rape, I deserve to know what I'm up against. As to cruel. You've cornered me, and I don't like it. Now I'm cornering you to get at the truth."

"You've been drinking. I smell it."

"That's right. But I'm not drunk. And I'm not like Ben. I don't intend to hurt you, so stop looking at me like a scared rabbit." Her stricken expression made him sigh, then back away.

She skirted around him, then dropped onto the bed, her back as stiff as a corpse. Her teeth nibbled at her lower lip while her tangled hair fanned over one shoulder. In the lantern light, her pert nipples

were visible beneath the muslin. So was the swath of red on her delicate neck. The sight of it sickened him. The first thing he'd like to do is
confront Ben Irons, after which he'd be swimming.

He turned his attention to the broken bolt, managing to lift it into
place. It would do little to keep out an intruder. He'd see it got fixed
tomorrow. After he turned around, her fingers were threaded against
her lap. He fastened on his gun belt, then shoved a bench close and
straddled it.

"I'm listening. Let's hear it."

"Yes. I admit I took money from the safe at the Silver Star Saloon in
Virginia City. He and I were partners in two establishments, including
the Red Lace in Fort Benton. I cashed out."

"And?"

"He declined my offer to sell him my half unless I agreed to a concession. Took matters into my own hands and left with my share. I
hadn't expected him to track me this fast. Just like him to send his hired
men after me."

"What concession?"

"I don't want to say. Besides, I'm tired."

"What concession?" he repeated through gritted teeth.

"What difference does it make?"

Gus raised his eyebrow. When she averted her face, her cheeks
flamed red. She took a moment to compose herself before she
faced him again.

"Since you're so persistent... he'd give me my half if I agreed to continue to work for him. Special clients. In other words, I'd be a captive to
a life I didn't want anymore. Never again will I be used."

"*Jesus.*" His head tilted, then he pinched the bridge of his nose. "Does
Ben have an accomplice on the ship?"

"No one I recognize. But he and another man have been
watching me."

"I'll talk with the captain. He'll see to your safety. Then get that bolt
fixed. For now, the only thing I can do is bunk on the floor tonight. The
money. Where is it?"

"In the captain's safe."

Gus grinned. At least she'd been smart enough to think of that.

"I'm sorry. I hadn't wanted to get you involved. I hadn't counted on anyone finding me. What did you mean about a deal? What do you want in return?"

"I am both angry and rude. Never mind what I said. You left me no choice but to push you more than I wanted. Otherwise, I wouldn't be able to help you. Get some sleep. I'll be on the floor. You're safe, Tori."

She tossed him a pillow and a blanket from the bed as he turned down the lantern light. He lay on the floor, staring at the ceiling, while he listened to her tossing on the bed.

"Tori. Accordin' to the law, you stole that money. Wouldn't it be easier to give it back?"

"No. I'll never do that. *It's money I earned.*"

He swallowed while he listened to the steady rumble of the ship's engine below deck. There was a steady lapping of water against the planks of the hull. Finally, Tori fell quiet, her arms outstretched. He lay awake with his arms folded beneath his head while he contemplated what he'd do about Ben. Once he left her at Fort Randall, Ben was free to get his hands on her. Unless he made sure Ben wouldn't be well enough. Could he see that they both had an accident? That's when he grinned, thinking about all the pleasurable ways he could slow them down.

———

THE NEXT DAY, she woke to find herself alone. He'd folded the blanket and set it on the foot of her bed. The pillow rested beside her head. She stood in front of the wash bowl and mirror to examine the purple splotches at her throat. She'd have to wear a high-necked blouse to hide the discoloration.

As she finished dressing, the vessel lurched, sending her into a stumble. The hum of the engines quieted. The boat stilled. Men shouted, and boots thudded above her head. The repetitive thumps sounded like ropes slapping the hull. They'd likely stopped to take on more wood.

After she checked her reticule for her derringer, she picked up the key, made her way outside, then locked the door behind her. The bolt still hung at an angle on the inside. Looking both left and right, she saw no one. Loud voices could be heard from the opposite side of the ship.

Tori followed the sound of commotion until she reached the forward deck, then saw the boat was tucked beneath overhanging trees along the mud bank. Curious, she joined the passengers pressed against the rail, their faces intent on the goings-on. Seeing no sign of Gus, she squeezed in between two women and a child. Below, men lashed the boat to tow ropes hitched to a team of mules.

"We're stuck. Put in to load wood, and she dug into the mud."

Tori recognized the gray-haired waitress from the night before.

"Name's Margaret. Work in the kitchen."

The woman looked different in the sunlight. Not exactly young, but less sour.

"I'm Tori. We've seen each other." After a silent moment, she darted another glance at the woman, then followed her gaze to the men below.

"Yep. Didn't know if you'd remember me."

"How will we become unstuck?"

"The men are out there with teams of mules hitched to the bow, trying to drag this thing out of the mud and into deeper water. Once we clear it, we'll be on the way again. I seem to remember you with that big man. The one down there working alongside the crew. Can't miss your man. No shirt on. Surely is a fine-lookin' one. Never saw such muscles."

She searched the men laying out rope while others minded the mules. Gus was in the thick of the activity, a coil of rope over his shoulder, his muscles straining against the tug of the animals. Men cussed and hollered out orders. She smiled at the sight of him.

"Yes, indeed. He is quite a handsome man."

"Too bad about one of the passengers who'd been ordered to help. Got himself caught in a line after that big man yanked it a little too soon. Heard the man's scream just as he tumbled into the water below. Swear I heard the snap of his bone. Good thing he was standin' on the lower deck helpin' with the lines. That handsome feller leaped from the bank, then dragged the yelping fellow from the mud. Sure was a mess. There was a doctor aboard who set his leg. Seems it's broke."

"The man with the broken leg. Do you know his name?"

"No. Don't know how it happened either. One minute, he was standin' below, then the next he got yanked overboard. Or maybe he didn't hear a warning."

Tori gave thought to providence. Then gave thought to Gus and wondered if Ben had been the one who'd broken his leg. "Providence," she muttered.

"Providence, yes. But that man looked loaded to the muzzle with rage. From here, thought that squalling fellow might drown the way he struggled."

She cupped her hands over her eyes to watch as the ship broke free, then reckoned Gus found an opportunity and took it. *Yes, indeed. A dangerous man when provoked.* If she were more courageous, she might ask Gus if he'd meant to kill Ben. But she knew the answer. If he had, Ben would be dead.

Three Days Later
Fort Randall, South Dakota
Early July 1879

GUS LED HIS horses down the ramp to the rail beside the landing. He looked toward the fort, then shook his head at how many houses had sprung up around it. In fact, he'd heard it was more a town than a fort. He snugged the cinch on his saddle, then turned his attention to fastening his saddlebag behind the cantle. Grinning to himself, he still heard the captain's craggy voice warning him to disembark before he stirred up more trouble.

A broken leg would keep Ben Irons from Tori for the time it took her to reach Omaha. With a last check of the pannier lashed to the packhorse, he checked his revolver, then laced the reins of his mount through his hands.

He glanced in the direction of the Nellie Peck, where barrels and crates were being rolled up the gangways, then his gaze searched the ship's rail for signs of Tori. With no sign, he sighed with relief—though he'd miss her feisty nature. Still, her company came with trouble. That thought was short-lived after he started to lead his horse up the road to the fort.

The persistent woman in question was marching his way, dressed in a high-necked gray dress. As she drew closer, he gave thought to slipping into the saddle, putting distance between them. But the sight of her pretty face doused that intention. *Fool that he was.*

"Gus. I'd hoped I'd catch you."

"Tori. I'd suggest you board the ship before she leaves without you." They faced each other, the girth of his horse and saddle between them.

"I'm not leaving on the ship. My trunk and valise have been unloaded."

"Jesus. This is no place for you. You need to get back aboard. Omaha, remember?"

"You don't understand. I can't."

"Why? Ben Irons isn't a threat."

"You saw to that, I'm sure."

"Maybe. That doesn't matter. The point is this. The soldiers spend most of their time away, on duty. Gold fever is in the air, which attracts the kinds of men who aren't polite. In short, you won't have much help. I won't be around to pull you out of whatever trouble you fall into."

"I want to go with you as far as the UP. I'll pay you. Name your price."

"*No.* We've already talked about this."

"No? You can't mean you'd leave me here and just ride off?"

"That's exactly what I mean. Since that steamboat is about to depart, I'd suggest you hurry back to the gangway. Wave them before they haul it in."

Her mouth pursed. She whirled while his gaze followed her to where her trunk and valise sat at the bottom of the dock. That settled the matter as far as he was concerned. He swung into the saddle, snugged the dally rope around his pommel, then nudged his horse along. Fate intervened when he happened a last look across his shoulder to see a well-dressed man who'd gripped her arm.

His recollection flashed back to the two men he'd seen together on the ship. One now wore a broken leg. Gus gritted his teeth while she struggled to jerk free of the man's hold.

Her scream of pain sent his blood boiling. This had to be the other man, both sent by Silas. Manhandling a woman wasn't acceptable, even in these parts. Damn the woman. His good intentions had just dropped into a deep well. She found trouble with every one of her dainty steps. It seemed he'd be the only one to come to her rescue.

He dug his heels into his horse's flanks while tugging the pack horse behind. Before he reached her, he'd slipped his revolver from his holster and cocked it. Once he closed in on them, he brought his horse up, then leveled his revolver at the man's head.

"Let her go." Onlookers from the boat, as well as the crew, stopped what they were doing at the sound of his toneless command.

The attacker's blue eyes flashed in the sunlight. "This is between her and me. You best keep to your business. She's returning to Virginia City. She's a thief."

Gus wrapped the reins around his pommel. He poked back his hat with his thumb. "That so? It appears the lady doesn't want to go with you. As to bein' a thief. That's not the story I got."

Gus waited. Tori tried to jerk free but was held fast. She stilled then looked toward him, her expression resigned, her spirit wilted. "Do you want to go with him, Tori?"

Her pleading stare held his. "No. I'll go if it means trouble for anyone."

"I don't agree with your decision. I won't tell you again, Mister. Let her go."

"Gus. Please. I've got no choice."

"The lady gave you her answer. Now git."

Gus's body tautened like a bowstring. His finger squeezed the trigger. The loud retort sent folks scurrying for cover. With a sidelong glance, he saw men standing near the old stockade, puffing cigars. None of them moved.

Tori dropped to her knees, her glassy eyes on the man who lay on the dirt. He groaned, then pressed his hand to the side of his head where blood trickled from his ear. The man's other hand reached for his gun. Gus cocked his hammer—the man froze.

"You gotta' name?"

"Tom Willis. Work for Silas Gaines. He'll find you. In fact, he's on the way, expecting the money. He's not one to mess with. Especially after what you did to Ben."

"Welcome to try. Best get on the boat before I decide not to let you live. Don't ever let me lay eyes on you again, or you won't need no doctor. Tell Silas she won't be back. If he comes for her, he'll meet the same fate."

Once Tom wobbled up the gangway, the crew unlatched it to make way. Gus dismounted while Tori struggled to her feet. She brushed her skirt, careful to keep her face averted.

"Look at me."

She lifted her glazed eyes but kept them centered on his shoulder.

"This Tom Willis. He was with Ben Irons?" Now her stare met his.

"Yes. I suppose so. I didn't know him or recognize him."

He sighed at the sight of unshed tears. This woman tugged places he wanted to keep buried.

"If it matters, I'm sorry," she said flatly.

"No. It doesn't matter. Come on. Let's get you to the fort. A woman named Marie Leveau will put you up till the next sternwheeler to Omaha. I'll see your things get hauled up the landing road."

"Thank you. I'll find somebody to guide me to the closest rail."

"Look, Tori. You can't expect to find men willing to do that without them expecting something in return. That doesn't always mean money. There's a stage that goes on to Sioux City, or you can take the next sternwheeler. Those are your choices. You've got a few days to decide."

"Aren't you going on from here?"

"I am."

"I'll pay you to take me as far as the first train west."

———————

GUS FOLLOWED THE freight wagon, his pack horse plodding behind. Her trunk and valise had been loaded beside sundry barrels and sacks of goods. Tori sat atop the seat beside Hawk, a man of few words and having the insufferable habit of spitting tobacco over the side. She dabbed her nose each time the wind drifted her way since the man clearly had not bathed in some time.

Gus had given him orders to escort her to Marie's Dry Goods Store. Her trunk and carpetbag were perched just behind her, but between what she faced ahead and an unknown future, she found she needed Gus's security. After another glance, her shoulders relaxed because he was still in sight. Her head swam with ways she might convince him to take her with him. This man beside her certainly would not make a reliable travel companion or guide.

Civilization peeked through the trees from the bluff above the river. All manner of crates and clusters of settlers stood near the long pier sticking from the red mud banks like a meatless bone. She found herself staring at hard looking men wearing buckskins, much like those Gus seemed to prefer. There were groups of blue uniformed soldiers standing amid the folks who'd disembarked the Nellie Peck.

By the time they left the trees behind them, the fort spread out before her eyes. She studied the civilized appearance of the compound. Then, before she knew it, the wagon pulled up beside the sagging porch of Marie's Dry Goods.

Gus's deep drawl broke into her thoughts after Hawk vaulted down. "Marie will see to you from here. Welcome to Fort Randall, Tori. You'll be all right. Like I said, you can choose. This is good-bye."

"My offer still stands. I'd like you to see me on to the Union Pacific."

"My answer is the same. *No.*"

"Then I wish you safe travels, Gus Quaid. Thank you. For everything."

"Watch out for yourself, Tori Barrett. Remember to see if Marie Leveau can offer you a room above the sutler's. Tell her I sent you."

She swallowed hard after he dismounted then reached for her, swinging her to the ground. He held her longer than she'd expected, then wondered at the tender stroking of his thumb. She barely held back her welling tears until he leaned over her, then pressed a feathery kiss to her cheek. After he mounted, he gathered the dally rope then turned his mount, and with one last glance, he was gone. She released a halting breath. Now she faced what was ahead. Alone.

FOUR

THE DECISION

HER FLINTY GAZE tugged at the emotion that swept through him. His last look found her eyes staring at her boots, as though she were a lost child instead of that hard-as-nails woman he'd first met. He waited a heartbeat, then she turned in the direction of Marie's. One part of him wanted to guide her to the damned UP, at least to have a clear conscience. But the other reminded him of the rugged trek across wild country.

Even if he were fool enough to take her to the rail, he'd wind up having to leave her in Ogallala. For now, she'd be reasonably safe near the fort, unless she did something to draw attention to herself–which she had a penchant for.

He'd managed to slow the men who'd followed her, giving her time to disappear. It was up to her to take care of herself. He didn't need nor want the responsibility. Still, hidden behind those beautiful blue eyes were secrets that both intrigued and worried him.

Leading his pack horse, he rode to the freight corral. He backed his horses out of the way of the troop of ten soldiers coming his way. He pulled up then waited. A lieutenant suddenly halted, then twisted around in his saddle, waving the rest on.

"Gus? That you?"

Gus raised his hand, in recognition. "Jim Mabry," Gus said. He'd known a lot of soldiers. This one he didn't trust.

"You here to join us?"

"Not this time. Passing through to Nebraska."

"That so. Best be careful. Got plenty of Sioux still on the loose. The Poncas aren't much inclined to get along with the Yankton and Santee. Rounding up strays is hard work."

Gus nudged his horse closer to the lieutenant, not liking the man nor his tone.

"Seems like most stay to the reservations."

"If the agents weren't in cahoots with the traders, the Sioux would get the shipments promised to them then save us from traipsing all over Dakota lookin' for them."

"Wish I had time to join you. Not this time."

"You sure are good with negotiating. If you change your mind, see the fort commander."

Just as the lieutenant tipped his hat and turned his horse, Gus called out. "Any signs of any white women on the reservation?"

The soldier lifted his hat, then set it back on his head. "Sorry, Gus. While we're at it. Saw a woman with you. Seems like I've seen her before."

Gus shook his head. "Nope. Just happened on the same boat."

He cringed at the thought of Tori running into this particular soldier, which added to his mounting worry, because he had a reputation around women. As a soldier, he found Mabry callous. He watched until the troop rounded the bend to the river. Two long blasts announced the Nellie Peck was ready to leave.

The growl in his stomach reminded him he hadn't eaten in some time. After a meal, he'd settle for a few whiskeys, then some sleep before setting out for Nebraska come morning. Once he reached Yankton, he'd settle into a warm bed with a used woman... with every intention of burying any thoughts of Tori Barrett.

———————

TORI STOOD BESIDE the buxom, silver-haired Marie Leveau. Neither missed the large frame of Gus Quaid as he ducked through the flap of a tent. Fort Randall looked, for the most part, like a thriving town, while the presence of soldiers added to a sense of security. Gus was probably right about Omaha. Still, her money would only last so long. Thinking about what she'd do, she forgot that Marie stood beside her until the woman's husky voice broke into her musings.

"Why don't you come on inside? Got a small space you can use for sleepin' then my hauler will bring in your trunk. Best look into a ticket on the next boat out. This ain't no place for a lady to stay unless she's the wife of an officer."

Tori studied the older woman's deep-set brown eyes and rouged cheeks. Marie hadn't been innocent in a long time... at least, not by Tori's calculation.

"Giving thought to what I'll do. Maybe you could tell me what's in that tent."

Marie leaned forward, then cupped her eyes. "Hmm. Figured you had your eye on that Gus. He's a handsome man, though a mite intimidatin' with his size. That's where men go to buy beer or whiskey, honey. The commander isn't happy about it, but he's leavin' it there so long as none of the soldiers goes in there while on duty. As to Gus. Don't count on him. He's a loner."

"Now, as to you, I think I have a good idea you've got trouble followin' you. Long as it don't follow you to my doorstep, I'll put you up. I'm guessin' you could use some vittles. Come back to the kitchen once you get settled in the room behind the curtain. It ain't much to offer, but it'll do for right now. Can't keep you for long."

Alone, she'd be no match for Silas if he caught up with her. By now, he was already on her heels. All she could hope was that he'd be on his way to Omaha. She needed to find a way to go in the opposite direction. Following Gus into Nebraska held appeal. Since he'd refused her entreaty, it was up to her to find someone else. *A plan. She needed a plan.* If she made it to California, no one would find her. Marie might know just the person to see her to the rail heading west.

She lay on the cot, then closed her eyes, one arm beneath her head. If only she had been more careful. Ever setting eyes on Silas Gaines had been one of her many mistakes. At the hard rap against the wall opposite the curtain, her eyes snapped open. She swung her legs to the floor, then ran her fingers through her tangled braid. "Who is it?"

"Hawk. I come with your trunk and fancy bag."

"Please come in."

Hawk was the size of Texas, with a jaw as square as an axe blade. He carried her trunk into the makeshift bedroom, then dropped it with a loud thud. A few moments later, he returned with her valise. His face was as red as a beet from the exertion. What little hair he had stuck out in every geographical direction. His beady eyes pinched rather than squinted. His mouth smiled, revealing brown, broken teeth, leaving her stomach churning.

"Marie said to drop it all here. Anything else?"

"Yes. As a matter of fact. Marie said you freight. I was wondering if I could pay you to take me along if you're heading south toward the Union Pacific?"

A crooked, slow smile had her quiver at her stupid but desperate decision. His intent perusal had her question whether to withdraw her request. She straightened at the thought that she still had her derringer. Maybe she'd buy another revolver from Marie.

"I leave tomorrow for Yankton. You can make your way into Nebraska from there."

"How much would you require?"

Hawk scratched the back of his ear. His gaze moved from her boots to her head. "Depends."

"On what?"

"What you're offerin'?"

"I'll pay you fifty dollars in cash. Make no mistake, I plan to keep my gun handy so you will keep to yourself. If that's what you've got in mind, Mister Hawk. My person is off the table. You will not touch me."

"Just Hawk. Fifty dollars will do. Seems we got us a deal. See you early. Make sure to buy a hat and don't wear no fancy dress. The end of the line is Yankton. Just so you know."

"All right. I'll be ready."

The curtain swayed after his departure, while she trembled at her desperate decision. What had she just done? Until they got to Fort Yankton, she'd be at the mercy of a man she didn't trust. Sleeping would be impossible. She'd just have to make certain he understood she'd kill him if he touched her. A larger revolver would make her case.

GUS LED HIS Appaloosa and pack horse to the front of the sutler's. He'd given thought to moving on before he had a chance to change his mind about Miss Barrett. It would've been smarter to leave before he did something stupid. But his damnable conscience wouldn't let him go without a goodbye. At least, that's what he kept telling himself. He had no intention to babysit a woman with a hatful of trouble.

Just as he stepped onto the raised landing, the door was suddenly flung open. He found himself staring at a *boy. Until his eyes settled on his shirt.* Then his slow perusal met those pretty eyes, sparkling beneath the shadows of a new broad-brimmed hat.

She wore boy's blue pants, a white shirt that snugged her roundness, and a revolver tucked in her belt. He did his best not to chuckle at her disguise. Her mouth lifted into a wry smile while his eyes feasted on her cute dimples and sprinkling of freckles across her nose. "Tori?"

"Yes. Thought you'd be gone by now."

"Just dropped by to see if you're doin' all right before I head out." *Why the hell are you dressed in boy's pants and wearing that hat?* If she hoped the getup hid her womanly side, she needed more work. The disguise wouldn't last long. More worry was that revolver.

"Goodbye, then. As you can see, I'm about to *head* out myself."

"That so?" He perused her from her boots to her felt hat and found himself grinning at the image she made. "Boat isn't due in till end of the week."

"I won't be on the boat. I've found someone to take me to Yankton where I might find a means to the rail."

"Who might that be?"

"Hawk. He's a freighter."

"Christ! I *know* who he is." Just as she started to duck around him, he stretched out his arm, barring her way. "Just how much did you pay him?"

"Not that it's your business. Fifty dollars."

His throat closed over a string of cuss words while she pursed her lips, then lifted her chin. Without another word, after latching onto her arm, he tugged her to the stairs more roughly than he'd meant. The woman had managed to rile him once again, and it was still early in the day. She tried to yank her arm from his grasp but her attempts only forced him to grip tighter.

He knew how stubborn she could be, so he doubted reason would work. She'd be no match for Hawk. He'd take her money, then leave her stranded. Once they were at the bottom of the steps, he led her to the side of the building, then out of sight of gawkers, but she spit names and cuss words... some he hadn't heard before. Once they were out of view behind the building, he pulled her against his chest. "Have you lost your mind?"

"Let go of me... you brute. Scoundrel. *Horse's patoot.*"

With her eyes flashing like blue flames and her cheeks flushed, she was more alluring... pouting mouth or not.

"If I let go, will you listen to reason?"

"Yes. If you'll listen to me, in return."

He released his hold, then dropped his arms to his sides. "My reason first. Hawk is a no-account and not used to being with women who don't give in to his baser needs. He's probably factored those needs into the cost. You won't like it much."

He studied the rising blush of her face. "It'll be a long journey with him expecting more than fifty dollars. So, in short, you'll need to wait for the next ship to get you to Omaha. From there, take the train. But going with Hawk would be a big mistake."

"Don't you understand? Ben has more than likely sent a telegram to Silas. He'll come after me personally... and he won't be alone. He'll expect me to be on a boat to Omaha where he may have contacted the law to arrest me. That's where he's going. I feel it in my bones. I don't plan to be caught. I've decided to go to California."

"You are not leaving here with Hawk."

She whirled away from him, then after only two strides, he caught her arm, spinning her around. His fingers dug into her arm while her eyes glittered with temper. He'd never met a more irascible and unreasonable woman.

"You win. But you might not thank me."

"What does that mean?"

"It means I'll take you as far as Yankton, then you're on your own. I might add, it's out of my way, but this is what I get for being partly stupid. You're dressed like a boy, but you're not fooling anyone. That blouse is too tight. Tuck your hair under the hat. Take one valise with enough clothes and necessities. No trunk. No wagon. Can you even ride a horse?"

"Yes. I can ride very well. I'm also handy with a revolver and rifle."

"Did you give Hawk that money?"

"Not yet."

"You'll need to buy a horse and saddle. I'll go find one for you. Be ready in one hour."

He proffered his palm up. She reached into her pocket, then handed him the greenbacks.

"I'll wait here."

The tapping of her booted toes already gave him second thoughts. "One more thing. The riding will be hard, dangerous, and long. You best not slow me down, or I'll leave you behind."

"You haven't mentioned sleeping arrangements."

"That's easy. You'll have your own bedroll. I plan to keep to myself."

His mind spun with this harebrained idea of his. While he marched to the livery, his blood boiled until he figured it might burst from his eyeballs. In fact, he whistled a tune to keep his tongue from launching a string of cuss words. Making matters worse, he sensed her eyes bore into his back, finding himself wishing he'd kept riding. Instead, he'd given in to this loopy agreement.

The witch. He knew what he'd said about the sleeping arrangements. But once he'd cooled down, he knew it would be damned hard to be near her and not want her. Imagining her in his arms might be his undoing and her mistake. He'd told her he could be trusted. But he damned well wasn't a saint.

———————

TORI PLODDED ALONG on a roan gelding, doing her best to keep his big Appaloosa and gray pack horse in sight. She swiped at her sweat-dotted face and swatted at incessant flies. Once they'd left Fort Randall, they'd followed the Missouri for miles before he led them out onto open grassland.

As far as she could tell, Gus hadn't looked across his shoulder to see if she was still there. Because she understood his keen sense of surroundings, she'd bet he knew exactly where she was. Did he even care that she'd slumped or that she needed to stretch her sore legs? Forcing her eyes to stay open, she nudged her horse into a faster gait to keep up with his pace. *No, sir, Mister Quaid. I'm not turning tail.*

Gus had been right about Hawk. After the freighter found her in front of the store, he'd demanded the money. Her change of mind infuriated him. His mottled red face had her backing away. Just as he pinned her to the wagon, Gus appeared, then yanked the man around, landing a punch square into Hawk's nose sending her attacker flat in the dirt.

At the sight of her freighter's predicament, Marie opened the door and rushed across the distance, then she kneeled beside the groaning man. The woman flayed Gus with a litany of cuss words. Helpless to intercede, Tori watched the nearby circle of soldiers egging on the fight but Hawk brushed his pants, then stalked away, leaving Marie to follow.

So lost in her contemplation, she forgot her aching legs and back. On the other hand, Gus rode straight in the saddle, his attention ahead of him. After he pulled up, he gave her time to close the distance. When she was alongside, she regarded his gaze at the Missouri River, sensing these open spaces gave him pleasure.

"This where we're stopping?"

"We'll rest here. Dismount and drink. Stretch your legs. Best not fall asleep in the saddle, Tori. If you fall. Well, I don't need to tell you. We'll camp when the sun arcs lower. There's a place beside a trickle of a stream to bed down."

As she stepped down, her legs buckled, forcing her to grab the saddle to steady herself. She straightened, determined to persevere. Damned if she'd complain. After he'd dismounted, he led his horse near hers.

"You look done in."

She swallowed from her canteen, then thought better of what she really wanted to say. "I'm fine. Been a while since I sat a horse. How long till we reach Yankton?"

"Two or three days."

"Didn't realize we were so close. I apologize for taking you out of your way."

"Just so you know... dependin' on what's up ahead of us, I might change course."

She nodded, then gave thought to why he'd tell her that. Just as she was about to ask, he'd already thrown his leg over his saddle with the ease of the plainsman he was. Not a man of many words, he turned his horse, leaving her to follow. After one failed hop, she lifted her chin to see him in the distance.

Determined not to complain, she heaved her leg over the saddle on the second hop, then gritted her teeth at the effort it had taken. Without more delay, she urged her mount into a lope and followed the ornery man. Somehow, she was beginning to like him, nonetheless. If for no other reason, he held to his word. "Well, Gus Quaid, I intend to prove my mettle."

They'd settled into a routine together. She gathered wood while he hobbled the horses. She set out the coffee pot and fry pan while he produced a small grate for cooking. While she hadn't done much cooking over the years, she found she liked it. That was before her life had changed.

She'd survived back in Virginia then long after that. She'd survive now. After he tossed her a sack of bacon, beans, and flour alongside the fire pit, he'd left her to cook something worth eating. Her resolve set in.

Tonight, she'd try her hand at bacon gravy. The question was how to make biscuits without lard and baking soda. The thought of sparse food circled her back to her lovely dresses and shoes, left behind with Marie. The woman had been willing to pay a fair price for her finer things. Still, it would be a long time until she could afford to buy such things again.

Someday, she'd buy pretty dresses after she reached California. With the money for her clothes, she'd been able to buy a revolver from Marie. She'd tucked it between her clothes inside her valise and hoped she'd never need to use it.

She kneeled beside the fire when she heard his approach. Stirring the flour with bacon grease, she then stirred in the beans. They wouldn't soften much, but there were no options. There hadn't been time to soak them. After he cleared his throat, her regard drifted upward to find one of his eyebrows raised. More remarkably, his mouth curved into one of his rare grins. *Was he making fun of her?*

"You're full of surprises, Tori. Smells good. Got more beans. If you soak them tonight, they'll go down easier tomorrow."

She bit her lip, then handed up the plates piled with her concoction, hoping she didn't kill them both with these vittles. They took seats on the blanket he had spread out near the fire, the plates on their laps, the tin cups of coffee beside them.

In the quiet, she said the first thing that came to mind. "Gus, I'll figure out how to make biscuits with what we've got. Just so you know, I'm not the pampered woman you seem to think." His lopsided grin surprised her.

After his nod, he waved his fork. "Don't need fancy food. Could make hardtack, and I'd be glad to have it. I'm not expectin' much with what we got."

She fastened her eyes on the firelight, then watched how it illuminated the hard planes of his face. Using his fork, he scooped the food into his mouth, his focus on his plate. She stretched her legs, then crossed her ankles. She'd almost forgotten to eat, so fascinated by his attention to his food. One thing was for sure, he wasn't much for conversation, especially when he ate. Not that she wanted to talk because she'd come to be weary of hiding her secrets.

"Best eat and turn in. I'll stand watch," he said between bites.

Lifting her eyes, she stared in his direction. "What will you watch for?"

He looked toward her, lowering his fork. "Cheyenne and Sioux. Mostly Sioux. And anything else."

"Haven't they been rounded up and sent to reservations?"

"Most have. Not all agree with the terms. Our horses are enticing for the ones on the run. They've got grievances over allotments, among other things. They'll see us before we see them."

"Lordy. I hadn't given much thought to that."

"We'll do all right. I got a question that's been gnawing at me."

She set her plate of half-eaten food down on the ground beside her. "All right."

"How much money did you steal?"

She lifted her chin. "The truth is, I took one thousand dollars from his safe when I left Fort Benton. About eight hundred from Virginia City. Rightfully, it belongs to me. He'd agreed to it after we became partners."

There was a heavy silence between them while she held his frosty glare. Setting his plate on the ground beside him, he leaned back against his saddle behind him, then pinched the bridge of his nose. All at once, he stood and picked up his rifle, then offered her a hard stare before he was swallowed by the night shadows.

Did he believe her? The sense of his disagreeable mood weighed heavy on her. Along the way, they'd been congenial. As sudden as a summer storm, the mood had become heavy. If he thought of her as a thief and a liar, it cut her deeper than he knew.

She lay awake, staring at the star-lit sky, while listening to the horses snuffle. Stretching beneath her blanket, she closed her eyes. Maybe tomorrow he would be willing to listen to her explanation. *She wasn't a thief.* At least not the kind he thought.

GUS WAS DEAD on his feet when he finally rolled onto his blanket and closed his eyes. The last thing he expected this woman to be was a thief. He already knew she'd been a prostitute. Whether by choice, he didn't know. An outright crook was another matter. Sooner or later, he'd find out what was going on in that pretty head of hers before things got out of hand. Defending her from the law was a distinct possibility, and he wasn't sure he could do that.

Streaks of pink and yellow painted the sky after he opened his eyes at the smell of bacon and coffee. He sat up, ran his fingers through his hair, then searched the camp. After he stood, he strode to where the pan of potatoes and bacon simmered. It looked like she'd used cottonwood and dry grass to keep the fire alive. But where was she?

He turned in time to see Tori walking up from the river with an armful of twigs. Her hat was missing, and her freshly brushed hair was neatly braided, glistening in the dawn light. No man could mistake her for anything but a beautiful woman, pants or no pants.

He stood back before she dropped the wood beside the fire, then she brushed her hands against her denim pants. Their gazes held for a moment. As she started to crouch beside the steamy pan, he caught her shoulders and held her in place. She averted her face.

"Look at me." Her eyes slowly lifted to look into his.

"I need to know *why* you took the money. Tried to sleep last night, rolling it over and over in my head. The woman I came to know is either an accomplished liar or a victim of some wrong I can only imagine. Either way, start talking."

She sucked in a breath. "All right. Sit and eat. I'll do my best to explain. But I don't know why it's so important to you. We'll be parting company, anyhow."

He had to ask himself the same question. His nerves jangled while her fork clinked against her plate, where she stirred the morsels from one spot to another. The food was tasteless, but eating was the least of his worries at the moment. She began her story with her life in Virginia.

Bits and pieces of that time skimmed over her tongue, some bringing smiles to her face.

As she described the war around them, he surmised she suffered along with a family that had all been killed. His stomach roiled at how she'd been in the clutches of a scoundrel who'd lured her away from one difficult life to another of shame. A no-account had set her up in business in New Orleans for his own gain, then stolen her innocence.

Her halting words became whispers until he could only imagine what she was seeing in her vision of that faraway time—a victim. As the words fell silent, he could barely look at her taut face. Her cheeks were tear-stained. He knew all he needed to know for the moment. Silas wanted more than money. He wanted *her* back. Gus would make sure that never happened. His throat closed over a lump. Her story triggered the fury he'd once felt when he lost his wife. This woman deserved more out of life than what she'd been handed.

FIVE

THE TOUCH

NEITHER SPOKE OF what had been confided. She hadn't revealed all of the truth—*that she had married Connor O'Malley.* Her disgrace was unbearable. Every once in a while, Gus slowed his horse in deference to her short-legged mount, giving her time to catch up.

She'd become accustomed to his moods. Sometimes, he was withdrawn, perverse, and even teasing... leaving her to wonder what he thought or what his past had been. Since she revealed more about herself than she'd ever done before, his sideways glances wouldn't quite meet her eyes. She didn't want his pity, leaving her to agonize about what he thought of her.

Observing the blisters on her hands after they'd stopped to water the horses, he'd offered a spare pair of his gloves, which he tied around her wrists with twine. While she still didn't trust this fierce, reclusive man... she'd uncovered his large heart. But she'd learned he'd rather die than let anyone see his kindness. Whether he pitied her or not, he'd become more attentive.

They entered a deep, narrow gorge where they followed along a winding stream. Her horse trotted into the water to drink. Gus turned his mount to face her, waving her forward. She smiled, then she saw his attention change to the upper branches of a massive cottonwood.

Her horse's ears flickered and flattened back. The horse lifted her head, then jerked the reins from her grip, just as the horse reared. She tumbled backward over the rump, then landed hard as her breath whooshed from her lungs. In the next moments, she stared upward into the golden eyes of the cougar standing above her in the boughs. As she moved, the low growl signaled the sleek cat was about to pounce.

Fear knifed through her. Gus yelled something, but she was too stunned to understand his words. She dug her heels into the dirt, trying desperately to scoot over the rocks and twigs to get anywhere away from the animal above her. The cat's mouth yawned open, its growl so fierce her heart stopped with cold fear. Frozen where she lay, she could only hope death would come quick.

A powerful boom rent the air, and then, just as suddenly, the big cat dropped to the ground with a loud thump. Her eyes widened while the cat's hide twitched where it lay sprawled near her boots. Blood seeped from a hole in the animal's neck.

Gus was there, standing over the kill. He crouched beside her, then she found herself nestled against him. She tried to hold back her sobs against his shirt but failed. *How silly. How stupid she'd been.* The animal was dead. She was safe, rocked in Gus's arms as though she were a child. The gentleness of his fingers sifting through her hair comforted her, yet she still cried.

"You're safe. I've got you," he whispered near her ear.

"My new boots." Just another silly thought that spilled from her mouth without reason.

"Your boots are fine, but I'm going to lift you to your feet so we can walk away from here. No need for you to look at the carcass."

How long they walked, she didn't know. Time slipped away from her. Soon enough, she became aware of the two horses he led behind him, which meant hers was missing. After they stopped, he lifted his canteen from his saddle and handed it to her. She hiccupped, then pressed her hand against her mouth. He brushed a trembling hand across her brow.

She swallowed the water, then looked across her shoulder. "My horse. She's gone."

"We'll walk a little farther upstream. Then I'll look for your horse. Most likely didn't get too far from water. I'll leave you with the pack horse. Her name's Jenny, in case you need to talk. She's fair company. Keep the rifle in your hand. Don't be afraid to use it."

Pasting a misplaced yet faint smile on her mouth, she gripped the rifle in her shaking hands.

"Thank you for what you did. If not for you, I'd be dead. Jenny and I will get along just fine."

"You're welcome. I should'a kept better watch in them trees. The horses should'a let us know sooner. Jenny is usually the best alarm." With his finger, he lifted her chin. "You sure you're all right?"

"Just shaken. That's about as close to a big cat as I ever want to be again."

A grin started at one corner of his mouth until it had spread into a full smile beneath all of his scruff. Brazen, though it was, she brushed her gloved hand across his cheek, but he stilled it in his firm grip. His gaze stayed on hers for only a moment before he leaned into her with a kiss to her lips as gentle as a butterfly wing—a reassuring, sweet kiss. It meant nothing more.

Slipping her hand from his hold, it occurred to her this man had the power to break her heart. Saying goodbye will be hard enough. "I'm sorry," she murmured.

"I'm not."

There was a forlorn groan deep in his chest, from someone who preferred to hide his feelings beneath his scars. In her case, the capacity to love had been diminished by her own demons. Lowering his mouth to hers once again, he deepened the kiss while she lifted onto the toes of her boots. Her feet left the ground as he clutched her against his chest. Her arms wrapped around his neck. They held each other until he sighed, then he lowered her to her feet. After he released her, he studied her for a long moment.

"Stay here. I'll be back quick."

JUST AS HE'D promised, he found her horse and led the animal to where she stood like a sentinel beside the pack horse, his spare Remington firmly in her hand. With her white shirt dirt-stained, her hair tucked beneath her brown hat, and her boy's pants rolled to near the top of her dirty boots, she sure made a picture. As enticing as strawberries in summer yet as dangerous a creature as he'd ever come upon. *Because he wanted her.*

The day would come when he'd leave her. On that day, his heart would wrench. When he saw the direction of her stare, he looked over his shoulder to where the carcass lay. "We're not likely to come across another. In fact. Usually don't find them here. Must've been hungry enough to roam out of her territory. Let's move on. Camp in another few hours of hard riding. Think you can hang on?"

She offered a quick nod of her head. No one could miss the fact she was bone tired, and he admired her grit. They kept going until he saw her hunched over, about to slip sideways. Fear that she might drop from the saddle had him pull up. They dismounted for camp, and while she searched for juniper, he tended the horses, seeing them watered and hobbled.

With the bedrolls and blankets spread on the ground, he left her alone to tend to his personals–giving her the chance to do the same. From his observation beyond the shadows, she busily tended beans and bacon in the pan. The speckled blue enamel coffee pot sat beside the fire. He'd already decided she wasn't cut out to be a camp cook, but he gave her high marks for trying.

Filling the canteens at the edge of the stream, he became keenly aware of several things. The sun was beginning to set. There was stillness other than one coyote answering another. And his sense of being watched was never wrong. Tonight, he'd need some sleep and would have to depend on his horses to sound an alarm. Luckily, he wasn't a sound sleeper. If they did have unwanted guests, he'd be ready for them.

Standing, he walked toward the fire, brought up short at the sight of Tori where she'd sunk to her bedroll and fallen asleep. With knees bent, her hand tucked beneath her cheek, waking her seemed blasphemous. Yet she had to eat, or she wouldn't keep pace tomorrow.

Once he'd filled their plates with vittles and poured the thick coffee, he stroked a finger across her delicate cheek. She swatted at his hand, then wrinkled her nose. He leaned close and whispered near her ear. "Beautiful dreamer. Supper is served."

Gus hunkered beside her, then waited. Her slow smile entranced him, prompting him to wonder what she dreamed about. She sniffed, then swiped at her nose. Her eyes snapped open. When she jolted upward, her head cracked into the underside of his chin, prompting his yelp.

"Jesus, Tori. You've got quite a hard-headed punch."

"Is that supposed to be funny?"

"Nope. It hurts." To prove it, he moved his jaw from side to side.

"Oh, my God, Gus! I meant to stay awake. I only thought to close my eyes a few minutes. The food must be charred."

"You were done in. Food is fine, and I'm not mad. Just wanted you to eat. I'm used to cookin'. Besides, I've been pushing us hard."

Rolling to his feet, he held out his hand. After she grasped hold, he tugged her up from her bedroll, then he placed one hand against her back, holding her against his chest, hoping she didn't feel what she did to him. With her dark tousled hair and sweet mouth, he found it hard to look away, especially as she dropped her head back and favored him with a smile.

Someday, he wanted to know everything about her. For the life of him, he didn't know why it was suddenly important. Or just maybe he didn't want to know. They'd agreed to part company, and he intended to keep to the bargain.

She backed from him, then ran her hand through her loose hair. As he watched, his fingers flexed, imagining what her silky tresses would feel like against his skin. After she took a seat on a blanket beside the fire, he almost broke into a hearty laugh at the sight she presented with her legs crossed, wearing pants and a mud-splattered blouse. He envisioned her seated in a fine parlor chair, wearing that prim, high-necked black dress, her hair in a neat bun. A place and life he couldn't offer her.

As was his custom, he ate without talking. Besides, it gave him the chance to glance at her while she forked morsels into her mouth and afforded him time to formulate questions that could easily upset this contentment they'd found.

"Where did you say we were going?" she asked.

Soft as spring rain, her voice broke into his intention to stay quiet. "Yankton."

"We'll be parting there, I suppose."

"It's a growing town on the Missouri from where you'll be able to get on another sternwheeler to Omaha or wherever you've a mind to go."

"Once I can get to the train, I'm making my way to California."

He lifted his head at her air of confidence. She had no idea how long and dangerous that would be. "Seems like a lot of changing your mind. What happened to Omaha?"

"Gus. I've got to go where Silas won't think to find me."

Knowing there was no sense in arguing with Tori, he sipped his coffee, watching her across the brim of his tin cup. She averted her face, picked up her plate, then walked toward the Jim River. He tracked her movement, then called out.

"Best watch out for rattlers." *And just why won't you give that money back to Silas?* The question that had rubbed a sore spot through what reason he still had. She nodded but didn't look back, leaving him with questions circling inside his head.

That night, he made certain the fire burned low. He had no choice but to get some sleep, or he'd fall out of his own saddle. Watching Tori's form stretched out in the shadows with her hands folded beneath her cheek, she reminded him of a lost child. Considering the quiet of the night, he lay on his bedroll with his head resting against his saddle. Folding his arms across his chest, he stared at the moonless sky. At first, there was a faint rustle of grass. Then he heard the quick padding footsteps. The horses snorted.

Gus turned onto his stomach, then lifted his head to study the camp. His hand reached for the rifle beside him. The horse's movements stilled. Crouched, he made his way to Tori, then covered her mouth with his hand. Her eyes flew open with fear in them. He shook his head.

With one finger pressed to his mouth, she understood. He handed her his revolver, then used another signal, ordering her to stay flat.

Staying low, he managed to hide out of the light behind a few scraggly junipers near enough to the horses to see what was what. That's when he counted two heads on the other side of the camp, all eyes centered on Tori.

The sudden sharp pain at the back of his neck caught him by surprise. His first inclination was to face his attacker. The beaded hair ornament, bone amulet, and shirt identified him as Sioux, his sworn enemy. This was a young warrior with a blood-stained knife gripped in his hand. The fearful but determined look in the attacker's eyes gave Gus pause, until the knife was raised for a second strike. Left with no choice, Gus twisted the knife from his hand.

Once weaponless, the attacker looked to his side, seeking escape. In that moment, something about the boy seemed familiar. He'd seen many such boys over the years, but this one reminded him of himself. His inclination was to let him go as a defeated warrior. Suddenly, the boy made a grab for the knife. Dark, furious eyes stared into his. Gus hadn't lived this long to be cut down by a wild-eyed kid. Apparently, this young Indian was more dogged to have a last lick.

So was Gus.

Gus planted his knee into the boy's groin. That sent the shrieking attacker to his knees. Gus waved the knife in front of his face. These were more than likely boys trying to be men–out to steal horses. To them, it was not only a game but a road to manhood. But damned if he'd allow them to hurt Tori or steal their horses. The boy tried to move. Gus held him. There was fury in the Indian's expression before the boy stilled beneath his grip. Gus grinned.

"You have lost. *Letan kigla yo.* Get out of here."

Just as Gus figured on getting to Tori, there were two shots, in succession, from his .45 Colt. Her scream raised the hair on the back of his neck. The young Sioux warrior stared at him. Gus would be a fool to turn his back on this kid, but he had to get to Tori.

The attacker grimaced while Gus dragged him out of the shadows.

The sticky blood beneath his collar reminded him he had to finish this. If he had time, he'd like to squeeze the life out of this persistent kid, but there was something about him that he couldn't fathom. There was nothing left to do. He landed his fist into the attacker's jaw and sent him sprawling onto his back.

The boy staggered to his feet, then ran into the darkness, taking that moment to join his friends. He picked up his rifle, then trotted into the camp, worried about what might have happened to Tori. He knew he'd underestimated her when he saw the Colt leveled at three scared boys. At that moment, he was more than proud of her than ever. In fact, his heart had been captured by her fortitude.

"*Yah-pe.*" Gus ordered. They understood they were shamed and de-feated. Worse—by a woman. "Tori. Let them go."

The warrior he'd hit swiped his hand across his bloody mouth. Then the three of them melted into the darkness... a defeat that would long be spoken of, unless they kept it to themselves. But that would require some explanation for the cut mouth. The sounds of their horses faded.

"Are you all right?" he asked as he walked toward her.

"Yes. But they scared me out of my skin."

"You shot at them?"

She nodded. "When they tried to steal our horses. I think I hit one of those horse thieves. What did you say to the one you struggled with?"

Her proud chin lifted, and he wanted to crush her against him. "In short. Told him to get the hell out of here."

"Were they Sioux?"

"Yep. Not a war party. Just three young strays lookin' for some free horseflesh and food." He reached for the revolver still gripped in her white-knuckled hands just as her eyes widened.

"Gus. You're hurt."

He pressed his hand against the bloody slice, and it came away cov-ered in blood. "I'll be all right. Might think about gettin' my canteen and whiskey out of my saddlebag. The kid sliced me pretty good at the back of my shoulder. Probably wanted to cut my neck. Bein' tall has advan-tages, else I might be dead."

"This is nothing to joke about."

With his hand pressed against his wound, he searched around the camp, then checked the horses while she rifled through his saddlebag. Bone-tired and feeling a mite light in the head, he stumbled to his bedroll then dropped to his knees, setting his rifle beside him. The last thing he remembered was raw, stinging pain, then a sense of floating.

The whiff of lilies had him swipe at his nose. His hand drifted across a blanket until it met a soft, warm mound tucked beside him. Gus opened his eyes to find her hand resting against his chest, her hair fanned across his shoulder. After he turned his head, he was relieved the weapons were within reach.

The fire burned low across from where they lay. She mumbled something indecipherable. With slow movement, he lifted the blanket to find he'd been bandaged across his left shoulder. Bare-chested, he pondered how she'd managed that.

Squeezing his eyes closed, he couldn't shake the vision of her facing down those Indian boys. From now on, he'd make sure he stood watch. Soon, they'd be away from the reservation and on safer ground in Nebraska. Damn. Of all the luck. He stroked a finger across her cheek, then watched her mouth curve. "You're awake, huh?"

"A little. Been keeping watch."

"Thanks for bandaging me."

She pulled the corner of the blanket beneath his chin. It'd been a long time since anyone had tended to his needs.

"I took a few tucks in your skin with my needle and silk thread. Cleaned it with whiskey. Thankfully, you'd passed out."

"Could've been worse. Got to be more careful."

Her hand smoothed across his chest, stirring yearnings that he had no right to. Grasping her fingers, he stilled her hand. "You keep doin' that, and I might want to take advantage of you."

She lifted her head and touched his mouth with hers. The thudding of his heart in his ears drowned out all reason. Forgetting his best intentions, he tossed the shared blanket aside. Even as pain shot through his shoulder, he rose above her, then slanted his mouth against hers, taking the kiss deeper.

Desire ran through him like a raging river when she fingered his hair. Her warm breath stirred his base needs, sending his hands to the buttons of her shirt, plucking one free, then another. His gaze feasted on the lacy camisole like a starving man. She had surely driven him crazy. "I want you, Tori."

"Do I need to remind you about the knife wound? This isn't the time. Besides, I don't want my handiwork busting open."

"Right now, the pain in my shoulder is secondary to what I need."

"Then, this is the least I can do for you, Gus. You asked me once."

"Christ," he hissed.

He squeezed his eyes closed, then rolled to his back. She might as well have dumped a bucket of cold water over his head. Gus dropped his arm across his eyes, then wondered how he'd made a fool of himself. Turning his head, he moved his arm to see her on her side, braced against one elbow, staring. She waited for his explanation, he supposed.

He knew what she'd been before. But didn't want her *that* way. And especially not as payment. The fact she thought he did—sickened him.

"Gus?"

He gulped down his brewing disgust with silent cuss words. "Tori. I don't ever want you to *pay* me. *I want you.* Not because you feel you owe me something in exchange for my help. Can't you understand what that does to my pride?"

"I was a prostitute. I don't know much about pure kindness in men. Nor how to repay you. The men I've known want something. Always."

"Honey. You better not ever think like that again. You're damn well every bit a lady. I want *her.* The woman I see. The woman who left her past behind. The woman who keeps me awake."

He stared at the sky while he listened to the rustle of the cloth as she buttoned her shirt. Once she'd stretched out beside him again, she pulled the blanket over them. He sighed, then started to press a light kiss to her pouting mouth but changed his mind.

"I feel safe beside you. Mind if I stay?" she murmured.

"Even if you test my will, you can stay. I'll be up soon to check around. Dawn will be here soon."

"Mmm."

She stilled, then after a time, her breathing grew steady. He stood, tucked on his shirt, then buckled on his gun belt. With a last look toward her sleeping form, he grinned at her soft snore. He lifted his rifle, then set off to check the horses, among other things. *Yes, sweet lady. You are welcome to share my bed anytime. But only for the right reasons.*

SIX

TO YANKTON

S HE'D BEGUN TO count the number of times Gus slid sideways in his saddle, only to catch himself. They were only a day or two from Yankton, but he'd kept to himself since this morning. Her words had hurt him, but she had no idea how to overcome her past—one that stayed with her. He wasn't one of those men she'd learned to hate. That was the issue. She had no idea what a caring, kind man needed to hear. Did she even know how it would feel to love someone like Gus?

She looked ahead to see him rub his shoulder. Had the wound become infected? Is that why he seemed tired? Worry became her companion. Gus wasn't the kind of man who'd admit to any weakness.

After a short meal and few words, he'd kept a steady pace, keeping distance between them. Looking skyward, she figured they'd soon camp for the night. As far as the eye could see, they were surrounded by bluestem and switchgrass. She recognized milkweed and wild roses poking up along the gentle slopes.

The Missouri River was in the distance, the water glittering like a long satin ribbon, peeking in and out of the grassy knolls and sandbanks. Now and again, grasshopper sparrows would lift skyward from where they hid. Trees were sparse, leaving her to wonder why he'd shied away from the shelter of pine and cottonwood.

So captivated by the passing landscape, she'd lost sight of Gus. Nudging her horse into a faster gait, she urged the animal to the top of a rise where she'd last seen him. Below were both horses, standing beside his still form on the ground. Stifling an urge to scream, she sent her horse into a lope to reach his side.

After she'd dismounted, she dropped to her knees beside him. His eyes were closed, and his lids flickered. She touched his chest to find a strong heartbeat. She saw no blood. Tori shook him then called his name again and again, with no response.

"Gus. Please wake up. Can you hear me?"

After he didn't answer, she shook him again. Surely he hadn't fallen this soundly asleep. She touched his head. He was hot as the blazing sun. *A fever.* That knife wound must be infected. Looking to her right and left, she wondered where she'd find shade. The best place would be nearer the river, where they'd have access to water. But how would she manage to get him into the saddle? He was heavier than she could possibly lift.

She brought her horse close to his and unhooked her canteen. From her valise, she pulled out her only petticoat and tore a strip. Soaking it with water, she pressed the wet cloth to his forehead, hoping to revive him. He mumbled a few incoherent words, then after a moment, his eyes opened, and he stared as though looking through her. She released a breath when he grinned.

"What happened?" he grumbled.

"You've got a fever. I really need to get you up onto your horse. You have to help me."

"Bring my horse close. I'll manage."

She latched onto the reins of the Appaloosa, then led the horse to where Gus managed to sit. With more strength than she knew she had, she helped him stand, praying his horse wouldn't shy. Swaying, he almost toppled until he managed to drape one arm around her shoulders. He reached for the saddle. She helped him get his boot into the stirrup, then somehow, he heaved himself into his saddle... then he slumped forward. Biting her lip, she prayed he'd stay mounted until they got to the river.

"Can you hang on long enough to make it to the Missouri? I'll lead your mount."

He nodded from where his head rested against his horse's crest.

HE OPENED HIS eyes to a dark-haired, delicate angel bent over him. Something wet pressed against his head. From the corner of his eye, he saw an orange glow of fire. There was a strange aroma from somewhere nearby. "Fever?" he croaked.

"Yes. But from what I can tell, it's coming down some. I managed to get you to swallow some willow bark tea. Found it in your things."

"Tasted somethin' bitter."

"You had some other things in your medical bag. But I don't know how to use some of it. Picked sunflowers to make a fever brew. You'll need to drink more. If you feel sore, it's because I lanced, then cleaned the infection in that wound. Your whiskey came in handy. For now, it's not weeping any pus. The hole is closed up and stitched. Very red. So it'll need tendin' by a real physician."

"Thanks."

Her eyes softened as he reached for her hand. "Mean it. You're a wonder. Keep your gun close. How'd you get me here?"

"Wasn't easy. But you managed to dismount before you collapsed. Half dragged you onto the bedroll and blanket. Got a fire going and tended the horses. Found hardtack in a bag, along with dried salt beef. Made a kind of stew with a little bacon for flavor. Hardtack mush is easier to swallow. Think you can get some down?"

"Should be takin' care of *you*."

"You have. Least I can do after you rescued me from the riverboat. Besides. I refuse to allow you to die."

When she stood, his gaze followed her. The firelight made her fine-boned profile even more beautiful. She was in his blood, unless it was the fever. This sure was a hell of a time to come to the conclusion he'd have a hard time losing her. After she returned, she hunkered beside him, holding a tin cup between her hands.

"This should help you. The more you drink, the better."

He rolled to his side and leaned up on one elbow, dizziness threatening to flatten him. She tipped the cup to his lips while he sipped. He swallowed the bitter-tasting brew and hoped it didn't cause him to retch. After a few more swallows, she set the cup aside, then stood. He lay back, then closed his eyes, too tired to ask her how long he'd been like this.

Something soft and gentle brushed his face. The smell of bacon roused him from sleep. Through his lashes, he saw her kneel beside him, a cup and spoon in hand.

"It's not much. But it'll help nourish you."

"Smells good."

She stirred the concoction and pressed the spoon to his mouth. After the food touched his tongue, his first impulse was to spit it out. Instead, he managed to swallow it. She'd done a fine job of heating this mixture, but he reckoned she wasn't used to cooking. Besides, he couldn't fault her when he wasn't the best cook either.

He lied. "It's fine. Fillin' me right up."

"Best I could come up with after tending the animals."

It was time to turn away from the subject of food, he decided. "Tori. Think I'll be able to ride tomorrow. Close to Yankton."

She clasped his hand. "You sure gave me a scare. Maybe we need to wait another day or two."

"Did you think I'd die? Leave you to your own? Been in worse shape."

"For goodness sakes. I'm not that heartless a wench you seem to think I am. I'd not let you die without fighting off the grim reaper himself. You're too good a man to die. We'll find a doctor."

So. She'd remembered his unforgivable rant. "Should never have said what I did. You aren't heartless. But I've survived a long time without a sweet nurse. Just old crusty kinds."

"That so? Bet you had them swoon."

"Swoon? Not hardly. Most were sour pusses. By the way, you sure look pretty in that blue dress."

She brushed her nervous hands over the skirt, then grinned. "Those pants were mighty dirty, so I washed them in the river while you slept. I'll take the cups, then see to the horses. Both of us need sleep. Besides, if I sit here much longer, you'll make me blush. Soon as I finish, I'll need to look at that wound. My petticoats were good for something other than wearing."

When she started to tuck a blanket around him, he latched hold of her wrist. He held her gaze and then did what he promised he wouldn't. He tugged her hand. She finally conceded, then scooted close to his side.

"Lay beside me. Just for a few minutes."

Once she'd curled beside him, she turned... putting her mere inches from him. A calm settled into his soul. No matter what her motives, he'd still want her till he died.

"Tori. If I was feelin' a mite better, I'd take this further. Not for any reason except I want you. Do you understand what I'm saying?"

A soft sigh sent her sweet breath against the crook of his neck where she'd rested her head. Breathing in her familiar scent, he wondered what would become of her in California. Could Silas find her? If he did....

"Gus. How can you set aside my past so easily? Most men wouldn't."

"Everyone has a past. That's not a place where we should live. I've been tryin' to do just that for so long that it's become familiar."

"What was her name? Your wife?"

"Aubrey."

"A beautiful name. I'll pray for her."

He had no idea how to respond to that. Not even sure he believed in prayers. Sure didn't think she did either. Calling up his wife's name had reminded him that she could still be alive.

"Best you check the horses. Take the gun. Sorry I'm not much help tonight."

"Do you mind if I sleep alongside of you?"

"Be disappointed if you didn't. Don't be long because I'll miss the lady with more mettle than I've ever known."

"All of us find courage when it's called for. Don't you know that?"

She started to move away, but he tugged at her braid, bringing her mouth to his. She broke the kiss, then stood. But not before offering him a smile like the sun before she was gone.

"I'll be back," she said across her shoulder.

In response, he winked. There was no doubt he'd watch for her. He reached beside the bedroll for his rifle and revolver. Dangers were very real until he got them to Yankton.

———

SOMETIME DURING THE early morning, he'd managed to disengage himself from her arms, then tend his personals before he woke her. The horses were tethered to low-hanging branches of the cottonwood. The soreness behind his neck reminded him that he'd been careless, and he wouldn't let it happen again. A knife wound wasn't going to do him in.

He stroked a hand over his bristled face. There was still some fever. Regardless, he'd get the coffee brewing, then fill the canteens because there was no sense in staying here. He hunkered alongside the narrow river while he watched for anything or anyone moving. He became aware of her soft footsteps approaching from behind him.

"And just what do you think you're doing, Mister Quaid?"

With a quick glance across his shoulder, he jutted his chin in the direction of the water. Tori's hands were on her hips, her pursed mouth reminding him of an irritated schoolteacher.

"Filling canteens."

"Huh. I can fill them. You shouldn't be traipsing around. Besides, you need another day or two to rest."

"*Traipsing?*" His jaw ticked. "Had to pee and other things. You've done more than your share. Just so you know, I've lived through worse without a nursemaid."

There was a heavy silence. He wished he could take back his smug remark. Before he gave thought to the right words, she marched toward him like a uniformed soldier. He rose to his feet with the canteens clutched in one fist and waited for her barbed words. With the head of steam she had, it might be cuss words he'd never heard her use. Shoulders thrown back, her small frame stood toe-to-toe with him, her mouth pursed. He braced for a well-deserved slap, but instead, she lifted onto her boot toes and brushed his forehead with the back of her hand.

"Better. Not perfect. As long as I'm your *nursemaid*, I get some say."

Despite her irritation, he took her hand, then pressed a kiss to the back of it. "You're a worrier."

"I'll take that as a compliment. Seeing as how you're short on them of late."

"As you should. Please accept my apologies. You didn't deserve my smug sarcasm."

Since she didn't make any further comment, he had the good sense to let it go. Instead, he found pleasure in walking along the river beside her while they picked up twigs to add to the fire. Once they returned, they sat companionably over coffee, bacon, and beans. He'd settled on the fact it was time to leave, by mutual agreement, with his pretty nursemaid. Just maybe that's what riled him the most. Yankton was ahead. Where they'd agreed to part.

Things between them were calm until she insisted he drink that God-awful bitter tea. But since he'd already been tetchy, he deserved this punishment... even as his stomach threatened to revolt. She must've seen him pondering the stuff because her stare pierced his.

"Gus Quaid, drink up, or I'll have to kick up a fuss."

He saluted, then gulped. Christ, he'd had bad whiskey, but this topped all of them. After the stuff cleared his throat, he grimaced, as her eyes leveled with his.

"Gus. I have a question for you."

"Mmm. Figured you might."

"Will you tell me the truth?"

"Depends on the question."

"So you admit to lying."

"If the situation calls for it... yes." He didn't bother to hide his chuckle.

"I've been in and out of your saddlebags. I wasn't stealing. I wasn't prying. I was trying to find your whiskey and medical supplies."

He poked his hat back on his head, then stretched his legs out in front of him... resisting the urge to squirm. So, she'd found the leather wallet with greenbacks. And four sacks of gold dust. The tables were now turned, leaving him to suck in a breath. "Go on."

"You have more money than I do."

"Except it's not mine. It belongs to a friend. I'm delivering it to him."

"All right."

"That's it? You believe me?"

"Yes, though it surely isn't my business anyhow. Must be a good friend to go to all the trouble."

He exhaled at the reprieve, but he didn't plan to elaborate until her next question stunned him.

"One more thing. Why do you pretend to be plain-spoken? You read *War and Peace* and *Moby-Dick*. Those books are inside one of your packs. No one reads such things unless they have a command of English. Yet you use colloquialisms in some of your conversations. From time to time, you slip back to common words. You're like two people."

"That so?" He raised an eyebrow more in irritation than in surprise. Damn the woman. She was too smart. She'd pinned him like a bug to a wall.

"That is so," she mocked.

Gus pinched the bridge of his nose, then dropped his chin while he searched for how to answer. Lifting his eyes to hers, he handed over the truth as best he could explain it. "Yes. The pretense of being as un-educated as most I meet allows me to mix in. Learn more that way. Besides, I'm not usually around people who are refined or civilized. Being inside some circles is safer than bein' outside, though you might not get my drift."

She tilted her head, stared, then blinked. "Oh, Lordy. You are a co-nundrum. In some odd way, I do get your so-called... drift."

"Now that's settled, let's eat and be on our way. But there is one thing, Tori. I don't want what I'm carrying known. That means keep it to yourself, or we're both going to be in trouble."

He took her quick nod as her acceptance. He just hoped he hadn't run into the most wily but pretty thief he'd ever encountered.

After they broke camp, a shiver let him know he still had some fever. The clench of his stomach had more to do with her knowing his secrets. God only knew if she fancied the gold or greenbacks for herself. Still, deep down, he couldn't believe she had deceived him, which might be his undoing.

SEVEN

FAIR LADY

HER GAZE FASTENED on the frame and stone buildings as they rode down the center of the main street in Yankton. When her horse shied at the sudden blast from a riverboat, Gus reached to grab the halter, steadying her mount before he continued ahead of her.

Her regard then fell on the women in fine dresses who strolled beside men in fine suits. Some stopped and gawked in their direction while they rode by. At first, she wondered at their curiosity until she reminded herself her braid had fallen loose from inside of her hat. Worse, Gus had insisted she return to wearing pants. Riding astride and wearing pants just weren't approved behaviors by civilized folks. Yankton looked to be full of polite society.

A magnificent palatial building poked above the fine houses dotting the north side of town. The sign over the Gold Nugget Saloon proclaimed miners welcome. In a town this size, there had to be more than one saloon. Gus led them to the livery, where they dismounted.

"Stay here while I see to our horses and tack. Then we'll head for the Dakota Hotel just down the street."

"Will you see the surgeon?"

"*Maybe.* Stop worryin'."

Handing over her carpetbag, he led the animals into the corral, leaving her to study the busy street. The loaded freight wagons reminded her of Hawk. She looked along the row of wagons, but no one resembled that no-account. She hoped he wasn't here, else Gus might confront him again. In a town this size, he could easily wind up in the hoosegow.

She surveyed the row of seedy saloons, taking notice of the soiled doves peering over the balconies, plying their trade. They were to be pitied. As she had grown older, she'd finally had the gumption to escape the tawdry life she'd had.

Gus escorted her beside him, forcing her to skip to keep up with his long strides. With his saddlebag draped across his shoulder and the Gladstone bag gripped in his hand, his face was taut with pain. At his opposite side, he gripped his rifle. Hearing boots clomping behind them, Gus stopped. They turned to find a freckle-faced boy with his hands tucked inside his overalls.

"Hey, Mister. You need help?"

Gus nodded. "Tell you what. You carry my traveling companion's carpetbag. How's that? I'll pay you for your help."

Seeing the boy's vigorous nod, Gus dropped his Gladstone bag, then reached into his pocket for coins. The boy's smile melted her heart... especially after Gus ruffled the boy's curly hair. "You gotta' name?"

"Gilbert."

"A fine name."

Gus led them inside the cool, well-appointed lobby of the Dakota Hotel. The wood floors were polished to a gleam, while the brocade and velvet furniture settees and seats were fit for a mansion. Gus released her arm, leaving her and young Gilbert to wait beside their baggage. He stepped up to the lobby desk. "Two rooms." The haughty concierge sniffed, then looked down his nose over his spectacles.

"They'd be expensive. You might want something along the lines of Miss Crenshaw's Boarding House. That'd be about three streets down."

"I'll take two rooms here. *Now.*"

The pinch-mouthed man sniffed again, then adjusted his spectacles. "That'll be two dollars for each room a night. Includes supper."

Gus reached into his pocket, peeled out four dollars, then slapped the money down on the counter. Slow to turn the ledger for his signature, she watched as Gus spun the thick book around himself. After signing, he tossed the pen... narrowly missing the man's fine silk vest. All Tori could do is hold her breath, knowing Gus wasn't in his best mood.

Two keys were handed off, then Gus poked them inside his pants pocket. After he hefted his gear, he jutted his chin in the direction of the stairs, leaving her and Gilbert to follow. At the door to her room, he set his gear on the floor. As usual, he entered first, setting her carpetbag inside while she waited. There was tension in his face that she pondered. She worried her lip with her teeth. "Gus."

"I'm *fine*. Be in twelve if you need me. After I settle in, I'll attend to some business. In the meantime, I'll have a bath sent up. If that pasty-faced desk clerk looks crosswise, I'll deal with him."

"Don't. Please, Gus. Let's not borrow trouble."

"I'll do my best. Lock your door. Keep your revolver handy."

"Gus, is this your way of saying goodbye?"

He sighed. "Tori. We agreed that Yankton was as far as I was taking you. I'm leaving day after tomorrow. In the meantime, I'll be here if you need me."

"I'll need to find my own way to the train, is that it?"

"There's a stage or even a train from here to Iowa. The riverboat is prominent. You can go on to Omaha. There's a rail there."

"Will you be having supper? I'd like to have your company, at least for tonight."

"The restaurant downstairs is fair."

"Is that a yes?" she asked.

"Would seven suit you?"

"Seven, then."

Giddy with the hope she might still convince him to take her along, she had to do some fast thinking. Before he turned away, she said, "Seems like we'll have a better meal than what I cook."

His laughter ended as abruptly as it started. They faced each other,

her mind memorizing his remarkable face. She touched his arm. Then an odd, sad smile turned up the corner of his mouth before it faded.

She waited in the silence between them until he hefted his gear, then ambled to his door. It closed behind him with a firm click. She stepped inside of her empty room with the dreary sense of his loss. Tori had never been lonelier than she was at this moment. Nor had her heart ever felt so broken. Gus would be gone. Staring from the window, she watched the comings and goings of the normal folks while she wiped away her tears. This was for the best, she told herself. *After all, he belonged out on the plains.*

———————

"WHAT'S SO FUNNY?" Gus asked when he lifted his head at her laughter.

"I've been watching you eat. It amuses me at how much you relish every morsel. You study that food like it might try to crawl away."

"This isn't the first time you've watched me eat."

"True. But I think this is the first time you've really found the food appetizing enough to show pleasure on your face."

"Hmm. So you know, I've managed to watch you as well. You stir food around, then eat so dainty it makes me nervous."

"Then I guess we're both guilty of stealing glances."

He shoved his plate aside at the mention of stealing. The kind of trouble she might be in gave him more than one worry. She turned her head, her gaze intent on the dining room and avoiding his glare.

"You know, Tori. I'm leaving early day after tomorrow. This time it'll be just Warrior and Jenny for company. Expect you'll have enough money to buy a ticket on the next boat out."

She turned her head around to face him while she fussed with the fancy napkin. Those blue eyes of hers held a world of secrets. "Still haven't decided what I'll do. Don't suppose you'll change your mind about getting me to the first rail depot."

He leaned back in his seat, then folded his arms. He lowered his face, giving thought to her plea. Then damned himself for being tempted.

The plains were filled with dangers she couldn't imagine. Snakes, sun, storms, wildfires, and drinking water were serious problems for a man, let alone a delicate woman. She'd proven her grit. But the perils were too great. Besides, the greatest threat was liking her too much. Liking might become something else he didn't want to think about... not while his past gnawed at him.

"No. We'll say our goodbye. Might as well get it over, Tori. Would you like more coffee or pie before we leave?"

"No. Thank you. I'm quite full."

Disappointment was etched in the curve of her mouth. Still, he knew this was best for both of them. Those stormy blue eyes shimmered beneath the chandelier light. Her plain blue dress softened the hardness he'd often seen in her. "Sooner or later... we knew it would come to an end, sweet lady."

"Yes. I did. So, it has."

"Best we both get some sleep."

They stood at the same time. She didn't wait for him, but he caught her arm, determined to see her to her door. Neither spoke until they reached her room. After he'd unlocked it, he stepped inside ahead of her.

"Appears safe."

"Thank you, Gus. *For everything.*"

He bent and brushed her mouth with a gentle kiss. When he stepped back, he said, "I won't forget you. But I'm damned well going to lose sleep trying."

She swiped at her eyes and lifted her chin. "Take care of yourself."

EIGHT

TURN OF THE HEART

US STOOD AT the bar with only a vague recollection of how he'd gotten there. He'd wandered around, deep in thought, crazy with need for a woman he didn't deserve. A cavernous loss filled him, knowing he'd never see her again. One of the last patrons of the night, and only steps away from the hotel, he downed one beer then chased it with a whiskey, hoping the effect would be sleep.

Once he'd shuffled back to his hotel room, he removed his gun belt, shirt, and boots, then stretched out on the bed. After he turned onto his side, he focused his attention on his saddlebag, then glared intently at the Gladstone bag that represented another man's hard work. What he carried was too important to lose. His thoughts circled back to Tori and the money she'd stolen. Good God. He wanted to trust her. Here he was, with enough money to attract a thief. But she'd had the chance while he fought that fever. She'd stayed at his side.

A short while ago, he'd stood outside of her door. When he lifted his knuckles to knock, he dropped his hand away, then ambled back to his room. He'd told himself Tori had no place in his life. Aubrey had been his world. His carelessness had cost his wife's life.

If turning away from Tori was the right thing to do, why was he a miserable man? Gus Quaid always stood his ground. He always made decisive decisions. This time, his spurs were tangled no matter how often he found another excuse.

She'd been a paid woman, and it was a plain fact. While he didn't think of her like that, the hell of it was—*she did*. Deep down, he thought of those men she'd been with, wanting to kill each of them.

He rested his head against a bent arm. His rifles were in easy reach, the .45 on the night table. He might be the only one to protect her against Silas—the man who might not give up. Calling himself twice a fool, his thoughts ticked off reasons to return to her room. *She'd be asleep by now.* Staring at the door, he thought of her honey voice and sweet taste.

TORI WOKE FROM a restless sleep, tossed her blanket aside, then paced a few steps to the window. From her vantage, she watched as, one by one, lamps dimmed, then buildings darkened. A man stepped from the mercantile, puffed his cigarette, then dropped it to the street. After he looked along the street, he walked back inside.

She sat on the edge of the bed and tucked the ruffled collar of her nightdress snugly around her neck, remembering Ben's hands choking her last breath. Gus had seen to that he wouldn't follow. Even Tom Willis had been sent packing. Her trouble wasn't over so long as Silas still breathed. She knew him well enough to know she'd taken more than his money. She'd humiliated him.

Just as she thought about getting some sleep, footsteps outside of her door caught her attention. Lifting her Colt .38 from the night table, she worried her lip, knowing she wasn't sure how to fire the thing. Still, Marie had sold it to her at Fort Randall, and she'd damned well use it if she needed to.

She crept to her door, then pressed an ear against it, waiting for a sound. The only thing she heard was her heart pounding in her ears. Sighing with relief, she turned away but was stopped by a hoarse voice.

"Tori. I know you're on the other side of this door. Open up."

"It's late. Go back to your room. I can't say goodbye again."

"I'll stay here till you open. Got things to say to each other. There's a good chance we'll wake everyone if I stay out here much longer."

Her hand trembled when she unlatched the door. Gus stood before her in all of his glory. Taller than most men, he ducked inside and shoved the door closed with his heel. His unbuttoned shirt hung untucked from his blue trousers. His .45 was visible in the holster strapped at his hip. Perusing him from his long black hair to his scruffy beard, she felt an unease at his stare.

Her eyes moved deliberately over his lean, hard stomach, then paused at his bare feet. She lifted her chin to see his handsome, wry grin. He lifted his arm. She stepped back.

"For God's sakes, Tori. I'm not going to hurt you. I was just going to take that .38 from your hand before you hurt me. Or yourself. Where's the derringer?"

Looking to where the gun was still gripped at her side, she handed it over to him.

"Do you know how to use it?"

"I've shot revolvers before. But not for some time." In fact, she'd shot her husband. That miserable Connor O'Malley.

"If I had time enough, I'd show you how. That's a single action and generally has a hair trigger. Best keep to your derringer. Where'd you come by it?"

"Marie sold it to me. I've kept it inside my valise. Does that satisfy you? Besides, what are you doing here? Kind of late to discuss my weapons."

He released a long breath, then stared into her eyes.

"Well? I'm waiting. Surely you know why you came to my door this late at night."

He walked beyond her, then set the revolver on the table. When he turned, he opened his arms in invitation. She hesitated. His change in mood had grown tiring. In short, she'd been battered by his change of mind more times than she could count.

When she walked into them, her feet left the wood floor while his mouth settled on hers. She smiled against his warm lips, tasting whiskey. Tori damned her traitorous heart. Just when she believed she'd never see him again, he was here. If she had any sense, she'd turn him away. But she *loved* him—something she'd never known.

There was urgency in his kisses. He lifted his head, then cupped her face between his hands. "Christ, Tori. I need to *know* that this is not payment. This is two people who want each other for no other reason than one. What we feel."

Did she want to give him her heart? A man who might one day disappear from her life?

She'd gambled on two other men. But Gus was different. She was different. "You should know by now, I'm not for sale. You set me free."

As impossible as it would seem, his eyes looked darker than night. His steady gaze held hers. Then in this quiet moment, she settled her hand against his chest, feeling the thunder from his heart. His hand found hers. They threaded their fingers, understanding that for the moment, they belonged together.

"Gus, I will never try to hold you. I care too much to do that."

"God, Tori," he whispered. "Let's leave the talking for another time."

They kissed, then locked away their pasts and their secrets. *For now.*

HOW LONG HAD she slept in his arms? While he listened to her breathing, he contemplated the power she held over him with just her voice, her smile, and even her mighty determination. She'd made him afraid to think of a life without her.

Tori was like the ocean... ever-changing. Serene one moment, then storm-tossed the next. Like dark water, things hid in the deep sea, things not visible, yet they were there. Dangerous or not, he needed to know what was below her surface. For his sake... and hers.

His mouth nuzzled her ear, then her neck. She smiled, then turned toward him.

"Mmm."

"You're awake, beautiful lady."

"Indeed, I'm awake. Someone kissed me." Her fingers brushed his warm mouth. "Gus?"

He rolled to his back, knowing she was about to pepper him with questions, some of which he could already guess. "I'm listening."

Her head turned toward him. "What if I told you I love you?

His body tensed. "Don't."

"Why?"

"Because I'm not ready to hear those words. Because I can't say them without...."

She turned her back to him in the silence of his unfinished thought. By the time she woke again, he'd be far from Yankton, telling himself it was for the best. He'd lost his heart when Aubrey was taken. Now resigned to her death, he wasn't free from the burden of guilt. More, he wouldn't survive if he gave her what was left of his heart only to find out she'd hidden things from her past.

———————

THE FIRST THING she felt was cold. *His* warmth was gone. Tori twisted her head to be sure. The only sign that he'd been beside her was the hollow place in the pillow. Now he was gone without a word of goodbye. She still felt him.

The thought she might see him riding away prodded her to go to the window for a final glimpse. There was no sign of him. No doubt, he was well out of sight of town. Once she'd washed and slipped into a modest gray dress of simple muslin, she tucked her hair into a neat chignon. She lifted her chin to face what lay ahead. There were decisions to be made. Hadn't she survived all these years on her own resilience? Victoria Barrett would make her way to California and forget Gus.

After locking the door behind her, she took the stairs to the lobby, her chin held high. She was an independent woman. From this day on, she would never allow another man to reach her heart. Reticule in hand, she headed for the depot.

There was no point in hiding her misery. The steamship clerk at the landing repeated the outrageous price of two hundred dollars before it sunk into her head. If she paid that amount, she'd have to live on dry biscuits all the way to California. The weasel behind the desk argued it was a matter of supply and demand. Even factoring in the sale of the horse and saddle, she'd have to penny-pinch. The one thing she'd never do again is slip back into her past life.

Before now, she hadn't counted on the costs that were mounting up. One thing was sure, this hotel was too expensive. Sooner or later, she'd be flat broke.

"What can I get you?"

Tori lifted her chin to see a young waitress standing beside her, wearing a frown that most likely matched her own. After she glanced around, she realized she'd been sitting here for some time, mulling her situation. "I'll have two flapjacks and tea if you have it."

"'Course we got that. You want an egg?"

"No. Flapjacks will do." *And they were cheaper.* With her elbows propped against the table, she rested her head in her hands. Lordy, how she missed Gus. He'd still insist she take that blasted steamboat.

"Make that just coffee for me. Don't need nothin' else. I'll be joinin' this lady."

She dropped her hands to the table to look up. Gus was smiling like he'd swallowed the sun, and she didn't know whether to jump out of the seat to hug him or slap him. What was he up to? He towered over her, then dragged out the chair beside her, straddling it.

"Her food is comin' out. Guess you're mighty full after you ate so much earlier."

Gus looked sheepish at the waitresses' observation. After the woman moved on, she studied him. Gus slapped his Stetson on the chair, then leaned back, his arms crossed.

He winked. "Cat got your tongue? You sure look peaked. Did you sleep well?"

"Why are you doing this? Thought you'd left," she added.

"Doing what?"

"Taunting me. You've made it clear you wanted to set off alone. You're still here."

"Almost did. Once I loaded the panniers with food and such, I decided it was goin' to be a lonely ride. Jenny and Warrior ain't much company."

"What are you getting at? What game are you playing?"

"No games. I've had a change in thinking. You look beautiful despite that downturned mouth. Your face is mighty pink."

"I'm quite well, thank you." Darned if she'd admit to pacing the room with a broken heart.

He nodded, then leaned back while the waitress set her plate and cup on the table. A young boy handed him a cup of coffee. Once they were alone, neither she nor Gus bothered to hide their mutual study of each other.

"Miss Barrett. I was wonderin' if you'd decided to get on the riverboat."

"I gave thought to the cost. Two hundred dollars, in fact. I can't decide what to do. Except to sell my horse and saddle. Not sure it would be enough."

"That'd be a shame."

"I have no use for a horse."

"Maybe you do. If you wouldn't mind a traveling companion, seeing as how you've been anxious to get to the UP."

Tilting her head, she tried to assimilate what he'd just proposed. Maybe she hadn't understood. "What are you offering? Please spell it out."

"It'd take about four or five days or maybe more... of riding across prairies dotted with badger holes, snakes, and gullies. Won't be much shade. Not expectin' trouble with Indians. But buffalo stampedes, sudden storms, dry rivers, and prairie fires can happen quick. They'll be blowflies, grasshoppers, beetles, and yellow jackets to contend with. If we're lucky, the horses won't stumble and break their legs. Or one of us comes down sick from bad water. We can only hope neither of us gets bit by a rattler."

"Those prospects are daunting, but I think I'm up to it. Just where are you meaning to take me?"

"To Columbus. They got a nice hotel before we board the train goin' west."

"Train? *We?*"

———

GUS LAUGHED AT her wide-eyed surprise. With her fingers laced together, she pinched her mouth closed, watching him. There was a moment when her hunched shoulders started to relax. Her quick smile radiated heat all the way to Nebraska. Just that quick, she was back to stewing. To him, she'd never looked sweeter, no matter what was turning in that head of hers.

"You're teasing me."

"No. I'm not. Though you're easy to rile *and* tease. Usually, I enjoy it. But not today. I'm very serious."

"I can buy a ticket west from there?"

"That you can. The Union Pacific can take you all the way to San Francisco, if you've a mind to."

She reached across the distance and grasped the hand he rested against the table between them. He rubbed his thumb across her skin, then watched as those expressive eyes sparkled with youthful happiness. Touching hands like this in public was, at the least, scandalous. Gus Quaid never cared for the so-called rules of society. Her ears were turning almost as red as her face.

"Best eat. And change into your boy clothes for riding."

"You knew I wouldn't refuse."

"Maybe. Got your horse saddled and ready to go."

"Thank you. Pretty sure of yourself, Mister Quaid."

"You might not thank me after you've experienced what's ahead of us. Be sure to wear your hat, or you'll spoil your skin."

"I expect we have an understanding."

As he sipped his coffee, he watched her over the rim. There was no point in making clear his view of what was between them. Her *understanding* and his might be two different shades. However, yes, they indeed had an agreement that stood on shaky ground. They'd have to work it out between here and Ogallala, where letting her go might become impossible.

NINE

TASTE OF PRAIRIE DIRT

FROM HIS VANTAGE, her face was shadowed beneath her broad-brimmed hat. She'd tucked her hair into the crown, but it had long since dropped to her shoulders in wavy curls. Without a doubt, she was even more alluring with it loose. Her drawn face and slumped shoulders signaled she was bone-tired after only six miles in the saddle.

Wishing he could make it easier didn't change they had to push onward, else they wouldn't make it to water. The fact she hadn't complained earned her high marks for fortitude.

Lightning forked through the dark storm clouds ahead of them. Finding them a place out of the wind had him nudge his horse to higher ground to have a better look. He knew dry lightning had a habit of starting prairie fires unless accompanied by rain. Outracing a fire with Tori and the pack horse would require a miracle. Making up his mind to push on toward Norfolk tomorrow, he hoped the storm passed them by.

Sitting straight in the saddle, her face glistened with sweat. The woman had no quit, always trying to prove herself. There was no doubt, by the look of her, she was bone-tired. Most women would've whined by now. Given the need to give the horses a breather, he took notice of a gentle slope, then waved his hat to signal her to follow. She guided her horse alongside his.

"Setting down on this side of that ridge. Cold camp. Tomorrow we'll be at the Elkhorn River with plenty of water."

After they dismounted, he saw her wince. She hadn't asked for his help but instead grasped her saddle to steady herself. Damn. His heart ached for putting her through this grueling ride. Knowing she wouldn't accept his help because of her pride didn't make his conscience feel better. Tori had more grit than any woman and most men he'd ever run across. Leaving her back in Yankton would've been smarter. Where she was concerned, his judgment was impaired.

After he'd hobbled the horses, then set out their bedrolls, a streak of orange tinged the sky in the distance as the storm clouds drifted farther east. By the time he'd settled their horses, he found her curled on her side on her bedroll, her hand tucked beneath her cheek, looking like an angel girl in boy's pants. Taking his blanket from his bedroll, he tucked it around her sleeping form before looking around.

Despite the danger of setting the range on fire and the fact there was no wood close by, he decided to burn some chunks of dry grass for light and warmth. Digging out a pit with his spade, he dropped the clumps of grass into the hole then set it aflame. After adding some juniper he'd found, he retrieved the blue porcelain pot, spooned in a hearty amount of coffee beans, then proceeded to add water from his canteen. He set the pot at the edge of the heat, then waited and listened for signs that the storm was nearing them.

A last, faint smear of light faded in the black sky while he again coaxed the fire to life with enough tinder-dry grass to keep the pot warm. Just as he poured coffee into his cup, she jerked awake. She rubbed the heels of her hands against her eyes. Blinking, she looked in his direction.

"You should've wakened me. I'm not expecting you to serve me."

"You looked done in. I'm used to ridin' all day. Best I could do is coffee. Got jerky and what's left of them biscuits from back in Yankton."

"Coffee smells delightful. Biscuits are fine."

"My coffee won't taste like gargle wash. I like it strong."

She pushed to her feet then walked to where he sat, his legs stretched out before him. After he handed her the cup, he said, "Careful. It's hot." Thus far, he hadn't gotten her to speak what she seemed to have on her mind. In the silence, he turned his eyes skyward while the faint scent of lilies and coffee wafted between them.

"Tastes good. Thank you for doing for this... and everything else. The smell of coffee was what woke me. Still. From now on, I expect to pull my weight. If I feel useless, I'll get cranky."

Christ. The woman made him grin more than he'd ever done before. Setting his cup beside him, he leaned back against his saddle with his hands folded across his stomach, taking note there were no stars. That usually foretold of bad weather. When he returned his gaze to her, he grimaced while she sank her teeth into that hard biscuit.

"Might need dunking."

"Think you're right. I'm not complaining, mind you. Sure don't want to break a tooth. Thought you'd said no fire."

"Didn't plan to. Figured we deserved it. Cools down out here at night. The fire won't last much longer." *Besides. I wanted to try to make up for driving you so hard.*

Silence stretched between them once again while she swallowed the last of her biscuit then brushed the crumbs from her hands. He pulled a strip of jerky from his saddlebag and handed it to her. She daintily nibbled at it. Once finished, she set her cup beside her then covered her face with her hands.

"You all right?"

"You're staring at me."

"Maybe because you're easy on the eyes. Besides, I seldom have such pretty company."

"So you've said before."

"I mean it."

Whenever she worried her bottom lip with her teeth, he knew he was about to be pelted with questions.

"You must've loved her very much."

Raising an eyebrow, he wondered how she'd circled back to his wife. "Yes, I did love Aubrey. But she's dead. She's in my past. Doesn't mean I'll ever forget her, mind you."

"Understandable and honorable. I've never run across someone like you. Aubrey was a lucky woman to have had you."

Sighing, he folded his arms beneath the back of his head. He looked skyward, giving thought to how to respond. Comparing her with his wife wasn't something he was comfortable with.

"Tori. I consider myself tough and skilled. I should never have left her alone that day. I'm the one who might've saved her. The way I see it, she was unlucky to have ever met me."

"Gus! What a thing to say. No one could've predicted what happened. Guilt is a heavy burden to carry. Once, a long while back, my father shot our only milk cow while hunting. He missed the deer he'd aimed at and instead, killed the cow."

"My pa was glum for a long while until one day my mother told him if he kept fillin' all the buckets with remorse, there'd be no room left for something else in those buckets. If you fill what buckets you have, you've got nowhere left to set all your guilt, and it would eat you alive. If you'd been there, you most likely would've been killed too."

"Yeah. Well, that's the point. I'll never know for sure. What about you? You haven't exactly made your past clear. There's been Silas and the money. What else do I need to know?"

She tilted her head, her mouth curved with a sad expression. "I'm a survivor. Like you."

"Both of us with our secrets. Maybe if you trusted me enough, I could help you escape whatever it is you're afraid to face because I don't think it's just Silas. Am I wrong?"

"Do you believe me when I tell you I'm not a thief?"

"You admitted to taking the money. Without consent."

"I took what was rightfully mine."

Gus sat, his back arrow straight as his gaze fastened on her pinched mouth. "I believe you were *owed* the money you took. The law might not agree. Still, what I want to know is why you worked for Silas. What happened to make...?"

Jesus. He couldn't bring himself to say it.

"Make me a whore?"

He rolled to his feet and pinched the bridge of his nose, trying to find a way to express his thoughts about her past. Anything reasonable evaded him, especially when she looked up at him like a lost kitten. She drew her knees to her chest, then wrapped her arms around them. Thick silence settled between them. Her lips trembled.

"I don't think of you that way, Tori. God's truth."

She stood and faced him. His heart tripped at the sight of her unshed tears. Still, there was nothing he could do to change what she'd been. It had to be her fight. All he could do is stand beside her. He curved his arm around her shoulders, giving in to his urge to drift his fingers along her cheek.

"Thank you, Gus. I don't believe you do."

"Sooner or later, I'll convince you. Not all men are like the ones you knew."

"You're not just different, Gus. You're rare."

"And you smell of lilies and coffee, my favorite things."

"Might be you're conjuring the smell. Or it's just in my clothes because I surely need a bath."

"Might find that bath in Norfolk along the Elkhorn River. Be there by late tomorrow."

"In the meantime, mind if I share your bedroll? Like you said. Gets cold out here."

"I'd be honored, Miss Barrett."

With her face held between his hands, he kissed her eyes, nose, and mouth, then they settled beside each other on their bedrolls while the smell of burnt juniper and buffalo grass drifted on the air. A man could get used to this, he thought. After he heard her steady breathing, he got to his feet and picked up his rifle.

Once he was outside the circle of camp, he whispered to the air, "Tori, you take my breath away. You make me want you even when I should know better." His moccasins silenced his footfalls as he made the rounds.

———

TORI DIDN'T KNOW how cold she'd gotten until the shivers started. Throwing off the blanket, she stood then squinted into the darkness. Two horses lifted their heads at her approach. She scrambled for her rifle, then neared the skittish animals. They snorted as she drew closer, their eyes wide in the thin moonlight. The strong smell of smoke stung her nose. More concerning, where was Gus? His horse was gone.

Both horses' ears pinned back, and their heads turned toward something beyond her shoulder. Turning, she saw the glow outlining the horizon. Lightning streaked above a distant hill, giving her a clearer view of the fiery river of gold pouring down the hillside in her direction. *Oh, God. A grass fire.*

Just as she whirled with fright, Gus's shouts became swallowed by the shrieks of terror from the agitated horses. If they didn't remove the hobbles, the animals might break their legs. Riding bareback at breakneck speed, Gus looked like an avenging warrior as his horse skidded to a halt. Vaulting from his horse, he grabbed hold of the reins before Warrior yanked free.

"Prairie's on fire. Not much time," he panted. "Got to make a run south to the Elkhorn else we'll burn to death. Wind's got it headed our way. Got to keep ahead of it. Break camp. I'll get the mounts saddled. Hurry."

Following his orders, she scurried around the camp, rolling up blankets and bedrolls and dumping what was left of the coffee into the charred pit. A glance found he had his hands full, holding the horses steady. She moved beside him, then grasped the reins, while he did his best to keep them from fighting the saddles.

Once the gear was tied onto the panniers, they mounted and dug their heels into the horses, sending them into a ground-eating run. From across her shoulder, the flaming orange river flickered and crawled like an evil animal, lifting the pungent odor of burning grass with it. Her lungs burned with the smell of burning grass.

"Keep moving," he shouted. "Don't look back."

Her heels slapped at the flanks of the horse as she leaned forward on the saddle. She did her best to stay behind Gus, but she slowed long enough to hold a kerchief over her nose in the choking haze while she gripped the reins with her other hand. A glance in the direction of the radiant blaze that weaved in and out of the hills let her know they were in trouble. It was still coming toward them.

Suddenly her horse took the bit. The feel of the animal's bunching muscles beneath her legs warned her to hang on tight. Barely staying seated, her horse used long, pounding strides to keep up with Gus, almost unseating her. Bringing his horse to a slow trot, he circled until he was beside her while Jenny tugged hard to escape Gus's grip.

"Hang on. They smell the Elkhorn River ahead of us. They got the sense to know where to go."

Peering through a foggy cloud of smoke, she searched for the promised river. It appeared out of nowhere. She understood Gus's urgency to put the river between them and the fire. When they reached the bank, their horses plunged into the muddy river. Water splashed over them, leaving them both drenched. Beside each other, they guided their winded horses up the opposite bank, then paused to turn in their saddles.

Mesmerized at the sight of the tongues of flames in the distance, she cast a glance toward Gus, who'd remained quiet. "What do we do?"

"We wait and watch to see if it jumps the river into that cluster of trees on this side. Can't run these horses any farther without killing them."

Her eyes stayed on the flames, afraid to look at them and afraid to look away. Venturing a quick glance in his direction once again, the sliver of moonlight revealed his lopsided grin on his soot and sweat-smeared face. He swiped his face with his shirt sleeve, then dismounted, and she did the same. Grasping her canteen, she gulped enough to swallow away the taste of smoke. The horses stood at the bank drinking noisily, their hides twitching with fatigue. They both stared at the flames pouring in their direction from the hills. She knew without his saying… they were in real danger of dying.

———————

SHE LOOKED DARNED cute with char smudges across her nose and cheek. Still, he wouldn't tell her that—for many reasons. Standing beside the horses, he kept his eyes on the fire that raged on the other side, whipped by a south wind.

"Gus? Shouldn't we move on? If we don't, we'll die. This river isn't very wide. What if it reaches this side?"

Her soft voice broke into his thoughts as though she'd read them.

"We'll stay for now. Give the horses a breather. If it jumps the river, we'll be in a world of trouble. Between the box elders, willows, and cottonwood, the fire stands a chance of chasing us down. We can't outrun it. If that time comes, we'll cut the horses loose from the hobbles, then wade into the deepest part of the river."

Her chin tipped like she was in prayer, then she chafed her hands across her pant legs.

When she looked toward him, her eyes glittered in the dim light of the moon. "I'll do whatever it takes to keep both of us safe. *Believe that.* I'm betting we'll come out of this sooty, tired, and stinking. But alive."

"I do. Believe you."

There was a great crackling from the willows and cottonwoods on the far side of the river. Smoke rose in great black plumes against the dim morning sky. It was all they could do to keep the horses from bolting. Gus made the decision to keep the hobbles on. If this monster managed to jump the river, they'd need to have a means of riding away, even if the chance of staying ahead would require a miracle.

A whooshing sound sent flames and sparks skyward, sending burning trees toppling into the river, filling the air with hissing steam. He handed her a fresh kerchief from his saddlebag, then tugged another from around his neck.

"Wet it and tie it around your mouth and nose."

The time was now. Leaving the hobbled animals a little way from the river, he hoped they survived. Trumpeting their alarm, there was no doubt they'd try to break free of the rope hobbles and maybe break their legs. Turning back to her, he saw her glassy eyes riveted on the burning trees. Without explaining his purpose, he unbuckled his gun belt, then fastened it to the bedroll behind his cantle.

"Get your boots off."

He waited a heartbeat while she did as ordered. Then he sat on the mud bank, yanked off his own, before he heaved them beside hers.

"Gus. Why not cut the horses loose?"

"We'd be on foot. In this country, that spells death. I'll grant you, it's a gamble as to whether they won't break their legs trying to get loose. We're out of options."

Without giving her a chance to argue, he swept her into his arms. Wading into the middle of the river, he hoped to find a deep hole. When the water reached above his hip, he lifted her higher, urging her to wrap her legs around his waist. Her arms clutched his neck, and her eyes glimmered with fear.

"Tori. We might need to dunk. Be ready."

Sizzling, exploding wood was all around them. Sweat ran over his neck. She gazed fixedly into his eyes. He couldn't offer her a promise. A vision of Aubrey crossed his mind. God, he didn't want this woman to trust him. Because he might fail again.

Her silence was telling. The cool water and fright sent tremors through her body, which made the peril more real. With his hand against the back of her head, he pressed her against him while her legs wrapped around his waist. A flaming tree cracked and splashed into the water, then sent plumes of smoke and sparks skyward. Her body jerked. Ripples of water lapped against him. With her head pressed against the crook of his neck, he closed his eyes and prayed. *Damn his hide for bringing her into this danger.*

TEN

FIRESTORM

AFTER A WHILE, she leaned away and looked into his eyes. He saw the awful terror in hers but neither spoke. He looked beyond her just as a large drop of water splatted his nose, followed by another. Soon his head was pelted with life-saving rain. They both glanced skyward as a drenching rain soaked their faces, washing soot over their eyes and cheeks. Wet strands of hair framed her face. He combed his fingers through her dripping tendrils as he studied the outline of her face from beneath the drooping, soaked kerchief.

They pulled their bandanas down around their necks. That twinkle of merriment in her gorgeous eyes was further illuminated by the crease of sunlight beaming from behind the clouds. Her sopping blouse clung to every inch of her mounds. The better man inside him prodded him to return his perusal to her face. Her lips chattered with the cold, signaling it was time to get out of the river. After he slogged up the slippery mud bank, he lowered her feet to the wet grass. Water streamed over their faces, neither of them caring. God had granted a reprieve.

"It's rain! Oh, Gus. Rain."

He threw back his head and laughed while he enjoyed her dancing in a circle, her arms raised to the heavens while sweet girlish giggles warmed him in ways he'd long forgotten.

"Yes. It surely is, Tori. Guess we got the bath we needed. Best get into dry clothes if we've got any. Need to get warm."

Gus looked to where the horses were hobbled, seeming undisturbed beneath the rain. They contentedly nosed the grass, chomping as though all was right in the world. The river was hidden beneath clouds of smoke, ringed by scorched oaks, cottonwood, and junipers.

Legs stiff with tension, he looked to where Tori tugged clothes from her valise, then figured he'd best change into some dry things, as well. As he slipped on dry britches and shirt, he looked heavenward under the soft rain. He owed God for coming at the right moment. Still, he had to ask why He'd forsaken him before. Then he looked toward Tori, a girlish, contented grin on her mouth. She'd been right about those buckets of remorse.

"Gus, we must look a sight. But right now, I don't care."

"I do. I don't want you getting pneumonia. Your lips are chattering. Come on. We need to mount up. I've got a place in mind for the night. Won't be fancy, but we'll have a fire... that is, if the place is still standin'."

Gus tugged her arm, then helped her to mount. With one look at the steaming river, they set off.

BY THE TIME the two of them reached the outskirts of Norfolk, she felt light-headed, hungry, and mean of spirit. She'd managed to get into reasonably dry clothes she'd brought in her valise, then slipped into her slicker. Gus had wrapped a blanket around her shoulders to keep her warm until they got to wherever he was taking them. Turns out, he hadn't exaggerated the dangers they might encounter. From the stoic expression on his face, he was probably already thinking he shouldn't have brought her along.

"See that little farmhouse in the distance? We'll stop there. It's decent shelter."

She followed his gander, then squinted to see a dilapidated, forlorn homestead. "Gus, don't you think the folks will mind being awakened at this hour?"

"Nope."

"How can you be certain?"

"They're dead."

"You knew them?"

"Helene Haefele was a good friend and distant cousin of mine. She died a few years back. Seems no one claimed the place. Had no children. Her husband died the first year they settled here. Whenever I come by, I stop. From the looks of it, nobody wants it. She had been an oddity with her strange notions. Some probably thought she was a witch. So we'll make ourselves at home in a *witch's house*. She'd invite us and be glad for the company."

Once they pulled up near the door, Gus freed the saddlebags and pannier, dropping them beside the narrow porch. Rainwater dripped from the tattered roof as Gus led the horses to the lean-to. She hesitated at the front door as it swung back and forth in the wind. It was certain there'd be varmints making a home inside. Lifting her chin, she figured she'd lived through much worse.

The door creaked when she shoved it open. Squinting into the darkness, she blinked, hoping enough light would slant around the door to locate a lantern. *Did she believe in witches? Bash!* Still, her arms were covered with goosebumps.

The room smelled of grass, rotting timbers, and things vermin left behind. Darkness hid the source of the scratching. She stepped farther in, then froze, her lips shivering. She jumped when Gus touched her shoulder, then stepped around her. He'd come up behind her without her hearing him.

"Stay put, and I'll scrounge up the lamp. If it's still here."

His boot steps halted, then after he struck a match, his face glowed. The smell of sulfur preceded the sudden light, casting eerie shadows in the room. Shivering with both cold and relief, her eyes settled on the large kitchen with a simple stone fireplace. The floors were strewn with feathers and what appeared to be mouse droppings. Still, this roof over their heads offered a chance to get warm and rest. After her stomach grumbled, she was reminded of how long it had been since either had eaten a proper meal.

Gus circled the room, then stopped beside her. "After I finish getting our things, I'll get a fire goin' while you see about putting your bed together in the next room. You'll need the lantern until I locate another one. Best throw one of our blankets over the mattress. We can rustle up some beans, bacon, and fry potatoes we brought from Yankton. Figure once we get to town, I can buy enough coffee to see us to Columbus. We got enough for tonight."

She nodded. After he left, she pushed her damp hair away from her face, then wrinkled her nose at the smell of rot. She entered the dark bedroom with the lantern held high. In here were more feathers. The mattress was torn open and filthy. It would have to do.

Returning to the main room, she found Gus already hunkered beside the hearth, coaxing a fire. While he worked, she set out the pan, potatoes, and bacon on the floral-carved table, and she gave thought about the man who must've constructed this for his wife. *No. She couldn't have been a witch. Just a loner like Gus.*

Darting a glance to where Gus kneeled, his shoulders hunched, she watched him use a poker to stir the flames. After the stove was crackling, he closed the wood box, stood, then turned his attention to the stone fireplace. Tori used the paring knife from the sack, then proceeded to peel potatoes. While they cooked in the camp fry pan, she sliced into the slab of bacon. The damper screeched as Gus adjusted the air to the chimney. Working companionably, neither were in the mood for conversations.

Before long, they were sitting on the floor beside each other, warmed both by the stove and fireplace. Embers hissed and popped. Without chairs, they set their plates against their laps. In his typical way, Gus centered his attention on eating, seemingly ignoring his surroundings. *And her.*

She cleared her throat. "I've fixed the bed as best I could. Plenty of holes in the mattress. Where'd you find dry wood?"

"Left some in the lean-to the last time I was here. Seems it stayed mostly dry. Place has been abandoned for years."

"Gus?"

"Hmm."

"I don't think it wise for us to sleep together."

He lowered his fork, then rested it across his plate. His face tautened as he glared in her direction. "Have I offended you?"

"No."

"I'd already figured to bed down in this room. But since you made a point of making the decision, I'm wondering why. Seems the horse already left the barn, unless you'd forgotten."

"This isn't the right time to become more involved than we already are. My mind is set on going on to California, and you're set on returning to Belle Fourche. Whether it's true or not, it feels like we're trading favor for favor."

He forked potatoes into his mouth and chewed without comment.

"I trust you. You're a good man."

He scraped the last of his food into his mouth, then swallowed. A tic along his jaw warned her that the subject was closed. After she choked down another forkful, Tori had had enough... both of his silence and of his red hot glower.

"The well is still workable. You might want to clean up a little come mornin'. I'll bring in a pail."

"You're angry now. I see it in your eyes. I've offended you about our sleeping arrangements."

"No. I'm not offended at all. I'm just... stumped by this sudden change of heart."

Her mouth trembled. "I don't want to think about you leaving me. It's best we keep away. I'll make it easier to part ways. Still, I won't feel right with you sleeping on the floor with mice."

"*Mice*? I'm used to worse. You said you grew up back in Virginia. Was it a farm?"

"Yes. Bigger than this."

"Did you have mice?"

"Yes. And copperheads. Deer and raccoons. Squirrels. Occasional bears. But what does that have to do with our predicament?"

"Then you shouldn't worry about a few mice. I sure don't. Maybe you'd care to share what the predicament is?"

"I'm not a thief. I have a past you already know about. You never wanted me along. But since I'm here, I feel I need to repay you for your kindness. I don't know how."

His hard as nails stare left no doubt he was angry. When he abruptly stood, picked up his rifle, then marched outside, she was left to wonder if he might ride off and leave her.

After she'd seen to cleaning the pans in the water bucket, she tucked a blanket over the rat-eaten bed and used Gus's blanket to cover herself. Determined not to fall asleep until she was certain he hadn't run off, she kept watch on the lantern light in the kitchen until she sank into sleep.

Some hours later, she woke from sleep to find one corner of the blanket tucked beneath her chin. The lamp still glowed from the outer room. Dropping her legs over the side of the bed, she tiptoed across the room. Curiosity was met with surprise at the sight of Gus sitting on his bedroll. He had settled his back against a wide leg of the table where the lantern shed light on the book he had balanced against his upraised knees.

He wore spectacles perched on his nose, seeming lost in the words. He lifted his glasses from his eyes, folded them, then tucked them into his pocket. With his fingers pressed against his closed eyelids, he suddenly looked in her direction where she hid in the shadows. She'd never seen him wear glasses. Somehow that image of the infamous scout would never have crossed her mind. He was truly a man of contradictions.

"You should be asleep."

She jerked at the sound of his deep voice, then stepped into the light of the room.

"Didn't think you knew I was watching you."

One corner of his mouth lifted. His gaze followed her, but he remained seated on the floor.

"Christ. I heard the floor creak. I'm not one you'd find easy to sneak up on."

"I think you should be asking yourself the same question, Mister Quaid. About sleeping. Didn't know you wore glasses."

He looked up and grinned. "Moby Dick kept me awake. As to glasses. Wear them to read fine print."

"You are a puzzle, Mister Quaid."

Slapping the book closed, he rolled to his feet.

"No more than you, Miss Barrett. Time I check the horses. Go on back to bed."

"I'll wait for you."

"That right?"

"Sooner or later, I think we need to talk about the arrangement between us."

He set the book on the table, then before she knew what he was about to do, he grasped her shoulders and tugged her against him. She lifted her face, then watched his slow, impudent smile until it faded.

"You're one helluva' beautiful woman and smart enough to know I want you. There's a trust issue between us. If you have feelings for me, then prove it. For no reason except me. Not as payment for services. Just feelings. The word *arrangement* was yours. Not mine. Can you understand what I'm telling you? This is not an arrangement."

"Gus. I hear what you're saying. But if I woke one day to find the Gus I think I can trust has left, it would be like what I've already had. Betrayal. You have the power to crush my heart, my spirit, and anything else good inside of me."

There was hurt in his eyes, and he looked dumbfounded. "I'm not a man to lie or pretend. Stop comparing me to them. Or to anyone else." He turned his back to her. "One other thing. I don't recall that we'd be living together. Remember your own words. You're going to California. It's best we keep things simple unless and until you learn to trust me."

He turned and drew her close. His hands cupped her face. "Sooner or later, you have to trust somebody. I'd never go against my word."

HE LURCHED FROM the floor where he slept. Reaching for the revolver beside his blanket, he searched the room for the source of the sound that woke him. He pushed himself up, then glanced from the window. All was still. Then he heard the whimper from the darkness of the bedroom. In his stocking feet, he strode inside, his revolver still clutched at his side.

Mindful that she kept both a derringer and .38 nearby, he hesitated. Moving closer to her still form, he found her stretched out on her belly, one hand gripping the blanket, the other one in a tight-fisted grip of the pillow.

"Tori."

When she didn't move, he tucked his revolver into his waistband, then seated himself on the edge of the flea-bitten excuse of a mattress. He touched her back, only to feel an instant recoil. She rolled onto her side and lifted her head, her eyes vacant, looking through him as though he were a ghost.

"Hey. It's me. Gus."

Her eyes blinked.

"Gus?"

"I'm here. You had a bad dream."

Tori sat, then leaned against the metal headboard. After drawing her knees to her chest, she sobbed. He needed to touch her but thought better of it. She looked as fragile as glass.

"Does this happen a lot?"

She looked so far away he didn't know what to do. When she didn't answer, he touched her face with the back of his hand to her skin, dotted with sweat. Worse, she flinched at his touch.

"Christ."

Gus gently pulled her against him, startled at how limp and unresponsive she was in his arms. This wasn't Tori. He needed to probe inside her dark place to bring her out. With her head pressed against his chest, he whispered, "Talk to me, sweetheart."

"Bad dreams sometimes. This time, I saw the flames close. They were about to swallow this house. Silas was on the other side, pointing a gun at me. You started to walk into those flames, then I grabbed for you. You wouldn't stop."

"*Jesus.*"

He rocked her while his heart thudded nearly out of his chest.

"I'll make sure you're safe. The fire is gone. Silas won't touch you."

"I know you want to keep me safe. Sometimes, we have to let go."

Gus pressed a kiss against her head, then set her back, not knowing how to argue her point. "Will you be all right if I leave you? Best we both sleep before dawn. I'll be in the next room. You're safe, Tori. Tomorrow, we'll pass through Norfolk, and in a few more days, we'll make it to Columbus."

"Sleep beside me. Hold me."

Did she know what she was asking of him? He was a flesh and blood man. Damn. His heart belonged to her, and this was the wrong time to tell her. Just maybe there'd be no good time as long as she wouldn't tell him more about her past and as long as she was set on California.

She worried her lower lip between her teeth. "Please, Gus."

Shit. He couldn't deny her anything. At least, most anything.

"I'll get my rifle and gun belt. Be right back."

She was curled on her side when he returned. With his weapons within reach, he stretched out on the bed, careful to keep distance between them. Her soft breathing and sweet sigh let him know she'd calmed down. Just as he stared at the ceiling, her voice broke the quiet.

"Whatever you think of me, Gus. I hope you know I care for you. That hard woman you met at Fort Benton has a heart. You helped me find it."

"I know how tough you are, sweetheart. What I think is that you're beautiful, and any man would be proud to have you. Until you face whatever you're hiding, your fears will always follow you. I know because I've had my own challenges." There was a long silence.

"You know what I was," she whispered.

He turned his head to study her, her body curled beneath a blanket. Then considered his words before he spoke. "I'm not a perfect man, Tori. I've done things I won't live down. I've been with prostitutes over the years. I don't think of you like that. Never will. There's not any one of us who never had to face challenges. The difference is what you do about it."

"Gus Quaid is a remarkable man. You're handsome and kind and brave. And smarter than you let on."

"*Handsome?* Maybe to you. Still, I'm a miserable cuss when I'm in a sour mood. The hard part for either of us will be ahead. We have some deciding to do."

Her laughter cascaded over him like a gentle waterfall, tickling his skin and conjuring the sight of her running barefoot through a field of flowers. Leaning close, he pecked her on her head, then dropped back onto the bed.

"Sleep, princess."

When there was no answer, he turned to find her eyes were closed. A gentle rise and fall of her chest beneath the thin blanket let him know she already followed his order.

Later, he woke to find her arm draped across his shoulder with her foot snugged between his bent knees. Slowly, he disengaged his body from hers, careful not to wake her. He crept from the room, guns in hand. About now, he needed a smoke. Especially since his own words rang true. Hard decisions needed to be made.

After saddling the horses, sunlight burst on the horizon. Tori had already put together a meager meal of bacon and fried potatoes. Her sunny smile this morning let him know she'd set aside the nightmare but more and more, he wondered what other things churned inside her head. He might never know.

ELEVEN

PASSING THROUGH

SHE'D DECIDED NOT to speak at all to the man who rode ahead of her. Like quicksilver, his mood swung from warm to cold. Since they left the witch's cabin, he'd offered only a sidelong glance. Sooner or later, she'd have to stop and stretch her cramped legs but damned if Victoria Barrett would ask to stop. She lifted her chin, then kept her sights on the Appaloosa ahead of her.

She smelled it before she saw the smoke, reminding her of that awful prairie fire that had chased them into a river. This time, it looked to be chimney smoke, which meant they were near Norfolk. Gus waved his hat, then waited for her to trot closer.

Guiding her horse to the other side of the pack horse, she fixed her eyes on the distant horizon from the top of this hill. Cabins lined the banks and slopes below them. The Elkhorn River sparkled where it snaked beneath overhanging trees above the river. Squinting, she made out a semblance of buildings and tents along a dirt street of a very small town.

"Norfolk," he said.

"I don't suppose there's a hotel. Feels like I could grow potatoes in my hair. Sure could use a bath."

"Not that I know of. 'Course, things have a way of changing. We'll stop at Mathewson's Dry Goods Store first. They'd know. Besides, we could use a resupply... enough to see us to Columbus. Won't be much between here and there. I've got a hankering for canned peaches."

"Would you leave me here?"

At her direct question, his canteen lowered slowly. One brow lifted then he shook his head.

"Didn't cross my mind. Sometimes, Tori, you ask a question that makes me feel like what's on the bottom of my boot."

"Sorry. I never can tell what's on your mind, especially when you've hardly spoken since early this morning."

Without looking toward her, he hooked his canteen strap over the pommel. "Make no mistake. I'm a man who'll keep his word, and you'll be the first to know if I plan to leave. But it won't be in a town without a means of transportation. I'll lead out, and you follow."

Her horse trotted behind Gus as they passed log buildings and a couple of soldier's tents. She squinted to see two frame houses at the end of the road and set her hopes that one might offer a room for the night. Once they reached the hitching rail in front of Mathewson's Dry Goods, Gus dismounted without so much as a word, then he tied the horses and marched inside.

She dismounted, not knowing whether there was a reason he'd left her there. Or did he figure she'd take care of herself? But Tori Barrett wasn't about to be left to stand here waiting. Taking the steps, she trooped across the porch, then entered the building... to be immediately assailed with the smells of leather, tobacco, and sour pickles.

The shelves were stacked with pots, pans, sacks of sugar, and flour. Bean sacks were heaped beside crates of potatoes. Several pairs of boots were sitting on the wide window casement. Her eyes strayed to the dresses, blouses, and petticoats, all hung from a rope strung along the back wall—drawing her like a bee to honey.

A gray-haired shopkeeper spoke with Gus in low tones while her eyes took in the store's inventory. It had been so long since she'd seen women's store-made dresses, she felt like a young girl at Christmas.

"Tori. This is William Hausen. He was just askin' me if you need somethin'," Gus called.

"No. Thank you, Mister Hausen."

Damned if she'd admit to wanting to touch a few of the dresses. Maybe even try one on. Her pragmatic side reminded her that if she were to make it to California, she'd have to remain frugal.

Gus and the store clerk walked into the back room, leaving her to peruse. The sound of their voices and a few chuckles suggested they were kindred spirits. She smoothed her hand over a bolt of muslin, then touched the plain, coarse calico. If she could choose, she'd make a dress of softer muslin. What she'd brought with her would have to suffice.

"Let's go." Gus grasped her arm, startling her with his sudden appearance. "He'll get the flour, meat, and boxes of ammunition ready while we eat somethin'."

He ushered her from the store while her stomach reminded her she hadn't eaten much but camp vittles. The prospect of eating in a real restaurant again was short-lived. With her skipping to keep up with his stride, most of the buildings were behind them. She jerked her arm free, which forced him to stop.

"Where are we going?"

"There's an abandoned sod house on the other side of the post office. We'll stay there tonight."

"Did you ask Mister Hausen about a hotel?"

"I did."

"And?"

"Tori—you are the most persistent, stubborn female I ever came across. For your information, there is no hotel. We'll make do. I've lived a long while. I've survived out on these plains. I'll see you finally get on to California if you'd leave the getting to the train to me."

"You, Mister Quaid, are exasperating. Simple manners dictate that I'm owed an explanation of your plans. Why are you being mule-headed about that?"

"All right. We've got that all settled. Sometimes my plans change, Tori. I'm not a man who's used to telling anyone what they are. You'll only suffer my company for a short while, then we'll be parting company."

Tori felt like steam was pouring from her ears at his long-winded tirade. They stared at each other, not moving. "Anything else you've got to say, Mister Quaid?"

"That sums it up. If you got an objection, well, you can always wait for the stage goin' to Columbus. Maybe the store owner can put you up. The stage comes along in three days. Make up your mind because I'm ridin' out in the morning. Up to you."

"How much is the stage?"

"Be about sixteen dollars to Columbus, from my recollection."

She swallowed a long list of cuss words that prickled her tongue. "In that case... I'd be *delighted* to travel with you. The sod house will do. And I still don't know why you're so perverse."

"You know why. I'm edgy about what's been simmering between us. To top it off, you've been prickly yourself, Miss Barrett.

"How much is the hotel in Columbus?"

She didn't miss the roll of his eyes nor the smirk of his mouth.

"Tori. If it's a problem, I'll pay your way once we get to Columbus."

"No. I won't take your charity. How much?"

"The *American* will cost two dollars. I'll cover it."

"You most certainly will not."

"Christ. I'm about to get even more cranky on top of bein' hungry. Let's talk about this out of earshot after we see our accommodations. Once I get the horses stabled, I'll be back with enough food to make a fair meal."

After he left her in front of the forlorn sod house, she waited in front of the door, wondering what she'd encounter inside. It couldn't be worse than the so-called witch's house where they'd bedded down with mice, among other creatures.

She looked across her shoulder to see a town busybody leaning on her broom, glaring in her direction. Tori, in turn, offered her a narrow-eyed stare, which had the woman lift the flap of her tent, then disappear inside. Gus, with his usual long strides, walked toward her, reminding her they would be confined to this small building—each of them in a peevish mood.

SINKING HIS TEETH into the fluffy biscuit, he rolled his eyes with the pleasure of the taste. Turned out that Tori Barrett was one hell of a good cook when turned loose with decent provisions. Forking the tasty ham into his mouth, he closed his eyes and relished it after having spent more than he should for it. This sure beat bacon and beans. After he forked potatoes into his mouth, he tasted onion she must've added. Allowing the taste to roll over his tongue, he reached for the tin cup of coffee. All the while, he sensed Tori's intent regard.

He lifted his eyes from his plate. "Tori. You missed your calling. You're one helluva' cook. You just didn't have the provisions to work with. Mighty tasty."

Her mouth curved into a sunlight smile. "I'm good with a few things. I'm not much of a baker. Those biscuits are what I learned from my mother. Besides, this is the first decent cook oven we've run across. It's a Walker and Pratt."

"A fine cook she must've been. Your mother."

That quick, the ordinary conversation turned cold. For the life of him, he had no idea the mention of her mother would upset her.

She stood. "Best I clean up then turn in."

"The bunk mattress looks better than the last one."

She nodded but didn't reply to his attempt at humor.

"Tori. I'm sorry I mentioned your mother. It seems to have upset you."

"Nothing's wrong. I'm just tired. Got to think about how I'm going to get to California."

He slid his empty cup aside and got up from the chair. Taking her shoulders between his hands, he pulled her against him. She came willingly. He stared at the top of her head and said what kept going around and around in his head. "Don't go to California."

She laughed. "You've got somewhere else in mind for me?"

"We'll be on a train out of Columbus in just a few days. I'll be stayin' on in Ogallala long enough to conclude my business. Then I'm headin' for my home at the Belle Fourche River. You'd like Ogallala. Maybe start a business there. Besides, you'd like my friends once you get to know them. They'd look in on you."

Her shoulders bunched beneath his hands. As she tried to shrug away from him, he held her fast. Her face lifted and, he touched her mouth with his thumb.

"Don't go to California. You don't have to. Silas won't come near you because I'll make sure of it."

"No. He's my problem... not yours."

You should have protected your wife, his conscience reminded him. He dropped his hands away, leaving her to plunge the fry pan into the oak water pail, effectively ending their conversation.

They slept apart, depending on the low-burning fire in the old stove to drive out the night chill. Nothing could drive the cold that had formed between them. The faint lantern light allowed him to study her slender form where she curled on the bunk. A blanket covered her shoulders. Her eyes reflected golden light as she stared in his direction.

It was all he could do to keep from rolling to his feet and taking her into his arms, telling her how much he wanted her to stay with him. Conjuring the touch of her lips and the sweet scent of lilies, he squeezed his eyes closed, grinding his teeth with frustration. Once she was gone, he'd take a long while getting her out of his mind.

———————

TORI THOUGHT GUS was right. Norfolk hadn't been much of a town. This morning they'd set out with enough provisions to see them as far as Columbus, which, according to Gus, they'd reach in two or three days.

Her horse plodded behind the pack horse, then just as they neared a large, white-washed frame house, a silver-haired woman stepped outside to greet them. With her hands planted on her hips, she squinted beneath the wrinkled hand that cupped her eyes against the sun.

"Goodness, Gus Quaid. You ain't a sight for sore eyes. Bill told me you'd come to town. You sure have changed."

Gus grinned. "Maggie. You sure haven't changed. I got older."

"You look like you've been short on good vittles and sleep. Who you got with you?"

After a quick glance at her, he said, "This is Miss Tori Barrett. I'm escorting her to Columbus."

Maggie simply nodded. "Bill said you'd been attacked, then came across a wildfire." The woman's attention turned to her. "You couldn't ask for a better man to guide you, honey."

"Yes. I couldn't agree more, Maggie."

"Next time you come this way, I can put you up. Maybe we'll have a real hotel. The train is comin' this way. The spur line to Deadwood and even into Omaha."

Gus tipped his hat. "Some call it progress. Thanks, Maggie. Got to push on. Been away from my place too long. Time to conclude my business and get there."

Once they'd left Norfolk behind them, Gus waved her closer, then circled his horse to her side. He poked his hat back on his head and sighed.

"What is it? Spit it out, Gus."

"You sure were interested in that Quaker Gem Stove and a lot of other things in the store. Bill is a jabberer. So is his wife, Maggie."

"If you're trying to make a point, maybe you should get to it because I'm not sure I know what this is about. What was wrong with admiring that stove?"

"If you talked much longer, he'd have sold it to you."

"Don't talk foolish."

"My point is this. If, and I'm emphasizing, *if* Silas is behind us, you're leaving a lot of breadcrumbs behind. We both have been since we left Fort Randall. Bill and Maggie are gossips, and now they know more than I'd like. From now on, we keep to ourselves as much as possible."

She swallowed hard. If it weren't for Gus, she wouldn't have given it any thought.

"I take it back about you being mule-headed."

"Nope. I really can be mule-headed at times. This just doesn't happen to be one of them."

"Lordy. I hope I haven't put us both in danger."

"Set it aside for now. Besides, danger is something I'm used to. Best start thinking about what you'll cook up tonight now that we have eggs and baking powder. I've got a taste for some biscuits."

"No matter what you might think, I had to cook for myself. Even a saloon gal has to eat."

Only two camps, and they'd be in Columbus. The bite of loneliness ahead already took hold. The thought they'd say goodbye in Ogallala hurt more than she thought anything ever could again. Despite Gus telling her not to worry, she was more than worried. She was terrified.

———————

LEANING AGAINST THE trunk of a red oak, he puffed on a cigarette, then stared skyward at the milky trail of stars splashed against a cloudless sky. The warmth from the campfire chased the chill. He ran a hand across his full belly. Tori was right. She knew her way around cooking when given the chance. How she'd managed those fluffy biscuits without an oven, he didn't know.

While he waited for her to return from her ablutions near the edge of the Loup, he'd begun to worry at what was keeping her. The sand along the Loup was quicksand in places. He'd warned her, but Tori had a mind of her own. He hefted his rifle and tossed his smoke into the dying embers. As he trudged through the high bluestem, he saw no sign she'd passed this way.

The sun left a thin streak of red along the misty horizon. Squinting in the direction of the river, his mouth dropped open just before his throat closed. Gus Quaid gaped like a boy seeing his first naked lady.

Hunkering, he dare not move, swearing to keep this memory for his own. Knowing he was being rude, he couldn't bring himself to look away from the hand that sponged water over those luscious naked breasts, painted in nature's pink light. He was reminded of one of those Greek goddesses he'd seen in books. Perfection like hers was hard to look away from. He swallowed hard. If he were decent, he'd turn his back and leave her alone. Spellbound, he was powerless to move.

When she stood and shrugged into her white shirt, he clenched his jaw. She wrung out the towel then arched her back. Gus licked his lips, not moving a muscle, even while his sweat stung his eyes, ducking when she turned in his direction. Instead, he gave in to pure pleasure. They'd already been intimate... but this was different. Her movement was pure innocence... her body kissed by sunlight.

This goddess didn't walk. Instead, she glided across the grass like a phantom. As she drew nearer, he withdrew into the shadows, dropping flat against his stomach, and prayed she wouldn't find him slinking about like a schoolboy. Once she'd passed, he stood and brushed his pants. Strolling back into camp, Gus whistled a tune, pretending he hadn't just been to heaven.

He found her shaking her blanket when he ambled up from the river.

"I'd wondered where you'd gotten to," she said.

He cleared his throat. "Just making sure things were quiet."

"They are. Seems too quiet. Except for those crickets."

Nodding, he sat cross-legged while his eyes followed her every motion. When she sat on her bedroll, he wanted to ask her something, but the thought left him.

"Crickets," he rasped.

"You don't hear them?"

He supposed he did. Still, he hadn't been paying attention to them.

"Are you all right? You seem a bit out of sorts."

He cleared his throat. "I'm fine. Be careful around the Loup River. The grass hides rattlers. Be careful where you step. Quicksand can suck you under."

Sitting side-by-side on the blanket, he listened to crackling embers while he watched her plait her hair. His thoughts turned to how different she seemed from the woman he'd met at Fort Benton. Yet, he was still partial to seeing her in that prim black dress.

"Gus. Are there Indians out there?"

He sighed. She sure knew how to come up with the least expected turn of thought.

"There are some still roaming around, yes. Don't worry over much."

"Those Indians who took us by surprise managed to slice you. Why didn't you see a physician in Norfolk?"

"I did."

"When was that?"

"Bill, the storekeeper, is the only medicine man in town. He took a look in the back storeroom while you were perusing the what-nots."

"What did he advise?"

"Gave me some salve. Said someone did a good job of sewing it up. As long as I don't have a fever, it'll heal."

Tori lifted a brow and cocked her head. "I don't believe you."

"I'm a grown man, Tori. Not used to bein' mothered, though you have good intentions. If it bothers me by the time we get to Columbus, I'll see a physician there. I'll even invite you to come along."

"Tell me the truth, Gus."

"About?"

"Bill isn't a practicing physician, is he?'

"Tends to animals. Let's drop this subject."

"I have one more, Gus." He held up one finger.

"You don't like Indians much."

"That's not a question."

He folded his arms across his belly, contemplating what he'd say, then deciding on the truth. "It was a Brulé that took my wife. God knows how she might've suffered at their hands. So, your perception is mostly right. I've known good Indian scouts and plenty of honest, good men among the tribes. But I won't forgive the ones who took Aubrey."

She lowered her head then she said, "I'm sorry."

He leaned against his saddle and stretched out his legs then crossed his ankles. When she lifted her face, he held her gaze. "Tori, if it makes a difference to you, after scouting with the Army, I've found the Indians aren't treated fairly. Now it bothers the hell out of me."

He cleared his throat. "Your turn. Where did you come from? Figure you must have family somewhere. You mentioned Virginia."

There was silence. She rose from beside him, then walked to the edge of the camp. He could tell she stared up at the stars. When he saw her scrub her arms with her hands, he stood, then moved behind her. She turned her head. What he saw was the hard, cold woman he'd met at Fort Benton. Beautiful, serene, and bitter. The Tori he'd bedded was delicate, fragile, yet indomitable. She was two people. Her expression turned sullen.

"You deserve the truth. I *was* a working gal since I turned seventeen. My ma died. Think it was pneumonia. My pa was killed in the War. My two brothers were gone. I was left alone on the farm when Connor O'Malley came by our house. Promised me I'd find a good life with him. Being young, I didn't recognize a bald-faced liar. Took me to New Orleans and set me up with a *job*. That day was the worst day I'd ever experienced. I'd been too young to see through his lies. Worse, he'd said he loved me. A fool girl—I believed him."

"What happened to him?"

She shrugged.

His first thought was he'd like to find Connor O'Malley and kill him. His second thought was that he needed to tamp down his urge to retch. Her innocence had been stolen. Imagining her at that young age, a sweet girl with dreams. That her heart was trampled until the only way for her to go on was to wall off her emotions… sickened him. What soul he had left felt heavy in his chest. *That son of a bitch had turned her into a whore when she should have had beaus coming to call.* Clenching one fist, he lowered his eyes and pinched the bridge of his nose. There were no words sufficient enough to erase what had happened to her.

"I'm sorry, Tori. *Damned sorry.*"

"That time is over."

The coarseness in her voice had him search her tear-stained face. Was there more she hadn't told him? "Where did you grow up?"

"Virginia. A little farm. Church folks. Good, God-fearing people. My brothers were full of ornery. Always teasing. One older. One younger. Both set off for the War behind our pa. My pa rode home on his broken down horse, a bullet still lodged in him. He died within two days. Buried him out back. My brothers never returned."

"Something like the place where I grew up. My pa was a French trapper in Dakota Territory. We lived on the frontier. My ma was Osage. Aubrey and me... we met in Massachusetts. Pa made good money trappin' and then found gold. Got enough to send me off to Boston College. Aubrey was a student there."

"I *knew* you must be a well-educated man."

"Never finished. But I got to likin' books. We got married and came back home to settle.

He closed his eyes, hating the pity in her eyes. He heard her soft footsteps. When he opened his eyes, she had headed back to camp without a word. Hell, they'd both suffered.

———————

THAT NIGHT HE heard her stir. Before he knew it, she'd curled beside him on the bedroll. He dragged his blanket across them and listened to her soft sigh. Pure pleasure poured through him with her backside snugged against his groin. His lips touched her temple, and in that moment, he knew he'd never sleep again without imagining her spooned against him.

The time they had left was short. With each mile, some part of his heart crumbled knowing he'd spend the rest of his life looking for two women. The wife who'd been stolen and the woman who wouldn't stay because he made no promises.

TWELVE

SHOT

AFTER THEY'D WASHED down dried beef and biscuits, they headed out onto the grassland beyond the Loup. He'd handed Jenny's lead rope over to her. As her horse plodded behind Gus, she gave thought to her appearance. Gus promised they'd get into Columbus either tonight or tomorrow by late morning. Somehow, it worried her that she wasn't fit for civilized folks in these pants. Still, she could hardly see herself riding down the main thoroughfare wearing a dress hiked up to her knees.

She rocked in the saddle with just the sounds of thudding hooves, snorts, and the creak of her saddle for company. Tori pondered whether she should ever reveal the secret she kept about Connor O'Malley. If his name ever reemerged, he could destroy her. In truth, she hid her name to protect her family name, and what she'd done to Connor. Moreover, she might be a wanted woman. Now that she'd omitted the fact she'd married Connor, if Gus ever found out, it would be one more indictment. Gus was a man who demanded honesty. He'd never accept her excuses, even by omission.

She jerked her head up at the sound of Gus's horse running in the distance before he disappeared over the rise. Something had alarmed him, and she wouldn't be able to keep pace with Jenny in tow.

Wind brushed the bluestem and buffalo grass into swirling shades of green, while the clouds cast shadows across the rangeland. Looking over her shoulder, she could still see the sandy, quicksand banks far below along the Loup River.

Darting a glance to her right, she saw an Indian sitting a gray horse, just watching. Her heart thudded in her chest. Within a blink of her eyes, three more appeared beside the first. From this vantage, their long black hair and scant clothing were a fierce sight. They stared while she froze, not knowing whether to set her horse into a gallop, leaving the pack horse behind, or whether to stand her ground with a rifle.

Beaded black strands lifted on the wind, while she contemplated what to do. Her heart beat loudly in her ears when they started for her. She couldn't outrun them. *Where was Gus?* Each gripped a rifle. *He'd said they were on reservations.* Raising her chin, she nudged her mount into a trot, hoping they'd pass her by, leading the pack horse behind her.

She didn't need to look behind her to know they'd begun the chase. A quick glance showed they were closing the distance, taunting her with hoops and yips. Knowing she wouldn't outrun them with the pack horse in tow, she dropped the lead rope and dug her boot heels into her horse's flanks. The horse's muscles bunched beneath her while she slapped her reins. A slope was ahead of her. The horse was already winded, and knowing the futility, she drew up, hoping their game was over.

It was no use. They'd boxed her in, hooting and hollering. She reined her wheezing mount around. She drew her rifle, only to have one of the attackers grab it from her hands. Then she was wrenched from her saddle to find herself plunked in front of her captor. The rest rounded up Jenny and her horse. In front of her was the Loup River. Behind her was a bare-chested man, his words indiscernible. She tried to twist free of his strong arm, only to be gripped with enough force to push the air from her lungs.

When she turned her head, the black eyes of the dark-skinned man were inscrutable pools, while his expression was both unforgiving and stony. As he touched the hair at the back of her head, she tried to throw her leg over the withers, even if it meant being trampled. He held her fast against her struggle. The other three rode by, laughing and hooting. Her captor rent the air with an unholy, shrill yelp, leaving her ears ringing.

She blinked, determined not to faint. After a while, she gave up struggling. Instead, she fell into hazy acceptance, contemplating her next try at escape. And escape she would.

———————

SCREAMS SENT GUS'S heart into his throat. He brought his horse around in a circle. From his hilltop perch, the sight below jolted him. The sons of bitches had managed to circle around him. They'd set up false trails, and she was paying the price for his miscalculation. Now they were riding away with her—*just like Aubrey.*

This time, he had no intention of letting them out of his sight. They'd signed their own death sentence. Keeping out of view, he stalked them, parallel but hidden by the gulches and valleys between bluffs. They most likely figured he'd trail them.

At times, walking his horse, then other times, dismounting, he'd crawl on his belly to watch them, calculating their distance for range. Finally, when they pulled up beside a wide swath of sand beside the Loup, Tori was dropped to the ground like deer-kill, and he flinched at her shriek of pain.

One man watered the horses while the other three hunkered near her and, for the most part, ignored her. It appeared they'd muffled her with a hide thong between her lips. They drank from skin water bags but offered her none. Tori scooted along the ground, away from them.

"Good girl. Keep moving. I need a clear shot."

With his Winchester leveled on them, he squeezed off one, two, three and four shots levering so fast it was like the gun was part of him. The one closest to Tori lay in a heap, holding his side. The one near the horses mounted his pony and rode wildly across the river, slumped against his horse while the animal struggled to gain footing in the sand. There was a wide swath of blood across his back. The third vaulted onto his horse and followed the others.

Gus swung into his saddle, then nudged his horse to where Tori kneeled, while the wounded Indian near her swung up behind one of his rescuers, then they were gone. Her back stiffened as she saw him approach, then averted her eyes. After he dismounted, he crouched beside her. Seeing her shake violently, he feared touching her. The shock was in her eyes and in her bloodless face. *Damn. He never should have chased after those tracks, leaving her alone.*

He sliced the thong and tossed it aside. The heart pounding inside his chest was both because of his rage and misery at the sight of her chafed mouth. *God, how close he'd come to losing her.*

"Sweetheart. You're safe. I'll never let this happen again. I should never have let you come with me in the first place."

She leaned forward then he wrapped her in his arms, rocking with her as she cried. The trembling of her body scared him. She sniffed after he set her face back, then cupped her cheeks between his hands. Her gray-blue eyes were misted with tears. Tucking her against him, he feared he wouldn't be able to let go of her for a lifetime. Yet she deserved better.

"Say something, Tori."

She nuzzled her cheek against his neck, then she said, "I was scared. Don't like being scared."

"No one likes bein' scared. Had me out of my mind. They outsmarted me. If it would make you feel better, go ahead and punch me in the mouth. More than once."

She rubbed her head against his neck while he combed his fingers through her hair, pressing the silky strands between his fingers, satisfying himself that she was safe, giving his heart time to slow.

"Gus?"

"Hmm?"

"Did one of them die?"

"I saw him stumble to his horse and ride out behind the others. Blood was running down his back. Not sure about the other one. Two were definitely wounded. Could've killed them, but I didn't."

"They were boys, weren't they? Like before."

He shifted, sat on the grass, then situated her across his lap. "Don't matter—*boys* or men, they could have killed you. No matter that reservations aren't pleasant places for them. That doesn't give them the right to do what they did. Likely, they would have let you go rather than stir more trouble. Like you said, they were out to prove themselves and steal whatever they could. If they'd settled for stealing a horse and gear, that's one thing. Wouldn't blame them for that. But this...."

She rubbed at her mouth. "Itches."

"How about I get you some water? And salve."

She grasped his shirt, stilling him. "No. Don't leave me. Not yet. Just a little longer."

"Ahh, Tori. My heart near stopped."

"I reckon my heart did, Gus Quaid. Can I still punch you?"

She lifted her head, then offered a trembling, feeble smile. He couldn't resist whispering a gentle kiss to the corners of her raw lips.

"You have leave to punch me. Anytime will do."

"I'll think about it later. I've lost my hat. Marie sold it to me for more than I should've paid. I can't afford another."

Her serious turn of thought almost made him laugh. Instead, he mustered an empathetic frown. The things she thought to say always surprised him.

"I'll buy you the fanciest hat I can find."

SHE REACHED BESIDE her, and finding him gone, she lurched from her bedroll. "Gus?"

"I'm over here. Breakfast of coffee, potatoes, and smoked ham. Almost ready."

She shoved a tangle of hair away from her face, thinking about the touch of that Indian. Determined to set it out of her mind, she rolled to her feet, then strode to where he proffered the plates. She hoped he didn't notice how jangled she still was after her capture, but her blasted twitch always gave her away. He held her gaze as she took the plate from his hand.

"Did the salve help?"

"Yes. It did. Thank you."

From his pocket, he pulled out a fork and handed it over. She'd forgotten how hungry she was until she scooped the vittles into her mouth like she'd been starved, savoring every morsel. Until her raw mouth healed, every time she ate she'd feel the sting.

"They won't come back?" she asked around a mouthful.

"I doubt it. My guess is they'll be too ashamed to admit to losing their prisoner to do much more than bluster. Especially since it was a woman. They'd never live it down. Would like to hear some of the excuses they come up with for the wounds yet still returned without any stolen horses."

"Anyhow, we'll be in Columbus in just four or five hours if we push it. How's it sound to treat ourselves to baths, fine beds, and a view of the town from the Credit Foncier Hotel? Only been inside once. You deserve some finery with a good meal at a table with a white tablecloth. I aim to see you get them."

She stopped chewing. "Gus, I can't afford such a hotel. Besides, you don't need to mollycoddle me."

"I can afford it. Besides, I want to get cleaned up before I meet my friends in Ogallala. I'm sending them a telegram from Columbus to let them know of our arrival."

"That's where you and me say goodbye."

The silence was like a wall. His jaw tautened before he said, "You'll likely want to stay in Ogallala. Good place to settle if you give it a chance."

"Silas might find me. Or someone he pays will find me."

"Doubt he'd come all this way. If you want to be honest with yourself, Silas might find you anywhere. Sooner or later, you have to stop hiding. You don't know for sure he's following you. It's a long way to Virginia City, Tori."

She had no reasonable answer. He'd never understand how possessive a man Silas was. After all, it was her problem. Sooner or later, she'd have to be on her own.

"Gus. Like you, I don't want the hotel to be some sort of payment."

"Christ, Tori. If you ain't the most stubborn, one-track woman I ever met. I told you I don't consider you like that. The hotel isn't payment. It's simply practical."

Setting the plate aside, she lifted the tin of coffee to her mouth and considered how much she'd come to like Gus. In truth, he come to mean more to her than was wise. Because even he meant to leave her behind.

"Breakfast was delicious. But you should have awakened me. Once again, you sat there and watched me as I slept." She stood to gather the dishes, dodging his stare and avoiding the thought of his leaving her behind. He grasped her wrist to still her.

"Not so fast. I watched you out of sheer pleasure, painting the memory of you in my head. After tomorrow, you can make up your mind what direction you plan to go. So will I. We always knew this wouldn't be forever. Isn't that what we agreed?"

"Gus. I once asked you this, and you skittered away from it." She cleared her throat and said, "What if I tell you I love you?" There. Her tongue betrayed her, and her face flamed with embarrassment.

His silence said everything while he slowly unraveled his fingers from her wrist. She dared to look toward him. His mouth was a thin line. Snatching up his hat, he lurched to his feet, picked up his rifle, then waited for one beat.

"Tori. You don't know me well enough to love met yet. Moreover, I don't know if you trust me with whatever you're hiding. Best we get our things together."

After a time, she stood and glanced across her shoulder to where he saddled the horses. Remorse and guilt gripped him. Her cloistered secrets held her captive. Neither of them could break free. She'd been foolish to think anything would change... just because she cared for this man. It was necessary to let him go, for his sake as much as hers. Beneath her breath, she murmured, "Damn you, Gus Quaid. Why did you make me love you?"

———————

COLUMBUS WAS A rugged gem. A city that might have always been there, waiting to be discovered. There were shops, saloons, and even a four-story structure that must be the hotel. She had to admit she looked forward to a bath and dressing like a woman again.

"That's where we're staying... the hotel you've got your eyes on. Once our horses are stabled, we'll settle into rooms for the night."

Nodding her agreement, she hadn't missed that he'd said *rooms*. It was settled. They'd go their separate ways. Still, at the prospect of a comfortable bed and a bath... maybe she would wake tomorrow with a new life spread out before her—in California.

She stood in the shade of the livery, then listened impatiently while Gus haggled over the price. He had a decisive, persuasive manner she admired. But for the moment, her dirty pants and tangled hair might be a problem for that fancy hotel. She worried her lip, irritated that Gus was taking so long palavering.

Farther along the street, three prim-dressed women formed what she figured was a gossip circle. No doubt, she had become the center of their blather. Pointed fingers, angry glares, and wrinkled scowls were slung her way. Prune-faced women with narrow minds had crossed her path many times before. While their penetrating gazes might melt iron, those women would have to work much harder to insult Tori Barrett.

After all, she'd known their kind all her life. Still, she had to admit, dressed in pants, she was an oddity. She pasted a sweet smile on her mouth which sent those three old crows on their way, marching like soldiers on a campaign.

The smell of tobacco smoke turned her attention to the saloon across the street, where a dark-suited man watched her. His insolent gaze traced her from the top of her head to her boots. Tori's skin prickled at the notion he may have recognized her. Had he been sent to find her? Or did he remember her from her former life? In fact, how would anyone recognize her in this getup? Still, would she always wonder every time a man looked her way?

"Hey!"

She jerked, then spun around to find Gus staring in her direction, one eyebrow raised in question.

"You look like you went off somewhere. I called you, and you didn't hear me."

With his rifle gripped in one hand, his saddlebag draped over his shoulder... he gripped the Gladstone bag, then led the way. She bit her lip while she strode beside him, her satchel held in front of her. She averted her face each time someone passed until they reached the doorway of the stone building.

She drew in a long draught of air and said, "Columbus is more than I expected."

They paused while Gus shifted his weight from one leg to the other, then held her gaze. "Wait till you get a gander at this fancy hotel on the inside."

"Oh, Gus. I don't belong here. People are staring. I know what they're thinking."

"Figured that's what was goin' on in your pretty head. The Tori Barrett I know wouldn't run scared. Once you get out of those duds and into a dress, there won't be one gal in town prettier than you." He winked.

She couldn't bring herself to tell Gus she felt watched. When they parted in Ogallala, she'd have to turn to her wiles to survive. If only she'd never met Connor or Silas.

———————

BUBBLES FLOATED BENEATH her chin while her head rested against the wide rim of the copper tub. Lifting one leg, she propped her ankle, savoring the clean smell of soap and the soothing feel of hot water. If she stayed like this much longer, she'd fall asleep and drown. In her daydreams, she thought about California... a place of gold miners, saloons, ranchers, and farmers. There must be a place for her there.

"*Gus,*" she whispered. "This is divine." Her mind refused to think about tomorrow.

"I was wonderin' when you'd figure out I was here."

She lurched, then dropped her foot into the water with a splash. Stunned, she lifted her head from the rim, turned her head, and faced Gus's intent gaze. Legs outstretched, his ankles crossed, and his shirt unbuttoned, he looked like he'd been drinking. She dragged her eyes away and settled back in the tub.

"Should keep better watch, lady."

"You weren't invited. Why are you here, Gus?" she snapped.

"Hmm. Now there's a question. I knocked some time ago. There wasn't an answer. So... I let myself in. Your eyes looked nearly closed. I decided to make myself at home and see you didn't drown."

"You could have cleared your throat."

"Guess so. I liked watching you. Just so you know, I'm a red-blooded man, and you're a beautiful woman. I never made a secret about how much I want you."

She picked up her sponge and dabbed her shoulders. "I haven't drowned. You are free to leave. I'll be sure to lock the door from now on."

"It *was* locked. I have my ways."

"In that case, I'm inviting you to vacate my room."

She waited, only to hear footsteps approach. His shadow crossed her body where he towered above her. Her gaze traveled up his long legs and stilled at his slightly narrowed eyes. His lopsided grin left her weak. Fool that she was, she liked him when he teased. She dragged her eyes from his smile just as he kneeled beside her and took the sponge from her limp fingers.

"I'll help you finish this first. I've been itching to rinse the soap from your skin."

"I can manage. Best you leave." She fixed him with a serious glower, but his grin was so filled with boyish deviltry, she found herself enjoying this repartee.

"Had my bath, or I'd consider joining you. Though... I'd accept an invitation."

"You're randy."

He laughed.

"It wasn't meant as a compliment."

"I know. And just so *you* know, I lean toward *randy* whenever I'm near you."

Before she could think of a surly response, he'd dunked the sponge into the water. Closing her eyes, she sighed at the pleasure of it sliding across her shoulders just before he dragged it along her neck with a slowness that nearly had her jump from her skin, setting off sensations she didn't know she had. Shudders coursed through her, leaving her limp enough to drop her head back and close her eyes. The sponge rode gently across her skin until she grasped his hand.

With her mouth clamped, she swallowed a groan of pleasure. One listless arm dropped into the water, splattering his shirt with water. From beneath her lidded eyes, she saw the wet splotches on his shirt. He looked down at himself.

"Now you've done it. I'll need to take off my shirt and let it dry before I tend to your hair."

As he tugged his shirt away from his solid muscles, she swallowed hard. As her perusal trailed his many scars, she held back a gasp, knowing he hated pity. How he'd suffered for so long. While she recalled seeing some of his scars, the others had been shadowed or hidden beneath his clothes. Mindful that he was very private about his past, she thought better than to ask. Instead, she gave in to the pleasure of his fingers as they massaged her scalp.

She'd already drowned with contentment when he drew circles along her temples with his fingertips. She purred like a kitten. Her breath caught, and she swore she'd died. Clutching his wrist, she stayed his movement.

"*No.* Let me, Tori," he growled.

From beneath her slitted eyes, he was nearly a blur. "Mmm."

"That the best you can say?"

"Don't stop."

"If that's the best you can muster, I better work on my strategy."

"Still didn't tell me."

"Tell what?" he mumbled, leaning away.

"How did you manage to get in here? Specifically."

His eyes narrowed. "A key. Can we move on? I swear I get blindsided by the direction of your thinking."

"You have a key to my room?"

"I managed to retrieve one."

"Now I know why your boots are missing."

"Astute of you."

"Now what?"

"This."

Abruptly, he stood, tugged his shirt free, then tossed it aside. Tori offered him a coy smile as she regarded his hard stomach and corded muscles—a man respected by some and feared by others. He was a man who could break an enemy in half yet use those same hands to apply a gentle touch. At that moment, his dark eyes were hungry. She couldn't deny this man, even knowing this night would never come again. Neither could she deny herself these moments she'd keep with her forever.

Without warning, Gus plunged his arms beneath the water, grasped her beneath her buttocks, then lifted her into his arms as though she were weightless. Water dripped onto the floor and formed a wet path to the bed. He lowered her to her feet, turned away long enough to grab the towel, then he blotted the droplets from her face. She shivered, more from his touch than the cool air.

His unwavering gaze held hers. She tilted her head in question before tugging the towel from his hands and dropping it to the floor. His eyes raked her from the wet strands of her hair to her curled toes.

He lifted her to the bed, then turned away to dim the light beside the window. When he returned, he settled beside her. Neither could look away from the other.

"Your mouth is chattering with cold," he said in a husky voice.

"I'm a bit cold. Maybe scared too."

He reached for the blanket, then dragged it over them. She rested her head against his shoulder while one arm shoveled beneath her, holding her close.

"You said you're scared. Why? We've been together like this before."

"No. I'm just... nothing has changed. We still have things between us."

He lowered his chin. Her eyes lifted to his.

"Gus. I don't want to ruin our last time together, talking about things we can't change."

He leaned over her, then pressed a kiss to her forehead. "Maybe this shouldn't be the last time."

"Please, Gus."

Gus dropped his other arm across his eyes. There was silence.

"If you plan to have your way with me, you might want to take off your socks."

"I'm planning to do just that. You got anything else buzzing in your head?"

"Would you tell me the truth?"

"Maybe. As long as we haven't circled back to how I gained entry to your room."

"I didn't mean to imply you're dishonest, Gus."

"Really? Well, I do have something on my mind. Here is the truth. I intend to ravish you."

She shrugged. "You're paying my way at this hotel." *And wished she could call those words back.*

"You know how to punch hard without tryin'. I don't like repeating myself. I'm not interested in sleeping with a prostitute or whore or whatever else *you* seem to think you are. I don't want a paid woman. I'm interested in making *love* to the woman who takes my breath away. Even though she has a sharp tongue in the bargain. You got any arguments with that?"

Drawing the blanket across her bare shoulders, his arm tightened. She felt his pounding heart beneath her head. He'd said making love. Did he realize what he'd said?

"Since you don't have any objection, lady, my intention is to continue where we left off."

He dragged the blanket from her. There was a rustle of cloth as she gave thought to what he'd said. He turned her in his arms. Her eyes widened. His mouth brushed hers, leaving her wanting more. As though he'd read her mind, he applied a breath-stealing kiss, tasting of

whiskey and tobacco. He skimmed his hands along her neck, then captured her face between his hands... while his kiss deepened. He leaned
away and captured her eyes.

His finger outlined her mouth, setting off a quiver.

"No arguments, lady?"

She took one of his hands in hers. "None that I can think of."

THIRTEEN

TURNING POINT

HIS HEART RACED into full throttle, and his blood ran hot. He was a man drunk with her. She awakened every emotion inside him—at times anger, then at times a love deep enough to cut through his wall of defense. For the rest of his days, he'd never lose her from his every thought.

While his tongue traced those perfect rosebud lips and feasted on the curved corners of her mouth, he managed to coax a slow grin. The taste of her perfumed soap lingered. This woman gave as good as she got until he was a mass of vibrating flesh.

They fell through the stars together… leaving behind all of their unanswered questions and doubts. He was too far gone for that. With his fingers threaded with her hair, he spoke her name.

Her eyes glistened with contentment as he lifted her hand, kissing each of her fingers. Emotions played across her face. *Wariness. Contentment. Uncertainty. Pleasure. And Love.*

She'd said she was scared. Now he understood why. Because he was scared of what his heart was telling him. He swallowed and brushed a strand of hair from her face.

"Are you all right?"

She lifted her head from where he'd tucked her against his chest. "Why wouldn't I be?"

"I…." His throat nearly closed. "I know."

"Gus."

The red-pink sunrise painted their skin as it streamed through the long window. Shadows moved. She murmured words in her sleep… words he couldn't decipher. His world had tilted, but daylight would return them to the hard truth. They would part—she taking part of his soul with her to California. He would grow old with his herd of horses in Belle Fourche.

———————

THEY SAT ACROSS from each other over cups of coffee and half-eaten eggs and potatoes. The platter stacked with bread and slices of beef was hardly touched. She'd become accustomed to how he enjoyed eating. Today, he'd forked his food while darting glances in her direction, without eating as heartily as he usually did. While she was truly hungry, her mind wasn't on food, knowing their time was almost over.

She nibbled at a piece of bread, then stirred her food around on her plate, lost in thought. *She couldn't compete with a ghost. Aubrey watched.* For his part, he wouldn't leave her secrets buried. He'd dig at them until, one day, he'd know the truth. Then he'd hate her.

"You look far away," he said.

Lifting her eyes from considering the bone china cup, she held his intent gaze. "That's because I *was* far away."

He sipped his coffee, then set his cup down with a thump. Leaning back in his chair, he crossed his arms. "If I ask you where your thoughts were, I doubt you'd tell me. Maybe we need to talk about *this.*"

"This?"

"Don't play coy with me. You know what I mean. I imagine you have some idea about where we go from here. As do I. Things have changed between us."

Now it was her turn to search the depths of his eyes while she sipped. After setting the cup on the table, she folded her hands.

"All right. You go first," she said.

"Maybe we should talk privately."

Leaning across the table, she whispered, "There's only one other couple in the far corner. I doubt they're interested in us because they're far more interested in each other."

He stood, then dragged his chair beside hers, his back to the corner. After he reached for her hand, he folded it within his, then stroked her fingers with his thumb.

"You know most of my past. I've spent a long while searching for answers. Some might call my search a form of revenge. My wife died because I left her alone. Guilt eats at me, Tori. Just before I met you, I gave little thought to a future with another woman until you came along."

"I'm layin' my cards on the table and expect you to do the same. Show your hand, lady. I'm a betting man. And I bet that Silas isn't your only problem. Let's start with your name. Is it Tori?"

"Victoria Barrett is my name. Silas is *my* worry, not yours. If I get to California, I hope not to have to look over my shoulder again." *Liar. She'd lied again.* Her stomach clenched.

"If you think I'm willing to go with you to California, I can't. I have a small ranch, raising horses. If I ever considered taking a wife, I'd need to know she wouldn't go running off the first time loneliness sets in... or if an old enemy shows up at my door. I need to know what I'm up against. And it isn't just Silas, is it?"

Oh, God. This sweet man couldn't change any of it. Even the great Gus Quaid would be up against more than he could handle. The last thing she wanted to do was cause him more pain. The truth was too hard to voice.

"I have his money. Money I consider is coming to me. Silas had an agreement with me. I thought you understood that."

"Return the damned money... with the promise he'll let you go and leave you be. I'll see he gets it, along with your message."

"How can you ask that of me? For him, it's *not* just about the money, Gus. He wants *me*."

He lifted his hand away from hers as though she'd burned him. "I told you I'd protect you."

"It's *my* problem. Not yours. Besides, I'm not the only one with secrets. You haven't yet told me why you're so intent on helping a friend in Nebraska. It's a long trip for a friend. I already saw the money and several sacks of gold inside your Gladstone bag."

"*Dammit*. Keep that to yourself, or I'll have more trouble than I want. I've been lucky so far."

"I'm sorry. But as you can see, they've just left. We're alone."

"Let's save this discussion for another time. We both best get some sleep. Boarding at eleven. I'll need to get my gear loaded before we get seated. That is if you still want to sit beside me."

"Yes, I'd like your company." Loving Gus with all her heart could never erase how she'd lived before. *If only she could undo all the things she'd done to survive, she'd fight to keep Gus Quaid.*

———————

BEYOND THE TRAIN window, the old Pony Express depot and church at Cozad came into view. The short boardwalk in front of the dry goods store was deserted. Squinting through the dirt-caked window, his eyes settled on the small hotel where he'd recovered from a near-death injury. Thanks to a good Army surgeon, he'd survived the arrow in his chest.

"The train is stopping. Where are we?" Tori asked.

Turning toward her, he winked. "Cozad. Not much but a speck." They'd hardly spoken since last night. Neither of them wanted to circle back to what hung between them. He had no taste for the prickly topic of their pasts, yet it was between them like a looming storm.

"You'll see a few hearty farmers and ranchers come and go. Been some quarrels between the two groups. Best not to wander far from the train. Stretch your legs while the train takes on water then boards any passengers. So far, it doesn't look like there will be any."

"Where will you be?"

"Down by the livery. When the soldiers come by, they usually carry information."

"Why would soldiers be here?"

"Because they camp out on the Mullally Ranch near Cozad anytime they're on patrol."

After her barely perceptible nod, her mouth pursed, leaving him to wonder whether she'd been about to question why he wanted to talk to the soldiers. That was his own business. *Because they might've heard if a white woman had been recovered.*

"You got your little derringer in your purse?"

"Yes."

"You'll be safe enough at the dry goods store. They got a privy out back. We'll be leavin' here in less than an hour."

Taking her arm, he helped her step down from the passenger car. Two men stepped down ahead of them while Gus gauged where they were heading. When they continued to the old depot and then lit their cigars, he figured they weren't a threat. Satisfied they weren't heading for the store, he jutted his chin. "Millicent is the crusty old proprietor. I warn you. She's nosy. Be careful what you say."

Gus tipped his hat, then left her to make her way across the street. With a last glance across his shoulder, he watched her enter the store and close it behind her before he continued on.

———

TORI HELD HER reticule close, her mind still on Gus's warning. The little town was eerily quiet except for the nickering horses in the corral. Since there were few folks about, she figured most were working their farms. Bells jangled when she stepped inside to the smells of leather, tobacco, and sundry spices. A silver-haired woman looked up from behind the counter. Tori thought that this must be Millicent.

"Can I help you? Get travelers from the train all the time."

"No. Just thought I'd stretch my legs."

"Well, let me know if you need somethin'. Name's Millicent. Don't see many folks in the middle of the week."

"Thank you." Gus's warning about giving away information stuck in her head like briars.

Tori turned her attention to the shelves lined with pots, pans, sacks of potatoes, and cans of lard beside jarred peaches. A large coffee bean grinder sat on a table. She ran a hand across bolts of wool, chambray, and brown denim... thinking Gus could use some new shirts and pants. A fair hand at sewing, she'd had little time for it over the years. But they'd soon separate and most likely never see each other again. Staring from the window, she saw no sign of Gus.

"You seem a mite sad, honey. Life shouldn't be that grim. Too young for that. You lookin' out there for someone?"

"I have someone escorting me to Ogallala."

"That so? What's the name?"

Biting her lip, she again remembered Gus's warning about Millicent being nosy, then wondered how he'd know that. Turns out he was right about this woman. But it couldn't hurt to say his name. "Gus."

"Gus Quaid. Well, as I live and breathe. Never thought he'd be back here. Stays to hisself. Last I saw him, he was in a bad way. Healed up in a room over to the hotel. Such that it is."

Tori's breath hitched. "What happened?"

"He was scoutin' for the Army, and they were all ambushed by a bunch of Indians. Blamed hisself. He took an arrow high up in the chest. Lucky he pulled through."

"Lordy." She couldn't think of another thing to say as her mind played over the scars she'd seen and touched.

"That man is lookin' for his wife... poor soul. He's most likely talkin' to Kinsey Hanes, our liveryman. He would've heard the Army news. Gus scouts for 'em. Kinsey would know if any white women been found. Ever'body knows she must be dead. Still, he keeps tryin' to find her."

She nodded. "I suppose so." *Gus. You must have loved her so very much.*

A long blast from the train jolted her out of her meanderings. She turned to leave, only to be brought up short by Millicent's cheerful voice. "You take care, now. Gus won't let nothin' happen to you. Next stop is Ogallala. Glory Sanderson's place might have more things."

"I thank you for the company and the shade." The woman gave away more information than a telegraph key. But she'd learned something more about Gus.

"Always good to have someone to pass the time of day."

The bells jangled at the closing of the door. Just as she started up the steps to the passenger car, a hand gripped her elbow, startling her.

"Easy. It's just me."

Gus's expression was unreadable as he led her to their seats. He checked his bag and then hers before stowing his rifle beneath the seat but kept his gun belt on. As the train began to move, Gus doffed his hat, then rested his head against the back of the seat, his eyes closed.

"Gus?"

"Hmm?"

"There was no news, was there?" His eyes snapped open.

"How'd you know?"

She touched his hand. "I'm sorry."

"Don't be. Rather not talk about it. Damn that Millicent."

"She spoke of you kindly and meant no harm."

"Deep down. I know she's dead." His tired, resigned voice and the silence that followed told her more than words could. Thwarted once again at hearing nothing about his wife, left him looking drawn. Her heart broke at the sadness in his face.

———

FIVE HOURS LATER, Gus led her to the Ogallala House, then saw she was settled into a room. Before he left the lobby, he ordered a bath be sent up to her room. He was more than glad to hand over Bryce's money. For now, he needed more than a beer. He needed to settle things with her. First chance he got, he'd dig out the truth.

Damned if he didn't want to get drunk tonight. Bryce, Cort, and him would have mighty fine headaches tomorrow. Now that the worry about delivering Bryce's money was over with, he had another worry and her name was Tori. For now, she most likely soaked in a steamy tub with flowery soap. Unless she learned to trust him with her secrets, then he'd have to let her go on her dangerous venture to California.

Then his thoughts turned to her in those boy's clothes. He'd almost bitten his tongue in half at the sight of her in that pretty green dress she wore in Columbus, a stunning change by comparison. He was tempted to slip into her room just to watch her sleep... but not tonight.

HE LEANED BACK on the plump red velvet chair, his legs stretched out in front of him. Instead of getting drunk, he'd decided to surprise her with supper in the restaurant. After he'd fenagled a key to let himself into her room, he was drawn up short by the sight of her asleep.

For now, he was content watching her dark hair spilled across the pillow and her balled fist beneath her chin, looking like an innocent angel. Whenever she allowed herself to be herself, she became a pure sweet woman with a heart too big for her own good.

"Gus?" she whispered.

Dropping the front legs of the chair with a thud, he scrutinized her perfect skin peeking from the lace of her nightdress. God. Even with freckles sprinkled across her dainty little nose, she made a man's heart trip over itself. Her bright smile melted him into a puddle, but those girlish grins hadn't happened near enough.

"How do you feel?"

"Lost."

That was an odd response. "I'm here. You're not lost."

He stood and walked to the bed. Kneeling, he took her hand, pressed a kiss against her palm, then lifted an errant curl of hair from her face.

She tugged her hand free of his, then sat. With her arms clasped around her drawn knees, she dropped her head back. *She was about to pepper him with questions.* He knew it like he knew when a snowstorm was brewing.

"Did you meet your friends?"

"I did. We settled up the money and gold. All tucked in the bank vault."

"Thought you wouldn't be back."

"Wanted to make sure you ate supper. Did you?"

"No. Are you offering?"

He winked.

She slid from the bed, then grabbed up her dress. "I'll be ready in a few minutes."

He grinned when she stepped behind a screen, then heard the rustle of clothing. When she next appeared, she primped, turning this way and that before the Cheval mirror, as he took pleasure in everything about her except for the secrets she kept. The Tori he'd first met had changed. Or had she always been someone else?

"You look just fine to me. I'm goin' to have the prettiest gal in Ogallala at the table."

"My skin is browned. My freckles are growing. And my hair is tangled. I best not call you a liar."

"Nope. Best not."

"Just how many do you know?"

He leaned in, pecked her mouth with a quick kiss, then offered his arm. "Got me there. Lost count, I guess."

Her eyes flashed. "Did anyone ever tell you that you're conceited?"

He winked. "You'd be the first."

———————

THE DUMPLINGS WERE as fluffy and delicious as she'd ever eaten. The chicken with rosemary was divine. After they'd finished eating, he escorted her to her room, telling her he'd come by at breakfast. When evening shadows played across the walls of her room, her mind filled with decisions she needed to make. Pacing from one wall to the other, she gave thought to the mysterious friends he was meeting. Come to think of it, he'd never mentioned their names.

She ventured a look from her window at the town below, where street lanterns cast eerie shadows. Piano music, accompanied by hoots and hollers, meant the saloon patrons were having a good time. She cringed thinking of the years she'd spent in places like that. *But no more. Never again.* She wondered if Gus was there, enjoying whiskey with his friends. She'd bet on it. After all, he deserved some time with whomever he chose—without her in tow. Their time was over. Still, her curiosity niggled.

What harm would there be in a stroll? Maybe even a peek inside the Cowboy's Rest? With her reticule in hand, she opened the door, then stepped out into the hall, locking the door behind her. Chin raised, she made her way down the stairway and into the lobby.

Marching across the polished floor, she hesitated. Gus's familiar voice came from the dining room. From the arched doorway, there was no mistaking the large frame of Gus with his back to her. Two men sat across from him.

"Ma'am? May I be of help?"

Her body stiffened. When she pivoted to see the surly concierge glare in her direction, she was left with no choice but to cover her slinking around in the lobby. "Yes. There is something you can help with. Can you tell me in what room Mister Gus Quaid is staying?"

"I'm not supposed to do that."

"I'm with him. He's my guide."

The man jutted his chin. "Perhaps you should ask him."

Someone cleared his throat behind her. "Room two, Miss Barrett."

Her head whipped around, and her gaze followed the buttons of Gus's blue chambray shirt to his grin. "You have a habit of surprising me, Mister Quaid."

Grasping her arm, he led her toward the stairs. "I might say the same about you."

"Thought you'd turned in for the night. By the way, you look beautiful, even when perturbed."

"I'm not perturbed."

Once they'd reached her door, she turned. "Thank you for escorting me back. Will I see you again?"

"Breakfast downstairs. My friends are in a celebration mood, and I'm joining them for some drinks."

"Gus. That money. It isn't stolen, is it?"

"Already told you it doesn't belong to me. For your information, it was earned honestly."

He held open his palm. She dropped the key into his hand, leaving him to unlock it. She waited until he waved her inside, then he closed the door behind them. His stare was unwavering. When he crossed his arms, she took a step back.

"Now… Tori. What were you really doing in the lobby besides finding out my room number? Though you already know it perfectly well."

She pursed her lips then tilted her chin upward. "If you must know. I was thinking I might take a peek in the saloon until I noticed you with two men at a table. The nosy concierge asked me if he could help me. I devised an excuse for being there. It didn't work out well at all."

He sighed. "Sometimes, Tori, you worry me. Get some sleep. Pack your things. We're invited out to their ranch for a celebration."

Her eyes widened at the prospect of visiting folks she didn't know. "That's not a good idea. Besides, I'm planning to leave."

"They offered their hospitality for as long as *we* like. You'd be safe. They have lovely wives, and you'd like Lark and Hannah."

"Didn't you hear me? I'm leaving. I'm seeing about the train."

"Oh, I heard you. Maybe you don't understand how long a trip it is to get to California."

"Gus. I'm not used to being around regular people. Being with you is highly improper. We're probably the talk of the town as it is."

"I don't give a damn what others think. These friends are plain people with big hearts. They've brought a buckboard. Got the biggest ranch this side of the Mississippi, I reckon."

"Gus. This doesn't feel right."

"Give it time, Tori. This isn't a bad place to settle. Silas isn't going to follow you this far."

"You're going to the saloon, then?"

"No place for a lady. I've got things to discuss with them. Selling them some of my stock. Come morning, we'll be waiting for you downstairs. We leave early."

Drawing in a nervous breath, her stomach clenched. The longer she stayed, the harder it would be to leave. His pleading, boyish grin was impossible to ignore. After lifting to her toes, she gripped his shoulders.

He lowered his mouth in a brief kiss. "I have one condition. After this visit, you will bring me back to the train."

"If that's what you want."

"Before you go, Gus. You've never told me who your friends are."

"The best men I know. Bryce and Cortland Enders."

Her hand went to her throat just before her throat closed. She managed a wan smile, hoping he hadn't noticed her shock.

"Hell, you look peaked. What's wrong?"

She swallowed, hoping to find enough spit to speak. "Nothing. Nothing at all."

The door closed behind him as blood drained from her face. Tori sank to her knees, her body shook, and her mind filled with how she'd be able to escape. She couldn't let them find her.

FOURTEEN

DISCOVERY

THE BEER WENT down easy. Cort ordered another round. Gus's mind was still on Tori's strange behavior tonight. She'd looked downright unhealthy, her face chalky. What was she afraid of? The only thing he could come up with was the fact she'd been a prostitute. Could she be worried his friends might not accept her past? *But why?* They didn't need to know anything about her past life.

Through the smoky haze in the room, he didn't miss the scantily clad women. The old Gus would've bid his friends goodnight, then stumbled upstairs with one of the soiled doves. His mind might be fuzzy, but his memory of Tori beneath him was as clear as daylight.

Bryce cut into his meandering thoughts. "Can't tell you again how glad I am to get that money out of Virginia City. About time I paid off my brother. None too soon because Hannah is goin' to have our baby in another month. Virginia City is too far for me to travel while I get my ranch in order."

"Glad it worked out," Gus replied.

He'd just lifted his second beer to his mouth when Cort slapped his back, splattering the liquid across his mouth and shirt. He swiped his mouth with his sleeve. "Christ, Cort. Don't go slappin' my back while I got a beer in my hand."

"Sorry 'bout that. Won't take no to our invitation. Besides, Lark would have me sleep on the floor if I didn't bring you and your lady along. They planned quite a shindig," Cort added.

From his view in the reflection from the bar mirror, all three of them were swaying like willows in the wind. "Tori agreed to come along. She's a bit shy."

Bryce snorted. "Heard about a pretty woman you got in tow."

"Yeah. Trouble is—she's bound for California."

Gus eyed the beer sitting in front of him. His roiling stomach told him to call it a night. After he tossed down a few silver dollars, the three of them wended their way out of the door. Once inside his room, he unbuckled his gun belt, then draped it across the chair beside the bed. He yanked off his boots, then stretched out on the bed. His last reasonable thought was that he had to do something about Tori. One way or another. *Tomorrow.*

A HARD RAP on her door startled her. Already dressed and packed, she'd planned to slip from the hotel at dawn, then wait for the train at the depot. *Any train going west. To anywhere Gus wouldn't find her.* The entire night was spent in misery, knowing she had to escape from Ogallala before Cort and Bryce saw her. Moreover, Gus would wonder why she was dressed for travel. She couldn't let him see her.

The rap on the door grew more persistent. Backing several steps from the door, she waited. When it came again, she realized he wouldn't give up. There was no choice but to have this confrontation and get it over with. Unless she let him in, he'd wake the entire hallway.

With her chin raised, she slid the bolt. Then the door slammed open, sending her tripping backward. She gaped in horror at the bearded, haggard face of Silas. A scream lodged in her throat, knowing that if anyone tried to rescue her, they'd face his gun. She tried to move to the door, but he caught her arm, then wrenched it behind her back. She stifled her shriek of pain. Tori Barrett was trapped by the man who held all the cards. With his boot, he kicked the door closed.

"Silas."

He shoved her from him. "Tori, so good to see you. You put me through an awful lot of trouble finding you."

"How did you know where to find me?"

"Figured I'd track you to Omaha. But a fellow named Hawk was more than happy to tell me you'd gone off with a scout. Marie was glad to give me more particulars. Not to mention that old bird named Millicent."

"What do you want, Silas?"

"My money. You'll come back with me for all my trouble. In due time, expect to work off what you owe me."

"No."

His eyes flashed with fury just before his hand snaked out, landing a hard slap to her cheek, sending her backward several steps until she caught her balance. She pressed her palm against her face.

"No. You can hit me, but I'm not going with you. The money is in my valise. Take it."

With two long strides, he grabbed her arms, then shook her until her teeth hurt. When she tried to jerk free, he back-handed her, sending her stumbling to the floor. When he kneeled beside her, his hate-filled eyes burned into her as she licked her bleeding lip. All she had to do was get to her derringer. If only she could think of something to distract him. Suddenly, he slipped his knife from his sheath, then waved it in front of her face.

"Don't say anything else, or I'll carve your pretty face. Understand?"

Swallowing, she wriggled away, but he caught her. The cold flat of the blade stroked her face with practiced finesse.

"*Victoria. Victoria.* You led me on a merry chase. Two of my men are badly hurt, thanks to that big mountain man you're with. Whatever I ask... you will answer. Otherwise, do not say a word. Let's start with my money. Is it all there?"

"Yes. The valise is under the bed."

"Bought a new saloon. Sold the ones in Virginia City and Fort Benton. We're leaving for California. Right where you wanted to go."

"I hate you." His maniacal laugh told her what she already knew. He'd kill her before he'd ever let her go.

"What's the man's name?"

"Gus will kill you."

"That so? Think it's time I met him. Tell him how good you were in bed. And a lot of other things. Does he know about your husband? Connor O'Malley? The husband you killed."

"Don't. Please." Silas had found a way to keep her with him. The alternative was to go to prison or be hanged for murder. If she went along, someday she'd find a way to escape.

"Then you best be a good companion. All we need to do is get downstairs without a fuss. If he comes after you, I'll shoot him. Train leaves at eleven."

"I'll go with you. I won't cause trouble. Leave Gus out of it."

"Get your things together. You'll stay in my room tonight. That way, he won't find you here. Where's your derringer?"

"My reticule."

He dragged her to her feet, then shoved her to the bed. Hope died after he recovered her gun and shoved it into his jacket pocket.

"Why do you want me? You have your money."

"You're good for business. None were better than you."

TORI'S STOMACH FELT like it gnawed her backbone. Laying here, she stared at the ceiling. While she hadn't been to church in a long while, she prayed God would keep Gus from looking for her. The light of dawn speared through the thin, dirty curtains, reminding her that her time was almost up. *She'd be going to California, after all.*

The bed springs squeaked when Silas swung his legs to the floor. His thick beard and unkempt curly hair made him look even more sinister as daylight lit his face. Picking up the valise, he slipped his knife from the sheath at his waist. After he sliced through the bindings that held her to the metal headboard, he used his knife to wave her to the door.

"Let's go."

Back straight, she followed him from the room. Life drained from her. She walked, feeling as though her feet floated above the floor as she gave thought to the hellish agony ahead of her. Once downstairs, she stayed close beside Silas as he gripped her arm. Curiosity had her glance from the lobby into the dining room. Gus was there, his back to the doorway. Squinting, she'd hoped to see the faces of Bryce and Cort, but they weren't looking her way.

Silas walked her to the depot, where they took a seat on the bench to wait for eleven a.m. The Howard clock on the wall ticked out the minutes. *Nine o'clock.* And with each tick of that clock, she was closer to leaving Ogallala behind and one minute closer to hell.

———————————

"DIDN'T YOU TELL your lady we were leavin' early?" Bryce grumbled. "Where the hell is she?"

"I did. Don't know what's keepin' her." Gus was worried, especially since she'd balked at first. He thought about how pale she'd become before he left her last night. Had she decided to leave on the train without so much as a goodbye? He glanced at the wall clock. It was nine forty five. *The train would leave at eleven. Too early to be waiting at the depot.*

There was a moment of mad bordering on panic. If she'd left for the train, did he have any business following her? After all, it was her decision. His fingers rapped the table.

Cort cleared his throat. "Gus. You look like a fish out of water the way you're wriggling in that seat. Maybe go see if she's there."

He shot to his feet. "Damn right." Gus spun, then marched to the stairway with long strides, taking them two at a time until he reached the landing. His heart thundered in his ears as he jogged along the hall. When he reached her door, he rapped hard, several times. Then he waited only a heartbeat until he shouted her name, drawing lodgers out into the hall to see what the commotion was about. He gritted his teeth, then turned the knob. It was unlocked.

Once inside, it was clear she hadn't slept in the bed. Or else, she'd made it up. Opening the bureau drawer, he found her clothes were gone. A look beneath her bed revealed her valise missing, which meant she'd taken her money and everything else before leaving him behind... along with any feelings they supposedly had for each other. She hadn't even had the civility to tell him goodbye to his face. *Unless she'd been forced to leave?* Had Silas found her?

"Son of a bitch!"

He ran down the hallway, elbowing the mop lady out of his way. When he reached the lobby, he turned to the concierge. "Did you see a woman and man leave here a while ago?"

"That woman you're escorting?"

"Yes. Goddammit. Did you see her?"

"She left with a dark-haired man, and she didn't look very happy about it."

Turning toward the dining room, he didn't need to go far. Cort and Bryce stood in the arched doorway, both holding their rifles. Their hats were pushed back on their heads while each looked bewildered at all the fuss. They'd drawn a group of onlookers who milled around in the lobby.

"I've got to get to the depot."

Bryce snorted. "She left."

"Long story, and I don't have time to explain. Back me up. There's someone she's been running from, and I think he took. Against her will."

"Christ," Bryce said. "You won't stand alone."

Gus slid his revolver from his holster, then checked the chamber. "Cort. Keep hold of my rifle. I don't think I'll be needing it. My revolver will do just fine."

Gus's long strides carried him across the lobby, where a crowd of gawkers had bunched, most trying to find out what the aggravation was all about. He sure wasn't keeping his voice down. He was killing mad, and anyone getting in his way would be damned sorry.

Sensing Cort and Bryce behind him, he shoved passed the curious, alarmed town folks, now tagging along as he marched along the street. Charging into the depot, his glance skittered over the line of men, women, and children waiting for tickets. None of them was Tori. Worse, he didn't know what the hell Silas looked like. Passengers had already begun boarding. The clock was now at ten-twenty-five. *Which passenger car was she in?*

Gun drawn, he stormed down the aisle of one car. Not finding any sign of her, he made his way between cars to the next. At the sight of a gun-wielding man, notable gasps and screeches erupted from the startled passengers. At the front of the second car, he found her. She was standing beside dark-haired Silas, her face drawn with fear.

She clung to her valise with one hand. When she lifted her face and turned to face him, a knot grew in his throat. Her eyes were glazed with dread, appearing to have accepted her fate. Her defiant chin trembled. Tori's pleading eyes looked toward him, elevating his fury to red rage. She dropped the bag beside her feet. With an almost imperceptible shake of her head, she signaled him to let her go.

Silas grabbed hold of her neck in a vice grip before he brandished his steel knife. When Silas flashed the blade in front of her face, Gus watched her cringe. He understood the warning, but he had no intention of letting him take her. With iron resolve, he stared at Silas while passengers scattered and funneled out of the door.

"Best drop your six-shooter, or I'll kill her. One snap of her neck or a quick slice to her jugular. No matter to me," Silas said. The calmness in his voice was unsettling. Gus knew then that there would be no reasoning. *Silas was about to die.*

"Let her go," Gus ordered.

Gus took one step forward, keeping his eyes on his target. For an instant, his eyes left Silas, long enough to see her pitiful gaze on his face. Unless he missed his guess, she was about to faint.

"I'll only warn one last time. Let her go." Gus kept his voice level, but no one could mistake the deadly threat.

As she moved, Silas squeezed her throat. She gasped for air. "Not a twitch, Tori. *Not one twitch.* When I loosen my grip, tell him you *want* to come with me."

The world stilled. Both Bryce and Cort had taken positions on either side of him with their guns drawn.

"Tell him," Silas snarled.

———————————

EVEN AS SHE watched Gus's face through fireflies dancing in her eyes, she was sure she'd never seen such stark fury. Clawing at Silas's arm, he loosened long enough for her to offer a garbled plea. "Gus. Let me go."

"You heard her," Silas yelled.

Gus's face blurred, but she saw his rigid stance. Those black eyes of his didn't flinch from his attention on Silas. Her abductor's heart pounded beneath her. Watching with a sense of unreality, she saw Gus level his gun. The click of the hammer, followed by a sharp pain in her neck, had her clench her teeth. Warm, sticky liquid oozed into the collar of her dress.

"I'll kill her before I give her up."

"That so."

The deafening blast pulsed through her chest leaving ringing in her ears. With the smell of sulfur filling her nose, she grabbed for air as a crushing weight fell with her just before light faded into dark.

FIFTEEN

RECOGNITION

G US WAS BESIDE her when she opened her eyes to see his taut face, his streaked with either sweat or tears. She hadn't felt her hand in his until he squeezed it.

"Where am I?"

"Doctor Collier's office." She lifted her hand and touched the bandage at her neck.

"I'm alive thanks to you," she whispered. "I'm sorry for everything."

"No need to apologize. Turns out you were right about Silas being damned persistent. I'm the one should be apologizing."

Pushing herself up onto her elbows, she searched the room that smelled faintly of sage and whiskey. "The whole town must be talking about what happened. I must've fainted."

"You gave them something to talk about other than the weather, that's for sure. So did I. Not every day there's a killing."

She swallowed. "You look worn."

"Guess I am. There's a buckwagon waiting outside to take us to the ranch if you're up to it. The surgeon said you'll heal up just fine. Not much of a scar. Said to remove the bandage tomorrow but keep it washed. Silas didn't go deep, or you'd be dead."

After her gaze turned to the gun in his holster, her lip twitched. Gus had rescued her more times than he should have had to.

He took her hand in his. "Silas is stiff as a board and on his way to the graveyard."

"After all this trouble, I'd understand if we went our own way. Here and now."

"Well, I don't agree. In fact, I'm not letting you go until and unless we straighten out a few things. Starting with your real name."

She averted her face. "Must we talk about this now? You already know who I am."

"Tori. *Victoria Barrett.* That's what you say, but your eyes say different. No damned need to hide from Silas anymore."

Thankfully, he let the topic drop and helped her to her feet. A few folks stopped what they were doing to gawk at Gus and Tori while they made their way across the street to where two handsome cowboys leaned against the wagon, waiting for them. The broader of the two tossed his smoke, then ground it into the dirt with his boot heel. She stopped mid-step, then tried to shrug from Gus's grasp. No. She couldn't face them now. Or ever. Had they recognized her?

Neither could she look away from them. Bryce stepped forward, his intense scrutiny sending her stomach into flutters. Grown into a man, she still saw the boy who'd been her protector. Looking past him, Cort's gaze trailed over her as though some faint remembrance had occurred. Her little brother was leaner than Bryce. Once, Cort had a mischievous glimmer in his eyes. Now, his dark blue eyes squinted beneath his lashes. *He'd been the teaser.* There was no humor in his expression now. Both were rugged and sun-browned... hard working ranchers.

Gus's hand clutched her arm, then guided her forward, one slow step at a time. Curiosity kept her from turning and running. *Maybe they wouldn't recognize her.* For once, she hoped God answered her prayer. Once they were face-to-face, Bryce's mouth pressed into a firm line while his penetrating regard held hers. *Cort. Bryce. Oh, my God. Had they recognized her? Surely not after all these years.*

She pulled from Gus's grip once again, then looked left and right to determine which way to run. *But where?*

"Bryce?" Cort said hoarsely. "You seein' what I'm seein'?"

Cort looked from Gus to her, then back to Bryce, as though seeking confirmation. Bryce stepped forward, then took her shoulders in a firm grip beneath his large hands, preventing her from escaping. Frozen where she stood, tears welled in her eyes. While her brother's mouth remained taut, his eyes sparkled with recognition.

"Bryce? It's her, isn't it?" Cort asked.

She watched Bryce lift his eyes skyward as he nodded.

"Nora. Oh, God. It's you—after all this time."

All Tori could do was tip her chin to stare at her toes. She'd prayed this day would never come.

"You sure?" Cort asked.

Bryce didn't reply. Instead, he moved his shaking hand to her hair, touching it with the gentleness of light. She winced at his expression of tenderness.

"Yes. It's our sister. Now, it's time to hear why you call yourself Tori. You damn well know you're Nora Maril Enders... and don't try to deny it. Say it! *Say* it! My God, Nora. We thought you were dead. Given up hope we'd see you again. All these years."

"Yeah. I'd be interested in knowing that myself," Gus said. "You didn't tell me your real name. You've landed a punch to my gut, Tori. *Or Nora.*"

Up to then, dear Gus had stood aside, silently taking this all in. She understood his anger and disappointment. What he didn't understand was her reason. Cort pinched the bridge of his nose, his eyes closed. Bryce's hard stare was unrelenting until she looked away. Her gaze had been drawn to the sadness in Gus's eyes and the rawness in his voice.

She'd deceived him. He deserved to be angry. Trust was as important as breathing to a man like Gus Quaid. As to her brothers, they were rightfully shocked at seeing her. Maybe it was best to leave before things were said that shouldn't be said. At the moment, she couldn't find her voice.

"Christ. Can't you see she's been jolted?" Bryce shot. "Let's save the questions for later. In the meantime, let's get the hell out of here. We've already given the entire town enough to talk about."

Up to this moment, Cort had said little. "I was young when I left.

Now that I see her, she looks a lot like our mother. She's coming back to the ranch where she belongs. Neither of us will take no for an answer."

She raised her chin. It was time to speak up. They were all making decisions for her. Tori made her own choices. "None of you understand. I didn't want to be found."

She shoved Bryce's hands away when he tried to take her arm. Whirling, she marched passed Gus with hardly a glance. At the back of the wagon, she hefted her valise, then with her boot heels digging into the gravel, she headed for the depot mumbling beneath her breath while she ignored the nosy bystanders who'd probably enjoyed this show. She changed course when she remembered the next train wasn't until tomorrow. Swiping at her tears with her hand, she tramped in the direction of the hotel.

"*Tori.* Or Nora. Wait just one damned minute. Where do you think you're going?" Gus called.

"Anywhere. California. I don't care. Don't you see? I can't stay here."

With her head held high, she strode along the street with Gus behind her. She dodged wagons, skirted around shopkeepers, then reached the doorway where instead of Gus, Bryce caught hold of her arm and spun her around. Cort reached around her to snatch the valise from her grip.

"Nora. You aren't going anywhere but with us," Cort grumbled. "Not after all these years of worryin'. Even if I have to toss you in the back of the wagon like a spoiled child. Don't think I won't."

All the air and bravado left her chest. God, how she loved them. Bryce opened his arms out to his sides, and that's when the last of her fight left her. Once in her brother's embrace, she sagged against his chest, letting her tears roll across her cheeks. After a time, she darted a glance at Gus, who'd stood apart from her, his eyes unreadable, his expression stoic.

He finally had the answer he'd been digging at for so long. She was Nora Maril Enders. That revelation hadn't set well with him because she hadn't trusted him enough to tell him her real name. At least, that's what he must believe. There would be no way to mend the rift she'd created between them. Unless he could forgive her.

Town folks stopped to observe them as the wagon rolled along the street. Tori Barrett had died today while Nora Enders would be the talk at every supper table. Ahead of her was a ranch where her new-found family lived. Fear crawled inside her at the real possibility they'd find out about her tawdry past... a past that might rise up to bite them all.

Flanked between her brothers on the hard, bouncing seat, an odd, glorious smile poured through her and then burst to the surface. Her older brother, Bryce, still lived. *Praise the Lord.* Cort was bigger than life with his own stories to tell—a notorious gunman turned rancher.

She looked over her shoulder to see Gus mounted and following behind the wagon. Quiet, he was seated straight in the saddle, his long black hair lifting in the wind. A warrior and kind man who'd been her reluctant savior. The distance between them had been made wider because she'd kept her identity from him. She'd broken the trust they'd worked hard to establish.

If he ever found out that she'd been married but killed her own husband, he'd never forgive her for keeping that to herself. One day, she may have to face the law for what she'd done. But not now. She'd been granted time to sort out her life for as long as she held that secret from everyone.

Listening to her brothers while they chattered about their wives, children, and their plans for the ranch, she looked behind once again to see Gus's horse dropping farther back. No longer listening to her brothers, she worried her lip between her teeth, making Silas's punch hurt even more. Gus had been faithful, honest, and sometimes brusque, yet he'd saved her life several times over. In return, she'd lied and broken his heart. In time, could he forgive her? And did it matter? After all, she hid the biggest secret of all.

She pressed her hand to her stomach as they grew closer to the ranch. The unknown lay ahead. Would their wives accept a former whore to be near their children? Maybe it was her silence or her pitiful excuse of a smile that had Bryce suggest Cort jump down while he talked with her privately.

With the team pulled up, Cort vaulted, then untethered his horse.

After he swung into the saddle, he tipped his hat, then nudged his horse into a trot to join Gus at some distance behind. She clutched the edge of the seat, her gaze ahead while a new fear rose inside... like a black cloud. *Where was she going?* How could she look upstanding folks in the eye? Bryce slapped the reins and hollered at the team, reminding her she wouldn't escape. Besides, she didn't know if she wanted to. Even though she might have killed Connor, would the hand of the law reach her in Nebraska?

"Now. Let's have it. All of it," Bryce said.

"I've been Victoria Barrett a long time. Leave it alone, Bryce."

There was a storm brewing in her brother's gray-blue eyes when she chanced a look toward him. "Like hell. You're our sister, Nora. You best get used to it. What's going on?"

"I'm not *her* anymore. Please don't push me. I had my reasons for changing my name."

She flinched when Bryce held up a hand. "Nora. I wasn't going to touch you. Dammit. What's happened to you? Don't you know how worried we've been all these years? Where did you go? You'd left, and no one knew where."

"Where?" she said tonelessly.

Her humorless, bitter laugh was soul-wrenching, even to her own ears. "New Orleans. I wasn't someone you'd recognize. I was taught by the best in how to please men. *Is that what you needed to hear?* Do you still want me to meet your family?"

EVERY TIME SOMEONE scraped a chair against the floor, pain shot through Gus's head. The coffee helped some but not enough. Cort and Bryce looked done in where they sat, swilling coffee without saying much. Bryce was a bit more good-humored than either of them.

"Maybe you'd like to share your magic potion for drunken fools," Gus muttered.

"Well. I do know a cure."

Gus looked up. "What is it?"

"Raw eggs, hot pepper sauce, and a little oil. Hell... hard goin' down, but your day will feel better. Lark or Hannah will fix it for you."

Gus swigged the strong coffee. "I'll stick to this. I'm feelin' a touch better already."

"So, what do you plan to do about Nora?" Cort interjected.

"That's between her and me. In the meantime, I'll bide my time and try to figure it out. She lied about a lot of things."

"She lied because she felt she had to. There's a difference," Bryce said.

"What if she's lying about a lot of other things?"

"Like what?"

Gus pinched the bridge of his nose. Damn. What drove her to Virginia City in the first place? Why did she change her name? Where did Connor O'Malley disappear to after he'd taken her to New Orleans? Things were broken between them. It damned well wasn't his place to fill in her brothers. Still, he kept circling back to Connor, then whether he was the reason she'd changed her name.

———————

STARTLED AT THE sound of jangling traces, she sat up in the wagon bed where she'd slept. Cort looked over his shoulder. She offered him a brief smile.

He pulled up the team. "Sitting up here is easier than on that hard floor, you kno."

She slid from the back of the wagon. Cort was there to swing her up, and once he'd settled beside her, he offered her a quick glance.

"You sure must be tired."

"Guess so. After I ate biscuits and drank that coffee, I drifted right off."

"Well, we'll be home soon."

"Where's Bryce and Gus?"

"Ahead of us. All three of us had too much to drink at camp. You'd fallen asleep."

"Guess I was a topic. I shouldn't be going to your house, Cort. I have a dark past not fitting a family."

His sharp laugh startled her. "Sister. You'd be hard-pressed to top mine. Why do you keep reliving what's done and over? The past needs to stay there, Nora. If I could undo it for you, I would. I killed before, and if I'd known your situation, I would've killed anyone who touched you wrong. That's how I'm made.

"Meeting Lark mellowed me. My family comes first, and, Nora, that includes you. Whatever happened is over. Start living life, or it'll just go on without you. Why can't you put it all behind you?"

"I've done some shameful things. Things that might come back again. I'll never know."

He glanced at her and grinned. "I've heard about Virginia City. So you know, I haven't done the Enders name proud over the years. Spent time in prison as a pissant kid. Drank more than I should've and in one too many gunfights. My bad reputation has been splattered over newspapers and in dime novels. I've moved on but not so dumb to think it'll be forgotten. It won't. But I don't let it run my life. That's what I want for you. While we're at it, Bryce's life wasn't sterling. That's for him to tell."

She snickered. "The newspaper accounts about you made me proud. From them, I knew you were still alive. But I figured Bryce was killed. Ma would've boxed your ears for landing in the newspaper."

"Huh. So you read about me, did you?" At his quick glance, she felt her face flame.

"Yes. Didn't know exactly where you were, but it didn't matter since I had never planned to contact you. Last time I saw mention was in the Madisonian." *And only because a patron of the saloon left one behind.*

"After listening to you and Bryce banter, I think you both are lucky to be alive. Trouble seemed to follow you."

"That sums it up." He slapped the reins. "Ma might've boxed my ears, but Pa would have me mucking stalls for a year."

She frowned at the remembrance of how hard her father had been on the boys. Squinting, she cupped a hand over her brow to make out

Gus's horse in front of them. Sparing her only a few words this morning, he'd kept to himself.

Cort interrupted her musings. "You and Gus are a good fit. He's as tough as they come, and he's a good man. Known him since I was seventeen. Seems like you two are more than friends. Wish I'd understood what was going on with that Silas because I'd have relished shooting him dead. As it is, Gus handled the situation.

"So. Are you sweet on him?" He held up one gloved hand. "Before you say it isn't my business, *I'm your brother*. Brothers have certain privileges."

She squirmed under her brother's intent stare. "We're friends, Cort. Just friends."

"If I thought he'd taken advantage of you, he wouldn't be sittin' on that horse of his. He'd be walking the opposite direction, minus his horse."

"That's mean. No. He has not taken advantage of me. I've betrayed him. You know him. He's not a forgiving man."

"He'll come around. Gus lived a hard life. Back there, when I rode beside him, he looked mighty worried at the sight of you leaning your head against Bryce's shoulder. Nearly decided to catch up to the wagon to find out what the matter was. I stopped him."

"Gus is hard to know, isn't he?"

"On the surface, he is who he is. But deep down, he's blamed himself for not keeping his wife safe from the Sioux. We all know how it eats at him. For whatever reason, he can't seem to let go of his remorse. The only person who blames him is... him."

"Do you think she's still alive?"

Cort averted his face and cleared his throat. "No. I don't."

"Seems Gus and me both need to purge our pasts."

"You'll fit in with Lark. She's had her own woes. In fact, I'll tell you upfront that you'll see a scar along her jaw. She doesn't hide it beneath hats like she used to unless she's in town. But she doesn't like to be reminded of how she got it."

"Indians?"

"No. A vicious outlaw marked her."

She looked toward Cort's bearded profile to see his taut jaw and the vein pulsing at his neck. He stared ahead, while his fists clenched and unclenched the reins."

"You killed him. I'd read about you."

"Yeah. I'd do it again."

Drawing a breath, she felt both sympathy for Lark and pride in her brother. "She must be quite a woman. I can't wait to meet her. Please don't tell her what I did?"

"What you *were*. Not that it matters to us in the way you think."

"Please don't tell anyone."

Cort sawed back the reins and brought the team of horses to a halt. "There won't be discussion about it. No one needs to bring it up or talk about it unless that's what you want. But Lark would be good medicine if you talked it out with her. I don't keep secrets from my wife."

"Bryce seems mighty put out about me. He hasn't said much. But I can see it."

"Bryce had his own problems. You'll soon enough find out. While his wife, Hannah, is a gem, *he* has a past. In fact, the evidence of that is in their son. Reyes is the offspring of a mistake. That's about all I'll say. Nora, you're not the only Enders with a history."

———————

GUS WAS THE intruder. While he'd enjoyed the banter between Lark, Hannah, and all the rest, he hadn't been able to keep his eyes from watching Nora's reactions. Her grin in his direction had him smile in return out of politeness. He'd spoken her name only once, and he'd used *Tori*. Thinking of her as Nora Enders somehow made her into someone he didn't know. Moreover, it was a constant reminder that she hadn't trusted him enough to reveal that part of her.

While the family chatted and teased, he'd slipped away from the table to find himself seated in the shadows of the front porch. This was time for family mending, and he didn't need to be reminded he wasn't family. Once he was certain she was settled, he'd be on his way home to the Belle Fourche River.

He rested his head back to stare at the stars, leaning his seat on the back two legs. His fingers were threaded against his full stomach. A faint streak of pink swiped the distant mountains while the yips of a coyote reminded him of how often he'd been out there alone.

"Pretty this time of night, ain't it, Gus?" The gravelly voice came out of the shadows.

Gus dropped the chair legs. Peering through the dimness to the far end of the porch, he saw the outline of Zeke Waterson. Typical of the old man to keep to himself. He sat in his rocking chair as still as a statue. "Didn't know you were there."

"Maybe I should'a cleared my throat. Been here all along. You looked so glum at supper, I figured you'd make your way outside sooner or later. Me? I got a head start. Don't blame you gettin' away from all that hoorah and those clucking women."

"You must be used to it. I'm not."

"Got that right. So, you wanna talk about what put the burr under your saddle?"

"Nope. Besides, I don't have a bur under my saddle."

"That so."

Gus stood, then stretched his arms out to his sides. The bunkhouse seemed mighty inviting at the moment. If there was enough light, he'd read. If not, he'd sit in Cort's office to read one of those leather-bound books, and when he was tired enough, he'd find a bunk. Still, if he didn't throw the old man a bone, Zeke would gnaw at him tomorrow.

"Thinkin' I'll head for home day after tomorrow. Give my horses some rest."

"Uh-huh. You and that pretty Nora were passing looks at each other. Thought before long you'd set the room on fire. Maybe I was the only one who saw it. Doubt it, though."

"I got a home to get to. And horses to get back to. Got some jobs for the Army before winter. I'll be busy for a while. She won't miss me, what with gettin' to know her family again with a new life. I need to move on with mine."

"Sounds like you got a full life. You can keep tellin' yourself that."

"You are a snooping old man. Maybe you need glasses."

"Do you wear glasses, Gus?"

"As a matter of fact... yes. Where is this leading?"

"Maybe if you put them on you'll see what's between you two isn't goin' away even if you go away. Cort learned that lesson... the hard way. So did Bryce."

Gus walked toward the old man, then leaned back against the porch post while he considered an answer. He cleared his throat. "This is different. She's been through more hell than a woman ought. Now she has her brothers. A family. Something she needs. Hannah and Lark can help talk her mind out of where it tends to wander. She won't need me. I just came along when she needed help."

"Guess you know best. You'd be right about those two women understandin' what Nora might've gone through. Women seem to talk out their troubles. Men keep them to themselves. Makes them look stronger, like they can handle things. Still, I think she'll need someone to call her own... give her a home. Thought it might be you. Brothers are fine, but no substitute for a man to hold onto."

"Dammit. I'm still married to Aubrey. She might be alive, Zeke. I can't rest till I know."

"Then I feel sorry for you because you'll never know. Deep down, you got to figure your wife is either dead or part of the tribe. You know what that means. Besides, if you look in the mirror you'll see you're more about punishing yourself for what you couldn't control. Decide when you've had enough—before life passes you by."

Gus straightened at the verbal strike that left him reeling. Biting back every cuss word he thought to fling at Zeke, his jaw tautened. *What did he know about losing a wife?* "I'll say goodnight before I decide to grab you by the shirt collar and haul you to your feet, Zeke. *You* never had a wife."

Marching across the yard toward the bunkhouse, he felt Zeke's eyes burrowing into his back. He grit his teeth, then gave thought to turning back to apologize. Damn the man for stirring things up in his already muddled head. *What did Zeke know about anything?* Still... every word Zeke had spoken was the truth that he had been too much of a coward to face.

———————

"YOU'VE BEEN AVOIDING me. I want to know why." She waited until Gus looked up from the book he was reading.

After his curt nod, he stared at her for a long moment. "There's nothing to talk about, Nora. Is that the right name?"

He returned to his book, thereby dismissing her. She'd be happier with an argument rather than his calm indifference. By design, he was treating her as if they were simply acquaintances. Not to be put off, she closed the office door behind her with a firm click, then strode across the room to stand in front of him, where he held a book open between his hands. She waited.

He sighed, then lifted his eyes to look at her over the rim of his glasses, where they were propped on the end of his nose. He offered no indication he was interested in speaking. Well... that was too bad. Days had gone by, and each time she'd approached him, he'd found an excuse to escape. She wasn't having it. She wouldn't be erased.

"Well?" She crossed her arms and tapped the toe of her boot. "You're furious with me. Why not just spit it out?"

His head jerked up, and then he glared. "I figure you got enough to think about. Lot of years to catch up. I'm just your *guide*, remember?"

The lamp light revealed the sharp angles of his face. He held her study then he returned his eyes to the words of the book, on the pretense of reading. Nora refused to budge until they settled this. Gus slapped the book closed, removed his glasses, then pocketed them. After he set the book beside him, he offered her a grudging stare.

He sighed. "This isn't wise of you."

"Wise?"

"I'm leaving. You know that. There's nothing left to say."

The nervous twitch at one corner of his eye let her know he was dug in about something, and she was angrier than she should be. This man twisted her heart. She was sick of being a victim. "May I sit beside you?"

"Suit yourself."

At the tepid invitation, she almost decided to walk out, slam the door in temper, then leave him to sulk. But that would be childish. Besides, she'd already slipped in that regard after she'd cried out her eyes in her bedroom. Falling into self-pity was something she'd sworn she'd never do again. Instead, she lifted her chin and plunked down beside him, arraying her skirt across her legs.

"Don't remember that skirt or the blouse. You look captivating tonight," he said.

"Thank you. Didn't think you noticed me or what I wore. In fact, you ignored me at supper. My clothes are your clever way of avoiding this distance between us. Why not just get to why?"

"Oh? If it seemed like it, I had my reasons."

"Don't suppose you'll tell me your reasons."

"No."

"These clothes belong to Lark. I didn't bring much with me from Virginia City, as you perfectly well know. More, I didn't come in here to talk about my clothes."

The corner of his mouth rose, prompting a vision of him on their trek across the plains. She'd learned it meant either amusement or disgruntlement. In this case, he was peeved and something they needed to talk about. "I haven't forgotten anything. Maybe you have."

"Honey. I haven't forgotten one minute of it. But this is where you belong. *And I don't.* Which means I need to head out to give you time to settle with your family. This is the kind of life you deserve. Not what I can offer."

"Lark and Hannah don't know what I was before. They might not want me here if or when they find out. What if they don't?"

"Then you don't know them very well. Besides, do you think Cort and Bryce won't fill them in once they're alone? Those women will badger him to find out everything. Neither of the women will hold one thing against you. Just like I don't."

"They'll pity me. If my brothers told them, I can't imagine what they must think of me."

"Knowing them, they'll think you're tough as nails to survive. If anything, they'll admire you. I sure do."

"Oh, Gus. Maybe you should take me back to Ogallala to the train. It would be best. Better yet, if you'd reconsider my offer, I'd go with you. No matter the terms."

"Best for whom? I already told you. I'm not interested in the kind of woman you're suggesting. Sure wouldn't sit well with your brothers. They'd be the first to shoot me. Those brothers would find you, and if need be, sling you over the back of a horse to haul you back here. They aren't ones to mess with."

"From what I've heard of your reputation, you're the one to fear. I witnessed your justice firsthand. You can be merciless, Gus."

"Nora. I've lived out here a long while. Being merciless—as you put it—is sometimes called for. It's referred to as justice. In the case of Silas, it was called for."

He dropped his head back and sighed. His inscrutable expression and pursed mouth suggested he'd become tired of this conversation. Nora slipped her hand over his, then Gus threaded his fingers with hers. Resting her head against his familiar shoulder, she sighed. After a while, she thought he'd drifted asleep until his throaty voice broke the silence.

"When I don't see you is never. Your face, your eyes, the way you tilt your head, how you tend to bite your lip every time you've got something on your mind. Every inch of you beside me is a gift. A gift so tempting it hurts me to my core to have to admit I don't belong in your life nor you in mine—until I know I can give you my whole heart. All of it. Besides, you didn't trust me. You lied about yourself when you could've easily told me the truth."

Nora licked her lip, then searched for a rebuttal against his words... so filled with heartache and heartbreak. They'd return to her for the rest of her life. How could she contradict what was so real to him? His torment was real. But so was hers. He was right. They couldn't be together until he accepted his wife was gone. And she couldn't bring herself to tell him that she'd murdered a man she'd married.

"You think admitting my past, the reasons for my name, would've been easy? Yes... I should have been truthful. Gus, I was afraid. Ashamed that I'd been used, intimidated, and fooled by Connor O'Malley. As to Silas—he never meant anything to me except as a business partner. Things went sour from the start. His idea of a partnership was possession. So, once again, I'd made a poor choice."

"I'm trying to understand. That's all I can promise. Silas, the money, Connor... your real name." He touched her face, then lifted her chin to face him. With a gruff voice, he asked, "Are there other secrets, Nora?"

The sound of the gunshot, then Connor falling with a hole in his chest, were as real at that moment as if she were there again. Blood soaked his shirt. Did she have more secrets? Yes. To voice them would seal her fate. If anyone found her, she might go to prison. Gus had spoken of trust. Could she trust him to let that part of her past go? *I've told you my secrets.*

She decided to turn him away from her past before she revealed too much. "Speaking of truths. I don't know your secrets. Why do you scout for the Army? Why do you ask questions of the soldiers? Would you even tell me how your knife wound is healing? Gus, you keep things hidden."

"In Columbus, I saw a doctor. Like I told you, it wasn't deep. It's healing up fine. How's the one Silas gave you? You're wearin' high-neck dresses."

"I'm fine. Seems we have matching wounds."

He chuckled, after which they settled into a sweet, contented quiet. Her head rested against his chest while she listened to his thudding heart. Before long, he stroked her arm. If he intended to do more, she took the decision from him.

Lifting her head, she brushed a kiss against his lips. He deepened the kiss, then withdrew, his fingers tracing her mouth. His eyes squeezed closed, then opened to study her with a sadness that almost made her weep.

"Gus, I've been wrong about so many things. If I could go back in time, I'd do things differently. And for the life of me, I don't know why it no longer matters. I'll need some time. But I won't live on their generosity forever. Sooner or later, I'll leave here."

"Hell, no." He waggled a finger. "Your brothers won't let you disappear. Besides, one thing I know for sure. I'll return one of these days and hope by then we both healed from our hurt. Then we'll talk about what's ahead—for us. How long, I can't say. I've got four hands tending my horses. I'm needed. Besides, this time is for you to be reacquainted with your family. Something I don't have."

He touched her cheek, then picked up the book beside him. After he straight-armed out of the seat, he left her. She ran her hand across the place where he'd been, finding it was still warm. The taste of him lingered on her tongue. He'd said goodbye in his own way. She shook inside with the thought he might never return.

SIXTEEN

RANCH LIFE

"I JUST DON'T know how you manage to keep up with my nephew, this big house, and still find time to work in a garden." Kneeling in the black dirt, Nora swiped her hand across her sweaty brow, then ripped another thatch of weeds free. After she tossed them aside, she looked over her shoulder to see why Lark made no reply.

Lark pushed herself up from where she kneeled, shook her skirt free of the clods of Nebraska earth, then dabbed her face with her apron. Her glistening face looked toward Nora with a grin.

"Best we finish and wash up. We can get back to this tomorrow. Don't know about you, but my back is telling me I've had enough work for today. As to taking care of this big house, I've been fortunate to have Theresa and Nita. Adoeete and Alonzo usually lend a helping hand unless they're called for something else. Most of the women I've met age fast with the toils of farms and ranches. But worse is the loneliness."

"Suppose so." Nora pushed to her feet, then brushed her hands. "Sure need to wash my clothes. Don't have many to spare."

"I'll have a washtub outside before supper. Anything you need, don't hesitate to ask. Can't promise we've got everything. I do have some dresses that should fit."

Nora nodded. "I feel like I'm a burden. Sooner or later, I'll have to move on, Lark."

"Best not say that in front of either of your brothers. They're very happy to have you back. We all are. Besides, if you up and leave, they won't take it well. You're anything but a burden. You do your share around here. Little Bryce loves you, and we've got plenty of room. Heard Cort talking about having a small house built for you."

"I'd say that's too generous."

"I'm being selfish, I know. But I've grown to like having a woman's company. Hannah is nearing the birthing and can't get over here like before. Your company is appreciated. Anyway, you best not forget you are an Enders. Every one of us wants you to be happy."

Happy? Nora supposed she'd met her one chance at happiness. He was gone. Maybe bein' a spinster sister would provide contentment. Happiness wasn't in the cards.

At the sound of a horse approaching, she turned to see Mason wave his hat while on his way to the corral. Cupping her hand over her brow, Nora studied the horizon, just as she'd done since Gus had left—without a word. Every time someone rode near, she hoped it would be him. Her disappointment grew with each passing day.

A hand touched her arm. "Gus is on your mind. I can tell whenever you look toward the hills. We hold high regard for Gus, but he is a strange man. He's managed to chew on guilt and remorse for so many years, he just can't let go. But he'll be back. We saw how he looks at you. You are the best medicine for that man. For now, I hope he's feeling miserable."

"He made up his mind. If he returns, it won't be because of me."

Lark laughed and put her hands against her soft roundness where another Enders baby nestled. "Oh? Knowing Gus, he wouldn't come here unless he was drawn by something or someone important. I, for one, hope he hasn't slept since he left."

"You don't know what kind of life I've lived, Lark. Gus knows about my past. That's reason enough to reconsider."

Lark lifted her hand, palm up. "I know about your past. So does

Hannah. None of us holds it against you... least of all Gus. *None of us judge you.* Didn't even let Zeke in on it, but wouldn't be surprised if Cort told him enough to keep him from stumbling over the wrong topic.

"In time, you've got to set it aside. We all have things in our pasts. Look at my scar, Nora. Every time I look in the mirror for the rest of my life, I'll see the face of the man who did this to me. That doesn't stop me from being a wife and mother. We live with scars, inside and out. Just because they're inside, don't let them determine the rest of your life."

"You're a wise woman, Lark. I've got to figure out what I want to do. As soon as that time comes, you'll be the first to know. But it won't be back to what I did before."

"I've thought of something we can do besides pull weeds and sew. Let's get inside and clean up, then sit on the porch with cool tea. I've got something in mind that'll run crosswise with Cort."

Nora raised one eyebrow. "Sounds wicked. Might be fun to rattle my younger brother."

"Wicked? No. Just unacceptable by narrow-minded folks. For certain... Cort will dig in his heels and try to convince us to stay out of it. I'll need reinforcements."

Nora knew to always expect the unexpected from this determined woman. Whatever it was Lark planned, she'd join forces. If for no other reason than to keep Gus from her thoughts.

Once inside the bedroom, she dumped three pails of water into the copper tub. After shrugging from her skirt and blouse, she plunked into the warm water, then rested her head against the rim, reminding her of the night Gus had stolen a key and secreted into her room. That night seemed so long ago. She squeezed her eyes closed, wishing that when she opened them, he'd be here.

While she dressed, Nora's thoughts swung to Lark's cryptic plan. Tori Barrett or Nora Enders hadn't gotten this far by being timid. Standing against her brother might not be smart, but she'd found an ally and friend in Lark. Whatever the plan, it would help her set aside the man who'd left without saying goodbye.

"ARE YOU BOTH crazy from bein' out in the damn sun too long? Or did you both drink too much of my bourbon?" Cort chided.

Nora had been familiar with her brother's mannerisms as a kid. But as a man, whenever he was dug in about something, he folded his arms across his chest. Right now, it looked like he was dug in deep. *Well.* She was an Enders, and she wouldn't be bullied. Lark's boot toe tapped, and her mouth pursed... sure signs that she wasn't budging on her plan either.

Lark wagged a finger at her husband, which set him back a step. "Cort. You of all people have always shown sympathy for the plight of the Indians. You gave the Cavalry clearance to camp on our land while those poor families rest and recover. Haven't those defeated souls been treated badly enough? Least we can do is take some food and blankets and tend to the sick. Even Alfred Collier tends them, despite some town opposition."

Cort looked from Lark then back to her, then tugged on one ear. "Well. I'm sure you're wanting to have your say in this big sister. Might as well hear it all so I don't hear it again at supper."

Nora raised her chin in defiance, while her glare held his. "I agree with Lark. I think deep down, you do too. They'll only be camped for about five days, according to that Lieutenant you talked with. You said so yourself. Those Indians aren't getting treated fairly. They mean no harm. We need to show them our goodwill."

Cort snorted, then grimaced. For a moment, he studied his boots before he lifted his eyes, pinning hers. "That about it?"

Her brother's face held the same hard angles as their father's. And like their father, there was a gruffness about him that hid his softer side. "Yes. Unless I think of something else."

"That sounds about right. From the looks on your faces, I'm guessing neither of you will put this to rest until you go out there. Do you have any idea the danger involved? I was out there to see for myself. There's a mix of Lakota, Poncas, Cheyenne, Pawnee, and Arapaho that have an axe to grind with whites, not to mention each other.

"They left reservations because they didn't want to conform to the ways of farming instead of hunting. Worse, they see the white men, including soldiers, as enemies... because their people are being forced onto reservations in Colorado and Oklahoma. How can you expect me to allow you to traipse off to a camp seething with disease and hot tempers?"

"Theresa is going with us. Tangle and Adoeete said they'd volunteer to escort us," Lark said. Her gaze held her husband's in a battle of wills.

"Oh. That makes it all right? You have an army of one cripple, one good shot, and three women. Huh. That was kind of Tangle and Adoeete to volunteer, but they have responsibilities here," Cort said.

"We'll take our guns. The soldiers have the camp surrounded. Surely they can spare a few guards to help us with distributing food," Lark argued.

Nora saw a glimmer in her brother's eyes as Lark put a hand on her hip and inclined her head. This was a revolt, and she sure hoped that his wife won. Cort yanked his hat from the table and pivoted, but not before he reached for a folded newspaper from the bench.

"You two best read the *Omaha Bee*. It's about Standing Bear and the Poncas. Make no mistake... I'm in their corner. So are a lot of whites. But I still don't trust all of them." He tossed it to the table.

Lark waited without moving to pick up the newspaper. Neither of them spoke while he paced from one wall to the other. Nora's gaze followed his footsteps and figured he was trying to think of a compromise. Finally, the pacing stopped. He glanced in her direction, perhaps hoping she'd take his side. But Nora simply smiled, knowing they might have won this battle.

"Christ. I can tell you two won't give up this hair-brained scheme. I can't sit here all day to keep watch. So... this is my proposal. I'll give you three visits to the camp, on ranch time. Meaning, I'm goin' with you. Along with Tangle, Mason, Billy, and Adoeete. Three days is all I'll spare. *And by God*. If I hear one whisper of trouble, you'll get in the wagon, and I'll see that the soldiers move them off of our land. Do I make myself clear?"

"Yes, sir," she and Lark said in unison.

"Who'll take care of the baby and the cooking? Or haven't you given it a thought? Two other things. If anyone is sick, you won't go near them. I'll send Collier out to have a look. You're carryin' our baby, Lark."

"I don't have to be reminded of my expectant state. I promise to keep my distance from the sick. You didn't mention Theresa."

"She stays here with Nita to tend to little Bryce. He can be a handful."

Nora already read her brother's mind. He was talking himself out of the deal, using the baby as a logical excuse. In the instant he mentioned the baby, even she had second thoughts.

He cocked an eyebrow and looked toward her. "Well?"

"Agreed. We leave out tomorrow morning, then. What do you say to that, Lark?"

"I'll be ready. What was the second requirement you mentioned."

"No woman will carry a gun. It would be easy to take them from you if any of them decided to start an armed insurrection. Christ. I lost a battle to two women. Won't ever live it down."

Lark pecked his cheek with a kiss and offered him a satisfied grin, leaving Nora gazing with envy.

"Expect a better kiss than that tonight, wife."

Lark swatted his arm.

Both wistful and amused at their interplay, Nora wished Gus were here. She missed his banter. She even missed his moods. Knowing his deep disdain for Indians, he'd probably be madder than a bull without horns at the risk they were undertaking. She missed him. Yet, it still stung he'd left without a goodbye. And still with the question of her secrets and his guilt-driven search for his wife.

"Nora, I hope you know how Gus would take this," Cort said.

"Gus isn't here. Besides, I've always made my own decisions. He has no part in this one."

He threw up his hands, turned on his boots, then clumped along the hall. She winced at the slam of the door. Then, like Lark, she dropped onto a chair, giving her heart time to slow. They'd come close to losing the battle—one that had been both tedious and tiring. Yet, she felt invigorated with this new sense of purpose.

That night, she lay in bed staring at the ceiling, unable to sleep, thinking about where Gus had gone. Seven weeks and no letter. Cort mentioned his horse ranch. Other than that, she knew little about what he did. *How long should she hold out hope he'd find his way back? She couldn't stay here on charity for the rest of her life. Soon, she'd have to move on.* She didn't rule out he wouldn't forgive her for her deception. Little did he know, she hid a larger one. Another reason to leave here.

———————————

NORA SAT BESIDE Tangle in the lead buckboard. Cort followed behind with Lark at his side. They'd spent half of the day loading sacks of flour, potatoes, beans, and even cookware. Crates filled with canned meat wouldn't last long, but at least it was a start. Bryce contributed blankets, collard greens, and two pails of fresh milk, along with two beef cows that Mason would herd with the wagons. No doubt, the cows would be killed and the meat salt-preserved.

Bryce had been her stalwart defender when they were kids. Even after Cort teased her, Bryce came to her defense. From the look of disapproval on his face, he'd taken Cort's side this time. He sent along Hannah's apologies as Lily Raine needed her mother.

She couldn't be happier for her big brother, having sweet Hannah as a wife. Bryce appeared to relish his new role as a father, given he'd missed out on Reyes as a baby. The few visits she'd managed, though, filled her with special adoration for her niece, Lily. Being surrounded by little ones, she'd begun dreaming about having her own. But that would never be.

In her mind, she still heard the words of a physician in Virginia City. *"Miss Barrett. You don't need to worry one bit about having babes. You ruined yourself. That might be best in the long run... given your choice of callings."* In her mind's eye, she saw his beady eyes.

She was brought out of her meanderings when the swaying wagon slowed. An array of white Army tents were in odd contrast to majestic, painted teepees. Smoke plumed skyward from the various cookfires

throughout camp. The pungent smell of burnt mesquite and sage drifted on the air. But the quiet of the small settlement was alarming, given
there were so many poor souls living here.

Men with long black hair, some wearing standard white men's clothing of cotton and wool, watched them with distrust in their eyes. Other
men wore traditional beaded buckskin shirts with denim trousers, their
dull-eyed gazes almost lifeless. Many of the women stood beside large
pots, stirring aromatic concoctions with tree limbs. A blue-uniformed
soldier waved them forward as Tangle guided the team into the camp.

The smells of cooked meat and fat wafted through the air as they
passed beyond the common cookpot. Flat, glazed eyes followed them.
Hopelessness inscribed the children's vacant stares as they stopped
playing, now watchful. She could hardly look their way for fear she
might cry. Several women were gray-haired, yet they worked alongside
the young ones. While she gripped the seat, she averted her face from
the intent stares of the soldiers with their rifles. They walked alongside,
escorting the wagons to the center of the camp

Dogs lay on the ground, tongues lolling, and their flesh so thin,
their protruding bones left her with a sense of hopelessness. Hungry,
thin, and listless children sat in groups, tossing stones in some kind of
game. There were no horses in view.

Tangle pulled up, then set the break while she remained motionless
in a cloud of unreality. She'd grown accustomed to his spitting tobacco
over the side. This time, he didn't. She waited while he jumped down
before coming to help her from the high seat.

Looking around, Nora felt somewhat ashamed at wearing a simple,
but clean dress while so many here were in tattered clothes. The ones
who were dressed in white men's clothes had most likely received them
on charity or from soldiers.

Lark pressed her arm against her forehead after she'd come beside
her. "Is it worse than you thought, Nora?"

"Yes. They need so much more than we can provide."

Lark squeezed her arm. "We'll do the best we can."

The soldiers took charge of seeing that the tribal women lined up for provisions. Each woman received two loaves of bread, a sack of beans, a sack of flour, a few cans of meat, and a blanket. Potatoes were dropped from the wagon beds while women crowded each other to reach for them.

She followed Lark to where a circle of women were sewing and chattering. Nora decided to crouch beside them if they allowed. She praised the fine beadwork then waited for some kind of reaction, only to have them look from one to the other, giggling. It was clear she'd become the source of their amusement when she spoke in English to them.

She pushed to her feet when her attention was drawn to a mother, her baby nestled against her breast. Walking close, she bent to touch the downy black hair. The mother pulled the child closer to her but said nothing, nor did she meet Nora's gaze. She brushed the baby's thin, cold cheek with the back of her hand. Only then did she realize the child was dead. The mother rocked back and forth, seeming in shock, still cradling her child. *Had Alfred Collier tended to them? Was he even here?*

After they left the camp behind that day, she vowed she'd use what money she had to order bolts of cloth and medicines. For certain, she'd talk with Alfred about joining the cause. These people needed so much more than just two ranchers could provide. She looked up to find Tangle's drawn face because he'd been equally affected.

"We need to bring the doctor out here, Tangle."

"Yes, ma'am. Cort already sent Billy to get him."

Dinner that night was quiet, except for the fussing of little Bryce. Nora forked beef and potatoes into her mouth but didn't taste the food for the memory of what she'd witnessed. The freshly baked bread and smell of soap were in sharp contrast to the stink of the camp. If she lived to be one hundred, she'd never forget the images of the defeated.

"You two women certain you want to return for a second time? I warned you it wouldn't be pretty." Cort sipped his coffee.

She shifted her eyes from Cort. "I do. What do you say, Lark?"

"I'm more worn out than I thought I'd be. Theresa is filling in for me tomorrow. We should send more cattle out with the hands. They don't have enough to eat."

Cort's mouth thinned. "Already thought about it, Lark. Tangle and Mason will run some out."

Dropping her fork, Nora pressed a hand against her mouth and sobbed. Lark excused herself, saying she had to tend to little Bryce.

Within the heaviness of the air, she was left alone with her stoic brother. "Oh, Cort. I never imagined how poor they were. Those soldiers just sit with their smokes in their mouths, scowling. Are they blind? Don't they understand what's going on?"

"What would you have them do? Turn them loose? That won't help. They'd be rounded up again. Besides. I know several of those soldiers feel the same. Under orders, they have no say."

During the silence between them, she recalled one particular soldier. Something about him made her wary. He'd followed her until he was called to attend to other duties. Her imagination and weariness were playing tricks with her head.

The scrape and clink of dishes prompted her to head into the kitchen where she was needed. At the same moment, Cort gulped the last of his coffee, picked up his hat, then left the room. For the rest of the night, her thoughts returned to the sight of the dead baby.

————————

TWO DAYS LATER, Nora and Lark were busy baking bread to be sent along on this last visit. At the creak of the screened door, the women lifted their heads in unison. Nora's mouth dropped open at the sight of the tall, broad-chested, and clean-shaven man filling the doorway. Her regard trailed over him from his fine leather boots to his blue trousers, then to his clean gray shirt. He doffed his black Stetson and twisted the brim between his fingers.

"Hello," Gus said with a voice as thick as churned milk.

Lark said nothing in reply. Nora felt almost faint at his sudden appearance, and her tongue might as well be glued to the roof of her mouth. But here he was, the man who'd left her with a vague explanation for a reason. For her part, she'd figured he was still pining for his wife, believing she still lived. He looked from one woman to the other, then steadied his dark-eyed gaze on her face. With her insides quaking, she sank onto a chair.

"We'll leave you two to talk. I need to take Bryce Wade upstairs for some clean clothes. Theresa?" Lark prodded.

"I'm coming. Don't know if I can stand the sight of the man, the way he comes and goes," Theresa snarled.

After they were alone, Gus took the steps to close the distance. He cleared his throat. "Cat got your tongue?"

"I'm surprised. Just when I figured you weren't coming back... now here you are. You've been gone for nine weeks without a letter."

"Checked on my horses and cabin. Had business to take care of. Mostly, did some thinking. Had some work to do for the Army, while I was at it. Besides, I'm not much for writing, Nora. Whatever I was goin' to say to you had to come from me, not some words on a piece of paper."

"I'm sure Cort and Bryce will be glad to see you."

"Didn't come back to see them. I came back to see you, Nora Enders."

"Did you figure things out?"

"I did."

In one stride, he grasped her arms, then pulled her to her feet. His arms wrapped her in a warm embrace. His head dipped, and she lifted her mouth to meet his, easing into a kiss that deepened. Against her mouth, he murmured the words she had longed to hear.

"Ahh... Nora, I've missed you. You never left my mind."

"Why?"

He set her back, still clutching her arms. "*Why?* Guess it's plain enough. I love you. I'm about to ask you to marry me just as soon I can offer you a home... near your family."

"Can you tell me which month you have in mind? The marriage question? And the home?"

"The marriage question is coming right after supper. I'll have a better idea on the house once I close a deal with your brother. It's goin' to be a nice evenin' for a stroll. Cort already asked me to supper at three.

I'll be here. Then after supper, I'll claim that walk. You got any notion of what your answer might be so I won't be disappointed?"

"Got to say, Gus Quaid. This is all so sudden. You have a way of shocking me."

"Does that mean you don't have an idea of your answer?"

"Why... Mister Quaid. I do love you and think you can count on an answer that is agreeable."

His lips touched the top of her head. She breathed in the scent of leather, tobacco, and Nebraska grass, filling her with the kind of contentment that only comes around once. His lopsided grin warmed her to the core of her being. She didn't want to reason it, but she did. What had brought him to this decision without more questions about her past?

"There is one thing, Gus. I won't be able to have babies. Would you still want me? There was a doctor...."

"Shh. We'll shoulder whatever happens, Nora. You're who I want. The rest doesn't matter. There's no guarantee in life." He winked. "Until supper. Don't forget that stroll."

"I'll hardly be able to eat."

He turned and scooped up his hat from where he'd dropped it. As he started for the door, he stopped abruptly, as though he'd forgotten something. His head turned, and his focus steadied on the heaps of bread stacked on the work table. He swung around, then faced her with a quizzical expression on his face, one eyebrow raised. "Seems like a lot of bread for supper."

"We baked it for the camp. We head out early tomorrow."

"What camp?"

"The Indian camp. The one where a contingent of cavalrymen is escorting captives they rounded up. Seeing them to the reservations. Gus, they're in need of food and medicine. We're taking the last two loads before they're moved out with the soldiers. Oh, the shame of it all, Gus. You've never seen a more pitiful camp of hopeless people."

"Yes. *I have.*" His expression hardened. His eyes were as cold as winter. A twitch along his jaw expressed the blazing fury found in his eyes.

Even his stance grew rigid. "Just how many times have you been there?" She backed away at his flat black eyes that stared her down.

"Tomorrow is the second time."

"*You* are not going back there again."

"You can't stop me. Besides. You don't have a good reason."

"Don't bet on it, lady. I won't have you in danger. Already lost one wife. I won't lose another. Some of them are sick. Do you want to expose yourself to that?"

She opened her mouth to pose an argument. But he'd already turned and marched out of the door. It slammed with enough force to shake the hanging pans.

"Damn you, Gus Quaid."

SEVENTEEN

GUS COMES CALLING

THE SUPPER TURNED out to be a formal thing beneath the big chandelier. Nita scurried in and out of the kitchen with platters of pork, potatoes, and green beans heaped with butter. While his mouth watered at the sight of the delectable food set in front of him, sweat trickled beneath his collar. Nervous and far out of his element, he wanted to be near her. *Alone*, away from the furtive glances around the table.

Dammit. He'd stepped into the middle of a firing squad when he challenged her. This wasn't how he'd wanted to start out. There were only two things to do—apologize for his abruptness, then make damned sure she was safe tomorrow. At the moment, she appeared to be doing her best to give her attention to everyone but him. Was she still willing to take that stroll? Did he manage to ruin everything?

Couldn't she understand how he'd been gut-punched to learn about her getting involved with tending Indians who'd been on the run? No matter how generous or Christian a gesture—he had her welfare in mind. With a glance in Cort's direction, he planned to have a word with him about this whenever he had a chance. In the meantime, Nora settled her attention on the babies, her brothers, and anyone else except for him. *No, indeed.* He wasn't letting her off the hook. After spend-

ing weeks without hardly sleeping, he intended to settle the matter between them. *A permanent arrangement.*

"So, Gus. What's your plan once you finish up scouting for the Cavalry? Word is that most of the Poncas and Lakota have been rounded
up," Bryce asked.

Bryce was at his sister's side. Her chin lifted, her gaze intent on
him, as though she waited for the right answer. This moment felt
like he was expected to walk barefoot across hot sand. After all, she
had one of the greatest stakes in his decision. A lot depended upon
how he answered.

"I'll return to Belle Fourche. Sell off my stock except for my seed
horses and some mares, then herd them back here. That is, if your land
offer still stands."

"My offer stands," Cort said.

Bryce nodded. "I'd be glad to have a look at those horses once you
get back, Gus."

Gus noticed Bryce's hard expression softened each time he looked
toward Hannah. From the corner of his eye, Lark handed a biscuit to
little Bryce, which he gummed. The boy slobbered and giggled as Nora
looked on with longing in her eyes. While the notion she couldn't bear
children didn't matter much to him, he loved her. And he reckoned it
would be something he couldn't give her.

"Gus. The sights and smells of the camp were wretched. You've
worked with the Army. Isn't there something you can do?" Lark asked.

Cort sipped his coffee. Bryce tucked his baby against his chest. Both
left him to flounder for some kind of answer. He had to give the women
high marks for courage, and he was aware of the poor conditions. That
didn't mean he could do anything about them.

Cort cleared his throat. "Tomorrow is the last time we'll go."

"You promised three days," Nora blurted.

"A message arrived with a Private. Said they were pulling out day
after tomorrow for Colorado."

"Alfred Collier is heading out there. Said he'd look in on some of the
sick ones. He'll need more time," Nora reminded him.

Cort brooked no further argument when he repeated, "Until the end of the day, tomorrow—Nora, it's final."

Gus kept his opinion to himself since he was already walking a fine line. Setting off an argument would ruin the mood more than it already was. Nora was already seething beneath her brief smiles. Christ, he wanted to ask her to be his wife, and she was as cross as a snapping turtle. Instead, he turned his attention to the meat he forked into his mouth while she glared in his direction. Most likely, she hoped for his help. He'd be there, all right. But keeping her and the others safe was his first consideration.

Her narrow-eyed stare leveled on him. "You knew about this, didn't you?" she sneered.

She studied him like a bug she might decide to step on. With all eyes on him, he could hardly ignore her pointed question—the air around the table was charged. Gus lowered his fork. What could he say? The truth was… yes.

Nita took little Bryce from Lark's arms. Hannah stood, then walked into the kitchen with Lily. Bryce tucked his chin, staring at his plate, not moving. Cort folded his arms across his chest, waiting to hear his response. The only sound was of her fingers tapping the table.

Gus leaned back, his hands folded against his belly. His appetite was gone. "Yes. I was privy to the decision. I work for them. I'd heard but had nothing to do with their decree."

Her eyes flinty, she tossed her napkin down.

"Nora. I expect I know how you feel. But they can't stay here indefinitely. The soldiers have done their best to keep them comfortable with what they have. The situation is bad all the way around. Even if I spoke up, they'd follow orders. I have no authority to dictate to them."

"*Bad?*" Nora hissed. "They should be treated with more dignity."

"Can't argue with that."

"But you can still scout for them. Is that it? Perhaps you will join my brothers for a smoke while I help in the kitchen."

"I need to have some words with you. In private. Please."

Nora stood, her back ramrod straight. She turned and left him with the men. What should have been a celebratory evening had turned sour. What she didn't know was he wouldn't give up. Not by a long shot.

At the sudden creak of the front door, all eyes turned toward Zeke and Reyes, both standing in the threshold looking sheepish. Being late for supper was considered rude. But they'd also stepped into the middle of a battlefield, not knowing it until it was too late. Nora vacated the room in a huff, passing Lark on her way into the room.

Zeke cleared his throat. "Sorry, we're late. Horse threw a shoe. Took our time getting back."

"And I stayed with him." Reyes looked from Zeke to his father.

Gus was certain that Rey and Zeke were weighing whether to back out. They both froze while Lark glared in their direction.

"Sit down. Both of you," Lark snapped. "We were just having a discussion. No need to look all put out."

Gus drew a breath of the room's frosty air in the wake of the argument. Zeke and Rey sat in the vacated seats. While the two latecomers ate, Cort turned the talk to horses and cattle. Gus's shoulders relaxed, then found himself caught up in conversation with one eye on the kitchen door where Nora had escaped. How long would it take her to calm down?

After she returned with pie and coffee, the men kept to their discussion, sticking to cattle and horses. All the while, he glanced in Nora's direction, with hope she'd thawed. Biding his time, he intended to have her to himself before this night was over.

SUNSET PROVED SPECTACULAR. She hadn't known how much of the beauty she'd missed over the years until she'd come here. Those discontented years receded, now been replaced with hopefulness and contentment. With the exception of how the Indians were treated.

Everyone had retired, leaving her looking around the empty kitchen for some chore. Finding none, she headed for Cort's library to find a book and settle into bed for the evening. Gus had left abruptly, and thinking about it, she couldn't blame him. She hadn't given him reason to stay. She'd been unfair and prickly over things Gus couldn't control. His plan to offer marriage fell like a star from the sky, leaving her with some mending to do. But how and where?

As she skimmed the titles of books, the oak front door squeaked open, then closed. She turned, the book clutched in her hand, expecting Cort to amble in. Instead, she faced Gus, wearing a wool coat with his collar pulled up around his neck. His gaze settled on the book in her hand before he returned his intense regard of her surprised face.

"I thought you'd gone with Cort to play cards or some such thing."

"I don't go back on my word, Nora. I meant what I said. Besides, Cort doesn't play cards."

He jutted his chin at the hand that held a book at her side. "What did you decide on? The book, I mean?"

"Thomas Hardy. *Far From the Madding Crowd.* Are you familiar with it?"

He grinned. "Yes. Not a book I liked. Gabriel was far more understanding than I would have been. The characters struggle against time and change. The ending is unsatisfactory."

"Well. Then perhaps I should choose another."

"Surrendering so easy isn't like you."

Setting the book on the corner of the desk, she smiled. "In that case, I *will* read it. I owe you an apology, Gus. If you'd like to talk, best take your coat off."

"No apologies needed. So you know, I'm well aware of the Indian plight. I just don't want you to be in the middle of it." He sighed. "Now. Would you join me for a walk? We won't go far, but you'll need a coat."

"I'd like that. Yes."

After helping her with her coat, they stepped into the early evening air. He gripped her arm and led her beyond the barn. The last wisps of pink light smeared the ridges while lanterns burned in the bunkhouse windows. With the feel of his large, calloused hand holding hers... she hoped he'd get to what he had to say. After all this time, she was more than anxious to call Gus her husband.

He guided her close to the back edge of one of the hay wagons where they were out of the wind. Once there, he clutched her shoulders, then brought her close to him. His head lowered just before his mouth took possession of hers, their breath mingling. With her back pressed against the wagon, he deepened the kiss. When her hand brushed his face, he groaned and lifted his head before he enfolded her in his arms.

"That kiss was meant to convey my love for you. No matter whether I agree with some of your decisions, I can't stop loving you. Besides, I admire your independent thinking. We'll have our disagreements as well as joy ahead. We'll meet heartache, but we will do it together. Before we each die, we will share good times and bad with courage. We'll face death of loved ones with strength. I'll both provide for you and keep you safe. All I ask in return is your love."

He lifted her hand and kissed her palm, after which he cupped her face. "Will you be my wife, Nora Maril Enders?"

She touched a finger to his mouth, then traced his high cheekbone. His long, raven black hair, threaded with a few strands of gray, presented a rugged, wild look. Taller than any man she'd ever known, he emanated power... yet inside, he was a gentle soul. Those dark eyes were pools she could drown in.

"You already know my answer. It's been yes for a long time."

"So you know. I'm buying a large parcel of Ender's range about an hour east. We'll build a horse ranch there. You'll have a house on a pretty knoll. Might eventually drift into the cattle market. But I promise I will provide for you, no matter what comes along."

"I'll go wherever you are. Still can't believe I'd once been a saloon owner. You already know the other things about me. Now I'm about to become a rancher's wife."

"Don't ever doubt how much I love you, Nora." He pressed the side of her face against his heart. She smiled against him.

"Silas is dead. That other life is over."

"I know." The mention of Silas lent a dark premonition, almost ruining this moment.

"Tomorrow would be a good day to tell your family. Lark will want to have a shindig. The sooner the preacher gets here, the better, as far as I'm concerned," Gus said.

"Luck was with me the day I first saw you at Fort Benton."

Wrapping his arms around her middle, he lifted her from the ground and kissed her until she thought she'd circled the moon and stars. Once they returned to the porch, lamplight streamed from the office, creating eerie shadows.

"Tomorrow comes early. Last chance to help those souls."

"Seems it's best I get used to my independent woman. Another thing, Nora. I'll send a wire or two that might help." He tapped her cold nose. "No promises. Remember what I told you about bein' careful."

"I always am."

"Sure you won't let me share your bed?"

"I'll be careful. And no, Mister Quaid. Best remind you that Theresa is a force to be reckoned with if she were to catch us."

"I'm not a patient man, as you found out in Columbus."

"Gus. Don't mention that aloud. We were foolish."

"Cort is fast on the draw, and Bryce is wily with his punches. And both too smart to take a swing at Gus Quaid." He cleared his throat. "Foolish? I'd call it bawdy."

He winked and left her at the door. From where she stood, his lazy stroll, accompanied by a whistled tune, were signs he'd had a bourbon or two. Come tomorrow night, she'd bet Cort, Tangle, and the rest of the cowhands would have a headache on Cort's bourbon.

EIGHTEEN

THE DYING WOMAN

NORA LISTENED WHILE Theresa prattled about whether they'd brought enough vittles to feed the one hundred or so Indians. After which, she threatened to confront those soldiers about the dismal conditions at the edge of winter. Though Nora agreed, they'd talked about this until there was nothing more to say. For now, they'd done all they could do.

Lark remained home to tend little Wade, the name they'd all begun using so as not to confuse him with his Uncle Bryce. The boy had developed a miserable cold, and like all mothers, Lark's first obligation was to her son. Tangle guided the horses into the encampment, his frown mirroring his displeasure. She clutched the edge of the seat as the wagon bounced over clumps of grass and chuckholes. Nora watched her brothers ride out ahead to make sure things were as peaceful as they appeared, she guessed. From across her shoulder, she watched Billy slap the reins to close the distance between the two wagons.

Her brothers sat tall in the saddle, and she couldn't help but be proud of them. Hannah and Lark were fortunate to have them. The remembrance of her awful marriage, then everything else that had befallen her, were still raw reminders of her sordid past. Connor had been full of promises—promises he'd never meant to keep. She'd been duped.

Now there was Gus. Fear that she'd lose him kept her from revealing the entanglement. Besides, she'd waited too long to tell him.

Moreover, if he ever found out she'd been married, it might also come out she'd murdered Connor in her escape. While there had been a good reason for shooting him, Gus would only see her admission as distrust. Instead, she gambled that no one would ever find out that she'd murdered her so-called husband... a ruthless, heartless man. Still, she lied by omission... and truth was something Gus held high in his list of values.

"We're almost to the camp. Looks like they're packin' up by the looks of all that scurryin' around," Tangle said.

She counted five mounted soldiers, rifles resting across their laps. Ever watchful, yet keeping their distance from the defeated people. None of the captives would have the strength to go far, yet their pride still ran deep.

After the wagon slowed, four soldiers took positions on either side to escort the wagon into the center of the camp. The lieutenant who'd watched her before, looked up to where she sat, his piercing glare unsettling her. His medium height, sharp brown eyes, and thin hair were somehow familiar. Determined to ignore him, she turned her attention to the group of women who'd gathered around the food supply.

Out of the corner of her eye, she caught sight of a buckskin-clad man, a broad-brimmed hat shadowing his face. Strands of his long black hair were lifted in the wind where he sat proud atop his Appaloosa. Gus didn't spare her a glance. Instead, he dismounted and draped his reins over the rail of the makeshift corral without acknowledging her.

Tangle pulled up, set the brake, then leaped from the seat. He came around and helped her and Theresa alight, then tipped his hat before he headed to where Cort waited. She followed behind Theresa to the rear of the wagon, her gaze on the expressionless women who waited in line.

Cort stepped before the waiting women before he said something to them in their tongue. Between Tangle and him, the blankets and food sacks were divvied. She felt rather useless but was determined to find something she could do. As she walked toward the cook pot, Gus's voice caught her by surprise. She turned to face him.

"Nora. Do not go inside the tents," Gus warned.

"Why not?"

"They have certain social rules. Much like us. You have to be invited before you set foot inside."

There was no help for the hitch in her breath at the circumstances. Still, Gus knew these people better than most. Rather than offend, she'd follow his directive. "I'll remember."

"You might also remember this. Some of these men and women are sick. Don't get close to them. Collier is here, somewhere. Let him tend the sick. You stay outside. Let me know if you figure someone needs help, and I'll fetch him."

He gave her a last, hard look, then strode in the direction of the corral. Lifting her chin, she set her hat on her head, buttoned her coat to her neck, then joined a group of women at the stew pot. A few spoke in halting English. Another offered her a baby to hold. The little girl smiled and then gurgled, offering her a toothless grin. The elders giggled as they watched the squirming baby in her arms. The last time she'd touched one of the babies, her heart broke with the discovery it had died. This time, she gave thought at how she'd never hold her own.

After a few hours of wandering among the women, speaking with them as best she could, she hunkered beside a group engaged in laughter. She accepted she was the center of their jokes, but it didn't bother her. She smiled and moved on until she stood beside a craggy-faced woman sitting beside a fire, the woman's eyes staring at the distant horizon. A little boy sat on her lap, playing with a carved horse. He studied her, then tucked his face against the woman's breast.

"He's my grandchild."

Lordy. This woman spoke English. Nora hunkered beside the woman. "He's a handsome boy. Where are his mother and father?"

"They are gone."

"I'm sorry. How is it you speak English?"

"Soldiers teach some. And traders. And others."

Nora had no idea who the *others* might be but accepted it was best not to pry. She got to her feet, memorizing their faces. "I wish you and this little boy safe travels. A good life."

The woman said nothing more as Nora turned away. Startled when a shadow crossed hers, she looked behind her to find an unusually tall boy of maybe thirteen or fourteen. Coal-black eyes bored into hers. He wore wool pants and a buckskin shirt emblazoned with colorful beading, and his long black hair glistened in the sun. There was something so familiar about him that she had to shake herself, quite certain she'd never laid eyes on him before.

"Can I help you?" Not sure he understood, she looked to where the old woman had been sitting. She was gone.

"I speak English. My mother... she needs a white woman to see her. Will you come?"

Looking from left to right, she saw neither Cort nor Gus. Shrugging, she nodded. "All right. Show me where she is."

Marching behind him, she soon found it necessary to trot to keep up with his long-legged strides. He led her to a tent that was set well apart from all the others. Gus's words replayed in her head. *Do not enter a tent without invitation. Those inside carry sickness.*

"My mother is inside. She is sick."

"What is her name?"

"She is Walks With Thorns."

"And *your* name?"

"I am Three Hawks In Fire."

"May I enter?"

"Yes. I've given permission." He folded his arms as his piercing gaze drilled into hers.

Was he daring her to turn away in fear?

Nora Enders was no coward. Despite Gus's warning, she shoved the hide flap aside, then ducked inside to the smell of burnt sage.

The interior of the tent was warm enough, lit by a low-burning fire. As her eyes adjusted to the dimness, she saw the woman lying on a cot. Two blankets were tucked around her. Her dark, plaited hair was streaked with gray. Nora moved closer, then hunkered beside the woman whose eyes were closed. Touching the back of her hand against the woman's quiet face, she found it both hot and dry. Neither a good sign.

"Walks With Thorns," she whispered.

The woman opened her eyes. Even in this dull light, they were a sparkling blue.

"You are very sick. I'm going to bring the doctor. He can make you well."

"No. Don't go."

There was pleading both in her sunken eyes and her words. Her hand moved, and Nora grasped it between her own.

"I promise to return with Doctor Collier. Can you understand me?"

"Yes. I speak English. I'm a white woman. Taken many years ago. Three Hawks is my son. Before I die, you must know his white name is Steven."

"Do you have a husband?"

"My Indian husband is dead. White Hawk."

"What is your white name?" Nora held her breath because she already knew.

"Aubrey Quaid. Our home is Belle Fourche. Do not find him. He must have a new life."

The news was so startling, Nora caught her breath. Both relief and heartbreak washed through her at what this would mean for Gus. Aubrey was so very sick. This would be heart-wrenching to find his wife, at last. Only to see her near death, like this. A wife with sun-darkened skin, protruding bones, and near starvation. The woman's aging had exceeded her years. Worse, she was very sick with fever. *She had to find Gus. Then the doctor.*

This day would be hellish, shocking, and tragic for the man she loved. Stumbling to her feet, a dark sadness filled her every thought. *How terrible for this woman to end this way.*

———————

SHE HIKED HER skirt, then set off at a run as fast as her boots would allow. All the while, her stomach roiled as panic swallowed each breath she took. The time to cry was for later. Dodging soldiers, she continued running toward the corral while her lungs heaved with the exertion. Passing one after another, Indian and soldier, alarm swelled until they followed behind her.

Theresa turned with hands pressed to each hip, her face wearing a deep scowl. Men and women stopped whatever they were doing, some lurching from where they sat as she sprinted by them. *Dear God. She needed to locate Gus.* When Cort stepped into view, she launched herself at him, leaving him to grasp her arms, stilling her. She gasped as he held her firmly. "Find Collier. Right now. Take him to the last tent beyond the others—*and hurry.* Please."

Cort's eyes squinted in the direction she pointed. "What is it? The doctor is busy with one of the men."

"I don't give a damn. She needs him."

His hand cupped her chin. "You need to stop shouting and get hold of yourself. You're stirring alarm in the soldiers. We don't need that. Tell me calmly what the matter is."

"Aubrey Quaid. I found her. She's very sick."

Cort's eyes widened. "Are you sure?"

"I wouldn't lie about it."

"I'll find Collier. Then I'll go look for Gus."

"She might not live long, from the looks of her. Hurry. I'll look for Gus. Let me tell him. I have to be the one."

Cort nodded, then strode away while calling out orders to Tangle and Billy. With a hand pressed against her heaving chest, both soldiers and Indians stared at her as though she'd gone crazy. Aubrey Quaid was what was important. Never mind the rest. As she started toward the corral where she'd last seen him, her stomach clenched, knowing Gus's world was about to shatter.

Only in recent months had he come to terms with her death. Now Aubrey was here but *scarcely* alive. If Collier saved Aubrey's life, she'd give thanks to God, even as her heart broke into a thousand pieces. Her legs were like sticks of wood beneath her, both wanting to find him but not wanting to find him... not for selfish reasons but for the pain it would inflict. She could only imagine the depth of this crushing blow she was about to deliver.

The soldier who'd unsettled her stepped to her right, then called her by name. *"Nora."*

His familiarity irked her, but there was no time to give him thought. "Have you seen Gus?"

"He's over on the other side of the corral, getting horses ready for tomorrow. May I have a word with you?"

Her eyes narrowed. "I'm busy, as you can tell. I'd advise you to keep to your business, soldier."

She continued to the corral where she found Gus leading a sorrel out of the corral. He turned to see her. His smile of greeting died on his mouth, and he dropped the lead rope. He drew closer with long, quick strides, and she drew in her breath. His stare was unwavering.

"Christ, Nora. You look pale as a ghost. Did someone say something to upset you? What's wrong?"

She swallowed the lump in her throat. "Gus. I found *her.*"

"Found who?"

"Aubrey."

His eyes darkened, his jaw hardened, and his face nearly blanched. His frozen gaze held hers. He squeezed his eyes closed for a moment, then opened them. "You're mistaken."

"I'm telling you the truth. She told me her name. Go to her. Please."

He stepped back as though she'd struck him. *"Where?"*

She pointed. "The end of the row of tents. A lone tent, away from the others."

He swiped his mouth with his sleeve, then pivoted. At first, he took slow steps, until he broke into a run, then he disappeared from her sight. Her mother's words returned. *Fate is fickle.* And so it was true.

———————

GUS DROPPED HIS hat to the floor beside the narrow cot, then he paced from one side of the tent to the other. The physician's medical bag was beside Alfred Collier, where he kneeled beside Aubrey. Gus watched as he pressed his ear to the listening device, the other end firm against her chest. Collier called it a monaural stethoscope. For Gus, he didn't care what it was if it saved her life. Flipping back the blankets, the doctor moved his hands along her abdomen. When Aubrey groaned, Gus gnashed his teeth. If that weren't bad enough, her hacking cough had the familiar sound of pneumonia. From the shake of Collier's head, Gus surmised it was exactly that.

A shuffling sound had him look across his shoulder. A boy crouched inside of the tent flap, his gaze intent on Aubrey. He guessed him to be *her* son. He'd always figured she'd either been killed or taken as a wife. It appeared she'd been forced to marry and bear another man's child. Hatred and jealousy welled inside him... especially at the boy's audacious glare.

Drawing in a breath, he dismissed the kid, then crouched at Aubrey's head to await Collier's opinion. From her appearance, she'd lived a hard life. *And it was his fault.* Needless starvation. Running. Hiding. Walking for days. A hellish life—one that could have been avoided if he'd been closer to her on that fateful day.

With a glance over his shoulder, he looked to where her quiet son still hunkered. Thinking back, he'd seen this boy roaming the camp with his long, confident strides. He was very tall, his eyes as dark as his own. There was an arrogant stillness about him. Yet, apprehension was written in his tense jaw. It wouldn't hurt to find out his name.

"Taku nici yapi hwo?" Gus spoke in the Lakota tongue.

"My name is Three Hawks In Fire. I speak English. My mother taught me her language. I read too."

"Maybe you could tell me how old you are."

"I'm twelve summers. Years."

Gus calculated in his jumbled head. Even in his dazed state, the notion that this boy could be his... took root. If blood could chill, his sure as hell did at that moment. Rolling to his feet, the boy did the same. They faced each other with an energy that burned the air. Three Hawks *could be him at twelve.*

"You are my son," Gus blurted before he could call it back.

"My white name is Steven. My white father owned horses in a place called Belle Fourche. If that is you. Then… yes."

"Christ. She told you."

"She said it was my right to know."

"*My* flesh and blood. My father was Etienne. Steven."

Gus reached for him, wanting nothing more than to touch his own flesh and blood, but Steven backed away.

"I am Lakota. I will never live as a white. You cannot be my father."

Gus didn't have enough vigor to argue the point at the moment. Weary with the shock of finding his wife, he could hardly keep his mind on what he faced—let alone what he had to do. Aubrey was his first concern. The panic-stricken face of Nora flashed across his vision. *What must she be thinking?*

Someone cleared a throat. "Gus." Collier's hoarse voice brought him around to face the physician's stoic expression. With a quick glance in the boy's direction, Alfred shook his head. "Let's step outside."

"I don't want to leave her."

"No. I don't suppose you do. Best we talk outside."

As he followed the surgeon, his son's trembling mouth reminded him they both had a stake in Aubrey's survival. His boy's drawn face indicated his emotions were about to burst. Gus hesitated. "You want to come with us?"

"No. I will wait here."

Once outside, Collier minced no words. "You know me well enough to know I won't sugar-coat the situation. The dry fever and cough suggest a lung infection. Possibly pneumonia. She's also malnourished and emaciated. Worse, unless I miss my guess, she has a cancer in her abdomen. Nothing we can do but make her comfortable. That means taking her back to the ranch where she can be watched and given food… if she can tolerate it—though I doubt she'll be able to hold much down. I'll see she gets something to ease her pain."

"These damned soldiers let my wife die."

"No, Gus. Circumstances let this happen. If you stop to think… and

I know it's hard right now, she's been in these straights for a long while. Too late for help from these soldiers or even surgeons. I wish I could give you better news, Gus. We'll all do what we can. I don't give her more than a month—if that. For now, I'll tell Cort so he can get a wagon ready to take her to the ranch. I'll let him know she'll need to be quarantined in a separate room of the house."

Gus swallowed bitter bile that threatened to heave from his gut. Tired, cranky, and in shock... he still hadn't talked to his wife, just to hear her voice. She had to understand he'd searched for her. Before it was too late, he needed to beg her forgiveness. The word *son* was trapped in his throat. *God had it in for him.* He wished he'd died a long while ago rather than face this. He pressed his thumbs against his closed eyelids, then listened to Collier's fading footsteps.

Ducking inside, he found his son seated cross-legged beside his mother. She held his hand in hers. As her head turned against the pillow, Gus's eyes filled with tears. He swiped them on his sleeve, then whispered her name.

"*Gus.* You're here. Steven told me."

He kneeled beside her, then dropped his head in his hands. "Aubrey. God. Aubrey."

Tears spilled across his face until he scrubbed them away with his hands. A bony hand touched his arm. He sniffed before he grasped her thin, bony hand. Their gazes locked while she offered him a wan smile.

"I never forgot you," she croaked.

"Nor I you. I looked for you. *Everywhere.* Then grieved, thinking you'd died. Wanted to kill the ones who took you. My blood ran hot with revenge."

She was quiet, then slipped her hand from his. Her weak smile faded. "I had an Indian husband. White Hawk."

"I need to know. Did he mistreat you?"

"No. Not in the way you think. He was a fair man. A good father to Steven."

"Then I'll have to live with that. Steven is your only child?"

"Yes."

Again, he folded her listless hand in his. "I'm taking you to a friend's ranch. There you'll get the help you need to make you well again."

"Tell me the truth. No lies."

"It isn't good."

"I know. At least we see each other again. Steven is *your* son. He knows."

"Thank you for him, Aubrey."

"He's a good boy. Strong and tall like you. Stubborn. He will need you. Take care of him. Teach him to be a good man."

"You have no worries about that. He's my blood. He'll come home with me and want for nothing. I'm selling out Belle Fourche and building a place near here."

At the sound of movement, he darted a glance at his son. Defiance was carved in his hard mouth. "No. I will not go. I stay with *my* people. You have no say."

"Three Hawks. Stop this. You will respect your father as you did your Lakota father."

"He is too late to be my father."

Gus interceded. "Son. You will no longer use the tribal name some other man gave you. From now on, you will answer to Steven Quaid. Furthermore, you will live among whites and wear white man's clothes. Do I make myself clear?" Gus spoke in quiet terms, quelling the urge to shake the boy.

Steven looked from his mother's face to his and then back to hers. It was clear the boy respected his mother... even in this. Before Gus could think what to say, Steven stormed from the tent.

"Christ." Gus rubbed the back of his neck. How did he think he could raise a defiant boy—almost a man? Besides being surly, he'd been taught the whites were enemies.

"He is headstrong. Be patient," she whispered.

Aubrey's chest lifted on a racking cough. Gus held her hand until it subsided. "He is more like you than you know, Gus."

At the rasp of her voice, he swallowed a lump in his own. He dabbed her sweat-beaded face with a cloth, then helped her sip water from a beaded water bag beside her. "Right now, all I want is to get you away from this filthy place. Then I'll deal with him."

NINETEEN

THE WINTER COUNT

L ARK FELT A pall that sucked the air from every room in the house. Speaking became almost blasphemous in the heavy silence surrounding everyone as each faced the inevitable death of Aubrey. Three people occupied everyone's mind—*Aubrey, Gus, and Steven.* The tragedy so poignant and profound that even the toughest of cowpokes swiped at their eyes in passing.

Not one person stayed idle because to do so was to invite more sorrow. Averted eyes kept the unspeakable implicit. Lark kept the baby at Zeke's house through much of the day rather than disturb Aubrey's restless sleep. Gus's restless pacing above the kitchen was a constant reminder of his grief. Food was left outside of the door, mostly uneaten. Gus remained entrenched with his wife while the rest of the ranch could only hope she died peacefully.

Neither Cort nor Zeke had much appetite. Choosing to take their meals with Steven at the cookhouse, the men did their best to keep the boy's mind on other things. Lark recognized Steven's challenge as he faced straddling two worlds. While the boy hadn't been very congenial, he'd at least been cooperative and respectful... to a point. Lark's heart ached at Steven's quiet melancholy—a melancholy that settled like a blanket over the entire ranch.

Doctor Collier determined that helping Aubrey with pain was all that was left to do. Cort did his best to console Gus. Hannah, Bryce, and Reyes came by every other day, leaving a kettle of soup and bread. Each night, Lark heard Cort's voice while he spoke with Gus in low tones.

Steven Quaid and Reyes Enders found common ground, tending the horses, then listening to cowboy stories in the bunkhouse. The one person who seemed to have fallen into the background was Nora. Lark worried about her. She found her staring from the parlor window.

"You look far away," Lark murmured.

"Guess I was."

"I was about to go upstairs to check on Gus and Aubrey. But I think a visit from you might help him with his grief. Alfred seems to think Aubrey isn't contagious at this point."

"I'm the last person he'd want to see, Lark. You go on. I'm fine."

"You can't hide a broken heart from me. Sooner or later, Gus's world will right itself. Then he'll need you more than ever. His feelings run deep."

When there was no response, Lark set a hand on her shoulder. "You know most of the story. This part, maybe you need to hear. While Sienna Harris was dreadfully sick, Cort still needed me to know something hadn't changed. Even while everything else had."

"It's not the same thing, Lark."

"I'll give you that. But Gus needs a kind word about now. Best it came from you."

———

THE DOOR CREAKED. Gus lifted his eyes and sat straighter in the chair. After a quick glance, he found Nora standing in the doorway, her regard on his sleeping wife.

"May I come in? Don't mean to intrude."

"You aren't intruding. I needed to see you." While he hadn't looked in a mirror, he figured he looked like the Devil had robbed him of sanity.

Nora dragged a second chair closer beside him. "Has she been awake much?"

"Enough to get down some broth. The doctor told me she wouldn't keep much down. That's why she's so thin."

"I'm so very sorry."

"I know you are. So am I. This has to be hard on you. Just regret I dragged you into this whirlwind. If the circumstances were different...."

"Hush. You didn't *drag* me anywhere. I made my own decision to take up with a rugged scout and Boston College man. Just because you've got troubles doesn't change my feelings."

He favored her with a quick grin. "For the record, I never graduated. We'd both been young." After a long silence, he asked, "Have you seen my son?"

When she flinched, he had his answer. While he'd expected it would be hard for the boy to settle on a white man's ranch and wear white clothes, he was in no position to do much about initiating rules or setting standards of politeness.

"He doesn't talk much to any of us. The good news is that he and Reyes seem bonded. Steven sleeps in the bunkhouse with the hands. They're fair-minded. Zeke doesn't make judgments, but he sure knows the right things to say. You have enough to worry about. Let us help with Steven."

He nodded. "Yesterday, she was lucid enough to ask me to take her home to be buried."

"Gus. She may die before you get there. Think this through. Cort said he offered a final resting place right up on the hill."

"I'll ask her." He groaned, then brushed his palms across his face. He had to admit Nora was right. Aubrey would be dead before he made ten miles.

"That you love her that much, Gus Quaid, tells me you are a rare man. God go with you and Aubrey. Whatever you decide."

When she stood to leave, he grabbed hold of her hand and felt it tremble. "Two things. My wife will live through our son. And never doubt my feelings for you."

She nodded, then left, the scent of lilies still with him. Gus squeezed his eyes closed, then sighed.

THE FIRST OF the snow fell the next morning, blanketing the plains. A desolate landscape matched the despondency cocooning everyone. He and Cort discussed burial plans. After several glasses of whiskey, Cort's sensible words repeated over again in his mind where he stood before the ice-streaked window. *"When she passes, she can rest right here. On the hill beside Wade and Sienna. And their baby."* With snow and ice pelting the window, he accepted he wouldn't be taking her home. This place would be her final place of rest.

"You are filled with so much... *sadness,* Gus. Because of me," Aubrey whispered.

He turned away from the window where he'd been silently cussing the weather. Taking a seat on the edge of the bed, he managed a smile for his fragile wife. Her eyes glistened from the effects of laudanum. "A snowstorm," he said.

"Ah. *Waniyetu.*"

He raised an eyebrow. "And?"

"It is the first day of the new year when snow comes. Winter counts."

"Well, with this weather, I won't be able to take you home to Belle Fourche for a while."

"I choose to stay here. It was a foolish, dying woman's words. They are your friends."

He lifted her hand to his mouth, then kissed her palm. "I raise Appaloosa horses on our ranch."

"Tell me everything, Gus. I need to think about them. My spirit will find you."

Then he did. Through choking sobs and a few funny stories about the irascible men he'd hired, she listened. She seemed to hang onto his descriptions of the long porch and large barn he'd built after she was gone. He spoke until his throat was raw, her lids grew heavy, and her eyes closed.

"Stay here. Good people," she slurred. "Tell Steven to see me."

"Yes. They are. I'll find him."

"And you love the pretty woman. Nora."

"Did you hear us talking?"

"Yes. Let me hear you say the words."

"I love *her*. And *you*."

"Good. My heart is filled with gladness. And content. Marry her after your heart is lighter. The babies you will have...."

Aubrey lifted her head with a violent cough that terrified him. Holding her against him, he waited. After the hacking subsided, she spoke again. This time her voice barely a whisper.

"Do not let him have his way. He will follow his uncle to the reservation when I am gone if you do not change his loyalties."

"That won't happen."

"My dear Gus. There is no one to blame."

"Except the ones who stole you from me. How did you teach English to our son?"

"You will laugh. Every skirmish or raid, the women were sent to clean out soldier's saddlebags. I stole books whenever I found them."

His chuckle was bitter. "Our time together was too short." Shifting her against him, she moaned. Just then, the door opened, and Steven walked to his mother's other side without acknowledging him. When he curled beside his Aubrey like a lost little boy, Gus swallowed, then choked at the sight of Steven as he stroked his mother's hair.

"Mother. I am here. Speaking English like you want. I brought your books with me."

"Listen to your father. Obey. Learn."

Father and son sat in the quiet of the room as night swallowed the white hills. And on the first day of the Lakota year, a gentle woman opened her blue eyes one last time. When they closed again, she breathed her last breath.

SNOWFLAKES CAUGHT ON Nora's lashes, and she brushed them away with her gloved hand. Fixing her gaze on the mound of black dirt, dusted with snow, her eyes filled. A strong hand squeezed her shoulder. Looking up, Bryce nodded in understanding. He'd always been the empathetic one, while Cort was more apt to hide his feelings. Flanked by Hannah on her left and Bryce to her right, she felt their strength as she struggled to keep her emotions bottled inside.

Gus and Steven stood apart, distress written in the purse of their mouths. Cort and Lark were beside Hannah, their faces somber. Gloom pervaded everyone, mirroring the cold, dismal weather. After her eyes searched the row of cowhands, her stare settled on Zeke. From the few stories she'd heard about Sienna and Wade Harris, she could only imagine how Zeke's heart broke, standing here at the graves.

Lifting her chin, her eyes found Gus. As though he sensed her gaze, his somber regard held hers for a moment. Steven stood tall, his face stoic. Relief washed through her as he sidled a little closer beside his father. Gus's eyes were intent on the grave as the preacher droned on, reading from Psalms that promised life beyond. Nora wondered if either father or son trusted in the words—or if they even heard them. In fact, she couldn't focus on them either.

The urge to stand beside him was set aside. The link between them was broken for the time being. With her gloved hand pressed against her quaking lips, she saw Gus start toward her until he thought better of it. His hands were balled into fists at his sides, but he managed a brief nod before he returned his attention to the preacher. When the preacher's words ended, the world seemed to hush.

A line of friends closed around Gus and Steven, offering condolences. Cort took her arm and led her to where Gus stood. Lark, Hannah, and Bryce followed behind. There were whispered offers of support from Cort. Gus squeezed her hand, then released it.

"Cort, Nora. All of you. My son and I thank you for all you've done. We owe you a debt of gratitude."

"Wish we could've done more," Cort said.

Bryce cleared his throat. "It'll be a while to get over the shock, Gus."

Hannah took Gus's hand in hers, squeezed it, and then hugged Steven, drawing a look of surprise from the boy. Lark stood on her toes before she wrapped her arms around Gus's neck, whispering words to him that Nora couldn't hear.

Lark touched a hand to Steven's shoulder. "We have food set out at the house. And it's a lot warmer inside than out. Come along, Steven. Your mother is now in a good place."

Steven looked from Lark to his father. After Gus nodded his approval, the tight-lipped boy followed the others alongside Lark, leaving Nora beside Gus. One by one, each of the family made their way down the slope beneath the gray sky. From the corner of her eye, she saw Zeke make his way to the three Harris graves, where he stood, his head bowed.

Gus cleared his throat. "Thank you, Nora. Appreciate you being here. Can't be easy for you either."

"Wouldn't be anywhere else."

"You're beautiful. I just wish I could hold you. Tell you what's in my heart. Somehow it doesn't feel right. Not now. Not standing here."

"I understand. I'll be waiting whenever the time is right."

"That may be a long while. Leaving in two days for my home. Taking Steven along with me. He needs to see where his mother once lived. Besides, I need the chance to get to know him, without the people he'd lived with. I'll be selling off most of my herd and bringing back some of my prime stock."

"I'll miss you. And worry."

He brushed her face with the back of his gloved hand. "You know me better than that. I know the land. I'm tough. Missing you will keep me awake at night. I'm raw inside, Nora. There's no room for anything else, for now."

"I know you are. You wouldn't be the man I love if you weren't. Write to me when you can."

"As soon as I find a post office. Most likely Fort Meade."

"Gus. This is so hard."

"For me, as well. This thing with my wild son may be even more than I can handle. You might be wise to find someone else. Someone who won't saddle you with a son that needs taming."

"Now you're talking foolishness." She shook her head. There was no point in arguing because he wasn't rational at the moment. Then he cupped her face, his gaze searching hers.

"I'd like to feel you in my arms. Nothing is right at the moment. Best we don't walk together back to the house."

"You go on, Gus. I'll follow with Zeke. He looks like he could use some company."

He looked to where Gus stood, nodded, then left. Lost in thought as she watched Gus's tall frame walk toward the house, she hadn't heard Zeke approach her. She lifted her eyes to his.

"Mind if I escort you to the house?"

"Not at all. I'd be grateful for the company. Figured I'd wait until your visit at the grave was over."

"Have to move slow with my arthritic legs." He jutted his chin in the direction of Gus. "Don't worry none. He'll be back. Now and again, I like to tell a story or two. Did I ever tell you how I lost my best horse in a heavy rainstorm that killed a hundred head of beef? Still got a limp."

Leave it to kindly old Zeke to lighten the grim moment. Jabbering most of the way to the house with each story more unbelievable, he kept her from bursting into a mass of tears. She'd be forever grateful.

TWENTY

GONE BUT NOT FORGOTTEN

Spring, 1880

FTER SUPPER, NORA sat on the top stair of the porch and drew in a deep breath of the sage-scented air. This was home, and she hoped it would stay that way. She understood why Cort and Bryce had this place in their blood. She tugged her coat collar around her neck against the chilly air, then gazed across the many hills dotted with cows and calves. The grass had begun to green after an unusually hard winter. Cort, Bryce, and the cowhands were scouring the gullies, searching for strays and carcasses for the winter count.

She'd spent a good amount of time watching over her little niece, Lily, while Bryce and Hannah moved things from the old ranch on Rocky Creek to the much larger house. The sweet baby girl had lighter hair and clear blue eyes like those of Hannah. Each time she held that sweet baby, a familiar yearning set in.

Nora cupped her eyes, then fixed her stare on the horizon, hoping to see the familiar Appaloosa crest the hill. Gus had left on the first of December, and it was early March. Doubt settled inside her head at whether he'd ever return. He'd sent her one letter after he'd arrived, though nothing more since then.

Just as she started inside, she caught sight of a black horse trotting toward the house. Her gaze stayed on the man as he closed the distance. After she recognized Alfred Collier, she pasted a pleased smile on her mouth to hide her disappointment. He dismounted, then handed off the reins to Adoeete. With his black medical bag in hand, he ambled in her direction, wearing a grin. After he'd stepped onto the porch, he doffed his Stetson.

"What brings you out here, Doctor Collier?"

"Checking up on Lark. That baby is due early April, after all. Glad you're here to help."

"Don't know much about birthing. But I'll do my best. Theresa and Nita know more than me."

"You'll do fine." He set his bag on a rocker, then waved his hand toward a chair. "Care to sit and talk a while, even if it is a bit cold out here?"

"Surely you'd rather converse with Cort or Bryce."

"Now, that *is* an insult. I'd much rather talk with a pretty lady any day than palaver about horses, cows, and beef prices. Besides, they're not here this time of year."

She laughed in spite of herself. "Put that way, how can I refuse? Can I get you something to drink?"

"No. Thank you. Maybe coffee before I set out. It's almost two days getting back. Glad for the use of that half-way cabin."

She took a seat while he sat opposite her. For the first time, she noticed more lines around his eyes as well as a few more gray hairs. Alfred was distinguished, both in the way he dressed and how he approached subjects. Gus was rugged and to the point. *Why did she find herself comparing them?*

"You'd be welcome to stay here for the night."

"Thank you. But I've got to stop at Henry Larson's place, so I'll bed down there. Or the cabin." He dropped his chin and studied his toes. He lifted his intense brown eyes. "How've you been, Nora?"

"Fine. Got to know the family after being cooped up all winter."

"I know the feeling. Even living in town, you don't see many unless they have a fever or broken bone. Most either too sick or too much in pain for conversation."

"You surely must be one of the most important people around, Doctor Collier. Invitations to supper are probably more than you can accept."

"*Alfred.* No formality needed. As to invitations to supper. They're far and few between. Got used to my own cooking."

"Then, I hope you like stew. That's what we're having for supper. Lark would insist you stay."

"Better than shoe leather that I cook for myself. I'd be glad to accept another time. I'm more interested, though, in whether you'd insist."

Her smile dissolved at what he intimated, leaving an uneasiness in the pit of her stomach. "Of course, I'd insist. I've stayed at that halfway shack. Can't imagine it would be stocked with much, other than canned goods."

"Have to say… it's mighty good to see your pretty face smiling again. Been enough gloom weighing down this ranch for too long."

"Thank you. But please don't concern yourself over me."

"Have you heard from him?"

"One letter from Fort Meade. Said they'd made it well and safe. Settling in for the rest of the winter."

"I see." He lowered his chin and staired at his boots again. "While it isn't my business, I understand he has a horse ranch."

She stood, then her chin lifted. "Yes, he does have a ranch. Doctor Collier. Is there some reason for this line of questions?"

"Just this. Gus has always been a loner. What if doesn't return?"

"It's no concern of yours."

"For your sake, I hope he does. Truly. I'm sorry I offended. So you know, Nora, I care for you. Think about that."

As she studied his frown, she counted back the number of times he'd been by on the pretense of checking in on Lark. She had no doubt he was a good man. But he wasn't Gus. However, he'd planted a seed of doubt in her head about whether Gus would return. The good doctor was playing his hand, and she didn't like it.

He cleared his throat. "Nora. I'm forty. In fact, I'll be forty-one before summer. Never been married. Almost was till she found someone wealthier than I'd ever be. Decided to come west. I've been alone and tired of my own company. You've made it clear how you feel about Gus. I'll abide by that. Still, make no mistake. I'll be here if you need me."

She lowered her eyes and stared at the floor. A lump in her throat kept her from speaking—even if she could find the words. He'd misconstrued her friendship for something else.

Before she knew what he was about to do, he took her hand and pressed a whisper of a kiss against her palm. Without a word, he reached for his medical bag, then started for the door. In a toneless voice, she stopped him. "You don't know anything about me, Doctor. My life is anything but what you'd expect. Whether Gus returns or not, don't wait for me."

"To be blunt, your past doesn't matter. I've had my own. You don't know mine, and I pray you never do."

The bitterness in his voice sent a coldness through her that had nothing to do with the weather. "I think we've both said quite enough."

"You have. I sure haven't. In the meantime, I'll wait for Gus. Right along with you."

Once the door closed, she covered her face with her hands. She'd damn herself for hurting one of the most decent men she'd ever known. Yet, she had.

May 1880

WITH THE STEM clamped between his teeth, Gus puffed his pipe. Steven had turned out to be confident around horses, assuring him that he and his son would make fine ranch owners. While they'd been here, he'd watched his son grow and settle into his life among the whites. Soon, they'd head back to Nebraska to finalize the purchase of a three thousand acre parcel from Cort... enough for a start. For now, they awaited the soldiers from Fort Robinson who would herd the horses he'd sold to the Army then use the proceeds to fund a house for Nora and Steven.

Tapping out his pipe against the porch beam, he looked toward the Belle Fourche River, a glimmering ribbon of water that weaved among the long-hanging cottonwoods. No longer did he need to ride with the Army. Aubrey was now a part of his past. He still had to begin again with Nora. They both needed to move on to a new future… if her affection for him hadn't changed. Expecting her to take on the raising of a boy who'd been raised in a different culture was asking a lot.

Gus stepped from the porch, then ambled to where his son sat atop the Appaloosa. There was pleasure in his son's eyes that couldn't be bought with money. They'd found trust between them in the common interest in horses. His son grinned as he waved his hat. The long trip here had been worth every mile because it had given them time to share their pasts but also grieve the loss of Aubrey.

Gus couldn't be prouder of the strides his son had made in accepting his new life. Still, once business was concluded, he needed to return to the woman he loved, who sometimes had a prickly nature, yet more courageous than most he'd ever run into.

He stroked the horse's neck and looked up at Steven. "Have a name for him yet?" Gus asked.

"We don't name horses. Until they prove themselves."

"I see. Well, by *we*, you mean the People."

"Yes."

"He'll get the chance to prove himself. We leave by end of the week."

"You want to go back to that woman."

Gus ground his teeth. In the realm of civility, there was still work to be done. "She is the woman I want for my wife. If she'll have me. Whatever happens, you will treat her with respect. It's what I want. So would your mother."

"She's white."

"So are you."

"I don't feel white."

"You will, given time. You will be by my side at my wedding. It is the custom. Do you understand?"

The boy shrugged, then turned his horse in a circle before nudging the animal out of the gate. After he was out of sight, Gus ticked off what he needed to get ready before they left. A neighbor was paid a good sum for this house and land. But one section, well north of here, would remain in Quaid hands—land not rich in grass but rich in gold. Gus hadn't put much thought into turning it into a business, just as his father Etienne Quaid hadn't. Somehow, though, he wondered if it wouldn't one day make a difference in all their lives. *Whether for good or bad, he wasn't sure.*

Cort had agreed to the sale of good Enders grazing land. All that was left to do was to get there. With some of the gold, he'd have enough train fare for the seed horses as far as Ogallala. With his son and two of his hands along, the trip would still be arduous. The vision of Nora had stayed with him. No matter what secret she kept hidden, he was ready to gamble on a future with her.

NORA HIKED THE bottom of her skirt to step over clods of dirt and clumps of Indian grass, hoping she'd find a few windflowers or wild pansies to brighten Lark's bedroom. After the difficult birth of Benjamin Lee, Cort's second son, his mother deserved a bit of cheering. With a basket in hand, she tramped back to the porch.

Thinking about Cortland, she swore she'd never seen a paler nor a more frightened man than her brother with Bryce pacing beside him. Hannah had been the cool head through it all. While Nora hadn't done much except to hand over fresh water and towels as called for, Hannah had been the steady one.

The sound of a horse riding up behind her had her twist to see who was coming. Mason tipped his hat.

"You all right?" he asked.

"Yes. Just seeing if I can round up some flowers for Lark."

"I'll keep an eye for more. Late May is still a bit cool for sunflowers. Her favorite." He winked.

"Is Doctor Collier still up at the house?" she asked.

"He is. Said he'd be heading back to Ogallala tomorrow."

"*Oh.*"

Mason grinned. "Keep watch for rattlers, Miss Enders. Best I get back to work before I lose my job." He turned his horse into a lazy lope, then waved his hat in farewell.

Once she'd reached the house, she turned to stare at the horizon. Her heart ached each time she didn't see his familiar buckskin-clad frame riding toward the house. Each day that passed left her less certain he'd ever return. Seemed that Alfred Collier's prediction was on the mark.

TWENTY ONE

THE WAIT

GUS LAY ON his bedroll near the campfire. Some people swore that the plains were soundless, but those were the ones who never listened. The brush of Indian and buffalo grass in the wind joined the occasional yip of a coyote. Whenever grouse took flight, they stirred the wind, usually a warning of a disturbance somewhere. All these things, and more, were proof that the plains were teeming with life.

Yesterday, he'd shot a few sage grouse, which they'd consumed for supper. Rolling onto his side, he searched his son's form, tucked beneath blankets, his chest rising and falling. Each time he studied his boy, he saw the vision of Aubrey. She would live on in him. But he was determined to begin his life again.

Gus sat up, rolled to his feet, then hefted his rifle, while his horses looked in his direction, wide-eyed. He walked around them, smoothing his hand across their necks to settle them. After he'd reached the perimeter of the camp, he found Dave Wilkins's silhouette in the moonlight, accented by the glowing tip of his hand-rolled smoke. Wally Blank was somewhere out there keeping watch on the small herd they'd hobbled.

When he returned to the campfire, he set his rifle down, took a seat, then considered sipping some coffee. He ran his hand across the place where he'd been knifed, the soreness still bothering him from time to time. Grinning, he recalled the vision of Nora with a revolver clutched between her hands, facing down three Indians with the coolness of a seasoned gunfighter. They'd been more afraid of her than she was of them. And in that moment, he'd fallen in love with her.

"You are quiet. But not enough," Steven said from out of the shadows where he lay.

Gus turned his head and grinned. "Had to check the horses."

"You were wounded."

"Many times. But the knife wound was the result of a group of Lakota kids out to prove their courage. One took a bullet before getting away." Steven rolled to his feet, then crossed his arms. After a brief hesitation, Steven took a seat beside him but remained silent. Gus figured he had something on his mind.

"I was there. Now I remember *you*. We thought we'd steal your horse. But instead, Tall Buffalo returned with a hole in his leg. We had no horse to show for our trouble. It must've been Nora who shamed him. If I'd known who you were, I would have defended you."

Gus's eyes narrowed, giving his mind time to process this revelation. "*You*." He dropped his head into his hands, his thumbs pressed to his closed eyelids. His tongue could hardly sputter a rebuke. He dopped his hands to his lap and glared at his son.

"*You* were the one who cut me! Christ, I might've killed you. It was a stupid thing to do. To think I might've killed my own son is enough to make me want to turn you over my knee. Or worse."

"I did not set out to attack you. My job was to hold the horses steady in case there was gunfire. But you came close to where I waited. It wasn't until we were far away that we found that Tall Buffalo was wounded. I watched Nora fire her revolver. Now I remember it all."

Steven's wary expression was off-putting, but Gus was still reeling. "You will live the white man's way. No more stealing. Tall Buffalo is of no concern. He's on a reservation."

"Surrender is just another word for dying. That's what my uncle, Nine Bears, says."

This was going to be the first of many battles Gus would have to fight. Nine Bears and all the rest of his Indian family still influenced Steven. It was disconcerting and maddening, but Gus was determined to win.

Gus wagged his finger with emphasis. "Remember, you are *my* son. Steven Quaid. You live with my blood in your veins. The ones who stole you from me are my enemies. But they are gone. You will live by my rules. Do not shame me or our family. That's horse dung about surrendering is the same as dying. Surrendering can mean you live to see another day. Dying means the sunrise is no more."

"It was my mother's wish to honor you. I keep my word."

In the quiet that followed, Gus drew a breath of relief. Steven's response was remarkably mature. He'd been raised by a very smart mother, and for that, he was grateful.

"Pa. Do you know why my mother was called Walks With Thorns?"

Pa. This was the first time his son had addressed him that way, and it felt right. Did Steven realize what he'd just said? He cleared his raw throat. "Never got the chance to ask her."

"She told me she tried many times to escape with me as a baby. Once, she ran with me in her arms because I was too young to run. They were close behind, tracking her. There was nowhere to go but through the briars. She tried to hide among them. The thorns tore at her flesh where she crouched, but she held me away from them. The men encircled her. She surrendered."

Gus looked skyward to prevent his son from seeing his welling outrage. He gulped, then said the only thing he could say. "A good woman sacrifices for her child. Aubrey would do no less."

June 25, 1880

HANNAH AND LARK settled the babies into their cradles, leaving little Bryce toddling around the kitchen, creating noise with pots and pans while jabbering in his baby language. Nita and Theresa were outside, hanging freshly washed bed sheets and blankets from ropes suspended between the house and privy. Nora left the women to their gossip and returned to the front porch where she'd left a book.

Zeke limped by the porch and waved as he headed for the cook-house for his usual coffee. Lately, he'd kept to himself more than usual. She made a mental note to ask Alfred to check on him the next time he was here. Book in hand, she walked to the end of the porch, then called out to him. He stopped and turned. That's when she noticed the pink flush along his cheekbones, just above his silver scruff.

"Zeke. Are you feeling all right?"

"Yeah. For an old man with arthritis. Coffee and listenin' to Reyes and Tangle blather will set me upright. Not ready to put this old man down just yet." Waving her off with one hand, he continued on his way.

After he was gone, there was a strange quiet… the kind before a storm. Most of the men were out with cattle or repairing corrals. She'd heard Cort order a check of the water levels. All any of them could do in that regard is pray for rain. Settling onto the swing seat, she gave it a shove with her boots, then eased into the gentle sway. With the book, *Life on the Mississippi* beside her, her eyes grew tired and then closed, giving in to memories.

Both Gus and Alfred crossed her thoughts. *Alfred deserved someone who could love him.* Yet he hadn't given up his campaign to convince her to give him a chance. For now, she'd been able to divert his conversations to local gossip, medicines, and new gadgets she'd heard about. While her thoughts drifted, a soft breeze touched her cheek. In her dreams, she sensed someone near. *Silly woman's thoughts.*

A feather tickled her cheek. Her eyes snapped open as she brushed away the offensive tickle that disturbed her dreams. She froze in disbelief at the sight of the man wearing a buckskin shirt, crouching in front of her. Stunned, her gaze moved from his grin to the blade of grass he dangled in front of her. A lump formed in her throat as she appraised him from his shirt to his moccasins, then she lifted her eyes to meet his stare. *"Gus?"*

"You remember me. Nora, you looked so peaceful, I just watched you, at first."

"You're almost more surprise than my heart can take. My God. You never wrote to tell me you were coming." The swing moved when he took a seat beside her. She tucked a strand of her hair behind her ear. "How long have you been watching?"

"For a while. From my vantage on the ridge, I saw you walking along the porch. After I got my herd to pasture with Alonzo, Steven, and my two hands, I came right here. By that time, you'd fallen asleep with Mark Twain for a companion."

"No letters. Just one," she scolded.

He tilted his head. "I'm sorry. Had my hands full with selling my horses and ranch. Then figuring out the best way to return with a few horses. Needed time to get to know my son and let him get to know me. Besides, I wanted to give you enough time to decide if you'd want to be saddled with a man with a son. Or even if I had the right to ask. Believe me. The thought of you never left me."

"I'd almost made up my mind that you weren't coming back. I might've left here."

"Two things I know for certain. You're one independent, decisive woman. No getting around it. I should've written. Moreover, I love you, Nora. Figure to cash in on that marriage agreement. If you'll still have me?"

"Yes. You should've written. Now that you're here, I can't muster an argument because I'm too happy you've returned. Now, tell me the details of the plans."

"Like I said. Sold off my land and house. Most of my horses, except those I'll use for breeding. Before I left, Cort and I came to an agreement on land. Eventually, I'll need more land. That's a matter for another day. First, I get that house started. Second, let's get the preacher here."

She rested her head against his shoulder, breathing in his manly scent of leather and horses. His arm held her against his side. "How is Steven?"

"I'm glad I got the chance to know him while we were away. Had many talks, even though he's a bit short on conversation. One thing still is bothersome... his loyalty to his past life. Need to work on changing that. It won't be easy, but so far, he accepts this new life."

"Good to hear. You've got to know he may see me as the woman stealing his mother's place."

"That will all work out, given time. He's my flesh and blood, and you're the woman I love. It'll be hard... for all of us, at first. Don't forget, I don't know anything about raising kids. We'll be learning together. But first things first."

Nora watched as he pushed from the swing and turned to face her before he offered a courteous bow fit for a ballroom. He tugged her to her feet, looked from right to left, and settled his mouth with hers. Gus leaned away, his gaze steady. She knew without any question what he would ask.

"Let's begin again. Nora, will you marry me? Soon?"

"Yes. Just as soon as we can get that preacher here."

They sat together, swinging while they spoke about everything from building a house to his son's natural skill with horses. Even talked about her determination to become a good cook. So engrossed in their discussion, neither of them heard the boot steps approach.

When she looked up, Alfred Collier faced them with a hard-as-nails glare. She'd been accustomed to the smile in his brown eyes... but today, that smile had vanished. Instead, his eyes flashed with thinly checked fury. A look designed to peel his hide had turned to Gus. After a moment, he swung his regard back to her. She felt Gus's body tense beside her as she shrank into the seat, not knowing how to ease the thick tension.

"I see you're back," Alfred drawled.

Nora cringed at the cold stares between the two men. Her mind searched for something to say to diffuse this ridiculous confrontation. Gus reached for her hand.

"You've decided to accept his excuses for staying away so long, haven't you?" Alfred snapped.

Her eyes flitted across the hard lines of Alfred's face, silently pleading that he wouldn't make a scene.

"Well?" Alfred persisted.

Gus's glare turned to her. With one eyebrow raised, Gus asked the pertinent question. "What's he talking about, Nora? Does he have some claim on you?"

"No. No, he doesn't. I think he just... misunderstood friendship for something more."

Gus looked back to Alfred's scowl. "Nora. Maybe you need to make that clear here and now."

"I agree. To be clear, Doctor Collier, I've never led you to believe we could be more than friends. I'd thought you understood my feelings for Gus are unshakable. You've made a wrong assumption."

"Christ, Nora. How do you know he won't leave you again?"

Gus dropped her hand, then straight-armed from the seat. The men faced each other like the adversaries they'd become. Nora had owned a saloon long enough to know when a fistfight was brewing. This wasn't over cheating at cards or stealing one of the upstairs girls. This was about her. She'd just about had enough of this. If she interceded, Gus wouldn't take it kindly. But it had come to that. Just as she stood, Gus gripped her arm and set her behind him.

"Alfred. I think the lady has given you an answer."

"Fine. Got no choice but to accept it. But don't ever hurt her, Gus. You're a fortunate man to have her."

In the stillness between them, she saw the hurt in Alfred's eyes. When he lifted his bag, he marched to the end of the porch without so much as a goodbye, leaving her shaken.

"Maybe you best start over. What's been goin' on?"

She drew a breath. "He's a lonely man. His trips here were about tending Lark and anyone who needed medical attention... until he seemed to make a point of spending time talking with me. It didn't occur that he'd become...."

"Infatuated? I'm pretty sure it sunk in now. I've staked my claim. And I intend to hold my ground, lady. Do you have an objection?"

"Please don't take it further, Gus. Let it drop."

Gus nodded. "That's my plan. Unless he persists."

NORA WAS AS happy as a woman could be, knowing she was about to become a bride... married to a man who was smart, kind, and as handsome as he was when she first met him. The confrontation with Alfred hadn't dampened this moment. She found herself more interested in ranch talk over supper, while Hannah babbled about fixing the wedding dress. She and Gus exchanged grins as his moccasin rubbed her calf beneath the table while heat crept from her neck to her face.

The dining table overflowed with plates of steaks and stew, bread and fresh butter, not to mention bottles of bourbon. The crystal chandelier lit the room like a noon sun. Each time she lifted her eyes to look toward Gus, he'd offer her a wink as he listened to her brothers drone on about cattle, horses, and drought.

In the meantime, she joined in discussions with Lark and Hannah about the nuptials. Steven and Reyes were engrossed with Zeke's crusty-voiced tales about the early days of the ranch. Lily Raine sat on Bryce's lap, stuffing pieces of potato into her rosebud mouth, her blue eyes flitting from one to another around the table. As the evening grew to an end, Alfred's hurt still played over in her mind's eye. Then she wondered if he and Gus would forever be at odds.

GUS MADE HIS way to the bunkhouse, hoping he didn't tumble on his ass. Cort and Bryce talked with him well into the late evening—over a bottle of whiskey. They'd covered everything from deeds, water, and building a house and barn. They expected the new place to be well underway by late Fall.

With his mind in a fog, he'd closed the deal and signed papers for a section of the eastern edge of the Enders's empire. As tired as he was, he longed to have her beside him. Sucking in a long draft of cool night air, he found himself looking over his shoulder at the house. A dim lamp burned in one room at this end of the building. *Her room.*

Instead of continuing to the bunkhouse, he swung around then strode to the large front door. Just as he was halfway there, he paused. He hadn't lived on the plains most of his life not to know whether he was being watched. Hair rose on his arms. *Dammit.* His sidearm was in the bunkhouse with his rifle. He stood stark still, his gaze fixed on the dark outlines of the hills. The horses in the corral were still, but their ears pricked.

A half-moon helped cast shadows around the buildings. Knowing he was in plain sight, anyone who wanted him dead would have already killed him. Maybe it was either willies or the whiskey playing tricks in his head. Still, tomorrow he intended to ride out to have a look for traces of the phantom who'd raised his hackles. For now, he had other things on his mind.

TWENTY TWO

PHANTOM

THE LIGHT. IT had to be the dim light from the lamp that woke her. Turning onto her side, she found Gus's eyes closed, his mouth slack. His long body was stretched out alongside hers, his bared chest a whisper away from her. Careful not to wake him, she burrowed her hand beneath the blanket, finding he still wore his pants. Still, her eyes widened at the audacity of the man. Hadn't she always known how impertinent he could be? If Cort or Lark found him here, she'd be mortified.

She lay beside him as the pleasure of him beside her washed through every corner of her being. How he'd managed to slip into her room was something she meant to ask. His leg moved. Her eyes widened as he boldly rubbed her calf with the sole of his bare foot. Her gaze followed his length, then returned to his dark, smiling eyes riveted on her face. One eyebrow rose. Slamming her eyelids closed, she hoped he hadn't noticed her brazen perusal.

"Too late, sweetheart. I know you're awake." His voice was thick, gruff with sleep.

"Did I invite you to my bed?"

"Yes."

"When was that?"

"You didn't need words. I read your suggestion in those blue eyes."

"You are bold."

"Uh-huh. And I want you. Do you object?"

"What if we're caught?"

"Cort was fairly drunk before I left. Bet he's dead asleep or busy with his own woman. Besides, this is none of his business. Now. Are you going to remove that frilly nightdress you shrugged into, or shall I help you?"

He swung his legs over the side of the bed, then padded to where the embers glowed in the heater. Dropping down on one knee, he added kindling and used the poker to coax the flame. While he attended to that, she slipped from her nightdress, then dropped it to the floor. Her attention turned to his panther-like walk in her direction as his eyes glimmered with something akin to hunger.

"Do you recognize anything different?" he asked.

"You're a tease. Since you asked, I don't see any new knife wounds or bullet holes on your chest."

"If I thought you didn't like my teasing, I wouldn't do it."

"Then, tell me, what's different?"

He held up two fingers. "Had my hair trimmed. And I have a future with a beautiful woman and son at my side."

She crooked her finger, inviting him to join her, certain her face flamed crimson while he whispered his plan of attack. One kiss wouldn't be enough as she smiled against each that followed… until they slipped into the heavens together with his blazing regard holding hers. His growl of satisfaction was the last she heard before she drifted with him to Earth.

Replete, she was enfolded within his strong arms, tucked against his warm skin. His mouth touched the top of her head, then caught one hand to press a kiss against her palm. Both were wrapped in the pleasure of the night.

Sometime in the morning, she shifted and woke to the sense of his warmth gone. She stood, then searched the room to find his things were gone and wrapped her arms around her middle, missing his arms. At the sound of clanging pots and pans from below, she was reminded she'd be needed in the kitchen.

After she'd brushed her hair, washed, then slipped into a simple calico dress, she started for the door. She'd found the girl inside of her... the girl who'd been lost... a woman too soon. Like so many times before, her darkest secret was still there, edging closer. It was a premonition that sent shivers through her at the thought someone might know her secret. Nora lifted her chin. She was too far away from that place and time for anyone to know.

Downstairs, she sliced bread and fried potatoes while Lark and Theresa gossiped like magpies. The oven door was slammed closed, and dishes were heaped with food. Her private thoughts flitted like fireflies in her head. All the while, she managed to join in the conversation about food, babies, and the nuptials. Little Bryce crawled to her, then clutched her skirt before dragging himself to his unsteady legs, a wooden spoon gripped in his hand. With his slobbery smile, her heart melted. With Cort's eyes, she was reminded of her little brother as they were growing up. She plunked a kiss to his chubby cheek and set him into his chair.

Cort appeared, nodded, then poured coffee from the blue enamel pot into a cup. Straddling a seat, he winked at her. "Nora, you're good with babies. Seems like after you and Gus tie the knot, you could sprout a few of your own."

Biting her lip, she felt the familiar sadness stir and simmer. *There would never be babies.* Nita walked in with Benjamin and set the baby in his cradle before helping to dish out eggs from the warming stove. Theresa took little Bryce, saying he needed a bath.

"I know you have to be hungry. You hardly ate last night at supper," Lark said. "If you don't eat, that wedding dress we got ready for you might not fit."

"Last night, I was still in shock at his sudden return. Gus manages to surprise without even trying."

Just as Cort started to fork eggs into his mouth, he lowered his fork. "Haven't seen him this morning. You happen to know where he might be?"

Flustered by her brother's question, she glanced at the wall clock, no longer interested in eating. Worry started to set in, twisting her stomach into a knot.

"No. If he wasn't here, I figured he was at the cookhouse."

Cort stopped chewing. At his quizzical expression, she shoved her plate aside. "Are you sure?"

"As sure as I can be. I was there going over the men's assignments. No one saw him. I checked, and his horse is missing. Thought he might've gone to Bryce's house. Zeke hasn't seen him either. Steven didn't know anything."

Goosebumps rose on her skin. "Maybe I better saddle a horse and ride to Bryce's place."

"*Nora.* He's a grown man. He wouldn't take kindly to bein' chased down. I have to check on water levels, so I'll have a look around."

"Something doesn't feel right, Cort."

Lark pressed a hand against her shoulder. "Let Cort find out. Knowing Gus, he's probably looking over his horses, not bothering to let anyone know."

Once Cort left, Nora stood on the porch. When she looked skyward at the swirling gray clouds, she'd bet they were in for a storm. They needed rain... but Gus was out there. The saddle horses had been moved into the barn. A thin puff of smoke rose from the cookhouse, and one lamp glowed in a window at Zeke's house. Even in her warm coat, she shivered at the ominous signs. *Where did you go, Gus?*

———

GUS HAD RIDDEN some distance away from the ranch compound, searching for whoever had been near the house last night. A half-moon had given him a view of the corrals and outbuildings from Nora's window. The hoot of an owl, though, caught his attention.

From the look of the sky, it was certain they were in for rain. If he didn't find any tracks soon, they'd be washed out. As he tried to decide whether to give up, a rider appeared. There was no mistaking the blue uniformed soldier. He waited until they were side by side.

"Lieutenant Mabry. What brings you out here alone? Thought you'd headed to Colorado with the camp of Indians," Gus said.

"I'm surprised to see you here, Gus. I was on my way to see Cort about a situation you can relay. One of those Indians escaped after stealing a horse and rifle. We don't have enough time or men to go looking for one renegade. Thought Cort and his hands best keep a lookout."

"And why would one Indian be of concern to us?"

"You should know that Nine Bears is the brother of White Hawk. Heard about what happened. Mighty sorry. That Indian might be lookin' for your son."

"I'll relay the message. He'd have no way of knowing where my son is." *Unless Nine Bears had been watching.*

Gus noticed the lieutenant hesitate as though he had something else to say. Apparently, he changed his mind because he tugged the brim of his hat and turned his horse. He watched until Mabry disappeared over the rise, then considered whether to follow the tracks until the rain. If Nine Bears was on the loose, he may have decided to come for Steven. That was something he wasn't about to let happen.

With that piece of information, he needed to expand his search, just in case Mabry was right. Steven was safe at the ranch, for the time being. After checking his revolver, he slipped his rifle from the boot, then rested it across his lap.

He nudged his horse forward, watching the ground while a thought niggled. *Why would a lone soldier be granted leave to deliver a message this far out?* Something didn't add up. There was more going on than one Indian. For now, he had to find the man who might be a threat to his son before he investigated Mabry's purpose.

NORA PACED THE parlor from one wall to the next until Cort returned from Bryce's house, Steven beside him. Neither had seen Gus. Her brother's face was taut. After both let in a hard downpour to question the men in the cookhouse, she took up a vigil at the parlor window. Nora could hardly see through the mist and torrent of water. At the sound of footsteps, she turned to find Lark setting a tray of tea and biscuits on the parlor table.

"Sit down, Nora. You'll make yourself sick with worry," Lark said.

"I'm scared."

"I know you are. That's natural. You know how Gus is. He probably hunkered into a shelter to wait out the storm. Maybe his horse threw a shoe and he's on foot, soaked, and madder than a rained-on rooster. For goodness sakes. You know it could be any number of common reasons that happen on ranches."

Nora sat, then rubbed her arms against the chill both inside and out. "You're probably right. Lark, something tells me he's in trouble."

"Cort will find him. But while we wait, how 'bout I share the story of Sienna and Wade Harris? It's a mighty interesting story. Betting it'll take your mind off this. And before you know it, Gus will come walking in, drenched and cussing."

"I'd heard pieces of the story. If you don't mind, I'd like to hear it from you."

Lark pinched the bridge of her nose before beginning. "I lived here as a companion for Sienna Harris. She was sick with a cancer. Cort was married to her. Did you know that?"

"Yes. The name on her stone is both Harris and Enders."

"Well. Sienna was a manipulator. But I respected her, and in turn, she became a friend in an odd way. There was always an unease between us, though. We had a storm worse than today. Rain poured down like God was throwing buckets. Sienna was a mighty strong woman—iron-willed and determined.

"She paced this very room with worry over her men, but she held a special fondness for Zeke. Most of the hands were out in the deluge with a wind blowing rain sideways—all to haze cattle away from the raging Blue River. Figured there'd be carcasses all over the banks.

"Zeke was out there with them when he went missing. Everyone turned out to hunt for him. That included Sienna. Even with cancer eating her alive, she hitched on her pants, then headed for the door, intending to mount a horse. Didn't get far when the three of us threatened to sit on her if she stepped outside. I convinced her I could take her place. Damned near lost my life. Fool that I was, I tried to rescue a calf from the middle of that swollen, roiling river. Cort found me just before I was drowned."

"Are you suggesting Gus might've drowned?"

"Nope. He'd be too smart to get out in the middle of that river. That's why I think he's holed up until the rain eases. Or hunkered at his new homestead."

"What happened to Zeke?"

"He was found near his dead horse... both with a broken leg. Zeke put down his mount."

"Maybe God is paying me back for my no-good ways."

Lark bolted to her feet, hands firm against her hips. "Best not say that again, or I'll lose my temper." The gold in Lark's eyes glittered like torches, telling Nora she meant what she said.

If it weren't for the seriousness of the situation, Nora might've grinned at Lark's grit. No wonder her brother fell in love with her. "I don't think I've ever known you to lose your temper."

"Just know it isn't a pretty sight."

"You and my brother are well-matched."

"As are you and Gus. I'm going to see about supper. You stay put."

From her perch at the window, Nora watched. She had every intention to stay put until she couldn't any longer. Then she'd do what Lark had the courage to do. Face off the weather and anything else that got in her way.

TWENTY THREE

THE RECKONING

G US FOLLOWED THE telltale tracks until rain washed them away. The shod horse could be an Army mount or ranch horse. Thinking back to last night, he was certain he'd been watched. It made no sense that Nine Bears would look for Steven. If he were, for what purpose? Or did this have something to do with Aubrey? *He wouldn't know she'd died.*

Tugging his brim lower, water poured over his drenched coat. The shirt beneath stuck to his skin. With only jerky and a canteen of water, he had to turn back. Any tracks were gone, and besides, he was chilled to the bone. Even his horse was worn. He kneed Northern until his tail was in the wind. Ahead was a narrow stretch of trail, a wall of rock on one side and a steep draw on the other. He looked over the edge to see how the rain had turned the gully below into a river of swirling mud. Rock outcroppings jutted from the slope, making this trail even more perilous. Northern took careful, jarring steps forward.

Gus snugged his coat collar around his neck. At the same moment, his horse stepped into a water-filled hole, almost unseating him. As he regained his balance, he struggled to keep his horse from whirling in panic. The water-soaked ground sagged, then gave way beneath him. He dug his heels into his horse's flanks to urge him into a jump before the ground took them over.

About to slide with an avalanche of mud, he kicked free of his stirrups, threw his leg over the saddle, then slipped to the ground. A river of roiling black mud sent him tumbling down the slope. His boot snagged on a rock until it broke free, leaving him grasping for the tangled branch protruding from between rocks. When it slipped from his grasp, he continued his fall, as he clawed at roots, hoping to break his plunge to the bottom. With his oil cloth coat torn and twisted around his legs, he hit something sharp, then bit back a yelp of pain. With no time to consider his leg, the ground rose to meet him, hitting hard enough to knock the wind from his lungs.

CORT SAT ACROSS from Lark, Nora, and Steven at the kitchen table, food hardly touched. Zeke was the only one forking vittles into his mouth. He darted a cautious glance at his sister when he noticed her stir potatoes around her plate without eating them. At any moment, he expected her to burst into tears. Lark chattered about the miserable weather and how the children were so fretful... most likely to distract Nora.

Anyone with eyes could see that nothing would be enough to turn Nora's attention away from her worry. Zeke's stoic expression and silence were out of character. Right about now, he hoped the old man would find his usual sense of humor to break the glum mood. Steven looked to be about to push away from the table, but Cort was more than ready to stop him, even if he had to hogtie him.

"Got to say. This reminds me of that hard rainstorm we had years ago. My best horse broke his leg in that one," Zeke said.

"We remember that," Cort said. "But it isn't the time to talk about it."

Zeke cleared his throat and continued his discourse, despite Cort's warning. "Just pointin' out how weather can get out here. Bet Gus is holed up, waitin' for the rain to stop. Can't figure why he'd go out under them clouds unless something bothered him. He's too smart not to come in from the rain."

Nora stood in her poised manner, then carried her plate to the wash basin. "I'll sit a while in the parlor. Need to be alone."

As she walked by him, Cort reached for her hand and squeezed it. "We'll have all the hands out come morning. We'll find him."

"I know you will."

Her voice was flat, her back straight. She left the three of them in silence. If he thought he'd have any chance of finding Gus, it would have to wait till tomorrow after dawn. That didn't help Nora at this moment.

"I want to go out now," Steven snapped.

Cort studied Steven's taut face, giving the boy high marks for courage. "Not in this weather. Too dark, anyhow. We don't need to have more people lost or hurt. There's shelter out there, and Gus knows where to find it. You will follow my orders. Just so you know, I got one of my hands watching the barn."

Steven shoved from the table, then stomped outside.

"I intend to join you. And don't tell me I can't," Zeke rejoined.

Cort nodded. "You're old enough to make up your own mind."

"Best I get to my place and sleep. If one of you leaves me behind, you'll hear about it next time I get you in sight."

After they were alone, Lark stared across the table at him. "Cort. I'm worried."

Cort folded his arms. "That makes all of us. I'm worried on all fronts. We should be making wedding plans for my sister. Instead...." He shrugged. "And Zeke's arthritis is bad. Doc Collier already told him his heart isn't good either. Now Gus turned up missing."

"Lordy, Cort. Things were going well, and now we're back under bad luck clouds."

DAYBREAK BROUGHT CLEAR skies while the men spread out in a wide arc, searching for any signs of Gus or his horse. Cort and his men took the point, their mounts swallowed by the gullies. Steven and Reyes flanked either side of Bryce. Three of the cowhands were dispatched to search the line shacks. He leaned forward and urged his mount up the other side to the rim of a gully. At the top, he caught sight of Bryce and the boys. He waved his hat, signaling them to meet him.

After they'd gathered, Bryce asked, "You find anything yet?"

"Nope. But just so you know. Zeke is following with a wagon in case we need it."

Bryce doffed his hat and swiped his forehead with his sleeve. "Christ. I'm worried about Nora."

"Yeah. She's pacing. Not eating. Crying. Then, sitting alone on the porch. She threatened to ride out to look for him, but I've got some men keeping one eye. They'd know if she tried to saddle a horse."

Bryce sighed. "Let's get to searching. Damn rain erased any signs."

SOMEONE SAT NEAR Gus, the breathing harsh. From beneath his lashes, he searched his surroundings. Rock and mud walls were above him. Water gurgled like the Earth sucked it into its bowels. Moving his tongue inside his dry mouth, he turned his head against the hard, wet gravel beneath him, setting off white hot pain. He blinked as he searched for the watcher. He squeezed his eyes closed against the sunlight. A damp cloth touched his head, stinging his skin like bees.

"I know you are awake."

The voice was hoarse. With a slow turn of his head, he opened his eyes to see an Indian crouched beside him, a cloth in hand. "You speak English."

"Walks With Thorns teaches many. Even me." He shrugged. "She was White Hawk's wife. *My brother.*"

"Sounds like something Aubrey would do. You must be Nine Bears?"

"Yes."

"Figured it might be you sneaking around. What's your plan for me?"

"Not killing you."

Nine Bears wasn't quite able to censor his humor in the quick curve of his mouth. Gus felt like chuckling, too, but it would hurt like hell. "My horse."

"Fool to follow me. Your horse was smarter."

"How did you know I was following you?"

His eyes glittered, but he gave no reply.

"So. You must've seen me talking to Lieutenant Mabry. He told me you'd escaped."

"Yes. Followed you to the big house. Then here."

"To find my son, I expect. He's *my* blood."

"He lived with us."

"Not now. He's white."

Nine Bears gave a deep sigh. "You will treat him well. I have no home to give him."

"Do you plan to keep running?"

"They will not find me."

"They won't look for you. I can promise you that. Even though we are enemies, I owe you. That is, if you plan to help me."

Nine Bears lifted an eyebrow. With surprising abruptness, he rolled to his feet, then stalked away. Gus called out. As expected, there was no answer. Nine Bears had said all he planned to say. "Leave me my horse. If he's alive," Gus called.

The only answer was a whisper of wind while puffy white clouds crossed his vision. He closed his eyes while the world spun inside of his head. He lay there for some time, listening to the rushing water, the occasional cry of a hawk, and leaves rustling in the trees around him. His hand fell to the wet cloth beside him. Gus lifted it to his mouth, then squeezed water onto his parched lips. A fly landed on his nose, and he brushed it away. After a time, he was alerted to the sound of chomping and the swish of a tail.

With a slow turn of his head, he focused his attention on his horse, seeming unhurt. The animal nosed the sparse grass. Except for his horse, he was alone, left to fend for himself. Nine Bears had done more than he'd expected of him, in trade for Gus's implicit promise to keep his whereabouts secret.

The man's sense of honor was strong. Gus would damn well keep his word, even while they were still enemies of sorts. In exchange, Nine

Bears gave him a chance to get out of here, knowing without his horse, he'd never climb out. Somewhere, there had to be a trail because Nine Bears had found it. Now, he'd find it.

He closed his eyes for a moment. His stomach growled, reminding him that if he were to survive, he'd have to get to his horse. After he rolled to his side, he managed to sit. His canteen lay on the ground. No longer could he ignore the drumming in his head. After he swallowed more water, he ran his fingers over the lump above his eye and winced. His lower right leg looked swollen beneath his buckskin pants.

When he tried to rise, his groan sent his horse sidestepping. The animal looked toward him, ears flickering. Knowing with any sudden movement, Northern might shy away, he looked around for something to brace his leg.

"Easy, boy. Counting on you to get me home."

A stout tree limb lay on the ground. He stretched his upper body until he reached it, then dragged it back to him. Pain shot through his ankle at his movement, and he sucked in a deep breath as beads of sweat dotted his face. Gus swiped them on his torn coat sleeve. With gritted teeth, he hoisted himself up, bracing one side of his weight on the crooked limb.

No more than four strides away from him, his horse looked ready to back. If he could manage to get to the animal without scaring him, he just might be able to climb into the saddle. There was no choice. Nine Bears had decided to leave him to finish this on his own... debt paid.

His rifle was in the boot of his saddle. If he reached it, he couldn't safely fire it until out of this hole, given the chance of spooking his already nervous horse. One step. Two. His heart pounded in time with the pulse of pain in his ankle. Since he was still able to put some weight on that leg, he didn't think it was broken. Gus drew another breath, then took two more steps. His horse shook his head and stepped back.

"Whoa. Northern," he said with an even voice.

With one last step, he grasped hold of the saddle and reins with his full weight on his good left leg. All he had to do was mount without hollering. He dropped his crooked cane and settled his left boot into the stirrup. His horse's hide twitched. One good hop was all he'd ask. *Just one.* The hop sent flurries of specks across his eyes... but he was seated. His bad ankle hung against the Appaloosa's flank. Now, all he had to do was stay in the saddle.

Lifting the canteen he'd slung around his neck, he swallowed a long draft. The wet cloth lay balled on the ground. Suddenly, he heaved whatever he'd last eaten. The horse's hide rippled beneath his legs, then the animal's ears pinned back.

"I'll be all right in a minute. Easy."

Sitting atop his horse, he waited out the nausea, appraising the rock-strewn ravine. The rain had turned the bottom into a good-sized river. He turned his horse to face the slide from where he'd tumbled, estimating he'd slid fifty feet through tangled branches and rocks. The massive tree roots had broken his fall. He must have hit his head before slamming against the bottom. There wasn't any way he'd be able to get his horse up that slope without killing them both. In fact, he wondered how his horse had escaped falling with him, after the ground collapsed.

Reining the animal around, he studied the narrow passage where the water flowed. It didn't appear that deep. Nine Bears must have come from that direction. The other side of the gulch was his best chance of getting out of here. Using his left knee, he signaled his horse to move to the water. There was no time to sit and ponder how smart or stupid his idea to cross the muddy water while clinging to his horse. It had to be done.

He couldn't help the thought of Nora not forgiving him if he missed his own wedding. Determination had him latch onto the saddle as his horse lurched, then found his footing before they splashed to the opposite bank.

Once there, he faced yet another obstacle—a wall of wet mud. He followed Nine Bears's tracks, leaning forward in the saddle and giving his mount freedom to carry him to the top, while he groaned with each swing of his right leg.

At the top, his horse yanked at the bit, anxious to move into a faster pace. He held the horse back and looked skyward, breathing in great draughts of air. Above the cottonwoods and junipers, fringed-winged vultures swooped and dove. They'd been deprived of the meal of Gus Quaid. Now would be the time to fire three shots if he thought he wouldn't spook his horse.

Nudging his horse into a walk, he headed in the general direction of the ranch compound and hoped someone would find him before he lost consciousness. The sun was high in the azure sky as his head dropped forward, his chin almost touching his chest. If it weren't for the rocking motion of his horse, he would've fallen asleep in the saddle and dropped into unconsciousness. Hungry and tired, there was nothing to do but keep moving. Nine Bears had taken his jerky. *Owed him that much. And maybe more.*

The sun beat down, yet he shivered. The terrain looked familiar but his vision blurred. He slumped forward and then shook himself awake. A flock of grasshopper sparrows took flight, sending his horse into a sideways dance while he gripped the pommel. Flickers of gray spots were in his vision. Shivering with fever, he clasped hold of his rifle, then slipped to the ground, managing to keep hold of the reins even as the horse tugged.

On his knees, he pointed the rifle skyward, firing off three shots. His horse yanked the reins from his hold, which sent him tumbling backward. He rested on his back with his rifle at his side. Then waited.

———————————

CORT'S BODY JERKED at the sudden sound of three successive gunshots. He cast a look toward Bryce, who'd stood up in his stirrups, scanning the horizon for any sign of Gus. Zeke's wagon bumped over the grass, coming to a halt to allow Reyes and Steven to leap to the ground. The boys untied their horses from the rear of the wagon and mounted. Steven set his horse into a ground-eating gallop, leaving the others to follow.

Northern was the first to come into Cort's view. Head down, the horse nosed grass and swished his tail. Just beyond the animal, he spied a tall man sprawled amid the Indian grass, face to the sky. Steven dismounted before Cort's horse came to a skidding stop.

"Pa!" Steven shouted, dropping to his knees beside his father.

By that time, the rest had surrounded him. Cort pressed his hand against Gus's chest to determine whether they found a sick man or a corpse. Gus opened his eyes, then looked from one face to the other. The lump on his head and his blank expression had Cort worried.

"It's us. Get you into a wagon, then home before you know it," Cort said.

"Thirsty."

Cort tipped a canteen to Gus's mouth. "Don't take too much, or you might vomit your guts out."

"Already did."

"Christ," Bryce snapped. "What the hell happened?"

Cort shot a steely glare toward his brother. "This isn't the time to talk about particulars."

Steven sat beside his father's head. "I'm here, Pa."

"I'm tough. Took a fall but don't think anything broken."

Zeke pulled up in the wagon, then slowly stepped down from the seat, pain etched on the old man's face. *Damnable arthritis.* A premonition passed through Cort, but he shrugged it aside. Running his hand along Gus's ankle, he figured it was either broken or twisted.

Zeke bent over Gus. "You look a sight."

"Stink too. Headache. Think my right ankle might be wrenched. Don't think broke. Hit my head. Horse set me on my ass. Slid into a steep ravine."

"Shit. We might've looked till August and not found ya down there," Zeke quipped.

"Let's get him into the wagon," Cort ordered. "Collier will need to look at the bump and your ankle. Maybe other stuff by the looks of the torn coat."

"Reyes!" Bryce called. "Tangle and Billy are somewhere near. You and Steven find one of them to go for the doctor."

Once the boys rode off, the men hefted Gus into the wagon, all while he cussed at the pain. After an hour of slow driving, the wagon drew up at the house where five glassy-eyed women stood sentinel on the porch. Cort dropped from the back of the wagon to catch hold of Nora as she flew down the steps toward the wagon. "No, you don't. Go inside. *All of you*. Get a bed ready. He's unconscious. You can see to him once we get him into the house."

Just as Cort expected, his feisty sister tried to shove past him. He blocked her way. Cort glared at her. "What we gotta' do is going to hurt like the Devil's pitchfork. Best time is when he's unconscious."

Understanding seemed to sink in at his words. He waited while Lark led Nora inside the house, the other women following. Once they were out of earshot, he did what he'd done many times over the years— set the twisted ankle and hope it wasn't broken. Or done more damage.

AS THEY CARRIED him up the stairs, Gus mumbled the word whiskey.

Zeke proffered the bottle of Cort's best stock. "Didn't think you liked whiskey."

"Do now." Gus swigged, then swiped his mouth.

"Pain killer. Use it myself on a daily basis," Zeke said.

"Nora? She's here."

Cort stepped close to the bed. "An army of women is about to descend with broth, soap, and stuff you don't want to know about."

"Don't want her to see me like this."

Cort snorted. "Figure you got no choice. Besides. She already saw you. She's tough. Besides, she most likely saw bruised-up faces before."

"Steven?"

"He's with Reyes up at Zeke's house. The hands are keepin' them busy for now."

"Cards, I'm guessin'."

Zeke chuckled. "Tangle, Billy, and Mason don't know how to play checkers. You about ready for us to get the pants and shirt off?"

"Not in front of the women. Got some pride."

THAT NIGHT, NORA and Steven sat beside him, her hand clutching his. He didn't care for all the coddling, but her touch sure felt good. Steven sat in stoic silence. Theresa and Lark visited with a bowl of broth and cool cloths for his head. One cowhand after another formed a visitor procession. Now he knew what a corpse felt like at a wake, if corpses still had enough energy to pay attention. Groggy, he fought sleep as long as he could before he dropped off.

When sunlight streamed through the window, he was forced to study the room from beneath slitted lids. From the other side of the door, there were whispered conversations. *Her* voice. *And Collier.* After the door opened, the doctor entered with Nora close behind—the man's expression tolerant.

"You're awake. That's a good sign," Collier said.

"I'm awake."

Nora stood at the opposite side of the bed. "Alfred is here to check your ankle and that bump on your head."

Alfred is it? Not Doctor Collier. It was plain to Gus how Collier felt about Nora. Apparently, Nora just as soon ignore the man's attention. But he didn't.

The doctor got right to work with his trade tools. He opened his bag, then brought out his stethoscope and roll of cotton bandaging. Wordless, Collier listened to his heart, then his chest. Lifting the edge of the sheet, he grasped his ankle, turning it. Gus braced for the pain, refusing to make one whimper in front of *her* or him. Instead, he gritted his teeth until the pain shot into his leg.

There was no swallowing the yelp and had to wonder of the good physician had done that on purpose. He hated the idea of having to depend on this man—the man who didn't hide his affections for Nora. She had no idea of her effect on men.

Alfred Collier snapped his bag closed. "That bump on your head is of concern. It should heal with a good-sized bruise. Might have some headaches for a while. Is your sight blurred?"

"Nope. I see plain enough." He looked from her to the doctor.

"Any headache right now?"

"A little. Comes and goes."

"Then I'm not too concerned about the head. In fact, I count you as one lucky man. Your leg and ankle are badly bruised. Suspect you have a sprained ankle that will be sore for quite some time. Avoid walking for the next few weeks. Use crutches. If it pains you to put weight on it, most likely you have a fracture. We can wait and see."

"Guess I should be relieved."

"Like I said. You're damned lucky. Mind telling how it happened?"

"Headed down a trail in a heavy rain. My horse balked. I tried to dismount to lead him. But the ground beneath me collapsed and sent me over the edge of the slope, rocks and mud tumbling with me. Snagged my leg on some roots which broke my fall. Don't know how long I was out cold. My horse somehow avoided the fall."

"How'd you get to your horse?"

"Alfred, you're asking far too many questions, don't you think?" Nora interceded.

"I'm curious. *Aren't you?*" One corner of the doctor's mouth curved upward in a faint smile.

"Maybe you should ask my horse."

Nora's gaze darted from the doctor back to him.

Her expression warned him.

"Managed to get off three shots. Help came running."

"I see. I'll leave laudanum in case you're in pain. Be back in a few weeks to see how you're coming along. They can send for me if the swelling doesn't go down by then."

"Thanks, Doc. I'll see you get paid once I get to my saddlebag."

"No hurry. But Nora... I really wouldn't mind that coffee and pie before I head out."

"Of course. I'll be downstairs in a few minutes."

The door closed behind the doctor. In the silence, she took a seat on the edge of his bed. "You don't like him much, do you? Mind explaining."

"Why would you think that? Especially since he as much as admitted to vying for your affections. While I was gone. Right on the front porch."

"I've told you I have no interest in him as a suitor. Can't you let it drop?"

"He's educated and looked up to."

"You went to Boston College. You're a valued Army scout, and your reputation is something books are written about. Stop comparing yourself to him. You're the only man I love. And we've already...."

When her face turned apple red, he filled in the rest for her. "Already been intimate."

"Now you're being crude."

He rested his head back and sighed. "Crude would be sex."

She stood, starting away from him until he grasped her wrist. "I'm frustrated. Our wedding has been on hold for the second time, and that pisses me off. When? Set a date."

"I'll have that preacher here as fast as I can get a message to him. In the meantime, please put Alfred out of your mind. He's a friend."

"Well, *your friend* is waiting downstairs for you. Better get him that pie and send him on his way." She pecked his mouth with a sweet little kiss, leaving him to stew in his self-pity, which he hated.

TWENTY FOUR

THE UGLY PAST

Four Weeks Later

"OF ALL THE damned stubborn mules. What are you doing?" Nora scolded.

"Hobbling." A grin plastered his bearded face.

"You came down the stairs with a crutch?"

"I guess I did. Seeing as I'm here. Alfred, as you remind me, told me I could get around without splints so long as I use my crutch."

"Think that you could make it to the kitchen table? For some coffee, that is."

"No pie?"

"Cake. No pie. And you are *still jealous.*"

"A little."

She harrumphed, then marched like a soldier along the hallway, leaving him to limp behind her. He dropped onto a chair while she took his crutch. Theresa glanced across her shoulder and offered him a brief smile before attending to her cooking. After Nora poured coffee, she slid the cup to his reach. Then his gaze followed her to where she cut a thick slice of cake.

He stewed over the fact she hadn't brought up the subject of their wedding for at least the last two weeks. By now, it had become a sore spot he kept rubbing till it hurt. After she set the plate and fork in front of him, he looked up to see that little twitch on her lip that usually meant she had something on her mind.

"Anything botherin' you?" he asked as he shoveled a chunk of cake into his mouth.

He was met with silence. Lifting his eyes, he lowered the fork. "Spit it out. What's goin' on?" Theresa cleared her throat, then left the room.

"Your new barn is up, and between your two men and some of the Enders's crew, the house is framed. Tangle filled me in."

"Is that something you're worried about?"

"You insist I'm worried when I'm not."

He waited. "All right. What's Steven up to? Haven't seen him."

"He spends most of his time at Bryce's house. Hannah teaches both him and Reyes. Those boys are fast friends. Beyond that, he spends a good amount of time with your horses."

"So that's not what's bothering you."

"No. I'm fine. Bryce is taking me and Theresa to Ogallala for some supplies. Be away about five days."

"Christ. Nora, I don't like you going there alone."

"I won't be alone. My brother will be there. Besides, Lark gave me a long shopping list."

Dropping his fork, he scrubbed his face with his hands before looking in her direction again. "So long as you take a gun with you."

"I always do."

After she'd left, he thought about how rattled she seemed. Something was wrong, and he aimed to find out what.

———————

NORA SAT BESIDE Bryce while he guided the team into a faster gait while she and Theresa settled into a companionable silence. More and more, she felt the specter of her past. Maybe she should have told Gus a long time ago. They were getting married in a little more than a week, and she still hadn't admitted to what she'd done. The truth was, she'd lied to Gus. How would he react if he found out she'd married Connor O'Malley and then killed him? *A rather big omission to have to forgive.*

Connor hadn't loved her because he'd been incapable of love. After she shot him, she never looked back to find out if he were dead—too numb and scared over what she'd done. *And if she admitted this to Gus... he'd hate her.* She'd already faced his disappointment when he'd found out she'd kept her name from him.

The thought gnawed that she might be wanted for murder. Was she a widow with a price on her head? If Connor were still alive, she had no right to marry Gus. She looked toward Bryce, his eyes on the team. Her big brother might be the only one to help her decide what to do—after he got over his fury.

GUS ROCKED ON the porch... right alongside Zeke. If there was one thing he liked about Zeke, it was that the old man was as straightforward as they came, a fixture on the ranch. Reyes hung onto the man's every word, and now, even Steven had begun looking up to the old-timer.

Zeke pulled a flask from inside his coat pocket, then swigged. "Care for a gulp?"

"I'm not much for whiskey this early in the day."

Zeke nodded before tucking it away. "Eases pain for me. How's your ankle?"

"Better all the time."

"You and Nora ever gettin' hitched? I'm sure wantin' to make my special bourbon punch."

"After she returns from town, I plan to press that issue. Got a ranch that needs my attention. Heard the barn and two corrals are done. The house is still going up, but we'll manage."

"Uh-huh. Well, not that's it's my business. But a lieutenant Jim Mabry stopped by with about five others. Had a message for you."

Gus's back stiffened. Christ. Had they found Nine Bears?

"What did he want?"

"Said he lost the trail of the Indian he was lookin' for. Thought you might've run across him. Told him you was laid up with a bad ankle."

"Don't know any more than he does."

"That's what I said. But I don't think your horse found his way down into that gully to rescue you without help."

Gus darted a glance in his direction. "You're pretty smart. I'd like to keep that information quiet. The Indian is important to Steven. And, much as I don't like to admit it, I owe the man my life. Keep it under your hat."

"I won't say nothin' at all. I got no real issue with Indians. Leastways, not anymore."

"Did Mabry have anything else to say?"

"Handed me an envelope addressed to Nora. Thought it kinda' odd."

Zele reached into his pocket, then pulled out the folded envelope, handing it over. Gus tucked it inside his coat pocket, sensing what was in the note was the source of her strange worry. In fact, he was vexed at Mabry's interest in his intended bride. More important, what was his intent?

"I'll see she gets it. Why didn't you give it to *her?*"

"Came by yesterday. She wasn't here. But thought you'd want to know. Hope it ain't bad news."

"Expect not. All her family is here." Still, Gus's fingers itched to open it. It concerned him that it might have something to do with Silas. While he gave thought to destroying the missive, he thought better of it.

"CHRIST! NORA... I swear to you my hand hankers to turn you over my knee. Bad enough you didn't tell me. *Married?* You mean you haven't told Gus?"

"I shot Connor after he hit me and tried to keep me from leaving. It was the only thing I could do. I think he's dead, and I'm a free woman."

"*Free?* If anyone found out about this... that you'd killed your husband, you could wind up in prison or worse. If he lived, then you're a married woman. If Gus finds out you kept this from him…."

Her brother's face was mottled with red rage. But she needed his help. "What should I do?"

"Get on with your life, for one thing. No matter how this turns out, Cort and me will stand by you. One thing for sure, I'm going to talk with Marcus Layton. He's a damn good attorney who'd hire a detective to do some snooping about Connor. It won't be pretty, nor pleasant. In the meantime, you tell Gus. *Everything.* He deserves to know. You should've been straight up about it before now. The man loves you. He'll get over this given some time."

"Oh, God. Bryce… I already kept my real name from him. He'll never believe anything again."

His arm tucked her against his side as they walked toward the restaurant where they planned to eat supper. Her appetite was gone. All she wanted to do was curl into a ball and cry.

As they ate in silence, she lifted her eyes and gazed at Bryce. His mouth quirked. There was no doubt Bryce was irritated by this turn of events. Finding out your sister might be a murderess couldn't be sitting well. She cleared her throat. "I'll tell him. As soon as we return."

He nodded. "So you know, once you're settled in your room, I'm heading for the saloon. I need a few beers."

"There was a time when I would've joined you."

———

WITH A SIDELONG glance at the torn envelope on the bedside table, he lifted the whiskey bottle and swigged. He'd lied to Zeke. Whenever whiskey was called for, he'd drink his fill. His better judgment betrayed him when he'd opened the note. Her story burned into him like a branding iron. *Married. Mrs. Connor O'Malley.* The woman he'd loved had shot her husband. In fact, she'd killed him if Mabry were to be believed.

He wanted her here. *Now.* This was a confrontation he yearned for.

The *good* lieutenant had known her in New Orleans. A sick disillusion-ment slithered through his gut and coiled there.

Forgetting the crutch, he paced, bottle in hand. His ankle pained him, but his thoughts of her pained him more. He wanted to shake her. The woman he loved was a liar. She'd managed to make him feel like a fool with her deceptions.

Lark had left a platter without her usual warm greeting. Cort walked in afterward, then tried to coax out what was bothering him... without success. No one understood his brooding. This was between him and his intended. Alone with his fury, he considered what was to be done about *her*. To think he'd been worried about Collier as her suit-or seemed almost laughable. Everything had soured.

It seemed he wouldn't be taking a wife, after all. Not so long as *she* had a husband somewhere. He pushed the crutch across the room. *Maybe she and Alfred were lovers.* For his trouble, Mabry would see his fist if they crossed paths again. *What was his game? What was in this for him? Why had Mabry reminded her about her past?*

———————

THERE WAS A light tap against the door. He opened his eyes and clenched his teeth. Sitting with his back against the headboard, he braced for the battle. "Come in," he barked.

When the door opened, she stepped inside, then closed it behind her. After she turned to face him, he saw her eyes were damp and overly bright. She licked her lips, looking like she'd prepared what she might say to him. Was this about her trip to town or her confession of deceit? One thing for sure, she looked scared.

He regarded her pretty green dress with a dainty white collar. So innocent looking, and for a moment, he wanted to forget her past. Far different than the prim black dresses she'd worn at their first encounter in a Fort Benton saloon. The black dress was more like the woman who stood before him—married and murderess. A liar. How many men had she duped? God. *He couldn't believe he'd been so wrong.*

Twisting her fingers against her stomach, she stood straight and waited. Her lip twitched while she offered him a faint smile. He crooked his finger, inviting her to come closer. She did, with slow, hesitant steps. "You look sullen. What's wrong?" she asked.

His jaw muscles taut, he ground his teeth, choosing each word carefully. "Have a seat. Tell me about your trip." His heart thundered in his chest as he waited.

She dragged the chair beside the bed, then sat. Those heart-stopping eyes regarded him before her lids lowered. She stared at her folded hands while the sound of his own blood in his ears drowned out his reason. He wanted to stop her from speaking, loathing her lies. But he also wanted to believe this was all some mistake.

"I figure you're upset with me. Is this about Alfred?"

"*Alfred?*" That man was the least of the problems. He sucked in a long breath, then did his best to keep his voice level when he continued. "No. *Not Alfred.*"

"I have something to tell you and hope you hear me out."

"I'm listening."

"There's something I should have told you a long while back. But I was afraid. Not that it matters saying I'm sorry. Just let me finish the whole story before interrupting."

When he remained quiet, she cleared her throat. He nodded. "Go on."

"After my brothers and father left for the war, my mother and I struggled to keep food on the table. She got very sick. Pneumonia, I suspect. After she died, I was left alone at sixteen, just as the war ended. I had no idea if my brothers were coming home. After waiting for months, I assumed they'd been killed."

She paused. His jaw ticked with impatience. "Finish."

"Connor O'Malley came along. You already know part of the story. Not all of it. He had an Irish accent and was always smiling. With his curly brown hair and twinkling blue eyes, he managed to convince me he loved me. Promised we'd have a good life together. We left, even as I wondered why we couldn't stay right where we were. He found an itinerant preacher to say the words. Then we arrived in New Orleans. That's where I found what he meant by a good life. It may have been for him, but not for me."

Where Gus sat at the edge of the bed, he dropped his head, not able to look at her or be drawn into her eyes. Shoulders hunched, he stared hard at the floor. "Continue."

"The horrid experience changed me forever. At first, he used his fist to keep me in line. Until the day came when I decided to run. He found me leaving with what little money I had stolen from his pockets... he hit me. I shot him. I'd bought a derringer just the day before. Not wanting to be caught, I ran—not knowing if he were dead or alive. I never looked back."

By that time, Gus lifted his head and pinched the bridge of his nose. Anger was tempered with how naïve she'd been. And how used. If what she told him was true, he pitied her.

"I'd like to kill him, myself. But none of what you're telling me changes the fact you kept it from me. After I'd asked you to marry me, you never once said, 'By the way, I'm legally married.' After I'd proclaimed my love, you lied. Now you tell me you killed a man, deserved or not. How do you suppose I can ever trust you?"

"Over the years, lies became part of surviving. I'd understand if you won't forgive me. But please try to understand my reasoning. I was so young and foolish. That doesn't change the fact I love you. That's all I can say."

"I've never given you reason to distrust me or my intentions. Building a life with you? I just don't know if I can forgive you. But *this...* is unforgivable. I was about to marry a woman who may still be married. Or a murderess. So you know, I'd already found out about Connor before you stepped into this room."

"Bryce wouldn't have told you. How did you find out? Who?"

He lifted one corner of his mouth in a sad smile. *"Bryce knew?* But you couldn't tell me?"

"I confided in him just two days ago, in Ogallala."

Gus picked up the note he'd read and reread until his eyes hurt. Crushing the paper in his fist, he threw it across the room. "Lieutenant Mabry stopped by and left the letter. Seems he recognized you. Was he a customer, *Tori?* He sure knew Connor O'Malley. Thought he'd let you know. *For old times' sake?* What his motive is, I can't say. Maybe you spurned him. Maybe he figured on getting money from you to keep it quiet. It doesn't matter."

Her tear-filled eyes sent him bolting from the edge of the bed. *Why had he said such mean, hurtful things to a woman who'd taken root inside of him?* At the moment, he'd like to slam his fist into the wall. He'd sure put his fist into that trouble-making soldier once he found him. Drawing in a breath, all he could do his stare at her. But the woman he saw was Tori.

"I'm sorry for saying some of the things I said to you, Nora. I can't talk about this right now. I've been kicked in the gut."

Nora gazed at the floor. "You called me *Tori.* That's how you must think of me. Once a whore, always a whore. Isn't that what you think? How many more times should I entertain you in bed before we call us even?"

Flexing his fists at his sides, fury welled, threatening to explode. The woman knew how to slice him to ribbons. She turned, then ran past him to reach the door, tears streaming down her cheeks. Just before she opened it, her back straightened. Gus was too raw to offer an apology for his awful words. Her next words gutted him.

"Tori will be waiting for you tonight. Then we'll call us even. I expect you'll be leaving for *your* new home. At least it offers distance between us."

"If you need me, I'll be working on finishing the house. One thing you got wrong... Nora. I've never thought of you like *that.* Never."

After the door slammed, her keening cry froze him and grabbed his heart. He limped across the room, leaned his back against the wall, then slid to the floor. How long he stared at the ceiling, he didn't know. Shadows filled the room when he got to his feet. Stuffing his belongings into his bag, he'd decided to round up Steven and move into his half-built ranch.

Gus, you stupid son of a bitch. What have you done to the woman you professed to love?

————————

THE DAY WAS sunny. Damn, how she hated the cheerfulness of it when gloom engulfed her inside and out. She'd lost him. Lost a future. She was inconsolable no matter how understanding each of the family members were. Oh, God. Loving this man had been a foolish dream.

Bryce's regard flitted across her face with an *I told you so expression*. Cort avoided the house in favor of his cows. Theresa brought her favorite foods only to find them uneaten. And Nita combed out her tangles, then spread out her dress, offering to sit with her on the porch. While dear Lark and Hannah admonished her that Gus would come to his senses, she ignored them all in favor of keeping to herself. In the mirror was a puffy-eyed woman who'd aged since he'd left without a goodbye.

Holding his pillow to her nose, it still smelled of him, even after more than a week. A sweet-pungent scent of whiskey pervaded the room. She still envisioned Gus and Steven leaving on the buckboard with two Appaloosas tethered behind. Posting herself at the window, she had watched until they'd become dots on the grassy slope. Lark's words replayed in her head. *He'll calm down. Then he'll come to his senses. That man loves you.* Now, sitting alone in her room, she heard the door open and close. Lark stood inside of the door.

"I knocked. You didn't answer, so I decided to come in."

"I was lost in thought, is all."

"*Gus.* I'd like to strangle him. But Cort knows him as well as anyone. He said he'll stew for a bit, then realize he's been a horse's patoot. Then be back."

"I can't count on that. Brought it on myself, and I have to live with my mistakes. Can you ask Cort if he'd do me a favor?"

"We'd do anything. Name it."

"I need to know for certain whether Connor O'Malley is dead. Else someday, he might come knocking on this door."

"Bryce already thought of that. Hired a detective through our attorney. No one needs to know about it. Better than that, Cort sent word to the commanding officer at Fort Sidney to find out about Lieutenant Mabry. Cort's killing mad. Best not show his face around here again."

"All of this would've come out sooner or later, Lark. Please don't let Cort get involved."

"We're a family, and we stand together. You up to baking? I always bake if my mind is heavy."

"Maybe another time. I think I'll join Zeke on the porch for a bit."

"I'm worried about him. Doesn't seem himself. He'd be glad for your company."

Tucking loose tendrils behind her ears, Nora stepped outside to the shaded veranda, taking note of Zeke sitting in one of the rockers. The smell of Lark's roses drifted on the breeze, blended with sweet tobacco curling from Zeke's pipe. Between that and the sweet smell of grass, she leaned against the rail, her gaze taking in the majesty of the place.

"Never gets old watching this, does it, Zeke?"

"Nope. Had me taken at the first look."

She studied the kindly man with a heart bigger than a mountain. Zeke's beard was thicker than she recalled, and his eyes were sunken. The flesh along his high cheekbones was ruddy.

"How are you feeling?"

He pulled the stem of his pipe from his mouth, then set it on the floor beside his chair. "Figured you'd get to that question. Don't need the ladies fussing around me. I'm doin' as fine as any old man would be doin' at my age. Doc Collier left me some medicine. Harpin' about seein' some doctor in Omaha. Hell. I got no interest in a long train ride. Besides, nobody lives forever."

"Maybe you and Cort could go there together."

"Tangle, he'd be more company than Cort. Grouchy lately."

"I've managed to stir up things. I'm sorry my past just won't leave me alone. Wish I'd decided to leave here rather than cause trouble."

"Hell. You ain't caused trouble, gal. That Gus has me pissed off. If I was younger, I'd take a swing at his nose. You can take my word he'll be back with his tail between his legs."

"He was right to be angry. I lied to him. By omission. Still, he deserved the truth."

"Me. Heard some of the story... the part about you once bein' married. I'm guessin' you were never married anyhow. Gus hobbled down those stairs and slammed out of the door. Expect you was cryin' your eyes out. Never saw that man so mad, but bet he was madder than you. I won't pry into how or why you got hitched years ago, but Gus is crazy about you. He just needs to put his fool pride back on straight."

"I'm telling you that soldier recognized me. If not him, then it might be someone else."

"Some men like to ruin things for others. Might have nothin' to do with you and everything to do with this ranch and what the Enders stand for. Gus had no business openin' a letter meant for you. I should'a kept it for you. Either way, he had no right. But maybe it'll work out for the best."

She hunkered in front of Zeke. "You're a good man, Zeke Waterson. You don't fool me."

"Wish I was younger. I'd ask you to dance with me. Might even pluck some posies to give you."

"He called me *Tori*. My other name. The one I'd used to protect the Enders name. Now, I've made a mess."

"You were never *her*. That was another woman. I know Gus can be a mule-head, but he has a big heart. Once he calms down, he'll figure he'd made one helluva mistake. This isn't just about you tellin' the truth. It's his pride. Give him a little time. Then you go find him and make him listen. He will. I know it in my old bones."

"You are a very wise and forgiving man. Don't think anyone around here could hold a candle to you. Including my brothers."

"That's horse dung. Don't go slinging those words near the cowboys, or I won't live it down."

Zeke grinned, and it occurred she'd never seen him smile. He was good medicine as well as the backbone of this ranch. "Were you ever married, Zeke?"

"Only in my head. She's buried up on the hill beside her husband, Wade. *My best friend.* Gave them time to be together. When it's my time to leave here, I get to lay beside her. This ranch and all the people on it are my family. Especially Reyes. He's like my own grandson."

She squeezed his thin hand between hers, not able to keep her mouth from trembling. There was a sadness in his smile. "Don't you dare think about dying. We need you."

"Too pretty to cry over me. You best go inside and get supper on. I might even join you tonight at that table." He wagged his finger. "And I plan to watch you marry Gus. Everybody expects my bourbon punch."

TWENTY FIVE

UNFORGIVABLE

SITTING ATOP A beautiful, smoky black mare, Nora rode beside the buckboard, rejoicing at the sunlit air. Cort drove the wagon, seated beside Theresa, neither of them their usual perky selves. Thinking back to last night's meal, Zeke had done most of the jawing about the changes in the ranch. Everyone navigated clear of mentioning Gus.

"Shouldn't we be getting close to town?" she called.

"About an hour. You doin' all right?"

"Yes."

"Didn't know how well you rode. Till now."

"Back in Virginia City, had my own horse."

"The one you're ridin' is yours."

"Cort, thank you. She's a beauty."

"Bryce's idea. Besides, everyone needs to be able to ride on my ranch."

Theresa harrumphed. "My backside is goin' to be sore. Once we get there, I'm goin' to get myself a hot bath."

Nora laughed. "Sounds like a fine idea, Theresa."

By the time they'd reached town, Nora had begun to wilt in the saddle. Like Theresa, her backside was a mite sore. Darned if she'd admit to it, though. Cort guided the wagon as far as Geist's Ogallala Hotel, then after he'd seen them both settled in, he left them to their plans.

Theresa leaned in close to her. "Cort. He's off to Tuck's Saloon to have a drink."

Nora grinned. After being a saloon owner, she'd never fault a man for taking a few drinks. Especially not her own brother. "Well. I like your idea of a hot bath. Got to admit, haven't spent that long in a saddle since...." *Gus.*

Inside the sun-dappled room, she looked at herself in the cracked mirror. Her plait had come loose and her skin was sun-browned after having helped in Lark's garden. As she stared at her reflection, his words returned. *Tori.* He'd called her Tori. She brushed her hair with more vigor than needed, the crackling with each stroke mimicking her mood. In short, his tirade had cut her deep.

Once she'd changed into a clean dress, she set out for the town, her reticule in hand. As she strolled toward the end of the street, her gaze fixed on a buckboard in front of the mercantile when she noticed a group of four soldiers who'd crossed the street, moving in the opposite direction. Relieved, she released the breath she held. *What if one of them was Mabry?*

She stiffened, then ducked back into the shadows, waiting until they'd gotten out of sight. When she was sure they were gone, she stepped inside the Sanderson's store to the sound of the jangling bell, grateful to have found safe haven.

"Hello there, Nora." The diminutive gray-haired woman with sparkling blue eyes beneath thick spectacles looked toward her over bolts of fabrics.

"Good to see you again. Didn't think you'd remember me, Missus Sanderson."

"Saints alive. I seldom forget a face. Now, what can I get for you?"

"I've brought a list from Lark. She's home with the little ones." Reaching into her reticule, she handed it over. Glory read over the list and nodded.

"I'll get these things together while you look around. Did Cort come along with you?"

"Yes. Plan to head back tomorrow."

"Just holler if you need anything else. We can have this ready. Macon can load it."

Nora found herself dawdling between the massive shelves, finding every kind of cooking utensil, from knives to hand grinders. Even had some dresses and men's pants. After the bell jangled again, she peeked around the corner of the shelf, hoping she wouldn't run into soldiers, although Mabry might not even be among them. Her mouth dropped open at the appearance of Steven, who'd headed for the counter, with no sign of Gus. Lifting her chin, she strode toward the boy, her heart pumping like a train engine. His eyes widened at the sight of her.

"Miss Enders. Didn't see you."

"How are you?"

"Good. Rather be at the ranch, though."

"That's understandable. You look like you've had a haircut, and you're wearin' new clothes."

"My father saw to it."

"He's well?"

"Still limps some."

"Where is he? I would have thought he'd be busy working on his new ranch house. How is it coming along?"

"You should come see. The walls are up. Doors and windows are in. Had to order more lumber and nails."

"Will you be leaving soon?"

"Maybe today. Maybe tomorrow. That's our buckboard out in front."

"Will you tell him I asked after him?"

"I will."

"In the meantime... what were you here for?"

"Pipe tobacco. He's over at the livery talkin' about ordering new saddles for the men he's hiring. He calls it dickering. Told me to come get his pipe tobacco."

"Dickering means to haggle. I'm sure he's good at it."

Her smile faded when the bell chimed again. This time, she confronted the very man she had wanted to avoid—wearing an impertinent sneer on his face. She clamped down on her back teeth. The urge to slap his face had her flex her fingers. There was no hiding from him. His eyes grazed her from head to foot. Then he bowed.

"Miss Enders. Lieutenant Mabry, at your service."

Then he had the audacity to wink. "Steven. Why don't you join your father? This man and I have some business to talk about." The boy's stare shifted from her to center on Mabry before he stormed out of the store.

"If you'll excuse me. I want nothing to do with you, Lieutenant."

"I do have business to discuss. In private. You read the letter."

"I did."

He grasped her arm, but she yanked free. "State your case right here. I won't go anywhere with you."

"You didn't recognize me at that Indian encampment. But I knew you were Nora O'Malley of New Orleans. Connor's wife."

"Not any longer."

"You shot him. Hear he died. You know what that makes you?"

"Again. What do you want?" She looked around, and thus far, Glory was out of earshot.

"Money. Gold. That Gus Quaid has his own little gold mine, I heard. He'd be willing to pay whatever I want to keep me from telling this whole town you're a trollop who killed her husband. Might get a reward."

"I won't be blackmailed."

The soldier's eyes narrowed. He lifted his hand just as she stepped back to avoid the blow. The bell jangled again, and this time, it was followed by the click of a gun hammer.

"Let her go and step back." Gus's modulated voice was deadly smooth. "Nora. Get behind me."

As she moved around Gus, their gazes held. Gus slipped his revolver into his holster, and anything Mabry was about to say ended with Gus's powerful punch, sending the man backward against the table, where he slid to the floor.

Glory and Macon were already behind the counter, Macon with his revolver leveled at the soldier. Mabry struggled to his feet, moved his jaw, then stood. When he made the mistake of taking a step forward, Gus levered several hard blows to the man's midsection, sending Mabry to his knees, groaning.

"Gus! Stop. Please."

Gus reached for him, then dragged the dazed man to his feet. Mabry's bloodied face and dull eyes told her that the man was in no condition to walk or talk. "Listen, so I don't have to say it again. You ever come near Nora again... *I will kill you.* If you figured on getting money from me, her brothers, or her, you'll regret the day you were born. So you know, I already know what was in the letter. Not hard to figure out what you wanted. If you set foot on Enders and Quaid land, you'll be sorry you ever did. Do you understand?"

While she rested an arm around Steven's shoulders, Jim Mabry's dispassionate, hate-filled gaze turned to her. "Yes," he mumbled. "Still won't change who she is."

Gus shoved him backward. "Stay away from me and mine. I'll see that your commanding officer knows what went on. You won't wear a uniform for long."

Mabry picked up his hat, then hobbled out the door, bent with pain. Gus turned on her, his glare unrelenting. Steven stepped back when Gus gripped her arm, then led her outside, brooking no argument.

"Where are we going?" she asked.

Steven's bootsteps tramped behind them.

Ignoring her question, he spoke over his shoulder. "Steven. Go check our wagon, then stay at the stable for a bit. I need to speak with Nora in private."

Once they grew closer to the doorway of the hotel, his grip loosened. "Just what are you doing here?" he growled.

She was held hostage by his frankly assessing regard. "I'm here with Cort and Theresa. You ought to know we occasionally need provisions."

He nodded. "Let's hope your brother doesn't find out what happened until we get a chance to talk. Got to keep watch in case Mabry's friends decide to exact revenge. I'm a good fighter. Don't know about four against one. What number is your room?"

"Nine."

———————

GUS WASN'T IN a social mood when he saw Cort walking toward them. He sure as hell didn't need a lecture about Nora. He'd already fallen into a pit of misery without being reminded.

"Haven't had much time to come see how your place is comin' along," Cort said in a way of greeting. "From the look of it, somethin' is goin' on. What is it?"

Gus felt her eyes watching him. "Nora and me have some talkin' to do. It's between us. No lecture from you is necessary, Cort."

"All right. She's a grown woman and can make her own decisions."

"That settled. I need a favor. Take my buckboard to the livery. Steven is there. Keep an eye on him."

"Sure."

At that moment, a stream of folks were running in the direction of the group of soldiers, half-dragging Mabry to the physician's office.

Cort raised one eyebrow. "Mabry?"

"I took care of what needed to be taken care of."

"So... that's what this is all about. I'll see what I can do to fix it. Turns out, the marshal isn't in town."

———————

SHE DIDN'T REMEMBER being squired up the stairway. Her head was spinning with what happened. Moreover, Gus's vicious side had been in full view of Steven. He took the key from her reticule, and once inside, he tossed both to the bed. She sat in a chair, then settled her head in her hands, not wanting to think, fighting the urge to cry.

Gus hunkered in front of her and drew her shaking hands away from her face, then lifted her chin with his finger. "I wish I could take back most of what I said. I was wrong. I've been sick over it. Figured I'd finish the house and then come begging you to forgive me. No more lies or secrets between us. God, how I hate Connor O'Malley. I'd kill him, myself. We can keep this all quiet. No one will ever come after you."

"*He* knows. He'll tell authorities just to get even."

"Not if he's a dead man, he won't."

"No, Gus. I won't let you do that. Before I'd let you get into that kind of trouble, I'd turn myself in."

"How 'bout we just see how it plays out?"

"There's enough blame to go around, Gus. So you know, Bryce has a detective searching for Connor O'Malley. We haven't heard anything yet."

"Once we do, will you be my wife? I can't wait any longer. Missing you is driving me crazy. That house I built will be mighty lonely without you in it." He touched her quivering mouth. "I love you."

His boyish grin lifted one corner of his mouth beneath his beard. His arms came around her then their lips met. He leaned away, tracing her lips with his finger.

"God, Nora... how I need you. I realized it the minute you ran out of the room. The minute I didn't see you again. I was vile for saying the things I said, angrier with myself than you."

"You scared me with your rage at the store."

"I might've killed him if you hadn't stopped me," he drawled.

"He admitted he wanted your gold. And whatever else he can claim. He was using my past to blackmail you. He knew about my killing Connor. I have no choice but to stay away from you until this is all settled."

"About the gold. He must have heard about it from somewhere. That worries me because it puts you and Steven at risk. Who would have told him? My men are loyal."

"You never told me."

"That was to keep you safe. A fine mess now that the word got out. The location is my secret. The gold is part of an old placer claim left to me by my father. Somehow, Mabry found out, and he saw a way to leverage money from me." She leaned forward and buried her face against his firm chest. He lifted her from where she sat, then rocked her in his arms.

"Christ. You don't know how miserable I've been. Even my hired hands and son have kept their distance. While you stay close to the ranch, I'm taking Steven to the fort to deliver a blistering message, in person, to the commanding officer about Mabry. He won't be in uniform once I'm through."

"Please be careful."

"I always am, you know that. You'll be my wife as soon as we clear up this legal matter."

At daybreak, she watched from the window of the hotel, hoping to catch a glimpse of Gus and Steven. A shiver had her anxious to leave for home. Her lies. His gold. And secrets… had conspired to bring about this hellish storm in their lives.

TWENTY SIX

VULNERABLE

Two Weeks Later

GUS HESITATED IN front of Doctor Collier's door in Ogallala. After he and Steven had gone to Fort Sidney, he'd left with assurances that the commanding officer at the fort would see that Mabry was discharged for threats he'd made against Nora. It didn't hurt that her name was Enders. The fact that Jim Mabry had left the fort in civilian clothes signaled the end of the issue. *At least, he hoped so.*

He had no choice but to return to Ogallala to pick up his lumber order. While he waited, he figured it wouldn't hurt to have a frank talk with the good surgeon. As he started to knock, the door swung open. The physician's eyes widened at the sight of him standing on the porch.

"Gus. What brings you here so late in the day? I was about to go to supper. Hope you don't have another bullet hole. Or did you break your fist?"

Gus flexed his fist. "Seems to be working well enough. I came because I owe you an apology."

"Huh. Come in."

Collier turned to leave him to close the door. Gus followed him into a neat parlor. A bookcase was lined with leather-bound books and stacks of newspapers. Gus took a seat across the desk from the tired-looking man, noting he sported several days of scruff. A glass of whiskey sat beside a stack of papers.

"Don't usually drink. Today. Well, I felt like it. Just tended to a family on their way west. Their little boy took sick with a fever. Think he'll pull through. They insisted on going on to California. Can I offer you a drink?"

"No. I'll get to the point. I'm sorry for how things worked out. *I do love her.* So you know, if she had decided she wanted you, I would have stepped aside. Can't say I'd like it."

"I already know that. If I thought for one minute she had doubts, I'd pursue her anyhow. Still. If you ever wrong her, I'll prove I'm no coward. I may not look like a match against you, but I can hold my own."

"That's plain enough. You got no worries."

"I was a fool to think I had any chance with her. But that's what loneliness does to you."

"I'm staying the night in town. Nora and I plan to be married as soon as we have a few things cleared up. I'd like to think we can be cordial, for her sake."

Alfred reached across the desk, then they shook hands. "Take damn good care of her, or you'll answer to me. You're a better man than I gave you credit for."

"I'm a man of my word, Alfred."

"I'll be out to see your place soon as I can."

"You'd be welcome."

HOME WAS ON the horizon. "You need to stop for a rest there, Miss Enders?" Tangle asked.

She looked toward the craggy-faced man who'd become family. "I told you to refer to me as Nora. In fact, I insist."

He tugged the brim of his hat while their horses walked side-by-side. "All right. *Nora.* Just over that rise ahead, you'll see the barn and that big house he's built. Think he has a crew of men workin' on a big bunkhouse. Those horses of his are the best I've ever seen. Think he'll do well by you."

"Gus isn't a cattleman."

"He's smart. That's all you need. My guess is he'll become a cattleman."

Just as they crested the ridge, she gasped. "Lordy, Tangle. Look at that long porch and the big windows sparkling in the light."

He winked. "Mighty big place if you ask me."

She studied the house, hoping to catch sight of Gus. That's when she saw him on the bunkhouse roof, shirtless and swinging a hammer. His browned skin glistened under the sun. So riveted, at first she didn't hear the horse coming toward them. Both twisted in their saddles at the same time to see Bryce walking his buckskin horse up to them. Nora watched as a lazy smile creased his mouth.

"See you came to gander at that fancy house Gus is building for you," Bryce said.

"That we are. Seems you're doing the same thing, big brother."

"Already saw it. Got some news for you, though. Cort told me where you'd gotten to."

Leaning forward, he handed her an envelope. She stared fixedly at her brother's face.

"Go on. Read the damned letter before I decide to shout it to the sky."

A soft wind lifted her hair as her hand trembled. Slipping the worn paper from the envelope, she held it into the light to read the scrawled words. At first, she couldn't believe what was in front of her. Reading it again, the words became pure joy, an ending to a nightmare she'd lived with. She swiped her tears, then released a long breath.

"Well? Aren't you goin' to hoot and holler? Hannah sure did. This calls for celebration, little sister."

She sniffed. "Gus needs to see this."

"Well, what are you waiting for? Get to it."

"How can I thank you?" His wide smile and sassy wink warmed her to her bones.

"Thank me by being happy and getting hitched to that tough recluse you seem to love. We'll wait till you ride down there before we head home. I think you'll be here for a while. *Talking.*"

Tangle tipped his chin, then tugged the brim of his hat lower as she glanced into his shadowed face.

"I love you both. No one could have a better brother or friend than both of you."

GUS DROVE THE last nail into the board and batten roof then sat back, swiped his face, then calculated in his head how much more work was needed. Before long, he'd have to see to sealing it with tar. For now, it would do. His men had already headed for the cookhouse to settle in for supper, leaving him to finish the last of this job.

A glance in the direction of the corral let him know two of his horses dozed. Come spring, he'd add more horses, expanding his herd. No doubt, the foals would grow healthy on this grass.

The sound of a rider coming this way had him swing around. He squinted, then grinned at the sight of Nora coming this way, trotting up beside the bunkhouse. This was the first time she'd been here, looking pretty in a white blouse, polished boots, and a riding skirt. He was too glad to see her to wonder why she'd come all this way alone. Her hair was pulled into a long plait, and a gray hat shaded her face.

He looked beyond her to catch sight of two men sitting atop the ridge, one waved a battered Stetson. It appeared she'd been escorted. After she'd pulled up and dismounted, he straddled the roof peak and tossed the hammer off the opposite side.

"I'll be right down," he called.

"Please be careful."

"Plan to."

Sliding along the peak of the gable, balanced with his knees on either side, he reached the end and dropped a small sack of nails to the ground. Stepping over the edge, he planted his feet against the first rung of the ladder before climbing down. Near the bottom, he vaulted the rest of the way. She stood before him, looking as sweet as a picture as she handed him his shirt.

"What do you think of the house? Didn't know you'd planned on visiting."

"It's beautiful. So very large. I didn't think you'd be interested in such a big house."

"Figured you deserved every inch of it. Even though Steven doesn't take much to living inside yet, he'll have the bedroom on the far end, facing the pastures. Want to come inside?"

"Of course."

"Plan to hire more men in time. Raising horses comes with a few more problems than cattle. There'll be some jumping fences. The house still needs a lot more work before it's done. Ready for that tour?"

Taking her hand, he led her across the grass to the long porch. "Before you go in, I don't have much in the way of furniture. Just a couple beds, a kitchen table, and some chairs. Figure you might pick out some things. Order whatever you need."

"I don't need everything all at once. As long as there's a good kitchen stove, we'll do fine."

Guiding her from one room to another, he felt like a show-off kid trying to impress her. He darted glances at her to gauge her impressions as he explained the layout of the house. Her ear-to-ear grom was enough to make a man puff up inside. He took pleasure as she ran a hand across the Empire wood stove and touched the few pots and pans hanging from the wall. Her fingers skipped along the long oak table where he'd sat alone, wondering if he'd ever have her as his wife.

By the time he'd led her through all the rooms, she looped her arm with his and tugged him back into the kitchen. Sliding out a chair, she sat. He leaned against the edge of the table and folded his arms across his chest. From her cheerful expression, he surmised she had something to tell him.

"I need to share something with you. It can't wait."

"What about?"

"About Connor O'Malley."

The mention of the name had him slant her a questioning stare. If she was still married to that son of a bitch, he'd have to do something about it. Slipping the envelope from her pocket, she slid it toward him.

"Bryce delivered this news."

He ran his hand over the paper before unfolding it. Squinting without the benefit of his glasses, he made out the postmark to be Louisiana. Cocking an eyebrow, he strode to a cabinet, withdrew his spectacles, then slipped them on. He paced as he read the words. His movement slowed to a walk while he read them again. After he reread, the news sunk into his head like good whiskey.

Tossing the letter to the table, he grabbed hold of her and lifted her from the chair before dancing with her across the room. After lowering her feet to the floor, he tucked her head against his heart, threading his fingers through her silky hair.

"Ahh, God, Nora. Your so-called husband died some years ago in a boiler explosion. Apparently he'd taken the job working riverboats on the Mississippi. Says he was survived by a wife and child. No mention of any other wife. Do you know what this means?"

Her head nodded against him. "It means that I'm not married. And I never killed him."

"Don't think you ever were. It was all a lie to control you. You *didn't* kill him. He lived to find *another* wife. I'm betting he was already married when he came across you."

"What should we do now?"

"Will you be my wife and mother to my son? Our son?"

She lifted her head and touched his face. "I have a dress fit for marrying. No sense in keeping it till the moths fill it with holes."

"I love you, Nora Enders."

"I love you more than you could know, Gus. We better head to Cort's place. If I know Hannah and Lark, the preacher will be there before the week is out. Maybe sooner."

He clenched his teeth, then did something he rarely did. He prayed that nothing else would spoil their nuptials.

TWENTY SEVEN

BLOOD IS THICKER

"ALL SET?" HE asked.

"I'm ready." She smiled and cupped a hand over her eyes. "Steven is as handsome as his father."

As the wagon jolted forward, he followed her gaze to where Steven rode ahead of them. "Handsome? Don't know if you can rightly call me that. But he sure has my love of horses and maybe a little of my stubbornness. He's set in his ways. I'm hoping time will erase his ingrained wariness."

"Just how will I deal with two stubborn men in the same house?"

Slanting a glance at her, he offered a lopsided grin. That throaty laugh of hers seeped into every crevice of his heart. "I expect by now the entire Enders clan is waiting for us. Do you realize that when you next come back, it'll be to stay?"

She nodded. "I'll be the very proud wife of the famous Gus Quaid, and I'll try to be a good mother to Steven. Gus. It'll be my privilege to honor Aubrey's memory by being a good mother."

"First of all, I am not famous. And second, Steven knows he's to respect my wife. Before long, he'll accept you. Aubrey was the connection he had to me and the white world. He seems fond of Hannah because she has a way with kids... being a teacher. You might start there."

They fell into thoughtful silence until she broke into his musings. "You still have the limp. I know it must still be hurting."

"It hurts some. No more than it did yesterday." Glancing across his shoulder, Wally and Dave waved their hats in farewell. It had started to niggle as to whether either of them talked too much about his gold claim. For now, he'd let it go because he had a wedding to get to.

About an hour out from the house, he began to see clusters of prime Enders cattle. September was about here, and if the winter was hard, many of the cows would die of starvation or freezing. The house should be ready before then. He'd already begun to calculate how much fence he'd need to keep most of his herd of horses from wandering too far. If they got into any of the valleys, they'd be trapped by deep snow.

Monotony set in while they bounced along the rough trail road in the direction of the ranch house. A warm day would turn sharply cold by tonight, and he hoped they'd reach Cort's place before sunset. From a ridge, he saw three riders heading toward them. No one could mistake Rey's long, dark hair blowing in the wind. Cort and Bryce rode down the slope ahead of him. After they reached the wagon, Gus pulled up the team while Steven brought his horse up alongside Rey.

"I take it this is the welcoming committee," Gus called out.

"Lark and Hannah kept nagging until we decided to make sure you were bringing our sister back. *Tonight*," Cort teased.

"For goodness sakes, Cort. What a thing to say." Gus bit his tongue rather than tease her about the rosy blush on her cheeks.

"Micah Jeffers, the preacher, should get here tomorrow or the next day. Sent Mason and Billy to fetch him. The women are circling their wagons to make sure everything is ready for the nuptials. Opened my best bourbon. While the women gab, we'll raise our glasses at the fact Connor O'Malley is no more."

Gus pulled the envelope from his jacket pocket and handed it over to Cort. "Just so you see it for yourself." Cort held the note up into the light. "Says New Orleans." Cort read the missive aloud.

"Connor O'Malley, a deckhand, succumbed to drowning when the steamboat *Stonewall* burned to the waterline at six p.m. of October

twenty-seventh, 1869. Mister O'Malley's wife and child were left desti-
tute, and there is no record of their residence. He was also wanted for
gambling debts."

Cort leaned from his saddle to return the letter to him. Gus tucked
it into his pocket, then winked at Nora. "Your brother looks mighty
satisfied. Don't you think?"

"They both do. Now, let's get to the house before I turn into an old
lady. Lark and Hannah will need help in the kitchen."

Gus tugged at the brim of his hat and hollered for the horses to
move along, smiling all the way to his boots. She'd be *his* by tomorrow
night if the preacher arrived. Right now, the touch of her hand against
his thigh was good medicine, not to mention enticing as hell. At the
sight of the buildings ahead, he breathed in the scent of chimney smoke
and freshly baked bread. This range and these people were his home.

Once they stopped in front of the porch, Lark and Hannah rushed
down the stairs, wiping their hands against their aprons. Cort and
Bryce dismounted, then handed the reins over to Alonzo. The two boys
led their saddle horses to the stable alongside him. Gus dropped to the
ground, then reached up for Nora. Adoeete heaved himself up onto the
driver's seat, then headed the wagon toward the barn.

"The women can entertain themselves. And so can our sons. Let's
get inside and warm up over a whiskey," Bryce suggested.

Gus's thoughts flashed back to Jim Mabry and the run-in they'd had.
*Why did something feel wrong? He'd mentioned his gold... not just mentioned it
but threatened to get his hands on it.* At the moment, a glass of whiskey might
be in order for this worry that niggled. Had he seen the last of Jim Mabry?

AFTER NORA SET out a platter on the long dining table, she looked
from the kitchen window to see a lamp lit in Zeke's office window.
The women's voices prattled on about food and dresses. For her, those
things were drowned in the worry or premonition she'd had about
Zeke. Was it just wedding jitters?

"Nora...?" When a hand touched her shoulder, she jumped. "You look like you're lost in deep thought. What's wrong?" Lark asked.

She turned to see Lark's head tilted in question. "How's Zeke doing?"

"So that's what clouded your happy smile? Got to say, we're all worried about him. His health isn't good. Collier comes by to listen to his heart, but doesn't think there's much can be done. Both Cort and Bryce seem to be braced for the worst. In the meantime, he keeps busy with Steven and Reyes. It's like he sees them as his own kin. We don't even mind him teaching them to play poker."

"I worry how his death will impact the boys. They've both lost so much already, Lark."

Lark's frown said what they all felt. "Zeke is the heart of the ranch. But his old heart is giving out. Let's all be happy while he's still with us. Let's not forget we're celebrating you and Gus. Let's put that upfront before we get all maudlin."

OVER THE NEXT few days, Gus put off talking with his son about the upcoming nuptials. He needed to make sure he knew nothing would be different between them. Right now, everyone was stretched thin with ranch work. Determined to keep busy until the preacher arrived, he spent his days in the saddle.

The second night he'd been at Cort's ranch, father and son reached a turning point that made all the difference going forward. He hadn't seen a change coming. Or at least, he pretended that it wasn't there. It wasn't something he could see but something he felt, like a shift in the wind before a rain was coming.

On a full moon, he happened to see Steven slipping from the bunkhouse, clutching a sack in one hand. Gus watched from the shadows as he left the corral on his unsaddled horse. *Where the hell was he going, and why?* One thing for sure, he was heading in the direction of Rocky Creek.

The why of it was disconcerting. He'd rather hear the truth from his son's own mouth, which meant he'd hunker down in the barn to wait.

As time ticked by, he swallowed against the lump in his throat while he braced for an unpleasant but necessary confrontation. Seated in the shadows, his back rested against the wall, moonlight streamed through the bale window. *Dammit. Maybe he should have followed him.* But there was already a thin line of trust between them.

Crossing his ankles, he rubbed the scar at the back of his neck that was a reminder of the fact his own son had been part of the attack. Things could've gone horribly wrong that night. *What was Steven up to now?*

Just as his eyes grew heavy, a nicker snapped him awake. His body tensed, and he counted on his moccasins to silence his movement while he ducked farther into the shadows. Steven's knee-high moccasins muffled his steps as he led his horse into a stall. After he turned to close the gate behind him, Gus stepped into view, making sure he blocked his son's exit. Steven's eyes widened, then narrowed. Caught, the boy looked left then right, finding himself trapped.

"See you're out for a late ride," Gus said.

"You watched me."

"Seems so."

Steven dropped his chin to stare at the floor. When he looked up, Gus read defiance in his taut jaw and his cocky stance. When he sidestepped, Gus caught hold of his arm with a firm grip.

"Nope. We're goin' to settle some things. Starting now."

The boy jerked his arm free. "Say what you want. I'm tired."

An urge to land a punch to end his swagger was born out of his experience with lawbreakers. *This was his son, for Christ sakes.* "It seems you've been gnawing at something for a long while. I should've seen it coming. As to bein' tired. So am I. Doesn't change the fact you snuck out in the dark for no real good reason, as far as I know. Let's start with where you went."

"I don't like living with whites."

Of all the things he thought the boy would say, this wasn't one of them. "That's too bad. Especially since *you are white.* Except for some of *my* mother's blood. You are counted white."

"I'm not ashamed to be Indian."

"Nor should you be. But you're *not* Indian except by adoption. I'm saying you need to understand both sides of your world are good places. To be respected. You've learned a lot from the People. Now it's time to learn from the blood you were born into."

"You are taking a wife. Why didn't you find us? My mother and me. And take us home?"

"Thought you'd get around someday to askin'. The truth is, I spent the last thirteen years of my life looking. I was sinking fence posts in a pasture when a band of Brulé rode off with her. After I heard her screams, I ran toward the house in time to find her clutched in front of a warrior. They rode away before I could reach my rifle."

"By the time I gathered guns and ammunition and mounted my horse, they were well ahead of me. But I kept going. My horse was slick with sweat and heaving with exhaustion. Finally, my mount went down from under me. And they were long out of sight, and I was on foot."

Steven's stare was intent. "What did you do?"

"What any man would do. I trudged back to the house and got together anything I'd need. Vowed I'd never give up looking for her. Went to Fort McPherson to file a complaint and to ask for help. They said they were stretched thin and couldn't send men out looking. But the commander of the fort offered me a job scouting for them. Turned out to be an opportunity to set out with soldiers, going from village to village. *Looking.* Always searching the faces of every woman I saw. Even while I continued to build my horse ranch, I took every chance I could to join Army forays... whenever they needed my skills as a tracker."

"You did not know of me. My mother told me."

"That's true. I love you. Even though I can be a hard man. Know that I'd die for you, son. She must've been traded to the Lakota. That's why I got thrown off the trail. Now it's your turn. How about you tell me where you got to and why? What was in the sack you had?"

He shrugged. "Nine Bears is my uncle among the Lakota. He came to me while I was working some cows. He asked about my mother and was saddened to learn of her death. Said he needed food. He told me my place is with him. To ride with him."

"So you stole food from our friends."

"Yes."

"No more. You will not be meeting him again. Nor will you join him."

"If I go with him, you can marry that woman, Nora. And forget me."

"I'll admit I love her and will marry her. You already know that. She's a good woman who'll treat you like a son if you give her half a chance. My marrying her has nothing to do with our relationship. You're my son first and always. Besides, I need your help with the horses."

"She will never be my mother."

"She understands your feelings, better than I do. In fact, I should've seen you were bothered by all the changes. The loss of your mother was hard on us both. I'd lost her before and then again. *I won't lose you too.* Nora asked me to have this talk with you and until tonight, I didn't understand how urgent it was."

"Reyes told me his mother died. But he likes Hannah. Still, he did not live like me."

"No. But you will fit into this world. If you have courage enough. From where I stand, I think you do. I asked you if you wanted to live at Belle Fourche or here, and you chose here. I took you at your word and accepted your choice."

Gus watched as he averted his face, seeming to consider what he'd said. When Steven looked toward him again, their gazes locked. His son's hand covered his heart. "I will stay as long as it feels right."

Gus squeezed his shoulder and grinned. "I'm damned proud of you."

After the boy stepped around him, Gus called him back. "Hey."

Arms outstretched to his sides, Gus invited Steven into a fatherly embrace. Steven closed the distance, and Gus wrapped him in his arms. His son's brief whimper constricted his heart and had him swallowing the lump in his throat.

"When do you meet him again?" Gus asked.

"Tomorrow night. He is leaving then for a reservation where his sister lives. He says I belong there. To come with him."

"Hell you will. This time, I'll be at your side. Do you understand?"

Steven stepped back and nodded. "Pa. Let me tell him that I am finished."

Pa. The sound of it felt as natural as breathing.

"BEEN LOOKIN' FOR you, Gus," Cort said from atop his horse. "Saw you ridin' along the river. Looking for strays?"

Gus stood beside his horse, the reins loose in his hands. "Had somethin' else I was keeping my eyes on. What brings you out looking for me?"

"Got a message. The preacher, Micah, is finally getting here day after tomorrow. He's been busy with funerals and births. The women got busy with food and frills, so I figured I'd get out of the way. Bet you want to get the whole thing over with. You and Nora sure had a lot of obstacles."

"Yep. So you know. I'm looking for Nine Bears."

Cort's eyebrow rose. Shaking his head, he lifted one gloved hand. "Just one minute. How did this happen? Is Bryce privy? Should'a told me before now. That's one serious hombre."

"Bryce knows. Tomorrow night I'm meeting that renegade. With Steven. The plan is to settle things then expect Nine Bears to head for the reservation."

Cort's body tensed then he tugged the brim of his hat. "Suppose you fill me in while we have a smoke."

Once Cort dismounted, Gus led his horse beside Cort's sorrel. After he'd told Cort the story, Gus watched the icy, hard stare of the gunfighter resurface. Without saying anything, Cort hiked himself into his saddle.

"Well?" Gus said.

"We'll be there. And I want it known. He won't be back. That's one thing we'll definitely settle."

GUS AND STEVEN followed a narrow trail to the lower part of Blue River, where it joined the Platte. Sitting atop their horses, they waited, but they didn't wait long. Wearing a deerskin shirt and Levi's, Nine Bears walked out from the trees with no horse in sight.

"*Ate´*," Steven said in greeting.

"You did not come alone."

"This is my true father."

"You deny the People who raised you?"

Gus's anger rose while his fingers hankered to reach for his revolver. At his son's nervous glance, he kept his tongue. Steven deserved to be a man. This was the moment he could demonstrate his mettle because Nine Bears was playing his best hand. *Guilt and loyalty.*

"My mother is not one of the People. She was a captive."

In the silence, Nine Bears crossed his arms. "You are one of us."

Gus's ire prickled. "He was a captive. Like his mother. He is now with his own people. That is his decision."

"Gus. The man who hates Indians," Nine Bears sneered.

"I hate the ones who stole my wife. We had done nothing to you."

Nine Bears's spine stiffened, then he stared hard in Steven's direction. "Let the boy choose."

Gus ground his teeth. This was his son's place to speak.

"I choose my father's people. My mother wanted that."

"You heard him. Go to the reservation or wherever you choose. I will keep my promise about your whereabouts. Our debt is paid, and we owe you nothing more." Gus slid his revolver from his holster when Nine Bears moved to Steven's side. The two of them studied each other.

"My brother taught you. Remember what you learned from us."

"I will." Steven handed him the sack with the dried meat and potatoes.

Gus held his breath until Nine Bears disappeared into the darkness. The sound of a plodding horse and a splash of water signaled the proud warrior was gone. Looking across his shoulder, he made out the outlines of Bryce and Cort, their rifles held at their sides.

"Likely we saw the last of him," Cort called out.

Steven twisted in his saddle. "He keeps his word."

Once the four of them left Blue River behind, Gus's shoulders eased. He'd never been prouder than the moment his son crossed between the past and present. Loyalties had been tested and there was a good chance that Aubrey looked down and smiled.

TWENTY EIGHT

THE OTHER SIDE OF HERE

CRYSTAL LAMPS GLOWED, filling the rooms with the festivity of the impending wedding. Mason and Cort were cornered by an animated farmer's wife and her craggy-faced husband, looking like he'd rather be anywhere but here. Tangle exchanged jokes with Billy as they sipped something that smelled distinctly like bourbon disguised as punch.

The preacher was seated in the parlor on the settee, sipping a whiskey he'd poured for himself from the decanter on the marble-topped table. Theresa and Hannah were ducking in and out of the kitchen with platters of frizzled beef sandwiches, bowls of potato salad, and slices of ham.

The cake was a delectable white fluffy thing that looked like it shouldn't be touched, let alone eaten. Hannah looked toward him with a dimpled smile and teasingly waggled her fingers. Tugging the tight collar of a borrowed shirt, that whiskey looked mighty inviting if it weren't for the dour expression on the preacher's face. Darting a glance at the stairs, Gus wondered if they'd ever get this shindig going.

"You look like you could use this," Bryce said.

With a raised eyebrow, Gus studied the proffered glass of frothy punch. He offered a tight-lipped grin before smelling it. "Christ, smells potent. What's in it?"

"Some berry juice, sugar, and as much bourbon as Zeke could dump in. This stuff has been a tradition since the Harrises lived here. Take a swig. It'll help you forget this is your wedding day," Bryce quipped.

Tossing back a swallow, Gus coughed as the powerful brew burned down his throat. "No chance of that." Gus swiped his mouth. "Took long enough to get to this day. I'll shoot the first person who gets in the way." He grimaced, then said, "You forgot to tell me exactly how much bourbon was in that stuff. It's lethal."

Bryce sniggered. "Used to say you only get married once. Now… in the case of you and my brother, we'll amend that. Should be old hat."

Didn't Bryce and the rest understand that a man about to get married didn't have much capacity for humor? With one last swallow of that punch, he thought he saw the chandelier sway. "Circumstances—my friend—change. What's takin' so long to get this over? Where's Lark and Nita? Not to mention Steven, Zeke, and Rey? I'd think Nora would be flitting around the kitchen, her wedding or not."

"Zeke is teachin' the boys the fine points of makin' ice cream. Somehow, he got his hands on enough ice, salt, and cream to put it together. They're out on the back step. I'd bet all three come inside with dirt-smudged pants and cream on their faces. That'll set off a loud discussion with the women. Nita is doing the tough work of keepin' our Lily and Cort's kids fed and occupied. Cornering little Bryce is harder than rounding up a bull chasin' a cow in heat."

The punch Gus had just swallowed nearly shot out of his mouth at Bryce's comparison. He laughed and drew the crowd of eyeballs in his direction. "Christ. A man like me isn't used to all this brouhaha. A nice quiet dinner would do."

Bryce tapped his shoulder. "Tangle, Mason, and Billy just picked up their fiddles."

Gus's spine stiffened. Was that his heart pounding in his ears? "Nora and me are goin' to run away and find a padre next time," he mumbled.

"Won't be a next time," Bryce said.

"Guess you tied the knot right here."

"Right here. In this room."

"Did Cort?"

"That's a complicated matter. Best I go relieve my brother from Jordan Cane and his wife. They started a farm on free-range. That wife is doin' all the talkin'. This'll be over soon enough, brother-in-law.'"

A headache marched through Gus's head. He set his empty glass on the table, then turned to see Zeke walk into the dining room, wearing a distinctly devious expression. The glow of the chandelier lit the old man's gray hair, turning it silver. One blue eye winked at him.

Gus watched Zeke make his way to the punch bowl, where he poured himself a glass of punch, then slugged most of it down without so much as a scowl. After he pulled a flask from his pocket, he poured a liberal dose into the bowl. Gus held new respect for the man's guileful nature. After a sidelong glance, Gus turned his attention to Reyes and Steven, both chomping into sandwiches while they eyed the cake.

Zeke joined him. "About time they got this thing over with."

"My sentiments."

"Nora is a fine woman. Got to know her a little. She sure gnaws on her past like it might come back and bite her. It'll take her time. Got to be patient."

Gus snorted. "Sometimes she wears a man's patience. I love her all the same. No one will ever come between us as long as I'm breathing."

"Good to know. Those two brothers are protective."

"Zeke. I gotta' question... you might not like hearing."

"Get it off your chest so we can enjoy this social."

"It's about *you*. Has Collier checked you out?"

"Yes. Not that's any of your business. No sense in worryin' about me."

"All right."

"You mean you don't want to know what he said?"

"I do. Like you said. None of my damned business."

"Put like that, guess I'll tell you anyhow. I know I'm not much help around here. Arthritis keeps me awake. Can hardly sit a horse so took to drivin' the wagon out to the holding pens. And I get a little short on breath. Doc said my ticker doesn't sound so good."

"Can he do something?"

"No. Said I could see a special doctor in Omaha. I got no interest in goin' on a long train ride. Age is somethin' we can't escape, Gus. I'm headin' to a new pasture before long. Every time I'm with Reyes, I think of myself at his age. He's become like my own flesh and blood. I'm worryin' about how he'll take it when I'm gone. Steven too."

"God, Zeke. Let's not talk like that. Especially now."

"Just want you to be nearby. Cort and Bryce came to be more like sons. Soon enough, they'll need somebody to remind them this ranch is bigger than any of us."

"I'm not goin' anywhere."

Gus held the man's glittering gaze. Why did it feel like he'd just said goodbye? For the life of him, he couldn't think of a response. As he chewed on that thought, the preacher's cane thumped. Zeke leaned close.

"Best get over there near the fireplace. That Preacher Jeffers means business after he opens that big Bible."

The preacher's voice boomed, signaling silence. "See that none of you is wearing a hat. No chewing tobacco or drinking during the ceremony. Tangle and the others with fiddles, you can begin. The ladies are waiting at the top of those stairs."

Gus forgot to breathe at the sight of Nora wearing a shimmering light blue dress with pearl buttons, holding a bouquet of Black-eyed Susans and cowboy's roses. Her dark hair was pulled up into soft curls draped along one side of her head, held with pearl combs. Her glowing skin had his fingers hankering to touch the silkiness of it.

Her descent was nothing short of regal, like the first time he'd seen her. She took her place at his left side, then he grasped her hand. His eyes flitted across her face, and at her faint smile, he winked. With her fingers trembling between his, he squeezed her hand. Steven stepped to his right, the ring clutched in his fist. He darted a glance at his son's rare smile. A wave of nostalgia rolled through his head at Aubrey's words. *Steven looks like you.*

Wearing a new white shirt and blue wool trousers, his son looked *civilized.* Words were spoken from some cloud where he drifted on the outside, looking in. Someone prodded him with a poke in the back, prompting him to look up. The preacher waited.

"I do," Gus replied in a hoarse voice.

Words droned on while his attention focused again on Nora.

"Do you take this man to be your lawful wedded husband, to have...."

Nora's husky voice responded, "I do."

He lifted her hand to his mouth, then pressed a kiss to her palm. After a nudge from beside him, he slipped the ring onto her finger, returning his regard to her smiling eyes. Preacher Jeffers gave his official permission to kiss her, and there was no hesitation on his part. A long, passionate kiss couldn't have left any doubt in anyone's mind that Nora Enders Quaid belonged to him. He'd never let her forget where she belonged.

Throats cleared, and the room filled with hoorahs, hoots, and whistles as he turned to shake the preacher's extended hand. Nora's rosy-red face, sparkling eyes, and soft gaze tempted him to forgo the well-wishing in favor of the bedroom upstairs. Her brothers shoved him aside, then pecked her cheeks with brotherly kisses. Lost in the crowd of people, he was forced to step back to relinquish her hand to all the cowhands.

Even crusty Zeke leaned in to plunk a kiss against her forehead. The women formed a line, each hugging her, then turning to him for the same affectionate embrace. When it was time for cake, the boys were first in line. Theresa was quick to chastise them for being impolite after they'd piled their plates with more than their share.

What man wanted to leave his new wife's side? None that he could think of. Bryce shepherded him to the porch, where Cort passed a box of cigars between them. Zeke took a seat in a rocking chair, then tipped his head back, seeming to be ready to drop into sleep. A tray held fine Jack Daniel's whiskey, prized by Cort and rarely handed out. Gus sipped, allowing the stuff to mellow the mood. The things he had on his mind wouldn't allow him to fall into a drunken stupor.

"Now that you're married, Gus, how does it feel?" Bryce asked.

For Gus, it seemed natural for the eldest brother to begin teasing.

But he'd rather escape to find his wife. "Like I have a legal right to do what any man would do with a gorgeous woman."

"Huh." Cort sniggered. "Just keep in mind. She's my sister. Best you not describe anything more."

Gus struck a match, lit the cigar, then puffed while Cort and Bryce did the same. They settled into quiet while clouds crossed the moon. Tangle stepped outside, leaned his back against a porch post, then lit the cigar clenched between his teeth.

"We're leavin' for our place later tomorrow. So you know," Gus said.

"How's the house coming along?" Cort asked.

Gus slipped the cigar from his mouth, studied it a moment, then stretched out his long legs. "Admit it needs furniture, rugs, and a few other things. My wife can order what she wants."

Cort squinted into the night. "Seems like getting your horse herd going will keep you busy."

"Yep. Got two hired hands from my former ranch and managed to hire on three men in Ogallala to build the cookhouse." Gus puffed again. It was plain Cort was digging around to figure out how he'd support his new wife. And he didn't blame him.

"I've got enough money from the sale of my larger herd and ranch land. Besides that, I own a parcel up north, I'd like to keep between us."

"Sounds like you're all set. Might think about cattle one of these days," Cort said.

Gus dropped the cigar into the water pail, listening as it hissed. "Maybe. We'll see."

Zeke's craggy voice came out of the shadows. "Cort. You got to give your brother-in-law credit. He's a good man and long-standing friend. Nobody better say nothin' about his claim. We all agree it stays with us."

Gus darted a quick glance in Tangle's direction, wishing Zeke hadn't mentioned that piece of information. Still. He trusted Tangle.

"We're agreed on secrecy," Bryce said. "Besides, nobody knows where it is. Up north is a lot of territory."

Zeke yanked a handkerchief from his pocket then mopped his face. "This early… heat ain't natural. Might be a drought comin'. Everybody knows the rivers are runnin' low. Best start plannin' for that, boys. Cull what you don't need."

"A drought is something to worry about. Lose a lot of cattle if that happens," Cort agreed. "Horses too. Don't remember it ever being this rain-starved."

"The grass doesn't look too green right now. Not a good sign," Gus added. "But, gents. I think I'll go see about my wife. I'm tired. That guest bed is calling."

A burst of laughter followed him after he stood, stretched, then made a point of yawning. Ignoring the hoots, he walked for the door, which Tangle held open, waving him in with a flourish.

"Don't want you runnin' through the door. Saw a bull charge a fence one time."

With a face feeling like he'd been too close to the oven, he marched into the house with guffaws and chortles behind him. He was getting too old for the bantering... especially at his expense. He left them to their drinking, then headed straight for the kitchen where he took Nora by the arm, then steered her to the stairs. The invited hands had already gone their own way to the bunkhouse, else he might be in for more ribbing. Nora looked across her shoulder until his grip tightened.

"Don't even think about turning back to the kitchen, Missus Quaid. Set aside your domestic inclinations for tonight. I've got other plans."

"I have no plans to desert you, Gus. Ever. Am I blushing?"

His gaze skimmed across her crimson face. "Yes. I find it tantalizing. And endearing."

TWENTY NINE

FAREWELL

THE SORROWFUL, SWEET strains of Tangle's violin drifted from below the window, bringing tears to Nora's eyes. She studied his crooked smile in the reflection of her mirror. The long legs of the man she loved were crossed at his ankles, one arm pillowed his head while he watched her in return. With only a thin sheet draped across his middle, she thought she'd never seen a more handsome man.

She twisted her hair into a loose braid while the strains of the song almost brought tears to her eyes. "It's a beautiful song played by Tangle. I never knew he had such musical talent."

"*Scarborough Fair*. An Irish tune."

"Pardon me? Do you mean he's played this before?"

"I've heard him on occasion. *Scarborough Fair* is one of his favorites. His Irish heritage. Seems a sad song for a wedding night. Said it's about a woman losing her love. I don't intend to die just yet."

Tilting her head, she gave thought to the soft music. She turned, then stood. "He's not playing for us. I think he's playing for Zeke. And Sienna."

"Maybe. This is supposed to be our wedding night. No tears."

"It is. I'm Missus Angus Quaid."

"I don't know why I told that pastor my full name. I'll never live it down now."

She walked to the bed, then curled beside him. He wrapped her in his arm as she nestled her head in the crook of his neck. "I love your name."

He tugged her braid. "I'm not goin' to leave your hair bound like that for long."

"Gus, do you feel sorrow in the air?"

"Huh? Well, I'm not of the mind to give thought to the ones up on the hill right now. Don't believe much in spiritual things. I'm more for the living."

When the last strains of the violin had faded, she sighed. "It was so beautiful."

"Glad the music ended else I might be tempted to pull on my pants and cut the strings. Don't need my new wife's eyes filled with tears."

His fingers loosened Nora's braid. "My... you are in a hurry, Mister Quaid."

"I am. I've been living out of a barn and bunkhouse long enough. When we arrived here, I was consigned to another bunkhouse. Figure we've been separated long enough."

"It couldn't have been that bad in the bunkhouse."

"Goes to show that you never slept with a bunch of men who groan or fart all night."

Nora leaned back to see a sparkle in his eyes, then she laughed. "I'm glad you set me straight." She turned in his arms. His warm breath touched her skin where he planted kisses along her jaw, then against her mouth.

"You're beautiful," Gus said against her lips.

Her fingers combed the hair on his chest, tracing the rough scars marring his skin. She felt him flinch beneath her touch when she found the heart-shaped scar on his chest, thinking it had to have been the arrow that Millicent spoke of. Her fingers drew lazy circles across the skin of his stomach, feeling it tauten beneath her stroke.

"Gus, you've suffered so much."

"No more talk." His fingers plucked each button of her gown. "Best get this off before I'm cranky."

Grinning, she said, "You? Cranky? Huh."

Drawing her silky nightdress from her body, he dropped it to the floor and then nibbled at her ear, whispering all the things he had in mind to do, sending a radiating heat through her body.

She kissed his neck, then his mouth. He deepened the kiss until they both shook with want of each other. He settled her beneath him, his eyes gazing into hers with such tenderness she swallowed against a sob. When he moved, the rhythm was as old as time, taking them both to the heavens... where they shattered into pieces, falling together until they were nestled in each other's arms. Each quiet in their thoughts.

As they lay face-to-face, his study seemed to devour her with his dark eyes. "What do you see?"

"My woman. My wife. With eyes the color of the ocean."

"Very poetic."

He chuckled. "Trying to please. Have you seen the ocean?"

"No. But I can take it on your word." She wrinkled her nose. "Is that bay rum?"

"You have an aversion to bay rum?"

"Not at all. It's just not the Gus I first knew at Fort Benton. Then again on the prairie."

Lifting onto her elbow, she watched as his gaze held hers. She traced his mouth with her finger. "You're a very handsome man, Mister Quaid. You stole my breath away the first time I saw you in your dress clothes. But I'm used to another Gus, wearing buckskins, carrying a rifle. The one who smells of sage, leather, and the land. The one who is every bit as rugged as these plains. Forever, I'll think of you like that."

He laughed. "And you are the most beautiful woman I've ever known, Missus Quaid. Now that you're mine, the rest of the cowpokes best keep a distance."

"I only love one man. He's here."

"Talking is for tomorrow. I need my woman."

A ribbon of pure pleasure wrapped them in sensations with each intimate touch and kiss, promising more until, at last, they plummeted to Earth, while his strong arms held her against his damp flesh. Their hearts thrummed together while she unraveled her fingers from the twisted sheet at her side. Unimaginable contentment filled her as her hand skimmed his solemn expression.

"Gus. What are you thinking?"

"How was I this lucky?"

Her thoughts turned to two women who'd crossed paths for perhaps some higher purpose or design. There had been a profound overlap of fates. The task of being a mother and wife were now hers... and she was determined to honor the past, present, and future.

"I wish I could give you more children."

He rested on his side while she curled against him. She felt him tense at her mention of having another child.

"Already told you. That doesn't matter. Whatever we're granted. That physician might have been a fraud. Or just plain wrong. Either way, all I need is you."

She sighed. In the silence that followed, she wished she hadn't reminded him of her past. "When will we start for home?"

There was no doubt he'd withdrawn when silence fell heavy between them. He lay on his back, his gaze on the ceiling. "Need to talk with Cort before we leave."

She sat up, dragging the sheet over her lap. "What is it, Gus? There's something you need to tell me. I can feel it. So, let's hear it."

"Figured it could wait till tomorrow."

"No. It can't."

He pulled her toward him, then nestled her head against his shoulder. Lifting a lock of her hair to his nose, he inhaled. "You have beautiful hair."

As she started to move, he stayed her with his hand. "All right. Have it *your* way. This might spoil the evening since I'm not done having my wife."

"No secrets. We agreed."

"You can be as stubborn as a miner's mule. You already know I bought one thousand acres from Cort and Bryce for my herd. Built us a house. Got a nice barn and bunkhouse. The cookhouse is still under construction. Did it occur to you where I'd gotten the money for the venture?"

"The sale of your ranch and horses."

"Not entirely. North of the Belle Fourche, I've kept something aside. Land that belonged to my father, Etienne Quaid. He staked it and deeded it."

"All right. You've made a brief mention of it before. What is the point of this?"

"My father was a trapper when he met my mother. Both were part Indian. He knew the mountains and did more than trap. He set up a sluice on the north end of the Belle Fourche River up in a valley. Gold was aplenty. Whenever he needed extra money, he placer mined. Kept the whereabouts secret and expected it to stay that way."

"You own a gold mine?"

"I own a large section of land along a creek rich in gold. So far, I haven't revealed details. Safer that way. Anytime I've panned some out, I leave no trail."

"You don't plan to go back there, do you? It could be dangerous."

"Not for the time being. That gold is a financial stake in our future, but it comes at a price."

She pulled away from his embrace and stood and then wrapped a blanket around her shoulders. As Nora stared from the window at the gray morning, she said. "*A price.*" Now, it became clear. *James Mabry had demanded money. He'd mentioned gold.* "Jim Mabry knows. Doesn't he?"

Gus yanked on his pants. "Afraid so. Now he's on the loose. Pretty sure he's not about to let go of his deranged vendetta. I'm the one responsible for getting him dishonorably discharged from the Army."

"But how did he find out about your gold?"

"Wally is a bit loose of the tongue if he's been drinkin'. That's the only thing I can think of. It won't be safe for you or Steven as long as Mabry is out there."

"I'm not hiding or running. That's final." She turned and raised her chin. "Non-negotiable, Gus. I will not be left behind. I'm going with you to my new home. Have you forgotten I traveled with you along the Missouri River and then across the plains of Dakota... outracing a wildfire. Nearly getting killed by Indians and a cougar. In case you don't recall, I can handle a horse. And gun."

"That's beside the point. I'll be working alongside Hersh, Trey and borrowed hands from the Double E to get these pastures fenced. They'll also need tending. Bought a hundred head of cattle, and they need rounding up to sell off before winter. Most nights, I won't be back till late, if at all. I'm shorthanded. Leaving you alone makes me sick in the pit of my stomach."

"Guess you'll just have to get used to the idea. I'm not budging. Steven and me will do fine."

"Stay here, Nora."

She lifted her chin. "I refuse to be run out of my own house by that sniveling, demented man."

"That damned gold doesn't matter. It's you and Steven I worry about. First thing I'm doing is to find out which of my two men talked too much."

"What would you do if you found out?"

"Send him packing."

"*Gus.*"

"This land is hard, and men like me, Bryce, and Cort have to be harder. This has to do with trusting the men you hire. If Wally put you in danger, he's going to be off my land."

Her eyes flitted across his stern expression. "He's been a friend for so long. I'd think you could forgive him one indiscretion."

"I'll decide once I talk with him."

His abrupt tone said he'd made up his mind, and there was no point in trying to change it. He crooked his finger, and she wrapped her arms around his neck as he leaned in to kiss her. With the soft light piercing the curtains, they recognized this glorious wedding night had ended and the new day had begun. While they washed and dressed, there was a light tap against the door.

"Breakfast is on the table," Lark called from the other side. After a moment, her soft footsteps faded.

Nora padded to the mirror. "Hope no one notices how my husband ravished me."

"I hope they do. Now, let's get to that food before Cort and me get to the plans for those cattle."

———————

BRYCE, HANNAH, AND Lily left in their wagon while Cort and Gus rode off to check water levels. While she and Lark finished the dishes, little Wade and the youngest, Ben, were bathed upstairs with Nita and Theresa's help.

"My goodness. Gus was quite taken at Tangle's serenade beneath our window last night," Nora said. "It was so sad a tune."

When there was no reply, she looked across her shoulder to find Lark's intent gaze out of the window as she absently wiped a pot. "We all heard it. Tangle is quite talented."

In the next silence, Nora dropped the towel and walked to where Lark stood like a sentinel. What she saw was Steven and Reyes beside the wagon out front of Zeke's place and wondered what Lark seemed so intent about. "Does something feel wrong?" she asked.

Lark sighed. "Expect Zeke is taking food and water out to the men setting posts for the fenced pasture. I'm worried about Zeke doing too much."

"I sure wish Alfred Collier would give him something. Should we send for him?"

Lark's face was drawn. "Something feels strange, Nora."

"I had the same sense last night. Maybe it was that sad music."

———————

ZEKE SLAPPED HIS broad-brimmed gray hat onto his head as he looked over the ranch from the shadows of his porch. Catching sight of Bryce, Hannah, and Lily as they rode by on their wagon, he waved them off. That little girl Lily would be quite a beauty, like her mother, he thought. He wished he'd be around to see her as a woman.

Reyes and Steven joined him for coffee earlier. Afterward, they'd headed to the barn to hitch the wagon... something he used to do himself. At least he was useful for something around here, delivering food and water to the men. It wasn't enough for an old cowhand to be out of the saddle.

For a moment, he hesitated to step from the shade into the heat. With a quick glance across his shoulder, it niggled that he hadn't been up to the weed-covered burial plots in a while. By staying away, he'd put off the acceptance of his own death.

He shook his head, then grasped the porch post to get his old legs down the steps to the waiting wagon where the team stood slack-legged. After he checked the wagon bed for the supplies he'd need, he limped to the front of the wagon. Each time he faced the wagon, he was struck by how much he missed working alongside the men. Menial tasks insulted this old man who'd fought off Indians and land-grabbers, not to mention rustlers... right beside big Wade Harris. Lifting his eyes to the corral, he squinted, wondering if he'd ever ride again. For certain, he'd rather drop from a horse than die a feeble old man in his bed.

"Mister Waterson. Got it all loaded. You want Steven and me to go along?"

Zeke jerked his head around. He hadn't heard those two boys come around the side of his house. "Nope. You two might want to stay here in case."

"Case of what?" Steven asked.

"In case Alonzo needs help in the cookhouse or Adoeete needs help in the barn. Or the women need you to fetch somethin'."

They looked at each other, then shrugged. After they trudged away, he was left to climb aboard the wagon. There was something inside him that needed to be alone. It came over him like a slow rising sun—this need to breathe in the sage and dry grass scent of the prairie, just as it was before the place became Enders land or Harris land. That same sentiment was coupled with a wave of sadness he couldn't explain. One thing was for sure, new blood was here to stay. That's what was important to *her*. *His* Sienna.

Lifting one boot onto a wheel spoke, he gave a last look at his house. One day, the place would belong to Reyes, where he'd raise a family. He gave a hop up to the seat just as a sharp pain knifed through his arm like it'd done last night. *Damned arthritis.* Dragging himself onto the seat, he tried to draw in a deep breath. It had to be this heat. Didn't take much to know they were in for a miserable drought. The pain eased while he inhaled a short breath of dry morning air.

He leaned forward and loosened the reins that were wrapped around the brake handle. After he released the brake with his left foot, pain charged through his chest like a bolt of lightning, leaving him gulping air. Spots formed in his vision. Through the darkening view of the team, he saw the horses looking back, waiting for him to make up his mind. Lifting his eyes, he thought to call out to the boys for help. For God's sake. *The last thing he wanted was for those boys to witness his death.*

Letting the reins slip from his gloved hand, he leaned sideways. The sky clouded over. *His time was done.* Yet somehow, he wanted to stay on a while longer. *Sienna. Last night we danced. Like I promised. Did you hear the violin?*

SITTING ON THE porch rockers, Lark and Nora shared stories of their lives. Some painful, others sweet. "Wonder what Cort and Gus are doing out there?" Nora said, more to herself than to Lark.

"Checking branding pens, river levels, men talk. We're in a drought. Don't know how bad it'll get."

Thudding boots jolted them from their seats. A winded Reyes appeared, his shirt sweat-soaked, his chest heaving while he drew in his breath. "Aunt Lark! Aunt Nora! Get Uncle Cort. Come quick. It's Zeke."

Lark charged toward him, taking his quaking shoulders between her hands. "Slow down. Tell us what happened."

"Don't know. Zeke just kinda' slumped over on the wagon seat. Steven and Alonzo are with him. He isn't waking up."

Nora pressed her hand to her chest, frozen with shock. Lark darted for the door, leaving her to hike her skirt, hop over the steps, then run as fast as she could to reach Zeke. From behind, the sound of Reyes's long strides kept pace with her.

Still winded, she froze at the sight of Zeke's limp body where it lay slumped across the wagon seat. Adoeete and Alonzo were lifting him down as carefully as they could. Reyes and Steven stood like statues beside her. As they carried him to the house, she followed beside them, biting her lip at the sight of Zeke's blue eyes, staring at nothing. His chest was still. The men were calling his name, getting no response.

Nora followed them on wooden legs as they entered the house. She swallowed the wail threatening to escape from her surging grief. The men settled Zeke's body onto the parlor settee, then stepped back before they doffed their hats as they bowed their heads. She squeezed her eyes closed against the sight. No one spoke because words were meaningless. But his words haunted her. *"I'll be headin' for a new pasture."*

She opened her eyes to see both Steven and Reyes, side-by-side, their expressions solemn. When a hand touched her shoulder, she turned to meet Lark's tear-filled gaze, her sister-in-law's face a mask of shock. She and Lark shared this profoundly sad moment, neither able to speak.

Nora moved close to where Zeke lay and kneeled beside the sweet man. Lark dropped beside her, both waiting in frozen silence. This was the man who'd always found the right words in times of tragedy and celebration. Now he was voiceless at the very moment they needed his words to fill the hollowness of this moment. Moreover, Zeke Waterson was the heart of this ranch, and without him, the history was lost. The melancholy was almost too much to bear. He should wake to tell them to stop worrying. *But he couldn't.* Nora pressed her hand against his heart and shook her head. The finality descended.

"Adoeete. Go find Cort. And Gus. Send someone for Bryce. Bring them back," Lark ordered on a sob.

The jangle of spurs and clomp of boots faded, leaving the four of them alone, cloistered with only the sound of the ticking clock. Steven and Reyes were on their knees, their eyes riveted on the white, scruffy-faced corpse... the man who'd become their grandfather.

Reyes set Zeke's hat atop the old man's legs while tears rolled over his cheeks. Nora could find nothing to say to make this easier. Steven took Zeke's cold hand between his, then spoke words in the Lakota tongue. A strange farewell for the man who'd lived through wilder times, fighting off Indians. Yet the sound of the words, though not understood, was strangely comforting.

"*Ake wancinyankin ktelo.* It means goodbye until we meet again," Steven explained.

Pressing her hand against Zeke's neck, she hoped he might have just fallen into a stupor or quiet sleep. There was no sound beneath his shirt, the skin unnaturally dry. Warmth was leaving him. Lark's wretched sob had Nora look up to where her sister-in-law now stood, her back straight, eyes spilling tears.

The agonizing, bitter loss cloaked them all, sucking air from the room. Theresa waddled in, drawing up short. Her wail was like a wild thing as Alonzo folded his massive arms around his wife, comforting her while she sobbed against his shoulder.

"Nora. He's gone. How can it be?" Lark whispered.

Pushing herself to her feet, Nora took Lark against her. They embraced and rocked together. The chasm was so startling, speaking was impossible, and so she cried with Lark. It was as though the heart of the ranch would never beat again. *But it had to.* What would any of them do without Zeke? He'd been here since the beginning, and now, he'd said goodbye.

Nora sobbed. "I'll miss him. Just as we all will. He taught us so much about living and dying. He wouldn't want us to grieve for long. It was fitting that Tangle played the violin last night. Bet Zeke's dancing with his beloved Sienna while Wade looks on."

Nora clutched Lark's hand and said, "Rest easy, Zeke. Keep watch over this ranch, like you promised you'd do." There hadn't been a kinder man alive except for Gus and her brothers.

THIRTY

WARM WIND

PREACHER MICAH JEFFERS returned to a far different event than the wedding. Every face was drawn, eyes of friends hollow. A pall settled over the ranch that washed through the toughest of men. Horses stood quiet in the corral, perhaps sensing something wrong. Today, the incredulity, the finality, was made even more painful at the sight of the grave where Ezekiel Waterson would be laid to his final rest.

Most of the mourners stood with hunched shoulders, heads bowed beneath the leaden sky. A light, grass-scented wind complemented the sadness. As he wanted, he would be buried opposite his beloved Sienna Harris Enders while his only real family looked on.

The front doors of both houses were draped in black bunting. There were ranchers from miles away, their wagons forming a line along the road to the house. Glory and Macon Sanderson stood beside Ginny Mc-Laughlin. Alonzo draped his arm around the shoulders of his sniffling wife. The cowhands were decked out in their best shirts and pants.

Nora imagined what Zeke would say about the fuss being made. Listening close enough, she could almost hear his gravelly voice tell them to *get on with it so he could rest without the gawking.* Tears slipped over her cheeks as Gus tucked her hand in his. Alfred Collier glanced in her direction, his face stoic, then after a moment, he returned his attention to the preacher.

The homily began with the twenty-third psalm. She looked toward Bryce where his fingers were threaded with Hannah's. The younger ones were in the care of Nita and a neighbor's older daughter, both keeping the rambunctious little ones occupied.

Nora was aware Cort bottled his emotions, and the weight of the effort was in his taut face and empty stare. From the stories she'd heard, Zeke had at first been Cort's adversary. But that all changed when Cort found a father, friend, mentor, and advisor in Zeke. At times, Zeke was the necessary, sometimes abrupt, voice of reason.

She lifted her chin at the sound of the tedious, deep-timbre voice of the preacher as he quoted verses from the scripture of John. From her time here, Cort hadn't spoken of faith, but his eyes lifted skyward when the sun burst through a cloud bank. Sturdy, strong Lark pursed her mouth in strained composure while her hand held his.

Closing his Bible, the preacher looked from one to the other. In his booming voice, he called everyone's attention. "And so, we grieve today. Tomorrow, we heal. As He guides us and keeps us steady and true, Ezekiel—Zeke Waterson's words—indeed, remind us of the circle of life. Mark this day as a moment to rejoice a fine man who gave us important lessons. I don't think a single man or woman here has been untouched by his kindness and sometimes his blunt assessments. Now, it's up to us to live by those lessons with God's hand. Before we commend the body to this grave, Cortland has a few words."

Gus squeezed her hand. She looked up to see his subtle wink. Straight-backed, her brother walked to the casket. Brushing a hand across the wood, he turned, faced the mourners, then lifted his chin. His gaze fell on each of his men where they stood in a row, their hats in hands, heads bent. Her heart thudded in her ears as she watched him swallow, hesitant to begin.

"If Zeke had a voice here, he'd keep all of you here till dark." He waited while the chuckles subsided before continuing. "I was just a no-account gunfighter and drifter, generally getting into trouble. Cocky and irresponsible, I had no real plans. Expecting life would turn around for me, in its own good time, until I happened to cross the prettiest ranch I'd ever seen. Wade Harris and Zeke Waterson took me under their wings and taught me what they knew. Which was a lot. Made me the man I am. Zeke always reminded me that this land got into your blood. He was damned right." Cort cleared his throat and shifted his weight from one foot to the other.

"I traded my pride but not my honor to hold this place together. Thanks to Zeke, I'll see this place goes on to prosper. But make no mistake, it will never be the same without him. He was my friend. A father. Just about everything in between. This ceremony would rankle him, even send him off grumbling about how the men should be doin' their jobs right now instead of wastin' time on a man who'd done his time on Earth, best he could."

Cort paused, and Nora dabbed her eyes, looking on as her brother continued. "Zeke was crusty, but he kept his soft heart hidden. If you found it, he'd deny it. He often quipped about dying. One time, he stood beside a dead cowpoke after he'd taken a bad fall. Just like him to say, he saddled a cloud and rode to the great beyond. The real truth is, this man is deader than a can of corned beef. That was Zeke's way."

After a few hearty laughs, Cort finished. "So. Rest easy, my friend. Sent you with your hat on to keep the sun off. Like you once said to me. You'd be a fool to run off and leave this place. And you ain't no fool. Expect you to stay on and look out for us."

The preacher crooked his finger at four men waiting beside the casket to lower it into the hole. Mourners filed past, brushing their hands over the pine lid, then headed for the house below the hill. She and Gus stayed behind with Bryce and Hannah. Cort and Lark bowed their heads beside the pine box as it was lowered with ropes. Once it was below, Mason, Billy, Tangle, and Adoeete shoveled fresh black dirt until a mound marked the resting place.

Once they'd finished, a gentle wind brushed Nora's face. The sun was low in the sky. This night would be for Zeke, along with all the memories he'd gifted them.

Almost Two Months Later

GUS DIDN'T THINK he could do it. Leaving her alone while he left with Cort and his men, didn't sit right. Still, the work needed doing, and his wife was a stubborn woman. While Wally and Steven were there to mind the place, he still worried. Rounding up one hundred head of cattle before winter would take some doing, but the Army paid good money. Short-handed, he'd gotten help from Cort and his men. Still, there was no getting around the fact he'd be gone at least a week... if not more. Every coulee and tree-strewn hillside could be hiding his cows.

After his gear was loaded onto his pack horse, he led his Appaloosa to the hitching rail before he stepped inside. Nora stood at the stove, her ramrod straight back to him. She was wearing that high-collar black dress she'd worn when he first laid eyes on her at Fort Benton. The one that made him want to know more about her.

"All set to leave. The men are waitin' for me at the cookshack, having their last smoke and coffee. Chilly out there." There was silence. They'd already argued over her refusal to stay at Cort's place. But he had a ranch to run, and her stubbornness kept her planted here.

She turned from the stove, her face taut, her lip trembling. "I know you can take care of yourself. You already saw that Steven and I can shoot if needed. Don't worry about us. But I'm worried this weather could change with you and the men caught in it."

Hell. It wasn't the weather worrying him. He'd already lectured her about keeping close to the house. He opened his arms out to his sides, and she walked into his embrace and rested her head against his chest. After he set her back, he tapped her nose.

"Remember to lock up. Don't wander off. Wally and Steven know to come runnin' if you fire shots."

"For goodness sakes, Gus. I'm not a child. I'll be fine. We all will. You just take care of yourself. Jim Mabry is probably gone from the territory by now, else he would've made his presence known before now. Still, I'll miss you."

"Used to like my own company before I met you. But you turned me inside out."

"You remember where I am, Angus Remy Quaid."

"I never should'a given that preacher my real name."

She grinned. "I like Gus better. Still don't know why you never told me."

"You never asked."

"Gus has a good sound."

"Agreed."

Leaning over, he pecked her mouth with a brief kiss and then hefted his rifle. Once he mounted his horse, he gave a long look at the house and barn. Wally stood beside Steven. Both held their rifles, assuring him all was well. If there was one thing he'd taught Steven, it was how to handle guns, and he'd been an avid learner. Wally had been in the Army and knew his way around weapons. If trouble was coming, he expected it would have already been here.

When he crested the ridge above the house, he turned for a last look while the rest of the men went ahead. His wife was a vision where she stood on the porch, a hand cupped over her brow, her gaze in his direction. Gus reminded himself that she might have a tender heart, but he'd also seen firsthand how tough and determined she could be. Still, he made a promise to himself that he'd work long hours to get his ass back here—sooner rather than later.

———

Three Days Later

THE DOOR SWUNG open, startling Nora. *Damn.* She hadn't remembered to bolt the door after she'd spoken with Wally about where he'd be today. She lifted the rifle, and her gaze leveled on Steven, standing inside the door with his rifle gripped at his side. Nora sucked in a breath, then pointed the barrel to the floor.

He slammed the door, bolted it, then leaned his rifle against the wall. "You didn't bolt the door," he said flatly.

"No. I didn't. You surprised me, that's all. What did you need to tell me?"

He tilted his head and reached for her weapon, taking it from her hand. After he rested it against the table, he waited for a long moment. "Saw to the horses. Left more wood beside the door."

It was clear that Steven hadn't warmed to her just yet, and she was beginning to think he never would. Standing there, with his arms crossed, he looked so much like his father. Gus had been short on words when they'd first met. In Steven's case, it seemed to have more to do with him growing to manhood in a new culture, along with having a different woman who'd taken his mother's place.

"Supper will be ready in a few minutes. Wash up."

Nora turned back to the stove but sensed he hadn't moved. How would she ever dig beneath this strained relationship? Gus had explained how the rules of etiquette amongst the tribes were different from the white culture. Had she offended him? She glanced over her shoulder to find him still waiting, one eyebrow raised. Dropping the spoon against the work table, she turned to face him.

"What's on your mind, Steven?"

"I don't know what to call you."

"Thought your father already discussed this with you."

"He said Mother or Nora. Said to ask you."

"I like either. I never intend to take your mother's place, but will forever want what's best for you. If using my given name, Nora, makes you comfortable, that's fine. I know what it's like to lose a mother."

His chin jerked up. "She's dead? Your mother?"

"Yes. Sit and eat. I'll tell you about it."

After he straddled the seat, she sensed his eyes followed her until she'd set out the plates and taken a seat. Nora bit her lip to keep from grinning. So, she'd managed to pique his curiosity. At least, for the moment, she held his rapt attention.

"Nora is a good name. My mother was Aubrey."

"Yes. And she was a strong, brave woman. And very pretty."

"Tell me about your mother."

Nora smiled around the meat she'd forked into her mouth as he leaned forward, apparently waiting for her to begin the telling. This shift in their rocky relationship was still tenuous, so she had to choose her words. Kindred spirits, they'd both lost a mother, and he found common ground in that. Up until now, she hadn't realized how deeply he felt the loss of everything in his past.

Between bites, she related stories of their Virginia farm and her brothers. But any attempt to explain the bloody conflict between North and South was impossible, given he had no understanding of political goings-on. He nodded when she described how her father and brothers left to fight, never to return to the house while she was still there. He listened intently, sometimes lifting his focus from the plate to nod or to comment. After she related how her mother had died of a lung disease called pneumonia, leaving her to fend for herself, he stopped chewing. In that moment, he must've concluded they had even more in common. Still, she saw no need to detail the rest of her miserable life.

"My mother was sick, like yours. While I lived with the Lakota, often the warriors would go into battle. Many did not return. Like your father and brothers." He waved his fork. "Tell me how you and my father found each other."

She smiled. If only Gus were here to see how they'd bridged a wide gap. She only hoped it lasted. When she went on to recount the harrowing adventures they'd encountered between Fort Benton, across the Dakota Territory, and then here... she watched his slow grin. From time to time, he raised an eyebrow as she proceeded to relate their harrowing adventures. It seemed she'd not only won over his curiosity... but even his respect.

After he slid his plate aside, he said, "You are brave, like my father. I see how he chose you."

"I think you are like him."

He nodded and smiled. "Thank you for the food. And for telling me your stories."

"You are welcome, Steven."

When he stood to leave, he said, "I'll be in the bunkhouse. In the morning, I'll stop to see if you need anything."

Disappointed that he still chose to sleep in the bunkhouse, at least they'd found common ground. Once she'd locked the door behind him, she rubbed her hands across her arms to ward off the chill. After she rechecked the bolted door, she lifted the lamp to make her way to the upstairs bedroom. Once there, she planted herself in a chair where she stared fixedly at the bedroom door. Eyeing her rifle, she drew in a shuddering breath. If anyone came through that door, they'd pay for it.

All that talk of Gus's gold and James Mabry gave her the jitters. The sounds of the night closed in, spooking her. Wild imaginings raced in circles while she watched the door. With nothing but sheer grit, she'd stared down Indians and escaped Silas Gaines and Connor O'Malley. After all, she was the wife of a rancher. Surely she would face anything that came through a door.

THIRTY ONE

THE WAIT

WEARING A THREADBARE gray dress, Nora hunched over the kitchen floor, scrubbing it with a vengeance, when the sound of quick footsteps caught her attention. Nora dropped the brush into the soapy water pail and scrambled to her feet to reach her rifle. After she unlocked the door, she stepped back.

"Who is it?"

"Lark."

Nora squeezed her eyes closed with relief. Taking a breath, she lowered the rifle, leaned it against the wall, then opened the door. Lark stood on the threshold and stepped inside, hesitantly.

"What do you think you're doing? I can't imagine the floors need scrubbing."

Nora lowered her chin to see her water-splotched skirt. When she lifted her eyes, Lark had turned her attention to the room. "Keeping busy. What brings you here?"

"Decided to see the house and check to make sure you're doing all right. No secret Gus and Cort were worried about you here alone. Is that apple cake I smell?"

"Still warm from the oven. Coffee is still hot." Smoothing her hands across her damp skirt, she was more than happy to have the company.

"I'd never turn down either. Mason is outside looking over the place. He'll see me back home in an hour."

"Not that I'd admit it to him, but I miss Gus. Got to get used to being alone."

"That's normal feelings. But you do look a little pale. You sleeping all right?"

"Yes. Just fine." She lied.

"Should I send Collier out here the next time he makes his rounds at our house?"

"That won't be needed, Lark. I'm fine. Just tired. Had a little stomach upset but no call to see Collier over that."

"Once you and Gus start a family, you won't have time to be lonely."

"That isn't going to happen, I'm afraid Lark. I've already been told a long while back."

Lark's eyes widened. "By a physician?"

"Yes."

"I don't know what to say."

Nora shrugged. "Speaking of children, Steven has been helping out. We're gettin' to know each other."

Lark narrowed her eyes. "How did that happen?"

"I shared how my mother died, how my brothers were separated, and how Gus and I met. We've managed to find mutual ground."

"Would you mind sharing that with me before Mason comes knocking on the door?"

Nora's face heated at the recollection of the burly man in buckskins who'd come into her private office—uninvited. "Let's just say it was memorable in more ways than one. In those days, I wasn't the kindest of persons."

"That you ended up finding your brothers makes the story all that much more intriguing."

Nora watched as Lark mounted her horse with Mason while Mason waited. Both waved and turned their horses for home. The loneliness set in again, leaving her to wonder where Steven and Wally were. Come to think of it, they hadn't been seen since this morning. Since they usually stayed near, her worry grew in pace with the ticking clock. With the door bolted, she waited.

———————

AFTER A TIME, Nora stepped out onto the porch, rifle in hand. She studied the hills of grass, hoping to see either Wally or Steven return from wherever they'd gone. It was unlike them to be away from the house for this long.

Rifle at her side, she strode to the barn. Once inside, the only sound was of her horse's nicker from where her mare stood inside the stall. The air was redolent with the smell of hay and manure. Light streamed through the bale window, and the milk cow chewed her cud but otherwise, undisturbed. When she turned, the floor welled up, leaving her to grasp at a barn post until the dizziness subsided. She shook her head. *Just nervous willies.*

After she left the barn, she looked up at the sound of an approaching horse. When she saw the buckskin walking toward the house with Wally slumped in the saddle, she hurried to catch the animal's reins. Blood ran over the side of his face from a gash on his head. A quick glance around let her know that Steven wasn't with him. Before the man toppled from the saddle, she led the animal to the hitching rail, looped the reins, and prayed she could help him down.

"Wally?"

He lifted his head far enough for her to see his chalk-white face and glazed eyes. "Got to find Gus and Cort."

"You're in no condition for that. Let me help you down."

He nodded, then slipped to the ground with a thud before she'd managed to help. She knelt beside him while she clutched the rifle in her hand. For certain, they couldn't stay out here if whoever did this might be near. Somehow, she had to drag him into the house. *Steven. Where are you?*

She lifted her rifle, pulled back the hammer, then fired a single shot into the sky. Setting the rifle against the porch rail, she said, "Let's get you up and inside so you can tell me what happened."

Wally managed to get to his feet, but he swayed, then stumbled. Half-dragging him through the door, her heart thundered against her chest because Steven hadn't answered the gunshot. Once the man was settled on the kitchen bench, she toweled the bloody cut.

"Steven. Got to find Gus," Wally mumbled.

"Steven will be along."

"No. Find Gus. Steven ain't coming."

Oh, dear God! "Is Steven hurt?"

"*He* took him. Couldn't get to my gun. Bashed me on the head. Last I knew, I was starin' up while he led Steven away. The boy was bound. Gave a good fight."

"Who?"

"That soldier Gus had a run-in with. Knows about his claim. My drunken mouth."

"Did he say what he wants?"

With a shaking, blood-stained hand, Wally reached into his pocket and withdrew a wadded piece of paper. "Says on this. I can't read."

Between shaking hands, she read the scrawled words of Jim Mabry, demanding gold and greenbacks in exchange for Steven. *Three days.* She had no idea how far away Gus was and, even if she were to find him, it might be too late. She bit her lip. This was one time she'd have to do this on her own.

The hitch was she only had a vague notion of where the old Rocky Creek cabin was located. But she was determined to find it. If he'd harmed one hair on Steven's head, she'd blast the varmint out of his saddle.

Wally appeared to be drifting asleep. "Listen to me. I'm going to patch you as best I can then leave you. Got no time for much more than to bandage this."

After she dropped the bloody cloth into the basin of pink-stained water, she reread the scribbled words. Gus kept greenbacks in his desk. She had to hope it would satisfy Mabry.

Wally's eyes were closed where he'd dropped his head against the table. If she made it to Bryce's place, there was no guarantee he'd be there. Her best course was to get this done because there wasn't much time. Still, she prayed she would run across some of Bryce's hands.

She shook the man who'd slumped against the table. "Do you hear me? Tell Gus the note is on the table."

"Can't let you go. He's a killer."

"I can handle myself. It's time to put a stop to his threats... for good."

"Help me up. Bring up my horse. I'll go with you."

"If you fell from your horse, I wouldn't be able to get you into the saddle. Tell Gus. That's all I need from you."

"Gus will have my hide for this."

"Don't worry about that right now."

Fury had a color. It was red. She left Wally sleeping on the parlor settee, a bandage snugged across the swollen gash. After changing into her riding skirt and a shirt, she grabbed an empty potato sack and stuffed it with biscuits and jerky before she unhooked her canteen from the wall. She propped the blood-stained note on the table where Gus might find it.

Yanking open Gus's desk drawer, she stuffed greenbacks into his parfleche. Beneath one of his books, she uncovered a sack of gold dust. That wouldn't satisfy Mabry, but at least she had enough to entice him. With her revolver tucked inside her jacket, she hefted her rifle and headed out the door, the scent of Wally's blood still lingering in the air. Outside, she led Wally's horse to the corral, then turned him in without unsaddling him.

Her heels dug into the gravel as she marched to the barn, rifle in one hand and the sack of food slung over her shoulder. Once saddled, she led her horse to the porch and tied down the parfleche. With a last look at the house, she mounted. A wave of dizziness caught her by surprise, leaving her to grip the reins tighter. When it passed, she nudged her horse into a trot in the direction of Rocky Creek. Mabry wasn't expecting her. He'd be expecting Gus.

What would Tori do? Tori was a hard woman who knew how to survive. A woman capable of riding and shooting. *A woman who could kill.* All she had to do was follow Rocky Creek. No matter the consequences, she'd find Mabry.

BOTH GUS AND Cort rode side-by-side with the Bar Q homestead in sight. There was no chimney smoke. In the unsettling stillness, Gus pulled up, and his eyes narrowed on the sight of Wally's saddled horse inside the corral. Cort rested his revolver against his pommel as both studied the house.

"Cort. Something's wrong."

"Feels like trouble, sure enough," Cort glanced around. "Nobody around is worrisome."

When the door creaked open, Wally staggered onto the porch, then clutched the post. Gus straightened when he saw the bloody bandage.

"Shit. You see what I'm seein'?" Gus grumbled.

"That's what I'm seein'."

Gus dismounted and rushed to where the man swayed. With his heart pounding in his ears, he flexed his fingers, wanting to wring Wally's neck. He was supposed to be guarding his family.

"Gus, go easy. Got to find out what's goin' on," Cort called out.

Wally backed a step, apparently seeing the rage on his face. "What the hell happened?" Wally opened his fist. Gus snatched the wrinkled, blood-stained paper from his hand.

Leather creaked beneath Cort's shifting weight while Gus read the blood-smudged note. The words and their meaning shot through him as if he'd been peppered with buckshot. He darted a furious glare at the bearded man who he'd known almost his whole life. For the first time, he wanted to throttle him. Mabry was intent on revenge. Moreover, he wanted payment to get his son back. Wally's bandaged head was soaked with blood, and Steven was missing. *Christ.*

"Where's Nora?"

"Ain't good news. The Missus left to find Mabry soon as she bandaged my head. First, I wanted to go with her. She said I'd slow her down. That polecat came up on me from behind. Clobbered me good. Damned sorry."

"Shit. You should be." His balled fists wanted to hit something or someone. Nora had put herself in the crosshairs of a madman. By God, if he hurt her or Steven, Mabry would face Quaid justice. Gus shook from the inside out, his anger growing into red-hot fury. He'd been right about one thing... he never should've left his wife and son. He'd regret that decision for the rest of his life. The damned gold was no longer important. *Mabry had signed his death sentence.*

Gus handed up the note to Cort and watched his friend's face tauten. When he lifted his eyes, the flat, dispassionate eyes of the gunfighter looked back. Then Cort crumpled the paper in his fist and tossed it to the ground. Mabry had just crossed the wrong men.

"Let's see if we can follow her trail. She's never been to that old cabin. Most likely, she'll be lost before long and goin' in circles. She better hope she doesn't find Mabry before we do," Cort said. "With any luck, she decided to get to Bryce. That is, if she had the good sense."

Gus tightened the cinch. "No time to switch horses. Mabry is cunning, but he doesn't have shit for brains. He can't be so dumb as to think we wouldn't come for him. This time, he's underestimated what he's up against. I'll see him in Hell, one way or another."

———

HANNAH STOOD ATOP a stool, where she hung a curtain, when the sound of an approaching horse drew her attention. Bryce turned from the coffee he was about to pour to look from the window.

"It's Alfred Collier."

Both stepped out onto the porch to greet this unexpected visitor. "What brings you this way? Nobody sick we know about," Bryce said.

"Was over at Cort's place. Alonzo needed a burn tended. Lark asked me to look in on Nora. Said a few days ago, she looked pale. Seemed edgy. Thought I'd let you know and see if you've been there. Might save me a trip."

"Not lately. Maybe I should go with you."

"I'm sure it's just her overdoing it. Heard Gus is away."

"Yep. Gus sold a hundred head of cattle to the Army. Better than lose them this winter."

"Then I best get out to their place and check before it gets too late."

"Got time for coffee?" Hannah asked.

"Nope. Thanks for the offer. I'll bunk with Wally and Dave for the night."

"Send word if we're needed," Bryce said.

Alfred tipped his hat, then turned his horse in the direction of the Bar Q.

Once he was out of sight, Hannah looked toward her frowning husband. "Something feels odd."

"Don't borrow trouble, or it'll find you. Just hope Gus doesn't find Collier visiting Nora. They don't like each other much."

———————

GUS LED THE worn horses to water. Neither of them were thinking straight after chasing cows, sleeping on the ground, and herding them for more than a week. Now they were hunting for a mangy son of a bitch. When he returned with the horses, he found Cort had a low burning fire going with the camp pot beside the flames.

"Coffee smells good."

Cort pulled his pocket watch from inside his vest. "It's about one. Give the horses another hour for a breather. Tempted to get to Bryce's place for fresh mounts. And an extra gun. Wouldn't hurt to have his help in finding Nora and Mabry."

Gus set his tin cup at his side, then dropped his head in his hands. "Christ. This is my fault. I should've killed that son of a bitch long before now."

Cort dumped what was left of his coffee. "We'll find them."

Gus lifted his face. "Should'a kept moving."

"Our horses are tired. Won't get far on foot."

"I'm beyond thinking about the horses. Let's douse the fire and dump the pot."

"You ain't thinkin' straight. *One hour*. I learned over the years if you go half-cocked, you'll get your head blown off."

"Nora. My son. What if he kills them both?"

Cort darted a glance at him. "Steven grew up among skilled warriors. He'd know how to escape. In fact, he might kill Mabry before we get the chance."

"*Maybe.* Once we set off, we need to split up. You go after Nora."

There was silence between them. Cort dropped his chin. Gus figured Cort knew what he was telling him. There was only one thing Gus could do. He planned to put himself between his son and the crazy killer because it was the only way to save his son.

Cort looked up. "Don't worry about my sister. I'll find her. She can't be too far, especially if she's riding in circles. I'm hoping she doesn't stumble onto Mabry's whereabouts. He wouldn't kill her until he'd used her to find your gold stake. Are you sure this is the only way?"

"You read the note. He wants me. That's what this is about. Just keep her safe."

HER SMOKY BLACK mare picked her way around the rocks poking through the grass. Holding her hat with one hand, she gripped the reins with the other, then pulled up to search the wind-swept hills. Dirt lifted with swirling eddies anywhere the grass had either been trampled or died off. Nothing moved except for a hawk circling above her.

Her horse pawed the ground. Any horse prints she'd come upon crossed each other. They could belong to any number of cowmen. *How could she have thought to track an experienced soldier? Steven. Where are you?* She lifted her chin. It wasn't in her nature to give up.

After she nudged her horse forward, she gave thought to making her way to Bryce's house. But that would mean more lost time. *Had Gus returned to find that note?* She doubted it. If he did, he'd already be on his way.

The longer she rode, the weaker she felt. Her head hurt, her body ached, and she had to admit she was lost. She licked her lips, her gaze intent on the telltale wisps of smoke rising from the direction of the

Blue River. Was someone following her? Or had Mabry gone in a different direction?

Tired and worn from the long ride, she dismounted, then led her horse into the shade of an old cottonwood. After she looped the reins around a stubby limb, she clutched her canteen and sat beneath the tree, wincing at the pain in her backside. Before she rested her head against the trunk, she tossed her hat aside and closed her eyes for a few moments. Lulled by the buzzing flies and swishing tail of her horse, she dozed.

KNEES BENT TO his chest, Steven watched his enemy pace. Mabry was jittery, making him less careful. This man was a fool to think his father would let him live. Over the years, he'd learned to study the enemy. Without moving his head, he slanted his eyes to learn the man's weaknesses. This soldier had many. For one thing, Mabry tied his wrists but left his legs free to run. His captor believed him afraid to try for escape.

All he needed was a chance to get to a gun. Nine Bears would tell him to wait for the best moment to strike. Like a snake, he waited. Hands tied behind his back, he wriggled them to stretch the binding each time his captor moved away. Once free, he would reach for the knife still strapped inside of his boot. *Stupid soldier.*

Mabry walked toward him. "Stop lookin' at me with those dark eyes of yours. Giving me the willies. I'm going to piss and check the horses. If you try to run, you won't get far."

"My father will find you and kill you."

Mabry turned in mid-stride, circling back. He hunkered in front of him. Steven read the man's arrogance. "Once he hands over the money, I'll kill him... then you. Bet Tori knows where your father's claim is. She'll tell me."

"Who is Tori?" His laugh was loud enough to send the horses jerking back from their tethers.

"Tori is the name your step-mama used. Don't you know she was nothin' but a whore?"

Steven had learned what a whore was. He didn't believe Nora was that, and he refused to be baited. No one would die but Mabry. The fool had built a fire anyone for miles would see. Time passed while he remained still, his eyes following the man while he walked in circles. After Mabry disappeared into the trees, he gave one last tug to his bindings, then slipped the knife from his boot.

———————

ALFRED COLLIER'S HORSE trotted in the direction of Gus's new house. He'd only been there once before, using any excuse to see Nora. *Fool that he was.* The selfish part of him wanted her for himself. But she clearly loved Gus, and he'd honor her decision. Even after both of them had come to an understanding, he suspected there would always be an unease between Gus and him. Still, Lark had handed him an excuse to visit, knowing he was heading for trouble should Gus happen to be there.

After an hour of riding, he pulled up, took a long draw from his canteen, then noticed his horse's ears swivel. Something or someone caught his mount's attention. After nudging his horse's left flank, he brought the animal in a loop while he surveyed the landscape, then he reined.

Within the shadows of a sagging cottonwood, there was no mistaking Nora's dark gray mare, standing slack-legged in the shade. *What the hell was she doing out here alone?* His heart tripped, imagining the worst.

Slipping his rifle from the scabbard, he walked his horse close enough to study the surroundings. Nora's back rested against the trunk, her eyes closed. His heart stopped. At first, he sat motionless, hoping to see a rise of her chest. Moving his horse at a slow walk, relief flooded him at the sight of the steady rhythm of sleep.

He dismounted, then returned his rifle to the scabbard before he walked toward her and dropped the reins. Crouched beside her, he skimmed the back of his hand across her cheek. There were shadows beneath her eyes, and she felt a bit warm. He shook her.

"Nora. It's Alfred."

Her eyes snapped open... then she did the last thing he expected.

She jolted to her knees and wrapped her arms around his neck. "Thank God. I need your help."

While he would've liked to believe she loved him, he was far too much of a realist to trust his foolish hope. He set her back from him. "What is it? What the hell is going on?"

"Jim Mabry paid us a visit while Gus wasn't there. Somehow, Wally was whacked unconscious. I need your help to find Steven."

Alfred could hardly keep up with the story... her words fired like bullets. At the same time, he was also trying to parse out the issue of her health. "Whoa. Slow down. What's this about Steven?"

"Mabry has him. He demanded gold or money from Gus in exchange for Steven. Wally managed to deliver a scrawled demand to the house. I tried to follow their tracks. Alfred... there were so many prints, I didn't know which way to go. I should've tried to get to Bryce."

"If Bryce knew what you were up to, he'd take you over his knee. I wouldn't blame him. Are you well enough to ride?"

"I think so. I'm tired, is all." *She planned to keep the dizziness from him.* "Don't know what came over me. Must be my worries."

"How long has this been going on? This tiredness?"

"Maybe one month."

"Jesus." *She was likely pregnant.* He'd save this discussion for another day. "Nora, seems like you best think about whether you're goin' to have a baby. We'll talk about that another day. You got any idea where Jim Mabry might've gone?"

"The Rocky Creek cabin. The demand note said for Gus to come alone. I took what money I found in Gus's desk."

He started to rise when she latched onto his hand. "About having a baby. It isn't possible."

"How do you know that?"

"A doctor in Virginia City."

Alfred grimaced. "Nora. I don't have time to explain why he might've said that." He wagged his finger. "You stay put. I'll be back for you."

"What are you going to do?"

"Fix this mess. Of all the stupid damned things you may or may not have done, traipsing after a deranged killer has to top them all."

She stood, then faced him. "I'm going with you."

"Like hell you are. I don't need to worry about you getting in the way of what I've got to do."

"He's dangerous. You aren't used to confronting men like him. I'll wait here if you insist. At least take the money."

"Gus isn't here. I am. More to the point, I wasn't always a surgeon. You don't know everything about my past. I'm not all you think. Won't be needing the money."

He gave her a last warning look before he mounted his horse, setting off at a lope in the direction of the old Rocky Creek cabin. One thing he was sure. Mabry would kill both her and Steven, given the chance. After that fight with Gus, Mabry was out for revenge. The plan made little sense. This was more about getting his hands on the gold digs that Gus is reputed to own. Once Gus and his son were out of the way, he might force Nora to divulge the location of that gold stake.

If Gus did leave gold for Mabry, which he doubted would happen, Mabry would simply wait in hiding then kill him. Gus must know that and would take a bullet to save his son. Christ. Gus was knowingly riding into a trap. Either way, this sharpshooter turned physician would stop Mabry.

Relishing this task, he was no longer the upstanding, moral physician of Ogallala. In fact, he never was. The townsfolk knew him to be a healer. But he'd been a killer, as well. At the moment, he searched the ground and horizon with equal intensity, just as he'd done many times before.

The enemy was out there. Like all the rest he'd ever killed, this one would make a mistake. Inside his head, he played over the smell of blood, the mortar fire and horses screaming like women. He shook the past from his head. A single target lay ahead. He smiled to himself while his fingers itched to dispatch Mabry to Hell. His skill as a sniper would serve him as it always had—for a more important reason. The Confederate bounty on his head held no meaning. If he died... so be it.

His jaw rigid, he thought about Nora and how she couldn't possibly divine what he'd been—nor could any of the good folks of Ogallala. Sometimes he woke at night... sweating and shaking at the memory. He hoped no one ever uncovered his past.

THIRTY TWO

THE SURGEON COMES CALLING

GUS RODE ALONE, following Mabry's trail while Cort split off to look for Nora. Sitting straight in the saddle, he walked his horse around the thin stand of cottonwoods and junipers, all the while hoping to God she hadn't followed Mabry. She wasn't a tracker, but she was a single-minded woman with a penchant for trouble. It would be like her to stumble onto him and face him down. The one relief was that he hadn't heard gunfire.

Through the trees, Hannah's old cabin came into view. The bean sack tied to his pommel was filled with fine gravel. He hoped Mabry would be distracted long enough for him to kill the two-legged vermin. The old cabin was a dilapidated shell, the roof half caved in, the barn not much better. Nothing stirred as his gaze moved from the barn to the porch.

Once he was beside the porch, he threw the sack. Then he nudged his horse into the shadows of the old barn to wait. Once Mabry showed up, he wouldn't give his enemy time to enjoy his bag of worthless rocks. He dismounted, rifle in hand, his eyes watchful. The only sound was of cattle bawling in the distance.

After an hour of hiding in the shadows, he was decidedly pissed off at this game. He swung into the saddle, then urged his horse out of the shadows to head downriver. Mabry had made a fool of him. This was about revenge, and gold was secondary. If Mabry got hold of Nora, he figured she'd tell him where his claim was. *But she didn't know. Steven knew.*

NOW WAS THE time, Steven told himself. Licking his parched lips, he knew his father would walk into a trap when Mabry used him as a shield. He'd already lost his mother. He wouldn't lose his father. Just as he thought about how to stop Mabry, the man left him alone. He reached behind for his knife before he rolled to his feet.

Without hesitation, he ran for the horses where a rifle leaned against the tree. Steven untied both horses, then mounted one of them. Before he bent to retrieve the rifle, he heard the click of a gun hammer. He looked across his shoulder to stare at the barrel of Jim Mabry's revolver. His captor grinned.

"I wondered if you'd decide to make a run for it. Got tired of waiting, in fact."

Steven swallowed hard, knowing his right hand gripped his knife, and Mabry couldn't see it. *Yet.* Still mounted, he considered charging. But he'd surely be shot. If he dismounted, he'd be used as barter. And if he turned the horse, he'd likely die before he threw the knife into the man's chest.

"Won't tell you again. Get down. You got nowhere to run before I kill you." Mabry closed the distance, his boots digging into the gravel.

The knife was still in his hand. Sweat trickled down the side of his nose. *It had to be now.*

"Drop your revolver, Mabry." Gus's flat, toneless voice from the shadows brooked no argument.

Steven smelled his captor's fear, as he enjoyed the man's look of surprise. But Mabry's gun was still at full cock, leveled at him. His father's hesitation and the slight lowering of his rifle signaled his decision to sacrifice himself, giving Steven enough time for escape. He clenched his teeth.

"Let him go. I left *it* there. At the cabin. Like you said. It's what you wanted."

"You know what? I want revenge more. I'll leave a dead son for stealing my career. And a dead husband… a gift to the whore you married."

Steven watched his father's eyes, figuring when to throw his knife into the soldier's heart. "Then I guess we end it right here. Steven. You know what I want you to do."

In the raw stillness, Steven steadied his gaze on his father's hard glare. At any moment, they both might die.

"Tell you what. I'll drop my rifle once you let Steven get off his horse."

"Get down. You heard your pa," Mabry ordered.

Steven threw his leg over his horse, then dropped to the ground. The flash of the steel blade caught Mabry's attention. Steven's arm lifted—the knife about to fly.

A rifle retort rent the air, sending Mabry's body falling backward, his scream of pain silenced by death. While Steven's eyes trained on the twitching body, his father came around to his side. Gus pressed the barrel of his gun hard against the dead man's throat. Steven's arm hung at his side, his prize hunting knife still gripped in his hand.

"Dead. But I never got off a shot. I'd hoped to get you out of the way so I had a clear shot."

"Then who did?" Steven asked.

His father stared beyond his shoulder. "Think I'm beholden to *him*." Gus jutted his chin.

Steven followed the direction of his father's gaze. A familiar black horse plodded toward them. The man seated atop the horse with his doctor's bag slung from one side, now held a rifle across his lap. The physician's piercing scrutiny was as unnerving as the indifference in his expression. Steven was certain this man of medicine had killed before.

COLLIER'S HUNCHED SHOULDERS and glassy eyes stayed on the lifeless man while Gus looked from one to the other, not knowing what to make of the man he'd known as a gentle surgeon. This was a man who healed. A man who never lifted a gun... to anyone's recollection. Now, his expressionless face held no remorse—neither within the killer nor the healer.

But there was weariness in his taut face. Alfred shoved his rifle into his scabbard. Behind the stoic façade, Gus recognized a battle raged. So far, the man who'd saved them hadn't acknowledged them.

"I take it you've been here. Watching the whole time," Gus said.

Collier's jaw hardened as he appeared to surface from a distant place. "Long enough. Waited for a clear shot, then Steven got in the way. Had to take my best shot. Been a while since I needed to."

The kindly doctor-turned-killer leaned forward on his saddle and rested his arm across the pommel. Gus had known more than one outlaw, and this man had once found killing as commonplace as breathing. *For some, it was.* But Gus would never have imagined the kind of coldness—usually reserved for men of the gun, inside of a man who was committed to healing. Collier had done this before, many times, and with skill born of practice and precision.

"I suppose there's a story behind your skill with that rifle."

"None that I'd talk about."

"I owe you. We both do."

"Knew both of you would've died. Don't owe me anything. Nora has her husband, and you have your son. That's all that matters."

"I'll send my men back to bury this carcass."

"If it were me, I'd leave him to the buzzards."

"Strange talk from a doctor."

There was a hint of a sad smile. "Not a doctor. *A surgeon.* Besides, nothing I can do for him." He shrugged. "I didn't like Mabry, anyhow."

"My wife is missing. Cort is off looking for her. Best we find her."

"She's fine. A little tired and in need of water, food, and rest."

"You found her?"

"Came across her. Mount up, and I'll lead you."

All the while they followed behind Alfred, Gus contemplated the contradiction between the *surgeon* and the gunman. There was a stoniness in his eyes that chilled a man to the bone. *A past he kept hidden.*

WITH A MOUTH like dry cotton, she opened her eyes, then squeezed them closed at the bright light. Turning her head against the pillow, she recognized their bedroom. She vaguely recalled being seated in front of Gus, held in his arms. Sliding her hand across her stomach, she remembered Alfred's warning that she best be more careful. What a fool she'd been to have believed that doctor in Virginia City. No wonder she'd dismissed the signs.

"Glad to see you're awake."

At the sound of Gus's voice, she levered up onto her elbows to find him seated on a corner chair, his legs outstretched. She studied his scruffy beard and sunken eyes. His gaze was strangely impassive, considering what they'd been through.

"How did you find me?"

"Collier found you. Don't you recall?"

"Yes. He ordered me to stay put while he looked for you and Steven. Let's not circle back to your disdain for him. We owe him a debt."

"I'm aware, and I agree."

"Was Steven hurt?"

Gus brushed his hand across his disheveled hair. "He's fine, except for his pride. He was about to throw a knife through Mabry's heart until Collier got his shot off. Wish I'd have hunted for Mabry instead of my cows."

"Don't think like that, Gus. This is a ranch. You have work to do and can't be expected to foresee everything. If that were the case, you'd never leave the house. Besides, Mabry would've found a way to get to us whether you were there or not. I'm a rancher's wife now. That means having the backbone to stand up to whatever I have to."

"You're a smart lady. But you could've been killed. As a man... and husband, I'm supposed to keep you safe. Dammit. You could easily have been killed. Lucky Collier found you."

"You said Collier got off a shot? Are you saying he killed Jim Mabry?"

"That's what I'm saying."

"Never thought he used a gun."

"He seems to be good at it."

"The last I remember is you holding me in front of you in the saddle."

"You're remembering right. Alfred led us to you. Cort found you and said you looked dazed... your face chalky white. Collier said you needed to drink plenty of water and needed rest because you weren't feeling well. Is that true?"

She swung her legs over the side of the bed, then stood. After shoving her arms into the sleeves of her wrapper, she padded to the window, her back to him. "You forget how strong I can be. What happened is over. This is a ranch, and I plan to be included in the work and trouble that may come our way. I'm not a wilting sunflower."

He shoved from the chair and moved behind her so close, she heard his breathing. She turned into his arms. His sad gaze held hers. "Yes. I wasn't feeling well."

"When I met you, I found Tori was a hard woman... one who knew how to take charge and handle things. But I've found Nora is every bit as tough. I won't make the mistake of thinking different because it's one part of you that made me fall in love." He pressed his mouth to her cheek. "But we agreed to no secrets. Are you pregnant?"

She nodded. "How'd you find out?"

"Why didn't *you* tell me... straight off? Lark told Cort her suspicions. She even sent Collier out to check on you. That happened to be lucky for us when he happened to see you asleep out in the middle of nowhere. Nobody told me. I pieced it together. Why didn't you tell me?"

"I didn't think it was possible. Don't you remember when I told you there'd be no children?" With his hands gripping her shoulders, his stare was unrelenting.

"I recall, yes. Still haven't answered me."

"Gus. I believed what I'd been told by a physician who'd lied. I'd bet Silas had something to do with putting the idea in my head, with the help of the town physician. Again, I've been a fool."

Gus brushed a stray hair from her face, then chuckled. "I can hardly believe I'll be a father at my age. Just hope it's a girl. Pretty as her mother. While I'm not happy about you going after Mabry, I understand why you did it. I'm to blame for putting those cattle ahead of you."

"You best know this ranch is important to both of us. Besides, I'm Gus Quaid's wife. As such, I plan to be at your side in building this ranch."

One corner of his mouth rose. "Thank you for this gift. Still, a thirty-nine year old man—almost forty, shouldn't be having another baby."

She chortled and gave his arm a swat.

"What's funny? he asked.

"How we met. We fought our way across Dakota Territory and survived. There were times I figured you wanted to rid yourself of me. I didn't let you. Now I plan to keep you. Even though you claim to be an elderly man, I haven't found evidence of that yet."

"You have a point. When will he or she arrive?"

"June."

"I'd like a girl. 'Course that would mean she'd be willful, sassy... just like her mother."

"And who is mulish in this family?"

"Sometimes I am."

Lifting onto her toes, she pressed a kiss to his mouth. When he deepened the kiss, she figured she'd been forgiven for the fool thing she'd done. *Not that she'd do different.*

He leaned away. "After more than a week of chasing cows, then returning to chase my wife and son, I'm mighty tuckered out. Still, I'd be happy to continue where we just left off after our friend, Collier, sees his patient."

"He's here?"

"Downstairs, last I saw. I'll send him up. See about some vittles while you two palaver."

"I suppose I might as well offer him our thanks."

———————

SHORTLY AFTER GUS left her, there was a tap. She cleared her throat. "Come in."

Alfred walked in, then closed the door behind him before he turned to face her. She'd never seen him so unkempt. Graying stubble framed the frown on his mouth. The usual straight shoulders were hunched as though he'd surrendered a cause. It was clear he hadn't slept.

"So. You're up and around. Looking rested."

"Can't say the same for you. Didn't you get any sleep?"

"Found out ranch life isn't for me. Those cowhands tend to snore and fart, keeping a man awake."

She laughed. "I've heard about the bunkhouse. As to me, I'm fine."

"From the look of your husband, haggard though he is, I'd say you gave him the good news."

She nodded, watching him as he opened his bag. "We owe you a debt, Doctor Collier. Thank you for saving our lives."

He turned with the stethoscope gadget in hand. "Something I knew how to do... other than doctoring. I'd do it again with any snake like Mabry. I guess Gus mentioned my dubious talent with a gun."

"It came up. Will you tell me how that is?"

He shook his head. "Not even you. Let me check you over, then I'll leave you to some good food and that worried husband of yours."

After he'd examined her heart with that curious device, he seemed satisfied. He snapped his bag closed, then lifted one corner of his mouth in a grin.

"Well?" she asked.

"Sounds good. Seem to be fit. Just don't overdo it. Before I leave, I need to know why the hell you went looking for an unhinged kidnapper in rough country?"

"I didn't give it thought. Doesn't matter."

"It does matter. Do you know how to track?"

"For goodness sakes, Alfred. I'm not addled. Anyone can see horse prints."

His mouth drew into a taut line and held her gaze. "I disagree. Still, I understand your sense of panic. Nora... when I found you on the ground, I...." His face flushed.

"Gus is my husband."

"I accept that. Both of us have settled our differences. Can't promise we'll ever be friends."

Before he opened the door, she stopped him. "Alfred, I hope you find someone to fill your life."

"I'd be a very lucky man if she were anything like you. I'm afraid I'm too set in my ways."

SUPPER WAS A quiet affair. Nora put together stew and biscuits for Steven and herself, setting aside a plate for whenever Gus finished watching over a sick horse. Steven used a biscuit to soak up the stew gravy, while he kept his eyes on his plate... unmoved by her study of him. One thing was for sure, he was like his father when it came to limited conversation over a meal.

He looked up. "Why isn't my father here?"

"One of the horses has a swollen leg. Said if the liniment doesn't work, he might try a poultice. I'm saving a plate for him. In the meantime, we can enjoy each other's company over a meal. How's that?"

He cocked his head, raising an eyebrow. "All right." After which, he returned his attention to his plate.

Nora lifted her fork to take a bite as the silence drew on. After several minutes of silence, she happened to look toward him to find his piercing regard.

"My father gave me a gift."

She found it odd Gus hadn't mentioned it. "What is it?"

With a suddenness she hadn't expected, he popped up out of his seat, opened a drawer, then returned to the table with a leather folder. "He wanted me to have a likeness of my mother. Would you like to see it?"

"Yes. I'd like that very much." She was cross-wise between his eagerness and the abruptness of his announcement. Steven slipped the framed tintype from the wallet, then handed it to her. Before her was the image of a much younger Gus standing beside Aubrey, both wearing church clothes. Aubrey's mouth wore a timid smile while her long, dark hair draped the shoulders of her pretty dress. Beside her, Gus beamed.

"Perhaps this should be on the dresser in your bedroom."

"He said he'll hang it on the wall."

"You know what? That sounds like a perfect place. Now, if you don't mind. I think I'll take that walk to find your father. See if that horse is going to make it."

"If the horse must be shot, then you shouldn't see it happen."

"I'm stronger than you think."

THE SUN WAS a pink crown of light on the horizon as she entered the barn. The smell of dry hay and horses filled the cavernous structure. Gus looked up from brushing his prized stallion. He glanced in her direction, then returned his attention to his horse.

"Thought you'd be with the sick horse," she said.

He jutted his chin in the direction of one of the stalls. "She's standing. Swelling is starting to come down. Got it wrapped in a poultice."

"Supper's on the table. We missed you."

"I'll be up in a few minutes, I promise. Is everything all right between you and Steven?"

"Steven wasn't a problem. In fact, we were able to learn a lot from each other. Since you brought up the subject, there's something I want to talk to you about. Can you look at me?"

Gus tossed the brush onto a hay bale, then folded his arms. Their gazes held. "Go on."

She sighed. "Gus... I made it clear before, and now I'm doing it again. There's no need to hide your previous life with Aubrey from me. Steven just showed me a picture of you and her on your wedding day. He's proud of it, said you'll hang it for him. Why was it kept secret? You and Steven don't ever need to slink around about the woman who first stole your heart—the mother of your child. I don't want you or Steven to think I wouldn't want you to speak about her."

"I think I already knew that. Somehow, I didn't want to bring my past up and upset you."

"What? I'm not jealous of her. That's first. Second, I admire her for her bravery."

"All right. Anything else on your mind?"

"You've been quiet since Alfred left here this morning. He still bothers you. Am I wrong?"

"Got to admit I'm nervous every time he's around you. I trust you. Just don't know if I trust him. Christ, the man loves you. He admitted it. Why wouldn't I be jealous?"

"I don't return his feelings. What set you off today? Thought you already came to terms with his notions."

"After he left this morning, I watched you pick flowers in the pasture, wearin' a pretty blue dress... lookin' like you belong somewhere else. He's a medical man. Graduated from a fancy Philadelphia college. Knows the right words. Fits in with people. You deserved a man like him. Not a horse rancher who lived most of his life on the prairie. That's what's bothering me."

"Gus Quaid. I happen to love *you*. Stubbornness and all. You're as smart as they come, and you don't even know it. A Boston College man who probably read more books than anyone in Nebraska. If socializing was important, I'd never have stayed on a ranch. As to refined? What I was in my past is something only you can make me forget. We will *not* speak of your fool-headed notions again."

"Come here." He opened his arms, inviting her into them. She rested her head against the rise and fall of his chest, hoping he'd somehow get over his sense of inferiority.

"Here's my decision. If you bring up the physician again, I will shoot him to end your misery." Beneath her ear, she heard the rumble of his chuckle.

"If I ever do circle back to him, I'll let you land a punch to this mule-headed man who happens to love an equally stubborn woman. We're well-matched, lady."

She leaned away, then stared into his unfathomable eyes. "Now that we've settled the matter, we best return to the house before Steven thinks we're arguing."

He grinned. "Doubt he thinks that. Hard to know what he thinks. But you're a damned good cook, and I'm hungry."

———————

July 1, 1881

NORA LAY ACROSS the bed with one lamp lighting the room. The ranch had several new foals in the pasture. Cattle grew fat on the Bar Q range. More importantly, Gus hadn't stopped smiling since Elias Wesley Quaid was born on June 18, 1881. At the moment, their son slept contentedly in his cradle.

The familiar night sound of crackling embers in the stove was comforting. The slam of a shudder against the attic window told her the wind had picked up. Running her hand across the warmth where he'd lain beside her. Gus was still the same rancher at heart, checking his stock at all hours of the day or night. Sometimes she watched him stare out over the grassland, divining what he was thinking. She knew the call of his other life was still part of him.

The Bar Q would stand as a legacy for both of their children. If God allowed, she'd like another baby. If not, she was happier than she dared to be. This land was in her blood, as it was through the entire Enders clan. Gus had pinned his hopes in Steven taking over the reins one day. But there was a wildness in his son's spirit. She'd watched a yearning in the boy's eyes whenever he looked at the horizon. One day, they might see him ride off. On that day, she feared Gus's reaction.

The night Steven had shown her his mother and father's portrait had been the turning point. He no longer saw her as a woman who rejected his mother. In fact, since then, he'd shared both pleasant and contentious moments between himself and Aubrey. Trust had grown between them, and there was no longer any hiding his mother's existence.

Lying here, she thought of Lily Raine. Bryce's only child with Hannah was a beauty. One day, she'd be a heartbreaker. Though spoiled by her cousins, parents, and ranch hands, Nora had the suspicion Lily would grow into quite a lady, despite it. Reyes was handsome and determined to run his father's ranch one day. Wade and Ben were still young but Cort was determined to hold them to ranching. Steven—he had both a remoteness and waywardness, perhaps born of the People he'd lived among, yet steadfastly loyal to his father. And to proving himself.

Padding to the window, the dawn light competed with the last of moonlight as it slanted across the hillsides. The heavenly stars were milky white across the ranch. She thought about the graves where Zeke rested beside the woman he'd loved. The Harrises held this land against all odds. Now it was up to the Quaids and Enders to keep it alive—just as Sienna planned.

So lost in thought, she didn't hear the door open. Sturdy arms wrapped around her middle, then Gus rested his chin against her head. "What do you see out there?"

She turned in his arms to face him. "The past. The future. Whatever is in between."

"Your lip's twitching. Sure sign you got somethin' more on your mind."

"Contentment. Happiness that maybe I don't deserve."

"Christ. You deserve everything. You paid a high price to earn it."

She shivered against him. "You brought the cold in with you."

"Expect you can warm me?" he grinned.

"Do you doubt it?" Her finger traced his firm mouth. "Still think you're too old for this?"

"Huh. Nope. Give me a chance to prove it."

Lifting onto her toes, she plucked at the buttons of his shirt, freeing them. "Best we get out of these clothes. Do you agree?"

"Whatever you want," he croaked. "As long as I draw breath."

EPILOGUE

THE ENDERS-QUAID CLAN

Mid-July 1881

O N AN UNUSUALLY warm day, Nora stepped back to observe the Enders and Quaid clans where they gathered in front of Cort and Lark's veranda. This was both a celebration of the family and a remembrance of Zeke. Amid the prattling and laughter, the men sipped Zeke's bourbon punch from the massive crystal bowl set in the shade of the porch roof.

With a clap of Lark's hands, her sweet, yet authoritative voice stilled the chattering... drawing everyone's attention to her.

"Everybody gather the children, then be sure to stand straight. Our photographer said not to blink, cough, or spit. And if you can't smile, at least keep your tongues still. No scratching either."

After several chuckles, Cort looked to Bryce, then both shrugged. They set their cups aside as Gus lifted their fussing Eli into his arms. Elias Wesley Quaid was not quite a month old and the center of their adoration. Both Nora and Hannah directed the family members to where they should stand in preparation for the flash of the camera. Bryce lifted his Lily Raine from her cradle, where she dozed, only to have her squeal at being disturbed. Nora smiled at her niece's tearful blue eyes while Hannah looked on.

Reyes took his place beside his father, while Hannah took her position on the other side of the boy who'd grown nearly as tall as Bryce. Wearing pressed blue pants and a white shirt, Rey was almost fourteen. A top cowhand, he'd earned the respect of the men of the Enders and Rocky Creek Ranches for his skills in roping and riding.

Gus took his place alongside her. She looked up at his grin just as he winked. She studied her husband's dark eyes, filled with hard-won contentment after all the tragedy in his life. The lines of time were evident, only making him look even more rugged. Steven took his place opposite her. His fingers stroked the downy hair of his gurgling baby brother, Eli. Nora couldn't help but notice how often Steven smiled these days.

Nita and Theresa were like family, after all, so Lark called out for them to take places behind the entire clan. A squirming Benjamin was held in Cort's arms, while little Bryce, now formally called Wade to avoid confusion, yanked on Lark's hand, wanting to be set free. Nora smiled at the fact that Lily Raine, the only little girl amongst them, would one day have to hold her own with her male cousins.

The photographer looked toward them and called out for everyone to stand perfectly still. The man had taken a good deal of time explaining the wet plate, though no one paid him much attention. Things like collodion, silver nitrate, and various acids sounded risky to most everyone. The men looked unconvinced but finally gave in. As long as the gadget didn't explode, Cort gave his approval. After all, it was an expensive gift for the women to have this family portrait. No doubt, Hannah would paint all of them in due time.

The photographer ducked his balding head beneath the black cloth. No one moved, apart from the confounded twitch in her lip. Staring ahead, she watched as the man removed the lens cap. "Stand perfectly still."

Good Lord. She didn't think the children would be still another second. It seemed time ticked endlessly onward by the time the photographer replaced the lens cap, then slid some sort of plate back into the camera.

"That should do it. I'll have this ready in short order. This is a fine looking family, indeed."

Nora exhaled before brushing a stray curl away from her face.

"How much did this cost?" Bryce asked Cort.

Nora tipped her head to listen, curious herself.

"Yeah. That's somethin' I'd like to hear," Gus interjected from behind her.

"On second thought, maybe I don't want to know," Bryce quipped.

All eyes turned to Cort to await his answer. Cort scratched one ear, then swiped his mouth with his sleeve.

"Seems he had to come all the way out here from Ogallala. Was on his way to the train when I caught up with him. Lark's been askin' for a family picture for a while. Wasn't about to let this photographer go without getting it done."

Gus laughed. "How much, Cort?"

"Twenty dollars."

"*Christ.* That's wages for one of my hands for a month," Gus snapped.

"I'll have a happy wife. We all will."

Nora decided she'd heard enough of the banter. After she joined the women at the food table, everyone busied themselves shooing flies and tending to fretting babies. Otherwise, they managed some gossip. As the afternoon drew to a close, most everyone started for home, leaving Nora standing in front of her brother's house to gaze over the hills and gullies, green with grass and painted with wildflowers. She gave thanks for the blessing of this place and for all those who came before them. The winter of 1880–1881 had been harsh. Snow and cold had killed at least two hundred head of Enders cattle. The heat this summer promised to kill more, as Zeke predicted.

In the end....

The floods along the Missouri River and Niobrara Rivers were followed by years of droughts on the Nebraska plains. The Enders and Quaids were pitted against both nature's wrath and the pressure of new arrivals on their dominion. Their determination was tested. They would suffer tragedies, but they would endure, always looking back to the days when the Harrises first set foot here, claiming this grassland and establishing a strong legacy to follow. Against all odds. And Lasting.